# About the Author

John Salter came to be an author after a long and varied career: firstly, a Jesuit education "which went in backwards" (as James Joyce would have it); then art school, before being a security guard and an art master in London of the "swinging sixties"; thereafter, a lecturer in the Sociology of Education; a teashop owner in Lyon (he had fled the destruction of England by Margaret Thatcher); and finally, "Professeur de Histoire/Géo" in a lycée, translator and "vacataire" for two Lyon universities. Upon retirement, he once more took up his paints and then put them down again to take up a pen when faced with the financierisation of the visual arts.

# Jackson Penn — an Uncertain Boy

# John Salter

# Jackson Penn — an Uncertain Boy

Olympia Publishers
*London*

**www.olympiapublishers.com**
OLYMPIA PAPERBACK EDITION

A CIP catalogue record for this title is
available from the British Library.

ISBN: 978-1-80074-023-5

This is a work of fiction.
Names, characters, places and incidents originate from the writer's
imagination. Any resemblance to actual persons, living or dead, is
purely coincidental.

First Published in 2021

Olympia Publishers
Tallis House
2 Tallis Street
London
EC4Y 0AB

Printed in Great Britain

# Dedication

This book is dedicated to Elizabeth Brown, a wonderful woman who nursed my battered ego through adolescence and gave it the courage to escape religion and obsessive Puritanism and become a real artist; to Marie-Claude Alamércery who took the place of Elizabeth Brown in my "mature" years in encouraging the artist to continue his fight against hypocrisy, cynicism and the rule of finance; my children; and finally, my friend Jacques whose companionship keeps me alive and living.

# Acknowledgements

I have to thank Dr Greta Arnott (my first wife and still a great friend), Carolyn Bear (cousin and author, full of writer's wisdom), Angela Hunt (good fun guru and editor) and Kate Mason (Angela's sister) for unremitting good cheer.

*Our life is an apprenticeship to the truth that around every circle another*

   *Can be drawn; that there is no end in nature, but every end is a beginning...*

   *And under every deep, a lower deep opens.*

   Ralph Waldo Emerson

# CHAPTER ONE

Jackson Penn was born in or about 1842 at Hannibal, Missouri. His mother was murdered eighteen months later and so his memories of her were extremely limited — just general warmth and the gentle feel of her hands. He was raised, if it deserves such a term, by his father's old, black slave, who had been purchased cheap for this purpose on his mother's decease. The old man did his fumbling best, as he saw it, cleaning, feeding and putting him to bed. When Jackson, hereafter to be generally known as Jack, was nine years old the old slave went thankfully to his grave. At which point his father decided Jack was old enough to take care of himself and also to take on the domestic duties, such as chopping wood, milking the cow, preparing food, making beds etc., which had previously been those of the slave. Food preparation was not a problem as his father was usually too drunk to eat.

Fortunately, or otherwise, for Jack, there were neighbours ready to intercede. The nearest neighbours were the Widow Wilson, her daughter-in-law, the Misses Watson, her son, Bill, a year older, perhaps, than Jack; and their slave, Dan, who was somewhere in his late teens or early twenties. They would give him a meal if he was looking too pale, thin and bruised and was sometimes clothed in Bill's hand-me-downs. Jack rarely found time to wash and his father often beat him. Thus, he was generally dirty, ragged and much bruised. From time to time, if he was ill or very sad and not too smelly, the Misses Watson would look after him for a few days; but this would make his father very angry when he belatedly became aware of the absence and he would come beating on the door, demanding the return of his son.

The house Jack shared with his father, Joshua Penn, had, with the years, become increasingly dilapidated as his father's drunkenness and his own ineptitude prevented any but the most superficial of patching up: cardboard for missing window panes; newspapers stuffed in draughty holes; string and glue for broken furniture; a bucket under leaks, etc.

The Widow Wilson finally decided to take on Jack's education. This largely consisted of reading, writing and prolonged homilies concerning bodily and moral hygiene accompanied by biblical citations. All this was not entirely gratuitous, as it had become evident that young Bill needed companionship other than that which Dan could provide. Dan, the slave, had been co-opted to become Bill's "playmate" from the child's earliest years. Dan found the exigencies of the little tyrant unsupportable and as often as possible would escape to the protection of his domestic duties. This would give rise to noisy tantrums that martyrised the fragile nerves of Misses Watson and which left her with the choice of having to do her own cleaning, milking and chopping, or passing time with the noisy, demanding infant. Usually, she chose the latter and sought alternatives, even Jack, who was about the same age, if he wasn't too dirty.

Thus, Jack became a "playmate", at about the same time as his ancient minder died, which he mostly enjoyed as he had long admired Bill from a distance and his mastery of his household and school friends. His submission to Bill's demands was largely a masochistic joy. He found something akin to affection in being continually bullied and bossed.

Dan, the slave, considered Jack, now that he was allowed

into the company of Bill, altogether more acceptable than Bill; as he demanded little other than a smile from time to time, which Dan gave willingly and even little hugs when nobody was watching as niggers weren't supposed to do that sort of thing for white boys even when nominally in charge of them. Above all he appreciated the relief Jack gave him from his Bill-minding duties. Attempting to control and limit Bill's mastery of the world and avoid the dangers and disaster it provoked led to constant conflict; but Jack seemed to be able to divert the child's monomania into less conflictual paths while satisfying his need to dominate. They soon became friends as, when nobody was watching, Jack treated Dan with respect and returned his hugs. Dan also came to provide him with refuge for escaping difficult drunken nights at home, as he had his own hut in the Widow Wilson's garden.

\*\*\*

On this present day in the early summer of 1855, Jack was sitting on the bank of the Mississippi, his back against a tree stump, an old muzzleloader across his knees, "borrowed" from the Widow Wilson. He was waiting for Dan, with whom he was going to run away. He was maybe fourteen years old and was, despite the dirt and the suspicion of an odour of old sweat and urine not entirely eliminated by a recent swim, an attractive child, with dark wavy hair and bright blue eyes set in golden, sun-stained skin. The Dan, he awaited, was to be along later that afternoon or maybe the next morning.

He was reviewing his life which, with little exception, was a miserable affair. He had been often hungry and mostly sad, but the real problem was his father, who would beat him, or lock him up and make clumsy attempts to rape him. There had also been murderous attacks with a knife, or whatever else was to hand when he was very drunk and mad.

Jack could not understand him, feared him and avoided him as much as possible — but that was his home, where he slept, that is, when he couldn't find elsewhere to go. His father's attacks, whether punitive or lecherous, had to be submitted to as he was usually only half drunk, mostly coherent and still much stronger than a boy; however, the more murderous assaults were brief and not difficult to avoid as at those times he was not only drunk but confused, unable to follow his own thought for more than a minute or two at a time and would, after a while, crawl into a corner, shouting and weeping and drinking until he fell asleep. Jack could see these attacks, that became more and more frequent, coming on and would flee the house, most often to seek refuge with Dan.

*** 

Thus, Jack's father was a man no longer himself. For many years he had been seldom sober. His past was mostly a forgotten page that would flash up from time to time to remind him of his decline, his decline into drunkenness brought on by the sickness that invaded him. His son was like the cat one kicked in order to express displeasure with life. His only solace was his hidden money and his pieces of gold. These riches were partially the result of an irresistible temptation and partially of having been born to comfort.

Once become an adult, Joshua had chosen to be a trader buying pelts from the Mandan Indians. This was not quite up to his parents' expectations who had envisaged a doctor or a judge or even a saintly calling. However, it provided a decent living without a great deal of effort.

The Mandan mostly trapped beaver, but occasionally there would be a mink or even an ermine in his white, winter coat. These two latter furs, the Indians mostly kept for themselves for decorative use. But Joshua became aware of this hidden store of luxurious little pelts as he was friendly with the Great Chief and even more so with the Second Chief, Four Bears, with whom he would often share a bottle of whisky. He and the Second Chief even travelled together. Joshua had also learnt of another, stranger hoard: a little collection of old coins in a curiously carved box that the Mandan thought of as their treasure, literal and spiritual.

At first, there had been no temptation as he made a good living with the beaver he purchased. He was an affable man largely appreciated by the Mandan as one of the few almost honest traders they knew. The carvings on the box reminded Joshua of things he had seen on business visits to England where he furnished hatters with the underbelly of beavers' pelts used in making felt for the manufacture of high-class headwear, military and civilian. One of these gentlemen, of Irish origin and claiming descent from a line of Celtic kings, had a small collection of torcs and bracelets. The designs on these objects resembled those on the treasure box. This fitted in with rumours he had heard about the origins of the Mandan, whose strange appearance, quite unlike any other American Indians, betrayed few signs of Asiatic origins, being often very pale of skin and with hair colour ranging from blond to black through silver and brown that could be found in any European village. The only missing colour was ginger or red.

Many held that this strange semi-sedentary, farming tribe, who then lived along with the Plains Indians on the banks of the

Missouri and the traces of whose unusual huts could be found down the length of the river Ohio before mounting the Missouri, had origins from a tribe escaping the Viking invasions of Ireland or Wales after the fall of Rome. The collection of ancient coins was held by the tribe to be Great Medicine that protected them as they sought redemption in following their White Saviour who came from the west.

For them, the most precious of these coins was one in gold, not quite round, that showed an owl on one side and the head of a female warrior on the other, both slightly off centre, which the Chief Medicine Man wore around his neck in a little silken sack. There were a few letters inscribed on it that Joshua, who had undergone certain elements of a gentleman's education (a little Latin and less Greek as the British would have it and, of course, being American, the arithmetic needed for keeping books), recognised as probably Greek. In discussing this with others of a little more learning, he was informed that the coin was probably Athenian of about the third or fourth century BC. Other coins of this little collection, some gold, some silver, were evidently of Roman origin. These coins were now in Joshua's possession and he simply hoarded them as he thought it too dangerous to attempt to sell them and, in any case, his main source of income came from having profited from the smallpox infection that decimated the tribe in 1832 and a legacy.

While the majority of the tribe lay dead or dying, he had confiscated the entire season's beaver pelts, along with the precious collection of those from the mink and ermine and, finally, the box of coins held to be of Great Medicine.

He had been persuaded to this action by his declining health due to a syphilitic infection acquired in England, and the ease with which the theft could be accomplished among the dead and dying Mandan. At about the same time his parents died leaving him with money which, combined with that coming from the pelts, created a small but quite comfortable income.

A brief adventure in London with an angel-faced lad of fourteen purchased on a street corner had been his downfall. He had never been a man of a greatly libidinous nature and mostly remained faithful to his Indian wife, the lovely daughter given him by his friend the Great Chief of the Mandan to comfort his often, prolonged visits to the tribe — otherwise, he was rather partial to the occasional adolescent boy, not hard to come across and impress in this budding nation of largely very poor immigrants. However, as time went on, and his sickness became ever more evident, access to such persons became difficult, as he began not to hear the commands from his enfeebled frontal lobe and developed an evil temper as well as ugly sores.

His small fortune, now converted into bonds, provided enough income to allow him to stay as drunk as he liked, necessitating only the occasional visit to St Louis to pick up the interest. His neighbours sometimes wondered about what he lived on and finally decided that he must be a man of private means, which meant that Jack himself, even if neglected and ragged, had to be recognised as only a kind of honorary "white trash" and once cleaned up would probably resemble a respectable child.

Jack had arrived, inopportunely, ten years after Joshua robbed the Mandan. His wife, who had survived her husband's infection, became a victim of one of his early murderous rages. Her body, he buried unceremoniously in the garden of his house after one long, wintery night of digging. The neighbours were tearfully told that she had abandoned him and returned to her tribe, which surprised nobody. They did, however, wonder why she had left the child behind.

***

Jack shifted slightly his position against the tree stump inserting his folded jacket between himself and the rough bark. Dan had still not arrived.

Then his thoughts returned once more to his life with his father and a night nearly two months before, when he had clambered from his bedroom window, not wanting to risk meeting Joshua raging in the room below. He had also wanted to breathe the free air away from the stench of damp and whisky that enveloped the house and the probability of his mad father coming up to beat him. He had wandered down to the river and looking out across the Mississippi's vast breadth had once more dreamt of escaping.

He began thinking of his now long-delayed intention of going west, to seek fortune in the goldfields and how he would descend the Mississippi down as far as the Missouri, which he would then mount until, once far out into the unorganised territories, he would find the trail to the goldfields. Could he persuade Dan to join him? But stealing a slave was a big crime and deeply offended what little of the Widow Wilson's moral teachings had found a place in his thinking. It could even be a hanging offence; but then Dan was unhappy and did not want to be a slave — a thought that reassured Jack.

The Widow Wilson had begun to talk of selling Dan down south, now that Bill was big enough to look after himself and to take over some of Dan's tasks. Thus, a generally good-natured Dan had become morose and sullen and there had been talk in the town of being well rid of him if she did sell him — particularly since he had got the Neilson's maid in the family way. Everybody knew it was Paw Neilson who was screwing her, and no nigger had a right to take over a white man's screw and now the Neilsons also had a maid who was crying and sulking round the house because she wanted to be with her Dan. Maybe it was not Dan's kid any way. They would see when it was born, because the girl was almost uncoloured — a "high yaller" as they said in the far south.

Dan was the only remaining slave in the reduced Watson establishment, a semi-poverty brought about by the departure of Bill's father gone to seek greater fortune in the gold fields in 1849. Dan's wife and two small children had been auctioned off three years back, as had been his mother, brother and sister some years before when Dan was only seven. Dan, embittered by these experiences and further embittered by being in thrall to the tyrannical whims of Bill, was only awaiting the propitious moment to run away and seek his freedom. Dan had also recently heard that his wife and children had died in a cholera epidemic that had visited their southern plantation. So when Jack hesitantly suggested that he accompany him on his own escape to the west, this moment seemed to have arrived. His thoughts, like those of Jack, had turned to creating concrete plans of escape.

One night, when Jack was standing on the riverbank, thinking on his hateful father and feeling relieved to have so easily escaped him, he noticed, rather belatedly, that the weather had changed. For some time there had been a faint rumbling on the eastern horizon accompanied by flickers of lightning. And now Jack watched a curtain of churning clouds advance rapidly across the starlit sky, creating a violent blackness as it came. Jack turned and ran towards the town, intent upon the refuge he had often used in times past when other refuges were not available —

the church. The oncoming storm promised to be very violent. He had almost reached the church when the rain and wind hit him. He was angrily aware that he had not re-acted soon enough to stay dry that night and he cursed the weather that tore at his clothes and buffeted him to one side as he ran. On reaching the church he prised aside the rotting clapboard behind the tub that caught the rainwater from the guttering and squeezed into the interior. Once inside he sought out the Winston family pew, the most comfortable of all as it had cushioned seats; however, it was already occupied.

There was his father deeply lost in his drunken sleep, an almost empty bottle and whipping belt still at hand. His quest, finding where Jack was hidden, was long forgotten. There was an unpleasant smell — not only had he vomited in his sleep but shat himself as well. Again, Jack cursed. He would have to stay clear for a day or two if he didn't want to have to help clean up Pap. The Winstons were not going to be very happy.

He went across to the Neilsons' pew, which was far enough away to escape the smell of his father. This was equally large, so that one could stretch out one's legs, but much less comfortable as it lacked cushions. He knew his father would be out for some time and therefore presented no immediate danger as his only thought on awakening would be to seek whisky. He settled down along the bench and began to consider going back to his bed for a few hours. He would wait, he decided, until the storm abated a little. Even though summer warmth pervaded the church, he shivered in his wet clothes. Outside, war had been declared. The old church shook beneath the cannonades. The thunder roared almost continuously, and the church was lit as if by a brilliant flickering candle that sputtered and flared with a sharp, cold glare. In one of the rare moments when there was no sound greater than the beating rain and wind, Jack thought he heard a movement. Perhaps it was his father wakened by the storm and so he raised his head. What he saw startled him.

There, indeed, was his father, but he was with a very big man. It was not anybody that Jack recognised. In the almost continuous light of the storm Jack had time to study the man's high cheekbones and hooked nose, his blond hair, beginning to turn grey, his Indian dress and the enormous strength of his hands. With one of these monstrous objects, he was holding Joshua, still largely asleep, upright against the wall of the church by his neck. With the other he was evidently searching fastidiously his clothing. Why would anyone want to search through his father's dirty, vomit-covered and shit-soaked clothing, Jack wondered. The scene looked like a robbery but then the filthy Joshua hardly had the air of someone with loaded pockets. Evidently failing in his search, the man savagely shook the inert drunk. He then looked around him. Jack ducked down into his pew but raised his head again as he heard the Indian-like man begin to drag his father down the aisle of the church. Jack saw them arrive at the stairs to the choir gallery; whereupon the huge man began to pull the inert body up the stairs by its legs, the head bumping on every step. By the time they reached the top Joshua was fully awake and he tried to sit up. It was obvious that it was only as he glanced about him that he became aware of his assailant. He gave a thin scream of fear and then started desperately trying to claw his way back down the stairs. The man still had him by one foot. By this he raised his struggling victim into the air without apparent effort and then, with the merest shrug of his shoulders sent him flying over the crude wooden balustrade to fall, a screaming bundle, headfirst to the church floor — where he lay silent.

At this moment Jack sneezed. It had been in the middle of a rolling clap of thunder; nevertheless, the man had heard him. Jack rushed for his hole in the clapboard, but the large man was very agile and caught up with him before he was halfway through and dragged him back. He took Jack by the throat, but then seeing the boy clearly for the first time, seemed to change his mind and pushing him from him, struck him a blow to the head that sent Jack rolling unconscious under the table that served as altar and Bible stand. Jack had been found there the next morning by the minister, with his father's bloody scalp attached by a string around his neck.

***

With his newly comfortable position against the stump Jack sought a further reverie and pushed away all thoughts of his father to seek out things warmer. The low, cloud-misted sun was comforting, and the water of the Mississippi moved slowly by, heavy and smooth, a yellow, lukewarm, flowing lead. The sky above was now of the same colour and weighed as heavily. He felt part of the torpid landscape of river, sky and the long straggle of dark trees. A pleasant, mildly exciting warmth began to fill him, along with a recently acquired sensation that started gradually, from high in his chest. His feet and his head seemed to escape this; but even they, while almost separate from the rest of his body, began to be unwilling to move, or to sense anything but the rhythm of the river. He felt his blood flowing like the river. It moved from his neck down to his thighs and from his ankles up to his belly, and there where the currents mingled, he was heaviest of all. As his body slackened, he recognised the embrace of his pubescence. The mingling currents grew warmer and even heavier and his mind wandered onto the past and those memories of events that complemented his mood and mounting sexual need. He thought of Mary Anne and then way back down into the very beginnings of his sexuality nearly two years ago; and then, even further down to the demands of his drunken father. But he didn't want to go back to that. No, Mary Anne was an altogether more pleasant moment in his young life. When he thought of his time with Mary Anne it was always with wonder, because it was not at all like the way these things normally were. It was not something to boast about, to tell Bill or the other boys. It was a secret just for him — the sort of thing others might have experienced, but they also would pretend they had not. He had been ashamed to tell Bill, because a real boy should not be able to feel like that and they hadn't actually done it together — he had been a bit too young, was his excuse and also that she and her family had soon after left the town. However, he remembered what Bill had told him about Beth, who was the daughter of the Reverend Doctor Winston, and how they had done it together one evening when they found themselves alone in the schoolhouse. But he knew that that was not true — at least, not as Bill told it.

Bill's story was that in the twilight of the classroom, lit only by the final dull glare of the sun just set, he had been able to make it with Beth. Bill had, of course, elaborated this into a scene of grand seduction, whereby Beth had succumbed to his heroic charms and lordly powers of persuasion. This most pure and virginal girl, her modesty protected by the growing darkness about them, had been victim of the demon lover and prince charming. The Don Juan of Hannibal, Missouri had scored. The problem afterwards, Bill had said, was to avoid too great an entanglement and to go on to other conquests. Jack knew otherwise. He had seen them and, besides which, there had not been other conquests that he knew of. And most of all, Bill did as she told him.

Joe Harper, Bill's best friend (Jack's status was too low to be that), was also the nephew of the schoolmaster, Mr Phelps, who made him school monitor. It became his job to tidy the classroom at the end of the day, to latch doors and windows, finally to lock up and deposit the key with his uncle, at which point sometimes he received a dime. But the job also gave him a more regular source of income. For a half-dime he would leave unlatched the little storeroom window, which could be entered by climbing on an up-turned log below it. Thus, young lovers could use the schoolroom as a trysting place, at weekends and on summer evenings. He would also leave the storeroom cupboard unlocked so that their artless couplings could be comforted by the exercise mats. Jack, knowing that the window was frequently left unlatched, would quite often spend the night there, rather than the church, when his father was too drunk or mad to be with; and when Dan's hut in the Watson garden could not be a refuge as Dan was engaged elsewhere — normally with some pretty, privileged, house slave with a bed of her own.

Thus, one evening, in April of that year, when his father was again seeking him, belt in hand, as whisky had not offered him total satisfaction, Jack investigated the schoolhouse and found the window unlatched.

He had settled in the furthest corner of the schoolroom on an exercise mat taken from the store. The sun was just set and the sky was still aglow, filling the schoolroom with a low, warm light except for Jack's own shady corner, when he heard movement and voices.

Bill climbed in through the window. He glanced round the schoolroom and then unbolted the school's back door to let in

Beth. He had asked Beth to come with him to the schoolhouse under the pretext of having her help him with a problem in his homework for that week. This meant consulting her homework which was already done and waiting in her desk. They both knew that this was simply a pretext — it was very unlike Bill to do his homework. He found being whacked with a slipper less painful.

They walked hand in hand to the front of the class, unaware of Jack's presence. Bill pulled Beth over to the blackboard and there, taking up a crayon, he wrote his name "WILLIAM ARBUTHNOT WATSON" and next to it a big heart pierced with an arrow and then handed the chalk to Beth. She began to write her name "BETHANY ABIGAIL WINSTON" and then adding the words "LOVES HER HERO" along the arrow in the heart; meanwhile, Bill had moved behind her and pressed himself against her. He then took hold of her raised hand as if to guide her. Jack knew that this manoeuvre of Bill's was solely a pretext to push his sex against Beth, who had been readily party to the ploy. He's going to cream his pants, thought Jack and he found another memory of Mary Anne, of their last long embrace before she left Hannibal forever and him sadder than ever. When Beth stopped writing her hand stayed aloft, unwilling to drop down and undo the pretext for their closeness, until Bill, much emboldened by the success of this approach, took her shoulders and turned her around to face him, but before he could pull her close Beth started giggling. She pointed to the bulge in Bill's light cotton trousers. Bill, disconcerted, blushed.

"So that's what it was, pushing me in the back," she said with a grin. Bill looked confused and bent forward slightly, trying to reduce the size of the protuberance.

Jack had been astonished at Beth's lack of embarrassment when confronted by the evidence of Bill's erect penis. Most girls would have pretended not to have seen it or said something nasty about boys, while Beth did not seem to mind it at all. For him, it was a new vision of girls. A new category had been created of feminine creatures as uncomplicated as boys — even more straightforward than some boys: Bill, for example, who was always avoiding real things and creating his own fantasies about them. What had he been thinking as he pressed himself against Beth? Was he a prince disguised as shepherd boy descended from the castle to seduce a fair shepherdess? He grinned to himself at this thought and was half-minded to rush out from his hiding place with a cry of, "why if it ain't Chief Bighorn!" and really embarrass Bill. Then Beth's next act astonished and destroyed another of his simple beliefs: that which held white womankind to be largely asexual except as something to do with marriage and the taming of a male. White trash women, he knew, were different, but not the well-brought up daughter of a Reverend Doctor. Bill had tried to embrace her again, partly, Jack was sure, to hide his embarrassment rather than increase his pleasure, but Beth pushed him away and, holding him by the waist, again examined his bulging trouser front.

"Can I see it?" she asked, in a voice that had a touch of pleading, "I've never seen one, never had a brother and cousin. Sam is only a baby, so it don't count." Her evident and enthusiastic interest in the object that had recently come to govern much of his time and thought helped Bill recover his composure.

"I dunno," he said.

"Go on," she urged. "Anyways, boys are always looking at each other's willies."

"How d'you know?" he asked. "You said that you ain't never seen one."

"I ain't, 'cept at a distance. I saw Joe Harper and Neil Jensen doin' it the other day behind the schoolhouse. They pretended to be fightin' when they a-saw me."

"That don't surprise me about them two," sniffed Bill. "A couple of pansies."

"Can I see it then?" persisted Beth.

"If you want," he said, still blushing and he began clumsily to unbutton his fly. He stopped, and with a cunning look, he said, "If'n you let me see your tits."

"They ain't tits, they're my bust," replied Beth.

"Okay?"

"Oh, all right then," and she blushed a little too, "but only a little look." Bill slowly unbuttoned her bodice. He could feel her begin to tremble slightly as he worked. The cotton cloth, patterned with little blue and yellow flowers, fell to each side as he reached the last button and her two half-grown breasts appeared. They were cream coloured, with a round pink and brown nipple and almost perfect little half spheres.

"My, they're pretty," said Bill, placing his hand over one of them and feeling the softness. "But they ain't very big."

"I'm only jess thirteen," said Beth hotly, "an' I bet your willy ain't too big neither."

"It's bigger'n Neil Jensen's (who was the oldest boy at school). I'm gonna be fourteen and a half next week."

"Let's see then." Bill hesitated. "You promised," she added.

It took a little effort to get the penis out from the tight trousers he had now worn for two summers and he had to unfasten the top button, but finally it was there, hanging a little by now. The struggle to extract it had somewhat tamed its ardour.

"It's prettier than a dog's or horse's one an' quite big enough," she said, "Can I touch it?" Bill nodded and thrust his hips forward slightly to aid her examination of the fabulous object. He was more than enjoying this sudden attention to his great problem and his body began to fill with shudders of excitement. She poked it gently with her forefinger and it jerked in reaction, suddenly recovering its previous rigidity. His excitement began to concentrate.

"Oh! How did you do that?" she said.

"I didn't do nothing," said Bill, "it's just like that."

Then she took it between two fingers at the head and bent down to examine it. This time it stood up as high as it could possibly go, and the head became a little more swollen. Bill's whole body stiffened, and he closed his eyes. The excitement hardened like a tensed muscle waiting to leap.

"Oh Beth, oh dear, oh my." She looked up at him as he spoke.

"Does it get any bigger?" she asked with a touch of anxiety. Bill had difficulty replying.

"Not much," he breathed after a second or two, fighting to open his eyes and control his voice.

"Can I see how the baby juice comes?" She stroked the head a couple of times as if it were a small animal.

"It, it's almost there," he managed to say. He had started breathing rapidly, heavily. His knuckles turned white where he held her shoulder.

"Hey, you're hurting me. Don't hold me so tight," she said and let go of his penis to pull his hand from her shoulder.

"Don't stop, don't stop," Bill urged desperately, "please, hold it again." She looked up at his face now all screwed up in a painful anticipation of the climactic moment when his hard excitement would at last rush out of him in jets of intense pleasure that were so close to pain. She smiled a little uncertainly. She took hold of him once more and nursed the swollen member between her hands, two fingers fondling it roughly under the head as if exciting a playful puppy. The head became so engorged with blood that it shone a little, reflecting the flame of the sky on its hard smooth surface. A tiny pearl of whitish liquid began to appear at the tip. Beth touched at it with one finger and smeared it across the tip to feel its texture. Somewhere in the root of Bill's belly and high between anus and prostate a star burst.

In his fascination with this scene, Jack had gradually raised his head above the desk that sheltered him. As he watched, Beth's breathing began to match that of Bill. Bill began trembling. Then he suddenly took hold of Beth again and pulled her towards him desperately trying to kiss her small breasts. As Bill did this Jack saw a stream of semen leap across towards him, to be immediately followed by a bigger, stronger jet that splashed across Beth's dress as they closed together. Bill was shaking wildly, barely able to stand, leaning upon Beth for support. She hugged him close, her own trembling racing along with his. They stood like that for a long time and in the silence and stillness Jack dared not move. However, he did start to stroke himself a little, because he too had become hard.

The sun was now long gone, and the silent dusk of the classroom was broken only by their breathing, a sound that gradually quietened. Bill spoke first.

"Wait here," he muttered and left her to return a moment later with an exercise mat from the storeroom. She had become quite pale. Inside her, her body still vibrated, and it ached to continue the embrace. She approached Bill and kissed him as he laid out the mat. As he turned to her again, she cupped his genitals gently in one hand.

"You messy thing," she said with a smile as she looked at the front of her dress and releasing his hardening sex, began to wipe at the semen with a handkerchief she had extracted from her knickers. Bill kissed her several times on the face and Beth returned his kisses. This continued for several minutes until Jack wondered at how long they could stand together doing that without getting bored.

"Can it do it again," Beth whispered. Bill nodded. Without letting go of his trousers he lifted the front of her dress until he could press himself against her soft body. He started pulling at the tight knickers of white lacy cotton that descended almost to her knees. He did not have much success. He let go of his trousers and his once more erect penis sprung into view. She threw it surreptitious glances, trying to catch sight of it without seeming too evidently to do so as he now struggled off her drawers with both hands. He lifted her dress over her head, then took off his shirt and laid it across the mat. Finally, they stood naked in the warm half-light.

"You're a very handsome boy," whispered Beth as she once more pressed herself against his belly and enfolded his sex. This might have been put in the future tense, for Bill was at that awkward stage of adolescence where the legs, buttocks and genitals are practically those of a man, while the torso and arms retain much of the frailty of boyhood.

Bill knelt down, pulling Beth with him until she lay face up on the mat and then gradually lowered himself over her. He knew, in principle, he had to be inside her, but wasn't quite sure how to set about it. He fumbled a little while, but finally, assisted by Beth's hand found where to place his penis, pushed and entered her. She gave a little cry of pain.

"You won't make me a baby, will you?" she whispered. He did not reply. He remained motionless, knowing he should be doing something active but not quite sure how to set about it, so it was Beth that helped him to a rhythm with the pressure of her hands upon his buttocks. She had seen dogs and horses at work.

*\*\**

Jack, still slumped against the tree stump, looked at the slow, yellow-grey river with sightless eyes. All vision was turned inwards as he replayed the last scenes of his reverie again and then again, until, with but the slightest aid from the tip of one finger, his semen began to flow — not in a wild and jerky rush, as had that of Bill, but in deep surges like those of the river.

Like those of the Bill that he had not seen so well, who found it impossible to fulfil his intention of withdrawing before the moment of ejaculation. His body forced forward when he wanted it to pull back. Caught by surprise he flooded into Beth with his every emotion in anxious conflict, with a sense of doing the forbidden that heightened his uncontrollable pleasure. She sensed his sperm entering her and also took pleasure in the foreboding of catastrophe it sowed along with it and, besides which, he was her hero. They had both feared to plant the seed but neither had been able to resist doing so. No one had ever said how, other than simply, not to. Their bodies had desperately wanted something, and that thing had seemed to happen by itself. Beth, replete in the arms of her hero, wondered why, as the preacher insisted, one had to go to hell for doing that. Bill simply looked forward to a future strewn with pleasure. How he had become her hero was another story.

# CHAPTER TWO

After he had shared Bill's introduction to the world of coupling, Jack drifted into sleep. He awoke an hour later feeling rather stiff and numb, got to his feet with the aid of the tree stump and started running on the spot and then jumping until his blood was once more circulating properly. He looked up and down the river wondering if, perhaps, he had missed Dan. This was not very possible as he had been in full view of the river and Dan could not have missed him. He returned to his stump, refolded his jacket and once more set about his watch. He decided that, even if Dan was an escaped nigger, he was his best friend and that was that. He once more fell into reverie.

*** 

One day Jack had stumbled across Joshua's treasure. This was a result of one of Bill's games, just as was Bill's being seduced by Beth after he had become her great hero.

Bill had been reading an account of the Fall of Troy and of Odysseus's later adventures and had been particularly taken with the story of his escape from Polyphemus, the Cyclops and so, one summer week when he had had enough of pirates, Indian fighting and knights in armour, he called together his band of followers to help him act out a modified version of Homer's epic writings. This took some days of elaborate preparation and even threats that implied the lessening of his friendship for the more recalcitrant older boys. The smaller boys were always willing to follow the school's most admired boy and bully.

For the drama itself, star roles were reserved for himself, Beth, Joe Harper and Jack. All the other boys had to do was fight each other with wooden swords and spears as either Greeks or Trojans and later on, Greeks and Cyclops, which pleased them as acting seemed somewhat schoolishly onerous, having to memorise some script, however short and violent and even a rather unmanly activity.

When the big day came, Bill felt that all should start with Achilles' fight with Hector (himself and Joe Harper), which took up the best part of an hour of "have at thee" and "take that" watched with little enthusiasm by the others whenever they took a rest from fighting amongst themselves as Greeks or Trojans. Nobody had wanted to be a Trojan as they were the losers and so it fell to the lot of the youngest, weakest and least popular boys.

Paris's cowardly action was difficult to extend beyond five minutes while Jack elaborately strung his bow, fired and did a dance of triumph.

However, Achilles' final agony took a good ten minutes more as Bill jumped about holding his heel, finally rolling about on the ground emitting hideous cries and calling upon Zeus for vengeance.

Beth briefly had a role as Helen meeting Odysseus disguised as a beggar (Jack, again because as well as being pretty he was rather unkempt and dirty). Beth kept her distance as he dramatically showed her in the form of another dance of triumph (which Bill thought he rather overdid) the little statue of Pallas Athena he was stealing in order to circumvent the "impregnable walls of Troy".

Then it was Dan's turn to play his role as the Trojan horse, by dragging a small cartload of boys on hands and knees through an improvised gate of crates and wearing a papier-mâché horse's head. He was helped along by Bill who would occasionally lightly thwack his buttocks with a riding crop, which Dan found rather irritating and taking on his role of child-minder, said: "Stop dat nonsense wid de crop, Massa Bill."

"What if I don't, nigger?" sniggered Bill giving Dan another tap.

"I'll take yah by yah shirt collar and drag yah home to yah ma."

Bill flushed. This flouted his general authority and menaced the slave/white hierarchy as he was verging on adulthood. Dan had been a sort of nanny to him and many of the boys around had had or even still had a nanny who controlled infantile outbursts of anger and frustration. Where this authority began and ended was ill defined and in the hands of family tradition.

"I'll do what I want," he shouted, giving another tap, Dan leapt to his feet tearing off his horse head. Two small boys fell off his back as he advanced towards Bill who backed away.

"All right, all right — only joking, Dan," cried Bill. Dan slowly and carefully put his horse head back on while glaring at the boy. He did not need a full confrontation while on such dangerous ground. He knelt down and at his bidding the two small boys timidly remounted his back. Jack and the others pretended not to have noticed the clash, while Bill stalked off to organise the sack of Troy

On the far side of the gate the rest of the boys prepared for another fight once the Greeks had left the horse. Bill changed sides and played Aeneas carrying to safety his father, Anchises (Jack once again as he was not very heavy — Bill was habituated to his smell), all the while fighting off Greeks with his free right arm and calling on the gods.

Then, towards the end of the afternoon, with the hot sun low in a sky that was black along the northern horizon and occasionally lit by lightning flashes, they enacted the finale: Polyphemus (Dan) being tricked by Odysseus (Bill, of course) with all the others as either Greeks or Cyclops. Bill's "mise en scène" for this final act was more than usually elaborate: a number of sheepskin rugs, waistcoats and other furry clothing had been gathered; Jack and Dan had brought large slabs of hearthstone, stolen from Jack's dilapidated house, that would create a good splash when thrown at the Greeks in the river; a large ball of garden and other rubbish stuffed into a sheet held together with string was Polyphemus's boulder; a "borrowed" skiff, Odysseus's boat; and finally the cave was a hole in the high clay banks of the Mississippi excavated by the river in the spring floods. There was, of course, a picnic representing Polyphemus' food store to be devoured by the Greek warriors. This food had been begged or largely stolen from the boys' parents — the painful payment for which had yet to come. Jack's contribution was reduced to a jug of whisky as food was in short supply in the Penn household and his father's ability to count jugs and bottles limited and, also, Bill had thought it unwise to have him multiply the thefts from his own home.

As all this was being prepared, the threatening blackness, the rumbling thunder, the now almost continuous lightning flashes remained in the north and didn't seem to want to advance upon them, but, at least, provided a dramatic background for Bill's climax. Then most of the boys, the smaller ones, walked upriver a little way to wait for the moment of boarding their skiff and the descent towards the cave. Dan waited out of sight with those boys that were to be Cyclops, that is, a small group of bigger and older boys with large eyes painted on their foreheads. As Bill had to be silent and heroic, Jack was given charge of the unruly band of smaller boys, as someone with the authority of being older, if not much bigger, and a close friend of Bill's.

On Jack's command, they started jumping onto the skiff. This almost capsized and Jack had to calm their enthusiasm. Finally, those that could not be fitted onto the boat simply swum alongside until the moment came to come ashore and mount stealthily to the cave. Beth, because she was a girl, was arranging the picnic in the cave. Once the picnic started those designated as Cyclops, the bigger, older boys, insisted that they were allowed to come and eat, which Bill reluctantly agreed to, giving them a temporary double role as Greeks. Dan, Bill decided, needing to reassert his authority, could not as he was too obviously not a Greek. He was also a nigger. Jack felt a little guilty about this, but then it was Bill who was in charge. When nobody was looking and all were a trifle fuddled by the whisky, he took a piece of pie up to Dan, who gave him a kiss. Jack liked this even if it embarrassed him and he looked around to ensure that no one had seen it.

Having eaten, the bigger boys re-became Cyclops and re-joined Dan to await their next intervention, while the Greeks lay down and started loudly snoring, which was Dan's signal to begin his role of ferocious monster. This part he could enjoy a little, as once he had rolled the boulder into place, he could get violent and act out eating a couple of the boys, who finally protested that he was being too rough. Jack giggled and Bill gave instructions on how to eat boys painlessly.

Then Dan played at being asleep while Bill, not very painlessly, enacted putting out his eye and blindfolded him.

"My name is Nobody!" Bill exclaimed as he ran for safety, hurling insults. Dan roared and screamed appropriately, and the Cyclops boys came to the mouth of the cave.

"What's the matter, Polyphemus?" they cried in unison.

"Nobody has done put out me eye and wants ta kill me," he shouted. At this, all the boys laughed, even though they had rehearsed the joke many times before, but it seemed to fit so very well in the mouth of a stupid nigger.

"Well, stop making such a fuss then," the Cyclops boys yelled as they left.

"Youse'll not git outa here cos I'll eat youse all," declared Dan as he turned towards the boys in the cave, beginning to really quite enjoy his role.

"No, you won't," shouted Bill.

The boys then draped their skins over their backs and all the while shouting "Baaah, Baah," started crawling past Dan, who stroked their furs and gave them a pinch when he found a bare arm or a leg or a tickle if he found ribs or feet. The boys replied by prodding him with the wooden swords. The "Baahs" became interrupted by giggles and shouts of laughter. The whisky was beginning to tell.

One small boy shouted, "Don't you pinch me, nigger."

"I'll pinch an' eat jus anybody I wants 'cos I'se a Cyclops," and he turned the child over and tickled him into laughter. The other Cyclops seeing that things were becoming fun returned and started helping Dan in wrestling the smaller boys who slapped helplessly about them with the swords. The entry to the cave became a shouting, laughing, disorganised scrimmage. One corner of a great social barrier was being lifted as Jack's creation took on a life of its own. He felt irritated and then anxious.

"Shut up! Fucking shut up. You're not doing it right," shouted Bill angrily almost regretting Jack's gift of whisky. He paused as silence fell.

"I'm gonna get Beth… er… Helen," he declared, which was

an essential addition to Greek mythology which seemed to have been missed out by Homer — the need for a damsel in distress to be rescued. This would also restore discipline, Bill hoped. So he picked up Beth (he was quite a strong lad for his age and she rather frail and light) and carried her out of the cave viciously whacking Dan with his sword as he went by and on down to the river. Then wading in a yard or two placed her in the skiff. He turned to wave his sword triumphantly at the Cyclops, who waved their fists and shouted curses at him — Dan with real anger. The whack with the wooden sword had hurt a great deal. Bill saw and heard hatred but didn't know what to do about it and so pretended not to have noticed, as did all the other boys — they had no experience of a nigger in revolt. Jack simply gaped open mouthed hoping nothing bad would happen as Dan began to advance down the bank towards Bill who froze.

"Bill Watson, I'se gonna really kill ya, one o' dese days," yelled Dan into the boy's face, along with a shower of spittle.

Dan then turned, wiped his mouth on his sleeve and hurried to the top of the bank where the hearthstones and other smaller missiles were placed and crossly enjoined the disconcerted Cyclops to get ready to bombard Odysseus's boat. The sheep by the cave began to take off their fur which they were forbidden to get wet, as they prepared to enter the river. The atmosphere had violently changed and the boys, not knowing what to do, set about pretending to be normal and were strangely silent. Suddenly, there was a distant roar of rushing water. Everybody turned to look up the river and saw a low tidal wall rushing towards them followed by a foaming turbulence. The storm in the north had created a minor flood, but of some violence, as the spring floods had narrowed the river a little at this point by causing the high banks to fall in. The boys already in the water scrambled for the shore and escaped just in time as the foaming ridge, not quite two feet high, picked up the skiff and Beth and raced them downriver. Beth screamed when the boat began to rock wildly as it fought the turbulence. Bill, still frozen where he stood, suddenly leapt into the river and started swimming after the skiff, which by then was a good hundred yards further downstream. Jack and the other boys simply stared. Unlike Bill, they had not seen the necessity for a heroic action needed to bring the day to its true apogee and he to his apotheosis. He was also glad to escape the drama he had created and the necessity of confronting Dan. The older boys, who had been avoiding Dan's eyes, ran to fetch adult help and thus turned the page on a situation they did not know how to deal with. Dan, who was arranging his stones with the aid of the smaller Cyclops, noticed nothing until Bill and the skiff were almost out of sight. He stood, a hearthstone in each hand, smiling down at his band of helpers, who smiled uncertainly back.

"You better join de udders," he said. They nodded eagerly and ran off.

Meanwhile, swimming hard, Bill was approaching the skiff. The current carried him as fast as the skiff, and his own efforts brought him gradually nearer to Beth who by now had calmed down as the boat ran with the water rather than fighting it. She could also see her Bill, whom she had long admired, gradually catching up as he became no longer a simple, attractive, dominating boy, but increasingly a great hero. She had missed the final face-off with Dan as she was settling into the skiff and adjusting her clothing to cover her bare legs. By the time Bill reached the boat the turbulence had stopped, the brief flood having been absorbed by the widening of the river. With Beth's help he clambered aboard, a glistening, muscular demi-god awaiting her arms.

But his first reaction, after a brief kiss, was dismay on finding that the skiff had no oars. They had been left on the bank near the cave. Bill tried paddling with his hands to bring them nearer the west bank of the river, but the current wanted otherwise and pulled them towards the opposite bank.

It was soon night and there was no moon to light them. The sky had become cloudy even if the storm had blown out as it finally descended from the north. They huddled together for warmth and Bill put Dan from his mind to let time resolve the problem. The picnic had fed them well and there was no lack of water and soon they stopped giving each timid kisses, increasingly adventurous caresses and cuddles as fatigue took over and they fell asleep. The hero's final reward was to come later.

They slept almost until the early summer dawn began to tint the air with yellow and pink as the rising sun cut through the river mists. Bill managed to fish a short plank from the water and began, under the adoring eyes of Beth, to guide the skiff to their home shore. Finally, they landed near a village a few miles south of St Louis and went to seek help. The folk of the village were much concerned and very kind and while they fed them, a villager rode to the nearest telegraph office to place a call upriver with the news of the children's safe landing. Then two days later the Reverend Doctor Winston arrived to take them home on a paddle steamer.

Overnight Bill had become the town hero and any whispers about his actions before the arrival of the flood became gratefully forgotten. His role of hero he exploited to the full with a bashful modesty that had the old ladies, and many young ones too, adoring him, especially Beth. Only among his male friends did he boast, adding all sorts of adventures and erotic hazards to the journey downriver. He also began to see much of Beth and they often indulged in the cuddling they had discovered in the skiff, to arrive, finally, at the culmination in the schoolroom as witnessed by Jack.

The Reverend Doctor wandered about the town informing all who would listen that Bill was "a fine boy".

\*\*\*

As Beth was being swept away by the flooding river followed by the heroic Bill, Jack and Dan had found themselves with the heap of stones that now were never to be thrown into the river. Jack looked uncertainly at Dan who smiled back and then, pulling him closer, gave him a warm hug.

"What's goin' to happen, Dan?" muttered the boy.

"Nuthin', I reckon. They'll all want to forget it, 'specially Bill."

"You think?"

"Yeah, they'll be more worried about what's gonna happen to them if'n the story got out — lettin' a nigger fight with them and cuss them, an' doin' nutthin about it... So what we gonna do wi' dese here stones?"

It was a rather suspicious heap that Jack didn't want his father to know about and so he decided to take the hearthstones back to the house. He and Dan loaded them back into the wheelbarrow in which they had carried them to the river and once back at the house they set about replacing them in the hearth, which meant further excavating in the sand that had been their foundation, so that the stones could go back in level. This almost immediately caused Jack to come across a buried leather bag and in the bag a box: it was Joshua's secret treasure, the box of ancient coins. Knowing little of his father's past and not wishing to have his find confiscated, Jack decided to say nothing, but took his find to the Reverend Doctor Winston (a Doctor of Divinity, but long given up on the Church where momentarily he had played the role of Bishop and thus, briefly becoming a cumbersome Very Reverend Doctor), who was impressed by what he saw and promised Jack to seek the opinion of a friend in St Louis, an amateur of numismatics. Jack took one coin, the Athenian one, to be his lucky talisman that he gave to the local blacksmith that he might drill a small hole in it through which to pass a leather thong.

Then a few weeks later and after Joshua had died in the church, there was another discovery. The Reverend Doctor had come to the house with Jack to see what of value might still be about. There were no more caches of treasure, but there was another rather larger tin box under the dead man's bed. It contained papers, which on examination suggested that Joshua had possessed money and was indeed a man of private means. There were references to bonds and several bank accounts. This explained why an old drunk, dressed in not much better than rags, never seemed short of a dollar or two to buy his whisky. The treasure of coins he had rarely if ever touched, as selling them might have drawn the attention and the interest of certain Mandan survivors.

The Reverend Doctor Winston suspected that Joshua was at the origin of the coins, but it wasn't certain, so ignoring them for the moment, he set about organising Jack's inheritance; which finally amounted to nearly eight thousand dollars, which to Jack's amazement could give him a bit more than a dollar a day in interest.

He didn't think much about any money that wasn't actually in his hand and was entirely indifferent to money in banks, as he now had more immediate worries. There was a growing rumour about town that it was he who had murdered his father to get at his money and had created the rather bizarre circumstances discovered in the church as a cover. Nobody really believed his story of a huge blond Indian. It was this that finally decided him to go west, at least for a time, while things in Hannibal calmed down. The Reverend Doctor Winston agreed and said he would, in the meantime, look after his affairs for him in Hannibal.

\*\*\*

Jack was once more on the point of dozing off as he lay against his tree stump, his moment of erotic pleasure having been mildly enervating, when he was startled by a sudden thud close to his ear. His drowsiness disappeared instantaneously, and every sense of his young body was alert. He glanced from beneath lowered lids to his left where lay the old muzzleloader that he had "borrowed" from the Widow Wilson. An old widow had no use for a gun. Still frozen in a position that denied the intense interior activity of his body, he awaited a further clue to the origins of the sound. It had been like the "thump" of a hammer hitting and vibrating the wood of the tree stump. If he had heard the crack of a firearm, he would have sworn that a bullet had hit the wood just behind his head. Keeping his eyelids lowered as in sleep he explored as far as possible to right and left through the mist of his eyelashes. He dared not move. If he moved, he betrayed his consciousness. This dissembled sleep was his sole advantage were there an enemy watching him. Any movement on his part could unleash he did not know what. Five minutes passed and nothing more happened. Then there was a faint rustle, not far from him, to his right, but at a distance that gave him the chance of acting.

Jack flung himself violently to the left, grabbed the barrel of the old rifle and with no real plan, simply in a defensive reaction, he swung it violently behind him as he rolled over. There was a dull thud as the stock hit the wood of the stump. Jack jumped to his feet, the rifle still in his hands, but with the barrel pointing uselessly behind him rather than in the direction of his supposed enemy. Standing barely ten feet from him was a grey-haired man, in one hand a bow and an almost empty quiver and in the other a wicked-looking knife with a long blade that reflected the yellow light of the river. He had evidently been startled into immobility by the sudden and violent action of the supposedly sleeping Jack. However, he was now in movement and sprung towards the boy with a wild yell that came, not from the throat of the western world of constraint and denial, but from a dark and bloody world of long-sought vengeance. Jack did not have time to manoeuvre his gun into its destined position and he simply raised it as a war club.

As the man came in, Jack stepped aside and swung the rifle down and across in a wide arc. It caught his assailant a glancing blow as he ducked to avoid it. The man, off balance, stumbled forward several paces past Jack, who was himself once more on the ground. The weight of the swinging muzzle loader, that had not properly found its target, had pulled him off balance. Despite his apparent late-middle years, the man turned and leapt back at Jack again, like a giant cat once more giving his shrieking cry. With no time for anything but a reflex of self-protection, Jack thrust the old gun towards the man. This time he held it by the stock. But he held it weakly. There was no force behind his grip.

And indeed, as the man fell on him, his knife raised high, the end of the barrel caught him in the stomach and the stock sprung from Jack's hands with a muffled explosion, striking him heavily on the chest. Jack's breath shot from him in an involuntary gasp and he felt himself slip off into blackness as his heart, shocked into stillness, fluttered towards death.

The man curved inwards upon himself and fell sack-like across the inert form of Jack, again jarring the boy's body. The young heart ceased to flutter and once more set to pumping blood to the brain.

Very slowly Jack began to re-find himself. His staring eyes gradually came back into focus upon the boughs overhead and their drooping burden of leaves that were buttery in the dull afternoon light. He became aware of the weight on top of him and a warm wetness that was spreading across him — not unlike the flow of sperm of an hour ago, body-hot and viscous, but this time in enormous quantities. Jack tried to raise himself on his elbows, but the man was very heavy for he was stone dead. Jack began to wriggle and squirm, slowly easing himself out from under the inert mass. After a while he was able to raise his shoulders a little and looked down across his chest. His shirt, other than the lower sleeves, was entirely red with blood and he could still feel it gushing from some severed artery and bubbling across his belly.

After a long struggle he had freed all but his legs. He sat up to better use the leverage of his arms for the final operation. As he slid gradually backwards, slowly extracting his legs, he saw pulled along with them a length of quivering intestine that gurgled forth a greenish-brown liquid the smell of which caused his nostrils to pinch and his throat contract with nausea. In a last burst of wild activity, he was out from under the body which exploded over his feet to form a trembling puddle of blood, mucus and excrement.

Jack gulped hard to hold down his stomach and he rushed towards the river. Whimpering like a puppy, he flung himself into the muddy waters in a splashing, red-smeared cascade until he was chest-deep. As he rinsed and washed, rinsed and washed, he sobbed silently, tears streaking his bloodied face, his nose as snotty as a two-year-old's. It was some minutes before he began to calm down and as reflection returned to him, he froze. Had that man been alone? He looked up towards the bank of the river and for the first time he saw the arrow embedded in the tree stump, not far from where his head had rested. He forced his eyes from the arrow and began a minute examination of the cotton trees that ran along the water's edge and on each side of the little clearing. There was nobody, or nobody that he could discern through the screen of weeds and bushes. At least there was no one who was going to attack him there and then.

It was only at this point that he began to ask himself who this strange man had been and why he had attacked him. He looked back at the arrow. It presented no answers to the mystery, merely deepened it. He was not unfamiliar with death and violence, but this was the first time anybody, other than his drunken father, had attacked him with murderous intent. And it was so strange: this big, old man with hazel eyes, using Indian weapons and uttering blood-curdling screams. Jack searched for meaning but found none other than that his aggressor reminded him of the man that had killed his father who also had been dressed as an Indian. He clambered from the river. As he stood dripping on the bank, he studied his victim more closely: his greying hair had been brown and not black.

Jack looked superstitiously towards the sky. It returned his glance blandly — greyly mute. Was the Widow Wilson right about jerking-off? She had said, "It's bad to touch yourself," when she had once seen him playing pocket billiards. This prepubescent activity was simply a sensuous comfort that had replaced thumb sucking when he was about four years old. He had never thought it had significance, but the Widow evidently did. She harangued him for a good twenty minutes on moral cleanliness and spoke vaguely if vehemently of the sin of Onan. Jack decided that this was obviously worth investigating and with diligence he finally learnt to masturbate.

Was this the vengeance of the Puritan gods, because he had jerked off thinking about Bill shooting all over Beth's dress? Why had God made his dick such a bother if he was not supposed to do anything about it? This question was posed with no real desire for an answer. Life and what happened in it was, from Jack's personal experience, in no way related to justice or reason; it just happened.

"Typical religious stuff," he said to himself. "Fucking old women's talk," he added uneasily. "Go shit all over yersels," he muttered to no one in particular. He was very scared.

Above him the sky was still a torpid, shiny grey: around him the river still heavy, slow and yellow. Nothing had changed. There was no sign of hellfire, no threatening, doomsday gloom flickering with red lightning, nothing but the ordinary. The afternoon remained perfectly as usual, except, of course, for the body, with its hazel eyes, its quiver, bow and knife and the arrow stuck in the stump.

Jack walked as calmly as possible to where the old muzzleloader lay. Quickly pushing aside his little sack of belongings which was on the other side of the stump to where he had been sitting, he picked up the powder horn and shot bag that were behind it and expertly reloaded his weapon. Only then did he feel a little more secure. Why it had gone off, killing the man, he did not know. Perhaps it had been put on a hair trigger by being thumped against the tree stump. If so, he had been lucky not to have shot himself instead.

He did not want to stay in the clearing with the body. But that was where he had agreed to meet Dan either that evening or in the morning — depending on how long Dan's business took to complete. He had to find somewhere to hide while he waited for Dan. Perhaps the man had been a lone lunatic, but Jack had a feeling that there were others like him and not far away. It was already late afternoon and while it was light and he had the gun he felt relatively safe, but in another hour or so twilight would come, bringing with it shadow and tricks of the eye that saw a phantom in every bush while real enemies could creep unseen to knife-throw distance and the silent arrow would grow more lethal. Despite the close heat of summer, Jack shivered a little. His chest hurt terribly. He opened his shirt and fingered the reddened area that was already becoming blue. At each touch he felt a jagged lance of pain. He could neither see nor feel any sign of broken ribs, but the area was so swollen; it was difficult to tell. But Dan would know when he got back. Dan was very good at bones and breaks. As he moved quickly towards the nearest wooded bank, keeping his back to the river, he thought about Dan.

He really loved that black man. Not that he would have put it exactly that way himself, for "love" in Hannibal was too sugary and had to do with mothers and girls untouched; but if there was another being in this world that he trusted even more than himself, whom he hardly trusted at all, it was Dan. At times he felt ashamed, in Bill's company for example, that he could be that close to a nigger. He also felt ashamed in Dan's company, but for another reason. He felt ashamed because he defrauded him. He deceived him, had many times disowned him and their love, both to himself and to other people. This was why he trusted Dan more than himself. Dan was always kind, loyal and so naive in his treatment of Jack, that Jack often felt trapped and angry. Why couldn't Dan do a mean thing now and again? It would certainly have eased Jack's conscience. Suddenly childishly angry, Jack began to cry again but almost immediately found this ridiculous. To be a child at this moment was not a good thing, he told himself, and after all he was about fourteen years old, or so. He sniffed loudly twice and rubbed his eyes clear with the back of his hand, stopped still and looked about him. It is very dangerous to cry, he thought.

Off to his left, leaning out over the bank of the river, was a large willow. He studied it expertly. It had the air of being a perfect hideout. Just what Bill would have chosen for a desperate fugitive: it was big, old and tall for a willow and it leant out thirty feet across the river. All around it hung a screen of weeping branches and Jack knew that once he was inside them, he would be practically invisible, but still able to see the clearing and woods about him. With difficulty, because his chest hurt so, he climbed into the tree and then out along a broad awkwardly horizontal branch that had at some time been almost cleft from its mother trunk by lightning, to where it forked. At this point a secondary stem had sprouted vertically and the branch reached once more towards the sky. Here he made his perch and was not too uncomfortable. The branch was flat and broad enough to sit cross-legged with his back against a more slender, vertical stem, to which, as he was beginning to feel very tired and weak, he attached himself with his belt, for to fall was to find himself in ten feet of swirling, yellow water.

As he sat there the pain in his chest began to trouble him more and more. He was also hungry. However, he felt a certain satisfaction, for even with a gun, somebody standing on the bank would have found it difficult to hit him. There were several layers of the tree below him that provided cover and the branch upon which he sat, being so broad and thick, also gave him protection in the direction of the bank. To have any real chance of getting at him from below meant entering the river which, at that point, was deep and fast flowing, or moving up or down the river to broaden the angle. However, at night, this would have meant losing him from view. All he had to do was to see that no one climbed up to him and with his old muzzleloader across his knees he was sure he could do that — provided he stayed awake. He adjusted his father's belt, a long leather one, with which he had often been beaten and which went twice around him in normal use and attached himself more securely to the upright branch against which he was resting. As a further precaution, he took a piece of string from his pocket and tied the old gun to the belt by its trigger guard.

From his hiding place, looking through the tree's branches rather than into them, Jack could see the clearing and even make out the crumpled form of the man he had killed. But soon the summer twilight began to deepen, and every object of the landscape settled into a grey indeterminacy that puzzled the eye and sent false warnings to his febrile brain. Soon his eyes ached and so he closed them to rest them awhile.

Suddenly he was awake. Terror petrified his body. In the bright moonlight he saw the glint of metal and the pale oval of a face that swayed slightly from side to side as it edged towards him. Beyond the fact that terror prohibited a coordinated reaction to this situation, he was numb from the immobility of four hours cramped sleep. He felt his heart race and leap and the stiff agony of his battered ribs, but his arms and legs, at least as far as his awareness of them was concerned, had ceased to exist. The face grew nearer; no more than six feet separated them. What would Bill have done? But then Bill had limbs that never slept. He tried to muster a voice full of threat and bravado. The feeble, shrieking result probably had a greater effect than any guttural roar might have done. His cracking, squeaking voice of a half-man took on a sinister, lunatic edge.

"Stop," he cried, "or I'll blast your fucking face off. I'll kill you deader 'n a dog." And, in a final rising scream that broke in two at the end, "Jump or I fire."

The face rolled sideways and disappeared from the branch. A quiet splash was quickly swallowed by the swirling currents below and Jack was alone. Agonising life slowly returned to his arms and legs as he forced the blood to start circulating. He would have fallen several times, dragged by the weight of his inert limbs but for the belt that bound him to the tree and the rifle would have been in the river were it not suspended by the string. When he was finally in sufficient control of his fingers, he retrieved the gun and thus reassured began to peer about him for evidence of the enemy.

The silver, moonlit landscape was almost as clear as day. However, its monochrome character hid many details and left much to be imagined. The clearing was a patch of brilliant grey, with here and there the detail of a clump of weed or fallen log picked out in satin white and deepest black. The interior of the woods was a confusing criss-cross of shadows with no relieving colour to indicate the difference between leaf or trunk or flesh. In the densest parts there was simply a shimmer of glistening greys that faded into a warm darkness. This darkness filled his imagination with fleeting objects.

From time to time he felt sure that he had identified something human, a movement, a sound, or simply the telepathic waves of a presence. But none of his intuitions assumed concrete form and the landscape remained still and silent. To his left he could make out the tree stump where he had dozed out his fantasy that afternoon. The arrow was not visible, for it was embedded on the other side, away from his view. He became aware of a missing element. He searched the ground between the stump and his tree, but there was no sign of the body of his assailant. He could make out a darkish patch where the man had bled his life away, but nothing more.

He had no idea how long he had been perched in the tree. It seemed to him that any moment the dawn should start to colour the eastern sky, but it remained obdurately colourless. Not the faintest tinge of pink or yellow came to hearten him. He began to wonder whether this night with its silver brilliance were not somehow part of a spell. His strange attacker from nowhere — a white man possessed, it seemed, by an Indian's spirit — could hardly come from the reality of Hannibal.

Perhaps Hannibal was not so ordinary after all. He shivered a little in his perch in the willow as he thought of the dead and felt glad that Dan had decided to come west with him. Were his father's scalp and the arrow somehow connected, he wondered. They were far from Indian territory and both men, the dead man and the huge man, were not ordinary-looking Indians, if they were Indian at all.

He began to long for Dan's arrival. It wasn't that far to St Louis that he really couldn't have returned before nightfall. But then perhaps he had found a girl. Dan had changed a lot in the last few months, since learning he was probably to be sold and in his new relationship with Jack and with Bill's unease after their Homeric confrontation, he now did independent things that he would never have done before, at least not without consulting Jack or Bill. He had even started cussing. Jack felt strangely jealous of this new man, Dan.

Jack longed for the comfort of his pipe. His chest was still hurting badly too. He felt like crying again. But he didn't. Once more his eyes made a searching tour of the moonlit landscape. He tried not to think of Dan. Thinking of Dan at any depth presented him with unresolved problems. He needed Dan's company, his support, too much to be able to begin an analysis of their relationship that required him to judge his friend, or even worse, himself. What was he doing with a nigger as his best friend anyway — and now lover? Not that Jack would have thought of it in that way. What had happened between him and Dan was simply a sensuous extension of their friendship.

A detail caught his eye. There was still no body in the clearing. He knew the corpse had disappeared while he slept but did not ask himself why he had expected it to be there now. Its presence would have reassured him. In the unreal silver of the night, he needed things to stay as they were. There was too much ambiguity. However, in recompense, he was sure the sky was getting lighter. Only upon registering this information did it occur to him that he was perhaps better off in the dark. In the moonlight, he was in the blackest of shadow and he knew himself more or less invisible to anyone outside the tree. He stifled this fear: whatever dangers the coming day might present, they were infinitely preferable to the deceptive world of shadows and moonlight.

Inexorably the sky grew lighter; at first the monochrome sky took on a greenish tinge towards the horizon behind him to the left. This spread slowly upwards, dimming the high, round moon as it went. Then the green gradually turned pink and suddenly the sky and the river became part of the same light. The river flowed into a brilliant haze that was both air and water that shimmered with the pale, warm colours of the returning day. Finally, the glittering edge of a feeble sun appeared and ate into the morning mist as it gathered strength.

Jack studied intensely the newly coloured landscape, searching for clues of his enemies, but even more for signs of the return of Dan. But all about him remained obstinately devoid of human life. There was a rabbit playing on the edge of the stain left by the dead man and high above a buzzard circled slowly on motionless wings. He longed for Dan.

It was not until about midday that Jack saw a canoe slipping along under the riverbank. His immediate anxiety was quickly relieved when he recognised the woolly head of his companion. Jack was still in the tree. He had not yet found the courage to clamber down to the bank. But now he began to crawl along the massive branch towards the main trunk of the old willow. His cramped legs moved unwillingly, and he realised that the canoe would pass under the tree long before he reached the ground. He stopped and standing up against the trunk prepared to hail Dan as he passed below. He felt mildly frustrated that he would have to let pass this opportunity to play a joke on Dan. There was nothing to hand that he could toss down on him, nothing that is that he did not mind losing in the river should he miss his target. Then he thought of his gun. Rapidly untying it from his belt, he searched the approaching canoe for a suitable target, but could not see anything he could shoot at without holing the boat. Reluctantly he settled for making a noise and a splash. Dan was searching along the bank as he floated by, looking for Jack. The old gun roared, and the ball splashed into the water in front of Dan who flung himself flat in the bottom of the boat.

"Hey, Dan, it's me," shouted Jack as the canoe disappeared out from under the curtain of the willow. And he scrambled down the tree, suddenly all agility and life.

As he ran out laughing from under the great tree, a puff of smoke appeared among the cottonwood on the far side of the clearing and the crash of a shot racketed through the bright morning air. Dan's head that was just appearing above the edge of the boat ducked down again. Jack threw himself to the ground, rolled over once and then lay still. He heard Dan's voice.

"Jack chile, you a'right?" Jack dared not reply. Dan called out a couple of times more, his voice fading as the canoe drifted quickly downstream. Then there was silence.

Jack was lying uncomfortably on his back with the old muzzleloader across his belly. He looked to left and right but saw only the tall stalks of the rank riverside grass. He closed his eyes and listened hard. There were voices gradually approaching, and as they grew nearer, he heard a language that he could not understand, but knew must be some Indian dialect. Soon he felt the shadow of someone standing above him. He opened his eyes slowly, not knowing what else to do. He did not feel frightened as much as ridiculous, but he did not see how else he could have acted. There did not seem to be any possibility for action. What a fool he had been to empty his gun as a joke! Dan was really going to have the laugh on him there. He was angry with himself and, once again, felt like crying. He forced himself to think about present problems.

There were two men: one was maybe a white man and the other an Indian in full war paint. The Indian was standing astride him. He said something to Jack that he did not understand, but which nonetheless sounded reassuringly neutral. It seemed to be an instruction rather than a threat. The Indian then squatted down until he was practically sitting on Jack's thighs. With his knife held as a warning against Jack's throat, he began to search through Jack's clothing. He gave a grunt of satisfaction as he came across the old gold coin that hung around Jack's neck from its leather thong. The Indian beckoned to his companion. Together they examined the coin. Bill had thought it had some ancient magical significance without being able to specify very exactly what it might be, while Dan said owls were good against witches. Jack's assailants, too, were obviously impressed by its qualities. The Indian astride Jack pulled the thong taut and started to manoeuvre his large Bowie knife between it and the boy's throat.

Suddenly, yet another shot rang out. Jack saw the white man reel past, one arm flailing for balance and the other, like a broken wing, waggling uselessly from a new-found joint halfway between the shoulder and the elbow. The man fell, his shocked, white face started screaming from a mouth distorted to a perfect "O". The Indian astride Jack had fumbled and dropped his knife at the sound of the shot. He gave a last desperate tug at the coin, retrieved his knife, jumped up and ran. Another shot followed and then another, but the man ran on and disappeared under the nearby trees, swallowed quickly by the green of the rough, riverside undergrowth. Jack momentarily caught sight of a third figure who had been waiting in the woods and who turned and ran alongside the fugitive Indian. He was tall and also appeared to be a white man. He carried a long gun of ancient form.

Remaining close to the ground Jack turned to look in the direction from which the saving shots had come. He saw nothing at first but a rapidly dispersing patch of blue smoke that drifted slowly across the bark of an old oak. He crawled rapidly in its direction, occasionally glancing over his shoulder towards where the Indian and his companion had disappeared. The wounded man had stopped screaming and was now moaning quietly. Suddenly, when Jack was about ten yards from the tree, Dan stepped out into the open, an enormous cavalry revolver in his hand which was still exuding a thin trail of thick smoke. He grinned at Jack.

"Dat's de first white man I ever shot," he said, with a certain note of satisfaction.

"Where'd you get that gun, you crazy nigger?" yelled Jack, unable to control an inbred reaction of disbelief before the vision of a negro with a gun who was not simply carrying it for his white master and who had, moreover, just shot a white man.

"Don't nigger me, chile," replied Dan with a smile as he proudly pushed the cumbersome object into the holster suspended at his hip. Jack glanced around, beginning to appreciate that his feelings were irrelevant to their situation, even if he could not completely dislodge the inner anxiety that accompanied them. He rushed the last few yards and threw himself joyfully upon his friend in a wild hug that forced Dan back against the tree, where the embrace was returned for several seconds. All the while Dan was anxiously scanning the forest on the far side of the clearing. Finally, glancing down on the boy, he placed a short kiss on the top of his head and pushed him away until he held him by the shoulders at arm's length. He studied the dirty, tear-stained face awhile.

"You'se still a goddarn baby," he said and wondered once again at the fine black hair and blue eyes, and the pale skin that never seemed to tan to a colour any deeper than a pale honey.

"What are we going to do with him?" said Jack, as he nodded backwards over his shoulder, towards the moaning victim of Dan's first shot. From the protection of the oak, they studied seriously the appearance of Jack's attacker, all the while keeping a wary eye on the trees across the clearing. He was a smallish man well into his middle years, with grey, almost silver hair. His skin was pale, as were his eyes which might have been blue or grey. It was difficult to tell at the distance. He was, however, dressed as an Indian and his hair, although slightly frizzy, was worn in long, thick tresses that had been tinted red. Lying on the ground next to him was a strange looking object: it was made of elaborately carved wood, thin and rounded at one end and at the other flattened into a broad curve, like an open beak, which held a heavy round stone. It was about two feet in length.

As they examined him, the man began to struggle to his feet with the aid of his one good arm. He glanced at them and then quite deliberately ignoring their watchful presence began a stumbling walk towards the trees on the other side of the open grassland. Jack tried to pull the revolver from the holster at Dan's hip, but Dan stayed his hand.

"Let 'im go, Jack," he said, "It'll keep de udders busy." Jack could see the sense in this and nodded. "Let's get de canoe, wese bin hangin' aroun' too long," added Dan and he turned and began to run down the riverbank beneath the trees.

"Wait!" yelled Jack. "The rifle, I forgot the fuckin' gun." Dan ran back towards him.

"Be quick then," he shouted and taking the revolver out he pointed it towards the woods. Jack ran bent double to where his gun and his tattered bag lay. He picked up both at the run and turned back towards Dan.

"Down," shouted Dan, seeing a puff of smoke across the

clearing, and as Jack threw himself to the ground two shots rang out and a ball cracked past above him. Jack jumped immediately to his feet so as to be away before the enemy had time to reload. Dan fired again, more for effect than in hope of hitting the enemy a hundred yards away.

As Jack ran past, Dan gave a last wary look across the clearing and glanced at the scar in the bark close by his head, before turning to run after the boy, his revolver once more trailing behind it a thin line of acrid smoke.

"D'jer hit him?" gasped Jack as they tore along the riverbank, tripping and trampling through the long weeds. Stringy lengths of briar and nettles lashed and scratched at Jack's bare ankles, until they were spotted with red. Dan did not reply, but simply grasped his friend's arm to pull him along faster. At last, they reached the canoe hidden under the riverbank, and scrambling aboard they pushed it out into the river and then lay as low as possible among the packages Dan had stowed in the bottom. The current picked them up and carried them downstream as fast as a man could run. For an hour they drifted like this and then finally sitting up, they both seized a paddle to propel the canoe across the river to where the currents were calmer. It was their intention to go downstream just as far as the Missouri and then turn west to mount against the current, for that was the direction in which they would find the goldfields.

# CHAPTER THREE

For many days Jack and Dan paddled slowly north-westwards against the Missouri current. Jack's chest healed rapidly having been no more than badly bruised. They discussed at length the events that had come about in that little clearing ten miles upstream from St Louis. At first Dan had been unwilling to fully believe Jack's account of what had happened. There was, after all, no dead body to be seen. He thought perhaps that Jack had finally been infected by the curious imagination he associated with Bill Watson and other "well brought-up" white boys, who seemed to lie about everything, for no real reason, and then accuse the black man of being credulous. Lying had its uses but nobody sensible did it as gratuitously as did some white boys, simply for amusement. But Jack had been so adamant, if seemingly little perturbed by his part in this death, that, in the end, he had to accept that pretty Jack, so pale and fragile, if somewhat dirty, really had killed somebody.

Pale and fragile he might seem, or even be, but inside the frail appearance of this adolescent, thought Dan, there existed a kernel of hardness. He may have been very frightened by that afternoon's adventure and was still nervous at every sound and shadow, but he faced up to the killing as calmly as most other people faced up to experiences which, while being strongly flavoured with mortality, were also everyday: for example, the birth of a baby or the death of an aged parent. It was as if the event were fore-ordained and Jack merely the medium used by this part of an inevitable destiny. Dan felt uneasy when confronted by such a terrible innocence that killed, even if justly, without remorse. There seemed to be missing somewhere a lesson in humanity that other beings had usually absorbed. Where, in Jack, demanded Dan, was the unconscious recoil before the idea of inflicting death? Jack was also very calm about other things that upset "normal" people. For example, he talked about his father and the way he had used him, as if everybody must have suffered similar experiences. As Jack loved Dan in his way, Dan also loved Jack, but more unconditionally. While Jack sometimes felt irrationally angry with his friend who no longer fitted his role of slave, what Dan experienced was a form of foreboding before the unpredictable, unfathomable, glacial qualities of this boy. Jack, he thought, had an ice-flower as a soul.

The other death he had confronted, that of his father, seemed to have left him equally unmoved. Admittedly, it would have been difficult to have felt any affection for the man that sabotaged his childhood. But even so, it was somebody he had lived with; but again, Jack showed no signs of fulfilled hatred, of taking pleasure in the demise of his great enemy and he had received his inheritance with equal indifference. It was not just the box of coins which might or might not have been his father's — it was a very old house and that hearth had been there for a very long time — but also a considerable sum of money that left him unmoved.

On that first evening, after the violence in the clearing, while they lay in the dark, fearful of lighting a fire, but nonetheless warmly wrapped in the blankets Dan had brought with him, they talked of Dan's mission to St Louis: and the meeting with Bill, made in order to organise the financing of the voyage westward. Bill was to have brought a hundred and fifty dollars from the Reverend Doctor Winston (an advance on interest to come). He was also supposed to help Dan buy the provisions, particularly a gun and ammunition which would have been impossible for a lone black slave to buy. Jack was unwilling to go himself, because of the suspicion that had fallen on him in relation to Joshua's death in the church. The Reverend Doctor had advised Jack to stay clear until the real killer was found, or things calmed down a bit; hence, Dan having undertaken the mission to St Louis with Bill, who was unaware that the plan for escaping to the west included Dan.

There had been less money than expected, or at least only a hundred dollars which the Reverend had sent as a sort of consolation. The bank where Jack's inheritance and also the money from the sale of the ancient coins was invested seemed to be suddenly in difficulties and no cash was available, only promises that all would be righted in the future, or so Bill reported. So with the hundred dollars (half of which still existed, in the form of two gold and two silver pieces) Dan and Bill had bought the supplies they needed. The cavalry revolver had been Bill's idea. It seemed to him an essential weapon for Indian warfare, a counter measure to the Indian's skill with the bow and arrow on horseback. Dan's pleas that Jack needed the gun for getting food and that he had no intention of fighting Indians on horseback were of no avail. Fortunately, there was still the old gun that Jack had "borrowed" from the Widow Wilson, and despite Bill's distaste for the prosaic, Dan's wish to buy powder and shot for it had prevailed.

Nevertheless, both Dan and Jack were secretly pleased with the purchase of the revolver, which had already proved useful; although it was the style of the thing that pleased most. Even Dan was forced to admit that for once the opinion of Bill had bordered less on lunatic imagery than usual. Bill, too, was growing up, perhaps. For several days they took it in turns to wear it. Finally, its cumbersomeness became wearisome and first Dan and a few days later Jack abandoned the joy of male swagger and it was relegated to an oilskin wrapping in the bottom of the canoe. However, at the least sign of a stranger and every night, Jack would have it to hand.

As they lay together under the blankets, pressed warmly one against the other, the banal everyday demands of their sexuality already appeased, Dan wondered mildly how Jack could be so cool about the probable loss of his fortune; while Jack, even when warm and sated, was as ever haunted by nameless anxieties that awaited new losses and he often reflected upon one of the important moments of their friendship and wondered if Dan's affection could last in the face of his cowardly betrayals. The probable loss of his inheritance didn't seem to matter very much; it had never been very tangible. And he still had his talisman.

\*\*\*

One day, almost a year ago, Jack and Dan had been for a summer, night-time swim. In the dark they could be friends. No disapproving eyes could see them. Their skins were warm and glistening. They were naked beneath a soft summer rain as warm as the air about them. Dan was bigger than Jack and about seven or maybe eight years older. Neither of them was very sure of his age. Jack was not long aware of his sexuality and his voice squeaked and cracked at every change of tone. Dan, on the other hand, had long passed that stage. He had definitely reached manhood a long time ago, as his lost children proved.

It was the first night they had caressed one another. Dan remembered clearly how it had started. He was lying on the warm wet grass, his shirt and trousers folded under his head, when Jack approached and rather than simply lying down next to him had jumped astride him with a laugh and sat on his legs, intent on teasing his friend. One of Jack's hands, originally there to seek balance, rested on Dan's thigh. Although they had been naked together before, the temperature had not ever been so exactly comfortable, nor the fine mist of rain so sensually soothing to the contact of their two bodies. Without thinking, like a child, Jack had started to caress Dan's thigh, his hand appreciating the smoothness of the skin under his palm, a sort of liquid silk in the rain. For Jack physical closeness, while very sensual, was still largely free of direct sexuality. His sensuality was still much that of the baby fondling its mother's breast, or even a puppy, or simply any object with a pleasing texture as had Dan's thigh. And after all Dan was a good nigger and a slave and thus a sort of pet. He felt a slight tremble in the legs that supported him.

"Hey, stop dat, Jack chile or I'm gonna get all stewed up," muttered Dan in a matter-of-fact tone.

"'Or what?" replied Jack, seeing a means of teasing Dan. His hand had been near the middle of his friend's thigh and now he moved it gradually higher up.

"Hey, do stop dat, Jack, Chrissake honey, lemme be." Dan started trying to sit up, but Jack leant forward and pushed him back down. As he had leant forward, his hand came in contact with Dan's penis, which he now grabbed hold of.

"Ooch!" Dan grunted part in pain, part in surprise. His penis was now rigid. Jack grinned mischievously at his victim.

"Why they're right about you nigger boys," he said mockingly. "It's very, very big. It's a wonder you don't split them poor coloured girls apart," and began to pull at it playfully. "I hope it don't get no bigger. I heard tell how you can kill a girl that way."

"Jack, goddarn it will yer stop. It ain't right to do dat, chile."

"I ain't doing nothin'," replied Jack, pulling even more rapidly and keeping Dan pinned down by putting his elbow under his chin as his struggles to sit up finally diminished. He was enjoying Dan's embarrassment. But it wasn't quite like when he and Bill and the other boys had masturbation competitions, sometimes autonomously and sometimes doing it to each other. This was different. He didn't know quite how. It was warmer and nicer, friendlier.

The social restrictions had meant that their relationship was played out at night and most often hidden in Dan's hut, which had forced them to share every sort of private moment and to tease his friend's penis did not seem, on that evening, any different from watching him scratch himself or have a pee in the river, this being an event that often became a game in which they competed to make the highest and furthest trajectory. As he continued this ambiguous warm teasing, he became aware of that relatively new feeling, that dull urgent ache in the pit of his bowels that heralded desire. It certainly wasn't at all like when he and Bill or other boys were jerking off together. This went deeper inside him, made him want to hug Dan to him. His guilt began mounting in measure with his desire as he realised that he too was erect and near ejaculation as he released the pressure on Dan's neck and simply lay across his belly and chest.

Each had witnessed that the other masturbated, but usually under the cover of darkness and hidden beneath a blanket, recognising the activity from the trembling, the controlled gasping, and the sudden stillness, the calm that followed. They were often naked together, but this was not strange and at the time it was simply a matter of getting to know the other, and the way a body expressed itself without words, speaking of trust and mistrust and of simply being at ease in each other's company.

Jack spoke again. His voice had become husky and his breathing rapid:

"Reckon I'm about to make you shoot real soon now, dear Dan," and pulling, now more gently with one hand, forcing the skin as low as it would go and then bringing it up again, he started caressing the tip with one finger.

"Aw, Jack, do stop dat will yer," muttered Dan without conviction. He had long ceased the struggle to get to his feet. Jack saw his friend's eyes close as he moved towards orgasm and he stopped.

"Right now, boy," he said, "are you gonna be a good nigger tomorrer and give your Jack all he wants?" There was no reply. Jack tried to keep the semblance of a joke going a little longer.

"That silence is gonna do you no good, boy, I don't care if you ain't grateful." But he found it was no longer anything like a joke. He recommenced gently the masturbation, wondering what Dan might think when it was all over. As Dan's orgasm came, he pulled Jack closer to him, hugging his head against his chest, his other hand clasping his buttocks, bringing the boy's erect penis hard against him. Then, as he trembled to the end of his climax, he began in his turn the gentle massage that would bring Jack to the same sweet paroxysm. Jack made no resistance as guilt and desire rushed towards the end that was to leave him confused and anxious as they lay belly to belly joined in a sea of semen and an affection larger than friendship.

Even as he had relaxed into Jack's caresses, Dan was troubled that a white man had seen him abandoned to pleasure and hoped Jack would not take too much cruel revenge tomorrow. But it was the little Jack he loved and the only white man who had ever treated him with even half-respect. It had not taken long to overcome the feigned reticence of the boy who so distrusted the world and who was sure it was not something one should be doing with a nigger. He had relaxed in Dan's arms as a baby relaxes into its mother. He clutched hard at Dan, his fingers pulling strongly at Dan's hair and digging cruelly into his flesh, just as the anxious baby bites the nipple that feeds it; and then, the crisis gone with trembling and little sobbing cries, he gradually relaxed, feeling the warm wetness between his belly and Dan's like a gentle pool of milk that had dribbled down his chest, or like the warm stream of urine that flows into the swaddling of the baby with all its needs replete. Then remorse came.

He remembered how he had then shut his eyes tightly lost in a struggle between the crime of hugging a black man to receive his love and the pleasure of being caressed; a pleasure that outweighed the simple sexuality of the moment, a pleasure that reached far back into his infancy when other hands that he hardly remembered had touched him, with the same tenderness. His guilt, because Dan was a nigger, mingled into his other anxieties. He began to weep quietly, for this tenderness was inextricably mixed with darker feelings and the conflict threatened to spoil the untroubled acceptance of the caresses he so dearly needed. He hated Dan's nearness and at the same time hugged him close: he hated the nigger and loved the Dan. His semen grew cold, as had dribbled milk and wet swaddling in the long distant past. Dan pulled Jack even closer and kissed him, wondering what strange things might be happening in the hidden thoughts of this child and how this act had seemed to proclaim equality; it being affection open to hurt — the beginnings of trust. But Dan was confused. What did this white boy want? What did he feel? Jack felt confused, at once very happy and fearfully guilty.

The next day Jack had not spoken to Dan except to make a spiteful joke or crossly demand a service. He felt dirty, an outcast from himself, someone who had betrayed and lost his whiteness. But as the days passed, he came to accept what had happened and even wished it to happen again in another world where there was only him and Dan and they were the same colour. Nevertheless, another month had passed before he sought, with a certain anxious diffidence, another opportunity to find again that almost forgotten warmth that he knew had existed somewhere far back in his life. In the end, on a day with the same warm drizzle, as if he had awaited this as necessary to the exercise, he simply laid his hand on Dan's smooth belly and said, "Can we do it again?"

And Dan simply replied, "Yes, I'd like that." And kissed him, and this time the kiss was returned, if a little hesitantly, but later very much more warmly.

\*\*\*

Dan had known a loving mother until he was nearly eight and so indeed had learnt to hate when she and his brothers and sisters were sold away from him; however, he had never experienced the darkness of the unloved infant that he sensed enveloping Jack like a curtain between himself and the world of others. Dan's distrust and growing hatred of the white world had taken another leap forward when in his late teens his woman and his two children had likewise been sold away from him.

He and Jack had pleasured one another like simple animals, but now they were both into a far more difficult moment of their friendship; and again, as he held Jack to him, much as he had held him that after-swim evening almost a year back, Dan's mind wandered from the prosaic paths along which it preferred to roam, but which unguided reflection would leave him still a slave, and he tried to situate Jack in his world of black and white and his flight from slavery.

As a slave boy, a child, he had had little apprehension of justice, equality, humanity or the dozen or so other concepts that now increasingly troubled him. Today he could not even look at a girl and desire her without having to make a calculation among the black and the white, to feel a sudden apprehension, a sudden fear when confronted by undefined grey areas open to instant cruel interpretation by his oppressors. He was not free, not even able, deep inside him away from white men's eyes, to enjoy the simple fantasy of making any girl his as hate inhibited love and accelerated violent desire. Since becoming an adolescent, he had begun to flee towards a private inner freedom, where he found himself having to protect this dangerous and complex new domain from his inbuilt inhibitions as well as from exterior attacks. He felt despised and imprisoned by the white world but then could find no black man's world to counter it — in the end there was just him and Jack.

When he had been a normal slave, a fatalistic acceptance of the world order sufficed to get by, provided the whites one encountered were not too brutal. But now, as a runaway, he would elicit the worst in all the white men he encountered. They would find his existence a threat. He was more and more often angry and frustrated. Jack had killed coldly but by accident. Dan began to recognise fearfully that there was a category of beings that he could easily kill, in cold reality rather than hidden in the heat of his imagination. He had learnt this after one pistol shot in the clearing by the river. But where was Jack in all this? Jack made his life complicated. It would have been much easier to live isolated from the world of whiteness, to relax into a total hatred of all faces that had no colour. But then Jack too had been a lesser being to the white men that surrounded him. Was not he an orphan whose drunken father raped him and who had lived with a mad drunk, all alone for much of his childhood, as the despised and forbidden but much used companion for Bill and the other boys of Hannibal? Jack was more or less white trash and even respectable slaves, the domestic ones, as he had been, ones that had learnt to read and write a bit were allowed to look down on this kind of white man. Even their white brothers accepted that a good, obedient slave might do so, but privately. Then Dan again realised the nature of their affinity: they were both alone except for each other. And for Jack, he felt, even that was not very certain.

\*\*\*

After seven weeks of struggling up the river Missouri, the memories of the bloody encounter with strange Indians were fast fading and the two had entered happily into a simple world of travel and hunting. No further sign of their attackers came to trouble them. Finally, they accepted that their flight downriver had deceived these strange men and that if they were being sought it was somewhere a lot further south and east along the Mississippi.

The sun was getting low down in the sky and they paddled slowly forward against the current, seeking a spot where they might pass the night. Just as the descending sun was about to force them to stop at any place that presented the least possibility of an encampment, they came across a small island. On one side it was separated from the bank by five yards of swirling water that would be impossible to cross without a bridge and on the other by a broad stretch of river that grew calm as it approached the island, where the water lapped mildly along a sandy beach. It seemed ideal: an angry moat on one side and on the other a stretch of water where any approaching danger would be long visible before it reached them. They beached the canoe and pulled it inside the cover of a double line of bushes. On the other side of these bushes, they made their home, a nest-like clearing surrounded by long grasses. Soon a bright, smokeless fire was crackling busily under a coffee pot and a pan of rich fatty bacon. They munched contentedly on their hunks of unleavened cornbread and listened to the wild rushing of the river on the far side of their little island. When each morsel of bacon reached a brown perfection, it was flipped out onto a piece of bread and as rapidly consumed. As the last vestiges of the twilight faded behind the trees, they took out their pipes and settled back to enjoy the end of the day. Jack gave a little yawn of pleasure.

"We ain't gone very far today," he said, simply for the sake of hearing his voice among the sounds of the wilderness. Dan simply shook his head wisely. It was totally unnecessary to discuss the wild river surging south-east like a rolling yellow field, that was filled with sharp snags and rafts of woodland debris amongst which they had sought to find the passages of calmer water that would allow them to fight their way a little further upstream. On both sides were high clay banks and clusters of cottonwood forest that clung to the river, ready at any minute to topple into the rushing waters that undermined their roots. Several times they had been forced to clamber from their canoe in order to drag it round a particularly difficult obstruction, the water, swirling around their chests and threatening to carry them and their fragile craft to destruction among the jagged dangers downriver.

A long day of excitement and exercise was drawing to a gentle close when they heard voices out across the river. They looked at one another, their faces suddenly stiffened with the beginnings of fear and as one being, they moved to douse the fire. It was quickly done, a blanket smothering what the remains of their coffee had not killed. They crept through the bushes to where their canoe lay hidden and peered out across the water. They could make out men with torches on the far bank and perhaps six or seven boats being pushed into the water. The light of the flaming torches flickered across the river and in the almost complete darkness of the moonless night cut a path of flickering brilliance across the water to the island. At that moment they began to regret the wild moat behind them that had at first appeared to guarantee their security. Now it was a dangerous obstacle to their retreat.

"Don't suppose they mean no harm," said Jack, without really believing it. "They can't be them looney Injuns, there's too many of 'em."

"Don't like the look on 'em," muttered Dan in reply. "Why they got all dem guns an' truck if they ain't up to no good?"

"What we gonna do?"

"Hide up an' hope they miss de island. I reckon they're gonna drift lower down by the time they reach this bank."

"There ain't much place to hide," said Jack uncertainly, "an' if they saw our fire we're done for."

The island was not much more than a hundred yards long and thirty odd wide and probably destined to disappear when the next storm waters rushed down upon it. There were bushes and perhaps four dozen trees. They hid their guns under the canoe and then camouflaged it; firstly, with their tent tarpaulin to break its shape and afterwards with branches and grasses — there were too many of them and too well armed to try a fight. As a hiding place, they settled for a tree at the furthest point upstream of the island and climbed high into its branches. From this point they could see the boats clearly: four skiffs and three large canoes. For a while it looked indeed as if they would miss the island, but the easy landing presented by the beach attracted the rowers in the first skiff and they pulled hard to reach it. As the boats approached, they went out of sight behind the other trees of the island. There was a babble of voices, of advice and counter advice as the seven boats landed. And then a single voice rang out.

"Goddarn, it's an island. Come on, you mother-fuckers, back to the boats."

Jack smiled secretly at Dan and gave his arm a squeeze. Dan nodded a reply. The confusion of men's voices, cursing the loss of an easy landing was suddenly broken by another cry.

"Lookee here, boys." The confusion of voices stopped and was shortly replaced by an earnest conversation, only the odd phrase of which reached the boys' ears, carried by the light breeze that moved about among the trees.

"Hey that's a new camp, them ashes is still warm ... More'n one I reckon ... That ain't a white man's baccy ... Must be runaways ..." A voice, high-pitched and threatening suddenly yelled:

"You hear us, niggers, we're comin' to get yer!"

Another joined in: "Better give up, you don't want us t' get all lathered-up looking for yer."

Jack tugged again at Dan's arm and signalled him to be quiet. He then quickly scrambled down from the tree and approached the noisy group that was beginning to spread out in line of search across the narrow island. He came into the light of the torches.

"What d'yer want?" he asked aggressively, "I ain't no nigger."

The line of men stopped and looked at him in surprise. An adolescent white boy was not what they were expecting.

"Well, well, ain't he cute now — an' where's the nigger, son?"

"There ain't no nigger."

"Don't tell me there ain't no nigger, I can smell the sonofabitch. I got a nose for a runaway nigger. They give off the fear sweat," and he laughed.

"You mus' be smellin' yersel," said Jack. One of the men sniggered.

"Don't you give me no sass, son, or I'll whup some manners inter yer."

He grabbed Jack by the arm and pulled him towards him, his right arm raised to strike him a blow. At that moment Dan appeared in the circle of light.

"Massa Jackson, Massa Jackson, chile," he cried, "It ain't right to go sassin' dese gennelmen, who is doin' dere dooty a-chasin' bad niggers. It ain't sartain dey wanna steal me."

Jack looked at him in astonishment as he caught the tones of a Dan that had existed two years ago, before he had felt threatened — or rather an exaggerated version of that Dan.

The man lowered his threatening arm and looked towards Dan, whose eyes turned to the ground while one hand nervously scratched at his stomach.

"Waal, waal," cried the man looking very pleased with himself, "told you I could smell a nigger."

"You cern'ly got the flair, Hank," said another shaking his head in respectful, mock amazement.

"Come here, boy," said Hank almost gently. "You look like

a good nigger. You care to tell me what you an' this gen'l'man are doin' here?"

"Is de Massah's island, we come to do a bit o' night fishin' sah."

"Oh yeah! Did'n know nobody had a property jess by here," muttered Hank, unwilling to believe the nigger.

"Yessah, Massah, indeedy, we jess moved over from de Missouri. Dere's lots o' dem farmers amovin' over har widdere slaveboys." Dan nodded vigorously, looking into the man's eyes with a wide-eyed appeal for belief.

"Waal, looks like they're on our side, boys. Another lot o' good Missouri bushwhackers come to kick them northern bastards out of the Kansas Territory." Hank laughed loudly and thumped Dan across the back with such earnest friendliness that Dan, taken by surprise, stumbled into Jack. He stuck out an arm to stop Jack falling. For a moment it looked as if they might fall together, but somehow, they regained their balance. Hank's smile vanished. His hand lashed out and caught Dan across the face with a sharp slap. Dan stiffened; his fists closed momentarily before he could recover his subservient posture. The man saw this reaction and hit him again. This time the blow was expected, and Dan could control his reaction.

"Don't you know to apologise when you touch a white man, boy?" Dan, head bowed, tears streaming down his cheeks, simply nodded; the second slap had caught him across the nose and he couldn't yet speak. The man raised his hand again, when a voice said:

"Ain't that enough, Hank? You don't have ter kill him. He ain't your'n, that you can damage him as you want." Hank relented before this appeal to reason. He turned to Jack.

"You wanna teach that nigger o' your'n manners, son, or he's gonna get headstrong. Young buck like him, really beginning to feel his balls, needs a lotta discipline." He looked around him and then picking up a wicked, spikey branch gave it to Jack.

"Give him a wop wi' that for me."

"Ain't none o' your business to tell me how to treat my nigger, mister. He ain't used ter gettin' hit, that's all." Hank turned aggressively towards Jack, his hand once more raised. Again, the voice of reason spoke:

"There's them that has thet theory, Hank. An' they's the right to their opinion. I reckon. Niggers is like horses, Hank, treat 'em right an' they quit buckin'." The man nodded sagely.

"Ain't my 'pinion tho'," said Hank lowering his hand. "Clear out o' here, son, 'fore I give yer summat for yer sass."

"Com'n Massah Jackson, Mistah Hank is bein' very nice."

"Where you think we're goin', Dan? This island ain't no more'n eighty yards long an pap's not comin' for us afore morning."

"Juss a little ways, so's not to bother dese gennulm'n."

"You stay right here," said the voice of reason, "we're a-goin' anyways."

"Goddarn right," said a third man, "we've wasted enough time on a 'scaped nigger that ain't." He stalked off towards the boats followed by the others.

"Not at all sure," countered Hank, "in these times, does a man leave an expensive nigger runnin' roun' with a little kid like him? Not at all sure we mightn't be makin' a mistake to leave 'em here. Even if they's honest, it's dang silly to leave 'em here." He smiled in a fatherly manner.

"Ain't sure we shouldn't take 'em back to his pap. I reckon he don't know how dangerous this country is for niggers wi' small boys."

"I ain't that small, Mistah," said Jack angrily, "an' we wanna stay an' do some fishin' like Pap said. Ain't no one's business anyways, 'cept ours."

"Aw, come on, Hank, we're wastin' time. The bastards at Lawrence'll escape us if we ain't there soon."

"Mebbe," replied Hank. "But I'm for takin' 'em along. There might be some profit in it. At least we could persuade 'Pap' to reward us for our trouble," and he laughed.

"Might be an idea," said a new voice.

"Who's for takin' 'em?" asked Hank and there was a ragged majority of "Ayes" and "Mes". The voice of reason shook his head but said nothing. Quickly, despite Jack's increasingly abusive protests, the boys were trussed and shoved separately into boats. Hank gave Jack an enormous cuff which shocked him into silence and put an end to his invective.

"Waal, ain't he a foulmouthed little fucker!" exclaimed the voice of reason.

# CHAPTER FOUR

Where Jack and Dan had been captured was along that relatively short stretch of river which divided the State of Missouri from the Kansas Territory. It did not take long to disprove the story Jack and Dan had made up regarding the ownership of the island and the fictive "pap". From then on Dan was shackled as an escaped slave and all his and Jack's protests that he was really a freeman were disregarded. Jack was under suspicion as a "nigger lover" and Northern abolitionist spy, despite his young years, and was thus also kept under close surveillance by the band of Missourians.

Jack and Dan had had the misfortune to be taken by a group of Missouri Ruffians, raiders intent on murder and pillage on behalf of the traditional values of the South. In moving into the Territory from the river, they met up with another slaver band and were now fifty strong. Jack and Dan had at first been unaware of the nature of their companions or the objectives of the raid, but when they were joined by this other group, who were more properly residents of the Territory, they then watched a farm burn and two farmers, innocent of anything but the wrong opinions, bushwhacked; and came to have notions of the recent bloody history of the Kansas Territory and to form their first appreciation of Ante-Bellum American politics. Not that politics was a word Jack would have used.

They were making for the town of Lawrence, the Free-Soil stronghold. The slavers had decided to retreat the year before from an assault on this town because of the intervention of Governor Shannon and their respect for Sharpe's new breech-loading rifle. But this time they were the law, and they were going to do the job properly. They had the legal backing of Judge Lecompte, who had indicted some Abolitionists for treason because of actions contradicting the Slave Laws. Their band was to be part of a sworn in militia of the Kansas Territory who were to arrest the indicted Free-Soil militia members in Lawrence. By the end of the week, Hank and his followers had joined up with the 800 other men on the same mission. Dan and Jack became part of a motley group of prisoners as the Missouri militia lay in siege about the town. Jack and Dan had been separated, Dan being sent to a group suspected of being escaped slaves.

\*\*\*

Jack sat in the back of a cart along with five men. They seemed to have been forgotten. They had been captives since the day before, without food or water and hadn't seen their driver since nightfall. The night had been long and uncomfortable with little possibility of sleep. They were bound hand and foot, their hands behind them and their backs supported only by the sides of the cart. Sat beside Jack was a young man named Sam who befriended him and helped while away the time. Jack wanted to understand all that was happening. He couldn't see why he and Dan had been treated as enemies rather than simple strangers.

Sam tried to explain:

"Well, you see, all this has been going on for about three years. It's about whether or not Kansas is to be a Slave State or a Free State as in the North."

"But don't everybody own a nigger or two?"

"No way! And you'll find it's pretty rare these days in the white world, where slavery has mostly been abolished and is even a crime."

"Yeah, Abolitionists!" exclaimed Jack, finding a reference he knew.

Sam continued, trying to explain how violence had gradually become generalised as raiders from the Slave States fought with the Free-Soil militia. And how in 1854, Senator Douglas, a Presidential candidate, had tried to save his Southern votes by refusing to apply the "Missouri Compromise" and the 36°,30' line, whereby slavery was geographically limited, and then the votes of the North by refusing Southern insistence on another Slave State in the new territories.

"Who's this Douglas?" demanded Jack.

"A guy who wanted to be President of the USA. But instead of solving the problem, he's made it worse. He has created a recipe for what was to be, in effect, almost a civil war."

"How was that?"

"The people of the Territory had to decide for themselves if the new state was to be 'free' or 'slave'."

"What's wrong wi' that?"

"Nothing, except the slavers cheated. Lots of Missouri folk came over the border to vote, when they didn't have the right as they weren't residents. And so, they outvoted the Free-Soilers and created a Slave State Constitution."

"So why didn't someone stop them?"

"Because, according to the law they're now the legal government, until proved otherwise."

"That's stupid. Everybody shoulda got their guns and shot the bastards."

"Well, that's more or less what's happening. Only they're shooting back."

"Why don't the President do summat?"

"Because he's stymied by Congress where he has to avoid upsetting the Southern States' Congressmen who are threatening secession if anyone tries to create antislavery laws and also there are few actions that might be described as battles so that the Federal Army could intervene, just savage reprisal following savage reprisal and now no man is safe.

"Us in particular," added Jack. "Sounds very complicated. Don't see what this has to do with me and Dan."

"Dan?" questioned Sam.

"My best friend — a freed man that these nasty bastards want to be a slave again," said Jack angrily, expecting disapproval and being troubled by his lie. But if he had told the truth, it was admitting to having stolen a slave.

"Hey! Hey! Calm it, son. I've no problem with your friend, although, in present company, you should keep it to yourself. They don't need reasons for lynching when it comes to black men or their friends."

"Why are you a prisoner anyway? You don't look like someone dangerous."

"I was in the wrong company at the wrong time. I had been wanting to write an article for an East Coast newspaper, for preference a bit amusing, on the pretensions of the Free-Soil folk, when I got caught talking to some of them by these border ruffians. Thus, I'm suspected of treachery and treason." Sam laughed.

"I reckon they gonna hang you too," and Jack laughed as well.

"You could be right, boy," Sam said, suddenly serious. "We'll have to escape."

"Pity Dan ain't here, he's good at that. Got taught it by Bill Watson." Though Jack couldn't quite see how Bill's intricate manipulations, taken from the literature of boyhood adventure, could help much in this situation.

"How old are you?" asked Sam.

"Not too sure, but I reckon I must be coming up to fifteen or so. I got some hair round me dick now." Sam laughed again. He thought that Jack didn't look much more than thirteen, if that.

\*\*\*

There was a chill in the early summer night which the prisoners' thin clothes could not resist and as the hours passed their bladders that had not been emptied since some time the morning before became too painful to control. If they had had no food, they had received some water during the evening. Just before dawn the first of them gave in to his need and a thin cloud of steam arose from his loins and he cursed aloud. The precedent having been created the others also soon lost control. Jack found himself giggling as he added to the puddle that had begun to gather on the planks of the cart which were well caulked with mud and dust. This caused others to joke too and their embarrassment gave way to good-humoured banter and mutual promises as to the thrashing they would one day hand out to their gaolers and in particular the one that had been driving their cart. The night progressed and slowly the clear cold blackness of the star-sprinkled sky began to brighten in the east and a bird or two began to sing. The driver of their cart came by as the first rays of the sun hit the top of a nearby tree and hitched the horses. However, he took no notice of the prisoners and their protests other than to mutter "nigger lovers", and having harnessed the horses and went away again. At first the sun had been welcomed as it took away the chill of the night and one or two of them had even found a little sleep, but now it blazed down on them as a relentless enemy. A strong acrid smell of stale urine pervaded the cart. There were sounds of cursing from the latest that could no longer control his functions.

"Fur crissake," muttered the despairing voice, "fur crissake, lemme near one o' them mother-fuckers an' I'll kill him. I'll make him eat his own shit." His trouble was worse than that of the night and the wagon became newly malodorous.

Jack sat in the pool of his own and others' urine and his buttocks became sore and stung. He was very hungry, but the pain of his hunger paled before that of his growing thirst. He wondered where Dan was. He had not had sight of him since the evening before, when he had seen him in chains heaving cannons into position behind quickly thrown up earthworks.

Suddenly a great shout rose up from the direction of the town, where the militia were awaiting orders to advance. Several shots were fired. Jack stretched as high as he could and twisted his head round in an effort to see over the edge of the wagon. A hundred yards away was a cloud of dust raised by whirling men on horseback, with arms raised, triumphantly firing off their rifles. The aimless whirling quickly assumed a direction and the mass of riders galloped away towards Lawrence, followed more slowly by the men with wagons. The horses that had remained harnessed to their wagon in readiness since early morning whinnied with impatience.

"Dang me, how them 'bolitionists stink," a nearby voice muttered slurily. "Ahnagonna need a powerful lot o' whisky to drown thet out. Them's pissin' animals them is." The driver laughed, pleased with his joke, as he mounted the wagon.

"Gi's some water, yer drunken varmint. We're adyin' o' thirst here," shouted one of the prisoners.

"Smells like you got plen'y o' water," said the man seating

himself on the driver's bench with a satisfied wriggle of his buttocks, once again spluttering into laughter and shaking his balding head.

"Reck'n the boy's 'bout dead," shouted another voice. The driver turned round and glanced at Jack who tried to look as near dead as possible without being totally beyond recall. He then nodded and taking a canvas water bottle from beneath his seat and threw it into the wagon behind him.

"Thet ain't no fucking good, you idjit — we're all tied up."

"Who're you a-callin' idjit, piss-arse," another giggle interrupted his anger. "Fer thet yer can all stay thirsty a bit longer or drink piss… like in the Bible," he added and laughing loudly, he shook the reins to start the horses.

"Mista, mista," murmured Jack, formulating with difficulty the four syllables in his parched mouth. The man turned round again and reined in the horses.

"Ain't nuthin' but fuckin' trouble, prisoners," he muttered. He clambered down and walked round to the back of the wagon, where he released the flap and lowered it.

"Jeesus, whatta stink, if it warn't fer the kid — JeeSUS." He took out a large dirty red handkerchief and held it over his nose and mouth while surveying the line of faces turned towards him.

"Aw no, can't stand thet," he muttered and seizing the arm of the man nearest him with his free hand, forced him over onto his face.

"Have drink o' that, mistah," he muttered, "most on it's probably yor'n anyways." And he laughed again, as well as he could behind his handkerchief. Then he took out a large pocket knife, which he unfolded with difficulty, being unwilling to uncover his face. He whetted the blade ceremoniously once or twice on his sleeve and then cut the man's hands free.

There were one or two mutters of "bastard", but nobody wanted to risk that the driver take offence.

"You give it 'em," he said to the man that lay face down on the wagon floor, "Ah can't stand the stink." He put away his knife, closed the flapboard again and clumsily regained his seat. Then after having taken a long swig at a bottle that he took from the store under the bench, he put the horses in motion, hurrying them along a bit to create a wind that it might leave the stench behind him. The man whose hands he had cut free was a pale, thin individual with a small moustache. He was the weakest looking of all that were in the wagon with the possible exception of Jack. He raised himself with difficulty, for his legs were still tied. He wiped his face as best he could with his sleeve and glowered at the company as if they were to blame for having seen his humiliation.

"Give it the boy first," said Sam. The thin man nodded. He worked his way up the wagon to where Jack sat just behind the driver and put the bottle to his mouth. Jack gulped greedily.

"Slow down, son, you gonna make yersel' sick," said his neighbour rather more worried about whether there was enough to go round than the fate of Jack's digestion. Jack stopped drinking and nodded towards the man next to him and the bottle continued on its round. In the end all six men had enough to quench their thirst for a few hours more. Jack realised that he had drunk more than his share and hung his head so as not to meet the eyes of the others. Their thirsts assuaged, the prisoners began to take an interest in what was happening around them. They had now almost caught up with the other wagons of the militia. The driver continued to take pulls at his bottle. He was in a friendly mood now and regaled the prisoners with doubtful jokes and boasts as to his sexual prowess.

"Never was a woman who could refuse me, nor one as complained," he asserted. "No call fer carr'ts nor broomsticks to finish the job arter old Ned Summers has bin there. A reg'lar terrier I am. Down the rathole so quick they's hardly got time to squeak. But ternight'll be 'ceptional. No fightin' to do an' fulla unspent spunk. Yup, no need to fight no more." He shook his head in satisfaction.

"What's up then?" Sam's voice interrupted from the wagon.

"You abloshonists have dun surrend'd," chortled the driver. "You've invited us inter town fer a drink. But dun recken we're gonna drink wi' no nigger lovers, no sir. Recken we'll burn the place down instead 'cos we're pretty ready and liquored up." He nodded to himself. "Yessir, reckon we're gonna burn that town down. Arter we've bin tucked into the wimmen that is." He once more burst into uproarious laughter and lurched sideways on his seat but managed to recover his balance and avoided falling from the wagon. He started singing a tuneless song that nobody recognised.

The prisoners looked at one another and the thin man, who had sulkily resisted all whispered suggestions that he untie his fellow prisoners, contenting himself with fearful but hate-laden glances at the back of the driver. But finally reassured by the man's evident drunkenness, he began tugging at the ropes around the wrists of the man next to him. Although the exercise was difficult, by the time the wagon reached the town all its occupants were free and the bonds that could be seen were simply arranged to look as if they fulfilled their function.

In Lawrence, all was confusion. Bands of drunken horsemen rushed to and fro' with loud shouts and much wasted ammunition. The driver did not seem to know where he was heading. He stopped the wagon and with a quick glance at his prisoners, disappeared into a nearby tavern. The prisoners began to feel their freedom approach. But, no sooner had the driver disappeared through the tavern doors than he reappeared again, tapping the side of his nose in a gesture of cunning. He came to the back of the wagon and undid the flapboard, then taking a thin rope from his jacket pocket he started to retie the hands of the thin man. Almost unconsciously, simply as part of his role as gaoler, he gave a testing tug at the rope around the man's ankles. It came away with his hand. He tried desperately to pull the revolver from his belt as Sam leapt at him and the two of them rolled to the ground. As they fought for possession of the gun the other prisoners clambered hurriedly from the wagon. One of them retrieved the driver's heavy whip and awaiting his moment brought its butt down sharply on the man's naked skull. The skin split, blood poured out and he lay still. Sam, who was the lighter of the two and had begun losing the struggle, extracted himself from beneath him. Everybody stood still for a moment looking at the inert form of their tormentor, undecided how next to act. Then the thin man picked up the revolver and with barely a second's hesitation fired it into the back of the driver's head.

"Ass'ole," he muttered, "an' I bet yore a' goin' where they drink piss all day long 'cos it's so hot." He walked off into the smoke of the burning town, the gun still hanging from his hand. Jack stared after him.

As if given a signal the other prisoners, with the exception of Sam, ran off in all directions.

"You got somewhere to go kid," said Sam. Jack shook his head.

"I gotta find Dan," he said.

"Isn't healthy round here for negroes," said Sam sympathetically, "No one wants 'em about.... Even especially free ones. They're forbidden in the Territory," he added with emphasis. "Slavers or Abolitionists, it's all the same. They aren't welcome."

"An' you?" said Jack.

"I'm not fussy. Reckon we're all some kind of human being once you take the skin off."

They had started walking down the street together looking about them at the ravages of the militia's rampage. They came to a horse trough outside a tavern.

"Reckon we should get cleaned up," said Sam, "Don't think we smell any too good, pungent as we are with the pestiferous perfume of piss." Jack looked at him admiringly. He had never heard a sentence like that before. That must be poetry, he thought.

"That's alliteration, son," Sam added. Jack nodded wisely. Even though he dearly wished to ask which bit was "alliteration", he did not want to reveal too rude an ignorance to such a cultivated young man. Jack jumped into the trough in order to take a thorough rinse; while Sam acted more delicately, simply lifted the tails of his coat and dipped his buttocks to a depth of about six inches.

"Yer coat's all pissy too, at the back," said Jack informatively. "An' more too," he added, "you was nexta the chap that dropped his gut." Sam sighed and joined Jack in total half-immersion.

"Reckon we should walk a bit to dry off and then seek accommodation," said Sam.

"Where at?" demanded Jack.

"A hotel, if any have survived."

"What we gonna do fer money?"

"I've made my arrangements on that subject," said Sam with a self-satisfied smile. "And some food and drink or I'll be dead before morning."

"But what about Dan?" insisted Jack.

"It's a bit late to go searching now. And first of all, we've got to hide away a bit, we don't want to be recognised by some drunken slaver and be used for pistol practice. They've probably discovered the body by now and will be searching for us. Reckon we'll be safest in a hotel if we can find one."

It started raining.

"As if we weren't wet enough," said Jack.

"It's a good thing. Will explain why we're all wet."

"We done look too smart," added Jack. The hotel, however, turned out to be burning along with the governor's house and the two newspaper offices. When Sam saw the smoking façade of the first of these latter buildings, he grew very indignant.

"Ain't those bastards never heard of the Second Amendment?" he cried. "What kind of civilised country is this?" and many more words in this style that gradually grew more vituperative towards those who did not respect the freedom of the press or the fact that a certain young man had been heading in exactly that direction in order to take up a temporary job in the very newspaper office they were now looking at.

"Band of barbarous butt-shoving bastards — ASS HOLES," he thundered as an end to his tirade. Once again, Jack was sunk in deep admiration for the felicity of the young man's language. A man who had a talent for both poetic "cussing" and a fine turn of phrase was a rare creature indeed and worthy to be his hero.

The centre of the little town was bright with fire and black with smoke. Drunken militia filled the taverns while others sought revenge in the streets for the murder of the gaoler. Jack and Sam escaped down the side alleys. Near the edge of town, they came across a stable where a man was still working. It was the first local inhabitant they had seen.

"Excuse me, my good man," said Sam as they approached, trying to sound even more East Coast than usual. The man stopped work and looked at them in an unfriendly manner.

"Who're you?" he said. "You ain't from these parts."

"No indeed, sir," answered Sam, "we're strangers in town, my young brother and I, and have been caught up in some goddam local brawl. We're looking for food and lodgings. Some ruffians seem to be burning down the hotel. Do you know of a good, clean house that might take us in?" The man shook his head. Whether in disbelief, denial or suspicion was uncertain.

Sam continued, "Yes, I suppose we are in a bit of a state," he added, pulling at his clothes to display them. "Our luggage is burning with the hotel and we were dumped into a trough by some hooligans who took exception to our accents."

"Durn right they was too," said the ostler with a sniff. "Too-clever-by-half folk ain't well seen roun'ere." He cleared his throat. "There's the Widder Johnson's place jess along the lane a bit. Yer could try there." He pointed the direction. "It's the house wi' yeller palings." He turned his back to continue his work and took no further notice of them.

The Widow Johnson, once having overcome her first fright at their bedraggled appearance, was quickly seduced by the urbane charm of Sam, the sight of a gold coin and the idea of having two men, even if one of them was still a boy, in the house on this night of fire and violence. She produced a bottle of acceptable whisky to help them warm themselves up and made a fire to dry them out. On the table she placed a revolver and an old rifle from the Mexican War, along with sufficient ammunition to withstand a six-month siege. Sam then remarked that trousers dried only with great difficulty while still on legs. Leaving them to finish the process of drying out in privacy, she went to make some supper. Sam and Jack stood there holding their trousers up in front of the fire. The smell of frying bacon drifted in from the kitchen. Saliva instantly filled Jack's mouth and the pain of his hunger flooded back into consciousness.

"Crissake, that smell's a-killin' me," he muttered and glanced up at his companion. Sam was looking at him intently, with a little smile flickering from his clever brown eyes.

"Why, I haven't really looked at you before. Now you're more or less clean and your hair brushed down, why you're as pretty as a girl." Jack flushed deeply. "My, my, I reckon you're going be a right little lady-killer, and probably a few men on the way too," and he laughed and slapped Jack's buttocks. The boy leapt away with a look of alarm.

"Just a friendly pat between friends," said Sam returning to the examination of his trousers and then gave the scowling Jack a large friendly smile, which Jack, relenting, returned.

"I ain't no faggot," said Jack.

"Who said you were, son? Who said you were? You can't help being a pretty young chap and I can't help noticing it — simple as that."

"You like boys then?" demanded Jack suspiciously.

"Not overmuch, but I'm prepared to make exceptions for the exceptional. But I don't really know if you're exceptional," and he looked at Jack with an air of trying to arrive at a difficult decision.

"Aw, take a runnin' fuck at yersel'," said Jack laughing, vaguely disappointed that he was not necessarily an "exceptional".

"Language, language — don't allow no cussing here," said the widow with a smile as she appeared at the door, a dish, heaped-high, held before her.

"Ooh, excuse me, gen'lemen," she then squeaked, pretending to have suddenly become aware of their naked legs and backed hurriedly away again into the kitchen. Sam gave Jack a wink.

"Think I might just have a warm bed tonight," he said. The two of them struggled into their still rather damp, but comfortably warm, trousers.

"All right now, Misses J," called out Sam. "We're as decent as nature will allow." The widow reappeared, her homely, handsome face, which a few years before had been very pretty indeed, brightened by a smile that welcomed. They sat down to eat, and Jack decided that this meal was the greatest feast he had ever known, a fact he confided to the widow, whose smile grew brighter, and then warmer by the minute as she replied coyly to the badinage of Sam. By the end of the meal Sam knew that they had arrived at an unspoken agreement. His eyes met those of the widow with an intimacy that needed no words. Jack noticed their absorption with one another and became slightly sulky, if not totally losing the good humour that pervaded his being now that he was well fed and comfortable — for that night at least, but who needed more. His thoughts rarely encompassed a future of needs greater than that required to bring the present day to an agreeable conclusion.

Jack was sitting in a big rocking chair by the fire dozing off towards sleep as Sam helped the widow Johnson clear the dishes from the table. Their hands touched from time to time in little accidental encounters that held electricity ready to develop into a full embrace. When at last they returned from the kitchen, where Sam had gallantly dried as the widow washed, they found Jack already asleep, curled up in front of the dying fire, a cushion from the settle under his head. With some little difficulty, for he was a big enough boy if rather too slight for his fourteen or fifteen years, Sam picked him up in his arms and guided by his new friend carried him upstairs to a little attic bedroom. It was the guestroom the widow kept and there were two neat beds with white sheets that looked cool and inviting. While the widow folded down the covers of one of the beds Sam struggled off the boy's jacket and trousers and then together they they put him naked between the sheets. During this operation Jack didn't show the least signs of consciousness, beyond a grunt or two, while being undressed. The widow gave him a motherly kiss and then looked at Sam. She blushed slightly and picked up Jack's clothes to take to the washhouse. Sam silently took her hand, blew out the candle beside the bed and led her to the door. At the foot of the stairs, he embraced her, and the kiss he received in return was in no way related to what he had seen placed so delicately on the cheek of the sleeping Jack. Jack's clothes were set to soak.

The widow Johnson's bed was as broad and soft as the widow herself and Sam sank happily into the luxury of them both. The last three of his twenty-one years had been spent on the frontier, which had not given him many skills as a lover. But he did not need them for the widow knew well the rites of love and after an initial period of shyness, during which she allowed him to assuage his first boyish passion, she took the matter of his education in hand.

Captain Johnson had been a happy husband, before his early death in the Mexican War and his woman a happy wife. Now Sam, who so reminded the widow of her ardent young husband, was to experience the same kind of happiness; he had rarely felt so loved in his life and certainly not since he last climbed down from his mother's knee. The plump little hands of the widow coaxed him gently from ardour to ardour. He could bury his head in her breasts with a little sigh. He could press his taught belly against the softness of hers with a little shudder of anticipation. He could feel the silky softness of her thighs, kiss her shoulders, nibble at her ears and all the while little fingers cajoled him and stroked him from root to tip and back again; lingering there, just beneath the head where sensation surged most strongly, moving away again before he could prematurely pour out his desire. Then, just as the intensity of this amassed desire threatened to become an agony of impatience, she placed him inside her where he could leap and writhe through the cascade of his pleasure, while she sobbed and shivered along with him. He learnt gradually some of the part he was expected to play — quite a few of the proper replies to each one of her caresses. And each time the final minutes were different: the first a frenzied soliloquy; the next a high-pitched note held between them almost forever; and the finale, a calm rhythm as they descended into rosy exhaustion. He emptied the last remnants of his passion from a body that then knew only an aching vacuum in the loins that hovered on the borders of pain as he dropped into a dreamless sleep.

\*\*\*

Jack had many dreams and the last flickering of his eyelids and the last sigh from his lips accompanied the pulsating flow of a little viscous pool onto his clean white sheets.

\*\*\*

The sun was already quite high when Sam awoke. He could hear voices below interrupted occasionally by the ringing laugh of the widow and the adolescent cackle of Jack. He gave a little smile of reminiscence and climbed lazily from the bed. The smell of fresh coffee drifted from the kitchen. He strolled naked to the tall wardrobe mirror and admired the soft glow of his hard white body with its arms, nut brown from the elbows down and a face of the same hue. The penis was long and heavy, still vaguely alerted from the night's labours. Sam smiled again, well pleased with himself and turned to find his clothes. There were none on the chair where he had thrown them the night before. In their stead was a woollen dressing-gown in a tartan pattern of autumnal hues that no Scottish clan would have recognised. It was just his size. He admired himself once more in the mirror before going downstairs.

The Widow Johnson and Jack were already at table when Sam entered the kitchen. Jack was wrapped in an old dustcoat. Their jackets and trousers, already sponged and pressed, were ranged on two clotheshorses around a pot-bellied iron stove. Their shirts, underdrawers and Sam's socks steamed slightly, suspended on a line above. On the table was a large pot of coffee, pancakes, butter, bacon and honey. Jack's face was greasy with butter and his fingers sticky with honey. These latter he licked between words as he chattered birdlike to the widow who watched him with a fond smile. She looked up at Sam, her cheeks flushed, her lips parted in welcome.

"Come and eat something," she said.

"Very gladly," answered Sam.

"Get tucked into them pancakes, they're f' famous," added Jack.

When breakfast was eaten and the widow had explained the events in Lawrence over the past year, Jack gathered the courage to speak of the subject that filled him with such a tumbling mixture of emotions that he found difficulty in organising them into anything coherent. The subject was Dan. He feared desperately for his friend and even more desperately he feared losing him. He felt warm and comfortable and longed to stay awhile in the house of the friendly widow and with the man called Sam and at the same time wished to leave that very instant to find his dearest friend, the only person he knew he might love and he knew loved him. He was ashamed to talk with concern of Dan because Dan was a nigger and he was ashamed not to talk of him with the warmth and affection he felt, as it was a terrible betrayal. He felt sick with this mixture of shame, fear and anxiety. The breakfast he had begun with such enjoyment became heavy and indigestible in his stomach. He forced himself to speak.

"When we gonna leave, Sam?" he asked, avoiding the eyes of the widow. Sam looked rather startled by this question. His own mind was on the possibility of prolonging his stay as long as the welcome lasted.

"That's not very polite," he replied and looked anxiously at the face of their hostess. She answered with a little smile that showed disappointment. Was there some plan she did not know of that was going to rob her so soon of this new moment of happiness that she knew only too well to be temporary?

"But we gotta find Dan," Jack blurted out, "I gotta find him. They mighta killed him. They might do anything to him an' even if they don' hurt him, they're sure to sell him downriver real soon an' then I'll never find him." He could not control his eyes and tears began to trickle down his cheeks.

# CHAPTER FIVE

Dan had seen the wagon that he knew to contain Jack lumber hurriedly off towards the town after the crowd of noisy, galloping horsemen. Later, he saw the smoke rising tall and straight into the still sky and heard the distant shouts and shots of the celebrating Missourians. He and seven other slaves were alone, supervised only by one of their number, a big, grey-haired man with a pick axe handle in his hand and a whip tucked into his belt. Dan looked down at his leg irons. He was the only one so encumbered. He looked towards the others, but they ignored him as if they read the threat of his escape in the way he stood.

One after another they turned away from the spectacle of the burning town with a shake of the head and restarted the now pointless task of throwing more earth on the earthworks around the cannons. The supervisor grumbled at them in his habitual manner, but without enthusiasm. Only Dan remained where he was, staring moodily at the towering column of smoke, the tip of which now started drifting off to the west.

"Shift yor ass, boy, an get ter work," the supervisor yelled.

"What's de point, they ain't gonna use dem cannon no more," answered Dan.

"Don' lip me, boy, or I'll whop yore hide." Dan shrugged and threw one or two shovels of earth into the air behind him. Satisfied that he had been obeyed, the supervisor turned his attention to the fire in the town.

"My, my don' dat burn bright," he said as a collapsing roof threw up a sheet of flame and a black cloud twinkling with sparks.

Jingling his chains behind him, Dan moved across to the next crescent of earth and its hidden cannon. Hidden in there also, Dan remembered, was an axe — if no one had moved it since the morning that was. He doubted it. There had been too much excitement for anyone to have felt tidy.

"Where's you off to, boy?" shouted the supervisor, his attention drawn by the clatter Dan made when he moved.

"I'm gonna add a bit to this'n here, it ain't as high as them others."

The supervisor considered whether or not this initiative in any way flouted his authority. He was ready to be annoyed, but then the heat of the afternoon was tiring, and he decided not to bother and simply turned away, once more to contemplate the fire and guess at the measure of the destruction it signalled. But then it was not his town and losing interest he gave a brief glance at the slaves as they went listlessly about their pointless task and settled himself down against one of the banks of earth for a little doze. This last year or so, little dozes had become increasingly appreciated.

For a moment Dan went cold with dismay. The axe was no longer in its place against the wheel of the cannon. He was about to shamble away with his disappointment, when his eye caught a glint of metal from the shadows on the other side of the gun. It lay in the grass, where it had been abandoned by the white man who had been cutting chocks to fit under the cannon wheels when he ran off to join in the fun in the town of Lawrence. Dan quickly placed his chain across one of the iron fittings of the gun harness.

He lifted his axe high and brought it down with all his strength onto the thin links. A link was dented, the axe had chipped, but the chain still held. He aimed another blow and then a second. The first missed the damaged link altogether but the second further weakened it.

"Hey what's you at?" cried the voice of the supervisor. Dan could hear him running towards his hiding place as he struck blow after furious blow at the chain. The link fell apart just as the supervisor appeared at the mouth of the earthworks. He could only see Dan's head and shoulders across the cannon.

"What's you a-doin, boy?"

"I ain't doin' nuthin'," answered Dan as he bent down and started rapidly pulling the chain through the lugs of his leg irons. He stood up, the loose chain still in his hand as the heavy man lumbered round the gun towards him.

"Don' do nuttin' silly, boy," he muttered, taking his pick handle in both hands. He stepped back hurriedly as Dan lashed at him with the chain.

"I ain't doin' nuthin' silly," said Dan, "I'm jus' cuttin' outa here. So don' try en stop me, ole man, if you don' wanna get hurt. Now clear outa my way cos I don' wanna hurt yer."

"Now you jes drop dat ting." The uncertainty of his voice belied the threat of his gesture as he brandished the stick at Dan. He weighed his fear of the desperate young man against his fear of the punishment that would surely follow if he let him escape; not just the whipping, that he had born all his life, but the loss of his privileges and the return to the backbreaking life of the working slave. Not to speak of the vengeance of the other slaves that was reserved for the supervisor fallen from grace. Raising the pick handle high he rushed upon Dan, hoping to get close quickly so that his weight would count for more than the other's agility. As he closed Dan brought from behind him the axe he had so far hidden. There was no time to measure his actions as he had to react before the heavy old man had time to close. In what was almost one sweeping movement the axe was revealed and then cleaving through the air to smash into the ribs of his advancing attacker. The old man felt the bones crack and crumple and he stopped, tumbling backwards under the force of the blow. He fell heavily and Dan leapt over him, axe in one hand chain in the other.

"Sorry 'bout dat, Grandad," he shouted as he ran off across the open ground watched in fear by the other slaves. The supervisor groaned to himself and hoped he was badly enough hit to die. He found to his satisfaction that he could not move and that he could feel nothing. The other slaves walked over to look at him occasionally throwing a glance at the retreating figure of Dan. The front of the supervisor's shirt was bright red, and a pink froth bubbled from his lips. On his face they saw a grimace that looked like a smile. Soon, they knew him to be dead. The older ones sat down fatalistically to await events. That the supervisor had fought the escaping slave and that he had died and that they had waited might go well for them, if their masters were not too drunk when they got back. The two youngest ones, after several minutes of hesitation, set out after Dan. They were not sure if it was to recapture him or to join him. They would decide later. But being young they knew that vengeance or punishment, it was the same thing, would fall primarily on them. In any case it might be better to be recaptured later by cooler heads than those that came from a drunken ransacking of the town.

*** 

Once he reached the woods, Dan stopped a while to recover his breath and plan what next to do. He saw the two young slaves set out after him and could guess their motives. He waited for them hidden behind the trunk of a large oak. Soon they came jogging up, looking uncertainly about them as they entered the woods. They were very young, not more than sixteen or seventeen years of age, dusky Jacks, but with sturdier bodies, the one very black with close curled hair and the other less than honey coloured with long straight hair. They chattered to one another in breathless whispers as they trotted towards him.

"What you run off fo'?" asked the darker of the two. "We'se done fo' now."

"Not if we catches him and brings him back."

"An' jes how we gonna do dat? He's gotta very wild look dat man," and he nodded to emphasise his statement.

"We'll foller him an' creep up on him when he's asleep."

"But it's gonna be dark. I reckon these woods is chock full o' evil spirits an' such."

"You bin listenin' to too many old mammies. I ain't never seen a spirit nor heard one neither."

With a wild scream Dan leapt out from behind his tree, his axe held high. The two boys tumbled into one another and fell to the ground where they sat rigid with fear. Dan burst out laughing and lowered his axe. The honey-coloured boy smiled uncertainly. Dan smiled back at him.

"What's yor name, boy?" he asked.

"Tinker, sah."

"That ain't no human name," said Dan.

"It's what de boss allus called me, when he weren't whuppin' me. Then he called me 'black bast'd' or 'wages o' sin'."

"What'd your mam call you?"

"She ain't never called me nuthin' cos I never seed her close enough. She lived up at de big house. It was ma aunt who raised me an' she called me anythin' that come to her head or 'whitey' if she were real mad."

"Ah, you're de boss's son!"

"Reckon so, but he ain't never said it."

Dan looked at him intently. "You bin taught to read an' write?" he asked. The boy nodded. "That's a sure sign," added Dan, "so what're you doin' here, boy?"

"The boss said I was gettin' uppity an' apin' white folk an' needed a lesson in how to be a regular nigger. An' so when dey was getting up a party o' niggers to look after the guns he volunteered me 'cos all the folk goin' on the posse really knew how to keep a nigger in his place. I think he's gonna sell me."

"Why's that?"

"Well, I was his butt boy and I later was to be a house nigger as his sec'tary. But he was losin' interest. I reckon I was getting too big and brawny. He liked his butt boys smaller and younger with squeaky voices."

"An so you're runnin' off?"

"I dunno," said the boy.

The other boy suddenly began speaking. His words bubbled with fear. "You cain't run off! Whada 'bout me? I'm really gonna get skinned if'n you shins off like dat."

"You ken jus' say you could'na stop me ... 'cos I'm bigger'n you is."

"Why don' you both run off?" asked Dan. "We can all git away to de North."

"What if dey catch us?" asked the frightened boy.

"I don' reckon it makes a might o' difference if we'se caught or if we goes back, which ever ways deys gonna whup us," said Tinker.

"Or worse," added Dan.

"What wivol' George probably dead an' all," agreed Tinker.

Dan suddenly felt very cold. Things had happened so fast

over the last twenty minutes, it was not more than that, that his thoughts had not yet gone back to consider the fate of the old man. His commitment to freedom was now mortal. He stayed free or he died.

"If'n he's dead de poor ol' bugger, he musta bin a real fragile ol' man." Dan shook his head sadly. He did not feel that sad. To him the old man's attack was like a suicide. He must have known that it was impossible that Dan would let himself be taken.

"Yup, his chest was so crushed in you musta cut his heart in two," the darker boy said matter-of-factly. He too had little sympathy for the old man, who was, after all a supervisor who held privileges at the expense of his own kind. He had not really resented him. In a way he had envied him his comfortable life; but he could not see him as one who needed his sympathy, even in death. Then fear redoubled in his staring eyes as he realised the impossibility of a return to the old secure if uncomfortable life. Tears of self-pity began to run down his cheeks.

"Ain't you got no pride?" demanded Dan brutally. "Is you already licked afore you've even tried?" But there was nothing he could find in his life that could have given him pride, much less hope or an idea of freedom. His world was the closed circle of a small plantation, where a rigid view of a divided world reigned. And in this world humility and stupidity were his lot: a message that had poured into his consciousness from all directions since the day of his birth.

Dan had known Jack who now talked to him as equal, Tinker had his capricious and guilty father, but this boy had received no intimation whatsoever that other interpretations of the meaning of life could exist. And he saw Tinker, who was the boss's bastard and even more so Dan as a couple of dangerous maniacs. He sat where he had fallen, cowed and tearful amid the ruins of a collapsed reality, a shattered nomos. There was nothing to sustain him. He had become an outcast from the only world he knew. As Dan and Tinker jogged off westwards towards the setting sun, he followed them, transferring his fate to those who had destroyed him as the only beings still there to be obeyed. He tried to imagine the dream that seemed to drive the other two towards destruction, but he could not. All he could see was the body of his brother, hanging by his arms from a tree where he had been flayed to death for attacking a sadistic white supervisor.

They had fled through most of the night. Where the woodland was close packed, they climbed trees and moved clumsily through the branches like giant, incompetent squirrels, trying to pass from tree to tree without touching the ground. Sometimes they made as much as fifty yards in this manner. Twice they came across a stream and paddled along it for a mile before continuing west and then veering north to circle the town. Near daybreak, with Lawrence ten miles south and east of them, they stopped to rest. No sooner had the two younger boys settled down into the nest-like clump of bushes and long grass that they had found than they were asleep. And the darker of the two was soon jerking and muttering in the grasp of his nightmares. Dan remained conscious a little longer and thought briefly of Jack before he too drifted into dreams, in which intentions merged with the images arising from his anxious unconscious: he had abandoned his new companions, who with their fears and uncertainty were already onerous, and sought out Jack to continue their journey towards the gold of the west. Their canoe rocked gently on the endless river and a warm red evening sun lit up the smiles that Jack gave him each time he turned to look at his partner.

Dan's sleep was shallow, and he was several times startled

into wakefulness by an unusual noise. Once it was the crack of a twig as Tinker rolled over and then the shriek of a startled bird. This sort of noise must have occurred many times, until a softer, more distant sound started ringing through his dreams like a feeble alarm that tugged him towards consciousness with increasing urgency. He was in a late sleep, more profound than that of earlier, for his body had at last relaxed away from its constant alert to descend into the obscurity of accumulated fatigue. He struggled against these warning sounds until at last he was abruptly conscious, as a primitive, insistent message that brought fear with it rose from the feeble but rising clamour of bell-like voices. It was a message of terror. All three of them sat up, startled, rigid with this horror as the noise came up over the brow of a hill not half a mile distant.

"Dey got dogs," squeaked Tinker, his voice re-finding the childish pitch he had thought to have lost forever more than two years ago. Dan got up to crouch behind a bush. He could see a group of seven or eight men and half a dozen dogs moving quickly down the hillside towards them. They were in open country. He could see nothing they could do but run helplessly until the dogs dragged them down. He looked at the others. Tinker returned his look with blank, hopeless eyes. The other boy was trembling as he wet himself in his terror.

"It's me dey wants mostly," said Dan. "You two hide up here under dis bush, while I leads 'em away." As he spoke he stood up, took hold of his axe and ran off through the long grass. The trackers quickly spied him and released the dogs, who rushed forward howling their view halloo. Dan ran hard, using every ounce of strength in his young body. He gradually distanced the men even if the dogs were steadily catching up. As they ran the dogs became separated from one another in a straggling line. The stronger ones surged forward to be first at their prey.

Soon Dan knew the nearest dog to be not far behind him and he turned to face it. The dog was twenty yards away. He had time for three great lung-fulls of oxygen, which sent strength to his arms, before the great beast was upon him. It was a vicious looking crossbreed between an Irish hound and a fighting dog, almost half the height of an average man and trained especially for slave hunting. Its coat was grey and shaggy, and a bib of saliva straggled down its chest from its gaping jaws full of large, yellow teeth. Fierce little red eyes regarded Dan warily as it came in, swerved and leapt from one side for Dan's throat. The axe entered the dog's body between the neck and shoulder to bury itself half a foot deep. The impact knocked Dan over and he had barely time to scramble to his feet and recover his axe before two more dogs closed in on him. These two were less hardy. And the men, who had seen the fate of the first hound, were whistling them back from the attack. The men too were now advancing more warily, their guns levelled before them.

Suddenly one of the two circling dogs attacked from behind, sinking his teeth into Dan's calf. Half a second later it lay paralysed with a broken back, its teeth still clamped on the leg. The other dog came in as the remaining three hounds arrived to join it. Dan caught it a glancing blow which broke a foreleg and the animal limped away howling to be attacked by its colleagues. Dan knelt down to force open the mouth of the dog attached to his calf, but it was like an iron clamp as the dying beast sought to fulfil its duty to its master. Dan was trying to hobble away, dragging the dog with him, when a shot rang out. He felt a harsh pain in his thigh and fell over. Another shot followed and the ball plunged into the ground beside his head.

"Stop that, will yer, I want the mother-fucker alive," called a voice that Dan recognised. It was Hank.

"But he killed my goddam hound. I spent three years teachin' that dog to be the best nigger hunter in the Missouri and he's goddam killed him." There was another shot and Dan's body leapt as his shoulder was pierced.

"I said to stop that, yer goddam idiot. I want that nigger. You kill him an' you pay me."

"But my Rufus, who's gonna pay for my Rufus?"

"Fuck your Rufus. He's done for my Abel too, ain't he? An' what about my nigger George?"

"He ain't no loss. Useless old bastard weren't worth his chow."

By now the men had reached Dan and, whipping the dogs away that had begun to worry his clothing, they inspected him warily. One of them kicked aside the bloody axe. Hank knelt down and stroked the head of the dog that was attached to Dan's leg.

"Poor old boy," he said, "you done your duty and you're goin' to the dogs in heaven." The dying dog looked up with adoration and Hank began to sob. "An' I'm gonna mess up this fuckin' nigger so bad," he stuttered with emotion. "B, b, by the time I'm through you won't know his ass from his face."

"Come on, Hank," said the voice of reason, who was also in the hunting party, "it's only a dawg, an' that's a val'able nigger. It ain't as though he killed a white man." Hank pulled a pistol from his belt and placing it against the dog's head, he fired and killed it. He then slashed Dan's face with the still smoking barrel.

"Where's the other two boys?" he demanded.

Dan stared back at him silently as he drifted between pain and nothingness.

"Are you gonna answer me, you murderin' black bastard?"

And he whipped Dan again with his pistol.

"That ain't gonna get yer nowhere better'n a dead nigger," said the voice of reason. "Probably cain't even hear yer."

Hank stood up. "What'er we gonna do with the motherfucker? He ain't in no condition to walk. Reckon I lost a nigger. We'll have to hang the bastard."

"Reckon so, but yer just might as well shoot him in the head, like you done the dog, 'cos he ain't gonna know about it."

"No, sir. That dog were a hero. This here's a low down 'scaped nigger and killer of noble dogs." He gave Dan a kick in the side which cracked two ribs. Dan was not aware. He drifted near the edges of life, where the world was pink and everlasting peace called him.

"We'll hang him anyways. An' if I weren't a religious man, I'd crucify the bastard." Having said these words with a nod of the head that affirmed his ultimate appreciation of holy justice, he beckoned over the man who had thought it his duty to bring a hanging rope — just in case.

"Get that round his feet and we'll drag him over to that clump of trees."

The rope was attached and three men, followed by the others, began to drag Dan towards the group of trees that stood on the brow of a small hill some two hundred yards away. As they approached the base of the hillock eight riders came out from beneath the trees. The man at their head seemed to be about fifty years old with hair flowing to his shoulders. He carried a long sabre which he held high above his head as he and his horsemen came down the hill towards Hank and his band. He rode towards them shouting:

"Halt in the name of the Lord. What are you doin' with this member of the lost tribe out of Israel?"

"Who the fuck is that maniac?" said Hank, at the same time cocking his rifle.

"Never seen him afore," answered the voice of reason. "Looks like a sort of preacher to me. Only he's got that there knife in place of a cross."

The rest of the slavers stared silently at this strange man and his band of young followers. They felt no presentiment or fear, simply astonishment, and their guns, with the exception of Hank's, hung unready at the end of limp arms.

The band of horsemen positioned themselves around the hanging party and their leader rode up to Hank, who held his rifle at the ready across his chest. He approached him at walking pace, his eyes staring blindly ahead as though they saw nothing but some powerful image of their own imagining. To Hank it seemed that for the rider he was not there and that he was about to ride over him. As Hank began a shout of protest, the man suddenly swerved aside and in the same movement his arm swept down and the sabre crashed into Hank's skull. Hank crumpled to his knees, the rifle still at the ready but the finger on the trigger did not move. Another member of the party hastily tried to cock his rifle, but a shot rang out and he fell dead.

"Drop your guns," barked the weird horseman and the remaining hangmen complied. He then moved amongst them and began to slash about him with his sword. The first victim fell with his face contorted in a silent howl as he tried to replace the cheek and ear that had fallen to his shoulder. The next blow was more deadly, and the man simply rolled over his head partially severed from his shoulders. The remaining three men began to run.

"Vengeance is the Lord's," screamed the rider as he chased after them, slashing wildly as he came up to his victims. His companions sat still and silent on their horses watching their father as he chased after his victims. He felled two and the remaining one suddenly stopped running and held his ground as he drew a pistol from his belt. The wild rider veered away. He was not near enough to ride the man down before he could fire. The voice of reason whistled up the remaining dogs and jogged away into the trees at the top of the hill. The rider watched him awhile and shaking his head returned to join his sons, who had made no attempt to join him. It was evident that the rider had not expected them to.

"Maybe there's some good in that man, the Lord decided to spare him." He sheathed his sabre with a blessing. "And there ain't no point in chasing about in the woods after a man with dogs and a pistol." He looked about him and seeing that the man with the severed ear was still alive, rode across and drawing a heavy horse pistol from the holster on his saddle finished him off. He then paid attention to Dan who lay moaning a few yards away. Dismounting, he knelt down beside him.

"This poor lamb is still alive." He gestured towards his sons. "Two of you boys, Salmon an' Watson, throw him across my horse." The two riders got down from their horses and picked Dan up by the feet and shoulders. A third started scanning the horizon against the possibility of a counter-attack.

"Hey, Paw, lookee there." He pointed towards the eastern horizon where two figures, silhouetted against the bright morning sky, were running as hard as they could away from the scene of carnage.

"What you see, Aaron?"

"Couple more nigger boys I reckon, Paw."

"Go fetch 'em, son. They'll find trouble running in that direction."

Tinker and his companion had watched Dan's capture and

the sudden descent of the avenging rider in wordless terror. Tinker was the first to speak.

"What they doin' to Dan now?"

"I dunno — let's get outa here," and the other boy began to stand up.

"Washy you idiot, wait." As he said this, he tried to grab the leg of the boy whose name had always been too grand for him, so that only his mother had ever used it in full and then only for the first few weeks of his life.

"Washy," he cried again in despair as the terror-stricken boy leapt away from him, "they'll see us an' they don't know we're here." But Washy was deaf to reason as to all else but the urgent need to flee from the horrors of his new life. He ran off and Tinker, more terrified of being alone with his visions than being caught by them followed him in despair. Soon they heard the sound of galloping horsemen behind them and tried to urge more speed from their tired legs. The only result was that first one fell and then the other to be gathered up by their pursuers.

"Ain't you two got ears?" said Aaron angrily. "We said we weren't gonna hurt you." The two prisoners stared at him suspiciously, the one frowning, the other trembling.

"The big nigger, he a friend o' yours?" They shook their heads energetically.

"That's likely," he said sarcastically. "You runaways?" Again, they shook their heads.

"We ain't gonna get no sense out of them. Come on, boys, let's take 'em back to Paw." He pointed to where the rest of their party awaited them and said, "You two walk ahead."

# CHAPTER SIX

"The best way is to just hang around until they bring the niggers into town. They might even be here already. There's no sense in getting all het up for nothing. Once we know where he is — then we can plan his escape."

All this sounded so reasonable that Jack immediately wiped his eyes and nose on his sleeve and headed for the door.

"Hey, hang on," cried Sam. "Watch out that you ain't recognised. And here, take this." He fished a dollar piece from his pocket. "Get us some bacca while you're at it, I'm clean out. Do you need anything, Misses J?" The widow shook her head and smiled; it seemed that life was to be kind and give her a little more time with this lovely young man.

Jack looked at them and reading the secret of their smiles, shrugged to himself and went out. He had seen Bill like this and he knew it to be useless to hope that his needs would be uppermost in Sam's mind until after he had supped long and well at the widow's inner table. She was a bit old. Maybe he would get bored quickly. With his hand in his pocket, discreetly holding down the penis that had become inconveniently erect at the thought of Sam and the widow's pleasure in one another, he marched quickly down the alley leading to the main street of the town. His walk began to slacken as he approached the end. He tried to decide whether it was worth going back to the house to find a quiet spot in which to satisfy this latest upsurge of aimless desire. He entered the main street slowly, his eyes registering only those things necessary for his safe passage. He was turning to go back, having decided that such moments were not to be wasted, when a hand caught his shoulder roughly and an angry voice said:

"You boy, ain't you the one that had the big nigger? Darn right, you is." The lassitude of anticipated pleasure fled from Jack's body as he stared into the face of the voice of reason.

"So what?" he said rudely as if the matter was without interest.

"So he's dead, or as near as dammit the last time I saw him."

"Dan's dead." His eyes stared. The blood left his face, which became pale and sunken, and his slight suntan a jaundiced varnish that heightened the sudden loss of the bright, boyish arrogance that had flushed his cheeks. Large tears welled to his eyes and began to flow down his cheeks. Even as this new emotion overwhelmed him, he cursed. He had moved from tearful pleading to cold calm, from calm to sudden, swelling desire, from desire to proud anger and now from proud anger to infantile desolation and each time his body over-reacted, pulled this way and that by uncontrollable emotional surges. He had wanted to be a man before this man and here he was, an instant inconsolable infant with the sour taste of his adolescent arrogance still in his mouth, a dying penis shrunken in his hand and his earlier tears still wet upon his sleeve.

"Come on, son, he ain't but a nigger and he done killed another too," offered the voice of reason, his original anger softened by the adolescent's collapse into desolation. Jack said nothing. He just stared, the silent tears now running down his neck and under the collar of his shirt.

"Come on, kid, come and have a drink." He led Jack into a nearby bar, where the customers waved in greeting to the voice of reason and stared at the crying boy. He ordered two large measures of whisky.

"You ever drunk whisky, boy?" he asked. Jack, who had many times tasted from his father's jug, shook his head. It was never a good thing to admit having drunk whisky.

"Ain't he a bit young," said the barman, "seeing as he ain't finished with blubbin' an all — shore he ain't pissed hisself." And everybody laughed.

"It ain't whisky for him, it's medicine. He's just had a nasty shock. Someone very dear to him got killed." A crowd began to gather round them, their laughter hushed to silence by the dramatic reply. "Right, drink that up, son, an' you'll feel better," with which words he swallowed half his own drink.

Jack began to suck at the fierce liquid and felt it start to warm his belly.

"Hey, Abel," for that was the voice of wisdom's name, "wasn't you gone to catch that boy that killed the old nigger?" cried a voice from the back of the crowd. "Where's Hank and the lads?" said another voice. Abel finished his drink and ordered another before he began to tell his story of the chase and the mad horseman. The crowd was at first saddened by the death of the dogs and then angered by that of their friends. They now understood Jack's misery and consoled him. Jack looked fearfully towards the voice of reason. Was he going to correct their mistaken assumptions? The voice of reason avoided his eyes but said nothing. Jack neither confirmed nor denied the suggestions made to him as to the identity of the one dear to him. "Was it his father or brother?" they asked. He defended himself with silence and found himself thankful for his tears for they gave good refuge. In any case, he very rapidly ceased to be the centre of interest as the men began to discuss the gathering of a posse to hunt down the murderers.

The posse began to gather outside the bar. Men and horses

appeared from all directions as the news spread that Hank and his companions had been murdered by Abolitionists. Jack managed to escape from Abel who was now fully occupied repeating his story to all comers and very full of whisky. He ran back to the widow's house. However, he discovered that Sam had gone out in search of tobacco, having despaired of Jack's return. After waiting a few minutes, walking round the parlour in a fury of impatience, he asked the widow to lend him her old horse as he feared that the posse would leave without him and that he would never know if Dan were really dead. Faced with the widow's reluctance he fished the gold coin from under his shirt and offered it as gage against the horse's return. Reluctantly the widow agreed seeing how desperate the boy seemed.

"But make sure you bring her back," she insisted, "'cos even if this here is real gold, which I don't doubt it ain't, it still ain't worth one entire horse, even an old'n like my Bessy."

"Sure, I'll bring her back, Misses J, sure I will," said Jack.

"Well, you go an' saddle-up an' I'll fix you some tucker."

Soon Jack had the horse ready and taking the small knapsack the widow offered him which felt unnaturally heavy on his back, he gave her a big filial kiss, jumped into the saddle and galloped off down the lane. Tears came to the widow's eyes as she thought of her baby son, who might have been just like this boy had he lived, but who had succumbed to the dysentery at the age of two. She watched the lithe young figure on the big old horse until they disappeared at the end of the lane and turned back into the house, suddenly sadder than she had been for years.

\*\*\*

Jack caught up with the posse as it was leaving town. He stayed well back, not wishing to be identified as an escaped prisoner who could have been party to the murder of the wagon driver. Abel had not mentioned this, but then maybe he didn't know that Jack had been in that particular wagon.

He followed the posse as they came to the site of Dan's capture and began searching the hills for a scent trail. It was a long job and if the dogs found a trail it was soon lost again as the activity of Tinker and Washy had created confusion. However, the scattered trails of scent finally took a single direction. Night fell and the posse made camp. Jack settled down fifty yards behind them hidden by a clump of trees. He ate sparsely from the food given him by the widow and thinking of her and Sam found his irrepressible penis already alert. With a sigh of resignation, he caressed it to the end it desired and then without being aware of it, fell asleep. He awoke with the dawn from a dreamless night, to find himself alone. The posse had already taken off for the hunt. However, he could just hear the bell-like howls of the dogs in the distance. The howls were continuous as now they followed an uninterrupted trail. Jack clambered onto his horse and raced after them.

Soon after noon a small, rough and ready farmstead appeared in the summer haze of the distance: a collection of half-built log cabins and tents; a group forming a protective circle. The posse halted and called in the dogs which were put onto leash. Then at walking pace and in silence they rode down to a small coppice less than a quarter of a mile from the farm.

"What now?" said a voice, impatient to be at grips with the nigger-loving killers.

"Don't rightly know," said another who had assumed the status of leader. If'n they're in there it's gonna be difficult to weed '\em out."

"Can't see no sign o' life," contributed a third. "P'raps we should wait 'til dark."

"If'n they ain't there that's gonna lose us a lotta time," said the leader.

"Ah ken speak Kansas. Ah could pay 'em a visit lookse," volunteered another.

"Reckon thet's the answer," continued the leader.

As Jack was watching a sole rider broke away from the group in the trees and walked his horse easily down towards the buildings; they brushed through long grass from which rose a cloud of pollen causing the horseman to sneeze loudly. A shot rang out and the horseman fell.

"They saw us comin'," said the leader.

"We gonna fetch poor Sid?" demanded another. There was a long silence as this proposition was considered. "The grass is long. We could crawl down under it."

"Go on then."

"I couldna pull him here all alone."

"I'll come with yer," offered the impatient one.

The two of them dismounted and moving to one side of the grouped posse, came to the further edge of the trees where they dropped on their hands and knees and began to push their way through the grass. It was at least two hundred yards to arrive at where Sid lay. After they had gone fifty yards another shot rang out and they flopped onto their bellies.

"We'd better separate. We move too much grass crawling together." And so, belly crawling they moved slowly apart. There was no reaction from the gunman, who having seen grass waving in a way unrelated to the fresh midday breeze, had tried his luck. Sid, who had lost consciousness momentarily having banged his head in falling violently from his horse, began wriggling his way back towards the coppice. He was unhurt having fallen deliberately if clumsily. As he moved up towards the posse, the horse that had been cropping grass alongside him began to follow his master. It even bent down to nuzzle him being somewhat puzzled by his behaviour. The gunman took notice and peered hard at the grass beside the horse.

"Sod off, yer silly bugger," muttered Sid trying to slap its nose. Another shot came and Sid cried out as it stung his calf, causing a superficial wound.

The other two, who had lain still as the shooting continued, realised they were not the target of this fusillade and that Sid was probably alive as dead men don't cry out.

Jack moved through the bushes to get a better view, not seeing the shadow that followed him. There was an animated discussion among the posse. There were those who wanted to charge the farm right away and those who wanted a more discreet approach at nightfall and one or two who wanted to go home. These latter were scorned. Finally, the advocates of the night approach won. Jack, who was satisfied that nothing more was about to happen, as the wounded scout and his two would-be rescuers returned to the posse, began to move back towards his horse. Suddenly his arms were pinned to his sides and a hand was across his mouth.

"Keep quiet and you won't be hurt," hissed a voice in his ear.

There was no need for this advice as he was numbed to silence by shock. The hand came off his mouth to be rapidly replaced by a gag and his hands were tied behind his back. Recovering from his fright Jack looked at his captors. They were three Indians, but again rather strange ones — two of them had blue eyes. One of them opened Jack's shirt and looked disappointed.

He muttered something in his own dialect and the others nodded. Jack and his horse were then led away down the opposite side of the hill to that of the farm. The air was very still, the slanting sun shone and the insects chattered. It was strange but he felt no fear and his escorts were very calm. One even smiled at him. This one had his arm clamped to his side by a broad bandage. It looked as though it hurt.

*** 

Dan lay on his back under a not very clean blanket. His legs and shoulder were bandaged, and he had a splint against his left thigh. He was very thirsty. As if reading his thoughts someone offered him a cup of water. He opened his eyes. His nurse was Tinker. His friendly young face warmed him, despite the shivers that wracked his body.

"Where is we, boy?" he asked.

"We're in the house of a loco man wi' the big knife who killed all the posse," whispered Tinker.

"Is Washy here too?"

"Yeah, he's in the kitchen tent helpin' make supper."

Satisfied that the world seemed to be turning towards the normal, Dan went back to sleep.

"How's he doin'?" called the voice of Owen.

"I think he's sleepin'. He's awfa hot an' shiverin'."

"He's gotta fever. Could be dead by mornin'. If not, he'll probably live — so Paw says."

"Where's everybody?"

"Fixin' up a s'prise for that posse. Them Border Ruffians ain't too bright."

"What kinda s'prise?"

"We gonna capture 'em. Do yer know how to fire a gun?" He wasn't sure of the boy's status. His honey-coloured skin and longish, almost straight, just a little wavey, black hair were difficult to place.

"No, suh. But I can larn it," said Tinker.

The posse spread out and advanced slowly through the long grass. The farm was silent and unlit except for a faint glow that came from inside the circle, where the reflection of lamp out of sight made the flattened grass glisten. Sid, despite his damaged leg, was leading the assault. The self-assumed leader had become the rear-guard. Silently they approached the entry to the circle. There was a nearly finished cabin on one side and a leather tent on the other. There didn't seem to be anybody on watch.

"Go an' look round t'other side, Luke," said Sid to the next man to him. "We'll wait here."

Luke went off bent low behind the tall tufts of grass and the others crouched down. There was still pollen in the calm night air that choked the sensitive who tried to muffle their sneezes as best they could. The constant song of the insects came and went in answer to their gasps.

Ten minutes passed and then twenty. Sid consulted his watch for the tenth time.

"What's happened to the silly sod?" he whispered to himself. "Has he buggered off?"

An explosive sneeze broke the night.

"Aw shit," cried Sid, "let's go an' get 'em," and three shots rang out from the other side of the farm.

They weren't fifty yards from the entry when further shots rang out from behind them and Sid fell dead and two others suffered wounds that felled them too. The rest of the group raced into the circle, which had suddenly become a refuge rather than the target of an assault. A voice called out from the roof of the only finished cabin.

"Drop yer guns or yer all dead." Another man was shot in the leg to emphasise the words.

"There ain't but four," yelled the leader, "rush the buggers," as he flung himself to the ground.

"Yeah, but where?" cried another. He dropped his gun as did all the others.

Three figures appeared from behind them — John Brown and two of his sons. And from the tents and sheds surrounding them came three others, two blacks and Tinker who was not very black at all. They were armed with rifles. Then Owen leapt down from the cabin roof.

The posse, or the fifteen left of them that were still whole, were grouped in the centre of the yard.

"I could kill you all, you sin-benighted ruffians," yelled John Brown as he advanced towards them rifle in one hand and sabre in the other; his Bible lay somewhere forgotten. "You think blacks are for whipping and buggering. You visit them with the blackness of your twisted hearts. The Lord created them men like you and me — or rather better than you. Their skin ain't as black as your festerin' souls."

"Festerin' yersel, you fucking maniac," muttered a voice from within the crowd.

Spittle sprayed from Brown's lips as he continued shouting. "I'll slay you like the chosen slew the Philistines." His wild eyes, gleaming red in the torchlight, seemed to start from his head. The sabre, raised high, trembled with his hand.

"No, Paw, don't kill anymore. We don't want more trouble. It ain't necessary. And it would be just murder."

John Brown stood still and lowered the sword. He looked

toward the blacks.

With a voice hoarse from its efforts he yelled, "Tinker, Silas and Abel, collect them guns. Where's that Washy got to?"

The prisoners were herded into the cowshed and locked in with a crossbar. A son, Watson, stood guard as the rest of them returned to the main cabin. It was difficult to leave black men to shoot escaping whites. That could really incite the whole county. A premonitory wind caused a shutter to slam and swirled dust about their knees as they entered the cabin. Tinker and Washy brought food in while the others settled themselves at the big central table.

"What we gonna do with 'em?" demanded Salmon. "We can't just kill 'em."

"Have to let 'm go, don't we? We ain't got the organisation for prisoners," added Jason.

John Brown glared around him. "We take their guns and horses, strip 'em naked and kick 'em back up the hill. Let God's will take care of 'em." He smacked the Bible he had re-found.

"Ain't that like killin' 'em?" Jason said. "They're miles from anywhere." He looked anxiously at his father.

"Aw, do what you like," and turning to Watson, John Brown added, "we've got business to do. There's a band of Missouri militia looking for trouble at Black Creek. That slavery fanatic Pate is leading them. They're a goodly number, near a couple a hundred I'm told. But I reckon we can raise some men in Prairie City. They ain't had time to forget Lawrence yet and you've still got some of John's Rifle Company. You lot come with me. We'll leave Owen and Salmon here with the niggers. They can follow on later with a cart for the big nigger and Salmon. Reckon we should meet up with Fred over there if he ain't gone too barmy."

At that moment a low rumble of thunder announced the incoming storm and a strong gust of wind slammed shut the cabin door.

***

Jack sat cross-legged between two of his captors. They were all seated below a great oak. They had untied his hands and given him to eat: a hunk of not very fresh corn bread, a slither of dried meat and a small apple. He ate quickly. Breakfast was now a long time away and the widow's knapsack had somehow got lost. Around them spread out on the leaf mould were the Indian's possessions. Jack's horse was tethered to a group of saplings some twenty yards away.

The still summer air trembled a little with the first grumble of far-off thunder. The Indians darted enquiring glances towards a distant darkness, the threatening herald of the oncoming storm. They talked excitedly among themselves. Then the smiling one turned to Jack and said, "We were going to camp here tonight but looks like we've got to find somewhere more sheltered." They started gathering their possessions into knapsacks.

Even though his hands and legs were free and he seemed to be forgotten in the rush to move camp, Jack didn't dare move. The wind began to freshen and some of last fall's leaves skittered across the ground before whirling into the air. The sky rapidly became blacker, with dark clouds driving in a circle as they rapidly approached. There were several flashes of lightning followed not much later by loud peals of thunder. A second for every mile, calculated Jack and decided that not more than four miles separated them from the storm.

The Indians were nearly ready when a simultaneous brilliant flash and enormous crash of thunder momentarily lit the forest lighter than day. The horse reared, shied and ran, tearing free from the young tree to which it was attached, its eyes wide and staring, then the topmost branches of the oak came crashing down spurting fire about them. Jack had leapt to his feet and was running furiously. He missed by inches being pinned down by a falling branch. One of the Indians was not so lucky and the others, being very occupied by the rescue of their fallen companion and their possessions, did not seem to see Jack leave, or the direction he took. The track up which he ran was not chosen but happened to be that whence they had come.

Almost immediately after the thunderclap, rain started, falling in thick sheets before changing into hail. Visibility was reduced to ten yards at most. The hailstones were not very large but even so painful and Jack crept under a thick bush to avoid them. There was no longer sight or sound of the Indians and the storm continued to batter and crash its way across the forest before finally calming down to occasional streaks of lightning, an almost continuous rumble of distant thunder and a soft heavy rain.

Jack crawled out from under his bush and looked around him. And there, not fifty yards away under the shelter of a massive hickory, stood the widow's horse, passively nibbling up at its fine leaves. He approached the horse slowly, making soothing noises and mounted. The horse didn't give any sign of its having noticed his arrival but responded quite willingly when he urged it forward into the rain.

Without much difficulty he found the remains of the track by which they had come and headed back towards the beleaguered farm. He must find Dan, but also, he had to give the widow back her horse and retrieve his lucky coin. However, Dan came first. Arriving at last, on the hill above the farm, just as the long summer night ended in blackness, he saw few signs of activity other than the faint glow of torches somewhere out of sight. The rain had almost stopped, and a cool breeze left him shivering in his wet clothes. Then he heard faint shouts.

# CHAPTER SEVEN

Jack dismounted and walked his horse down the hill. He thought that this would appear less aggressive than riding down. He was fearful of what he might find, but he had to have somewhere to hide as, no doubt, the Indians would come after him. As he arrived at the entry to the circle of buildings, he saw a group of half-naked men shouting and gesticulating towards four men with rifles, two of whom were black. The riflemen started urging them towards the opening in the farm's circle. As they approached Jack recognised members of the posse. He saw that some of them were wounded and had to be helped along.

One of the men with rifles shouted towards the main building.

"Tinker, Washy, bring them horses along."

"Yasmistah Owen," came a reply. And Jack saw two youngsters move into the light of the riflemen's torches leading a dozen horses. One of them was evidently black, the other difficult to tell at that distance. Attached to the saddles of the horses were bundles of clothes, boots and a variety of guns.

Owen spoke again. "On them horses are all your things. So don't go saying you was robbed. The only thing we've kept is your 'munition. That can't be helped as you're as violent bunch of nigger-hating roughnecks as ever to blacken a Christian soil. So now clear off out and don't stop to get your things and dress before you reach the top of the hill. Then, if after ten minutes we see anyone of you near here, you'll get shot."

"That ain't all our horses," the leader shouted, and others muttered assent.

"Some of 'em ran off, so you'll have to look for 'em," said Salmon.

"We'll be back to skin you bastards," muttered another, and the posse shambled off up the hill.

Jack chose this moment to move into the light of the torches, his hands in the air.

The four men were startled at his appearance and raised their guns.

"Who are you?" demanded Owen and pushed down the barrel of Salmon's gun.

"I'm Jack and I'm looking for my Dan."

"Who's Dan?" asked Salmon.

"He's the negro those men were chasing."

"Why 'my Dan'? He your slave or something?"

"No, no he's free. He's my friend. We was running up the Missouri to light out west for gold and all that, when some men like those there captured us. No, he was freed by Bill Watson's great-aunt, the widder Wilson from Hannibal. But them men wouldn't have believed it, so we pretended he was my slave. But that didn't make no difference an' they just took us to Lawrence where they was goin' to fight them Free-Soilers an' an'......"

"Okay, okay, son. I'll believe you."

A faint voice came from the half-built farmhouse. "Is dat you, Jack?"

Jack let go his horse, broke free from his interlocutors and ran into the building. He saw Dan lying on a mattress across the room. He ran over and hugging him close gave him a shower of kisses on his cheeks and forehead, tears streaming from his eyes.

"Well, he ain't a nigger hater," said Owen, who was by now standing in the doorway.

Jack stood up embarrassed by his own emotion in which he

had forgotten he was amongst strangers who might object to a white boy kissing a black. He saw only bemused smiles.

"He's my friend," he insisted and looked them in the eyes. "I've come here looking for him. I followed the posse when I heard who they was after 'cause he killed a couple of tracking hounds when those other men tried to catch him after he ran." He didn't mention the supervisor.

The four men, the black boy and the boy of uncertain origins were watching him closely. Jack looked at the two boys. He found the "uncertain" boy attractive and found himself wanting to kiss his neck which looked very smooth and warm. This surprised him. He couldn't remember having had that reaction before with a boy or even a girl. It didn't seem natural.

"You got any baccy?" he asked to change the subject.

"Here," and Owen tossed him a plug. "You look all done in, kid, and soaking wet. Take off them clothes and I'll give you a blanket. Then you can have a bite of stew."

As Jack abandoned his clothes Owen took them up and put them around a chair in front of the fire. "Salmon, don't just stand there, give the boy some food." Salmon grunted disagreeably, spooned out some stew from the pot over the fire and handed it to Jack. "Owen's always a sucker for a tall story." And he smirked.

"Don't take no notice of him, boy," added Owen, "He's been ill and become ill-mannered and pernickety."

"Thank you, sir," said Jack, whether towards Owen or Salmon was difficult to say and turned towards Dan. "What's happened to you, friend? You look bad."

Dan raised himself slightly on his bed. "Got misself all shot up by them maniacs who captured us, cos I kilt a couple of their hounds and an old nigger supervisor who was lookin' for suicide."

"Wow, you killed him?"

"Wid an axe. They wus more worried about the dogs. One less useless, agein' nigger to feed weren't bad news."

Jack was very impressed. He hadn't imagined Dan as a killer — the gentle Dan who mothered and caressed him. He had shot the white Indian but that was at a distance. To chop down someone with an axe was something else. He saw a new Dan — Dan the warrior. He liked the idea. He couldn't but admire this new Dan who had been fighting for his liberty. The slave was fast disappearing.

He squatted on the floor next to the bed and began to recount his adventures with Sam and how he had again been attacked by strange un-Indian-like Indians. Dan nodded and admitted that their interest in him was strange, even mysterious. Something Bill Watson might dream up as the obscure details of an adventure. Jack talked on a little longer until he realised that Dan's eyelids were drooping. He got up and walked to the fire, the blanket hugged around him. He smiled at Owen who seemed to be the gentlest of the Brown boys.

"Your clothes are still wet," said Owen. "And it's time for us all to get some sleep. We need to get up early. Seeing as you're not afeared of blacks you can share Tinker and Washy's tent. It's big enough and it's getting a bit crowded in here. It's the one next to the cowshed," he added, pointing in its direction.

Jack nodded and adding another "thank you, sir" splashed through the mud outside and made it to the tent. He pulled the flap apart and looked in. Washy seemed to be asleep but Tinker sat up and looked at him.

"Yeah," he said.

"I was told to come and sleep here."

"That's all right if you don't mind the smell of nigger," and laughed. "Pull up a couple of sacks," he added patting the ground beside him. "It's warmer close too and I've only got one blanket."

"Me too," said Jack, exposing his naked body to Tinker's view. He looked round and found some sacks stuffed with dried grass that served as mattresses. He pulled three across to where Tinker was sitting. Washy began to snore gently.

"He's already asleep," sniggered Tinker, "the sleep of the just... the just jerked off." He laughed, and Jack laughed too.

"He has sinned, I reckon," and he laughed again.

"You go for that sin crap," said Jack, "'cos anything that's worth doin' seems to be a sin."

"You're right there, boy. And no, I don't go in for no religion. That's just for old maids that never got a man and niggers who ain't got nothin' else. Like Washy here. Do yer mind if we share these blankets?" he added, "With the two on top of us and the sacks underneath we might get warm."

"Yeah, good idea," smiled Jack.

They arranged the bedding and wriggled down under it. After a bit Tinker's hand was on his arm. Jack turned towards him and waiting a minute to be sure it wasn't an accident, placed his hand on Tinker's chest. The feeling he had had on first seeing Tinker was still with him — an instant yearning. Soon Jack heard his companion's breath begin to labour. Jack's already stiff penis strained further, and he moved his hand across Tinker's left nipple and, after a moment, down towards his stomach and on to his belly, which twitched under his fingers. Then Tinker's hand went directly to Jack's erect penis and held it tightly.

"It's more fun with two," whispered Tinker, loosening his grip and beginning to move his fingers up and down, each time giving the head a little caress.

"I think you've done this before," giggled Jack and wanted to do the same for Tinker but was hindered by his trousers which he began to unbutton. Finally, he could push down the trousers. Tinker's penis came free which Jack started to fondle as he began to lose control of his mounting desire. Then, after a while, Tinker grasped Jack's buttocks and pulled him belly to belly. Jack was helpless. They began to move gently against one another, each little thrust sharpening the pleasure. Their breathing became increasingly rapid. Jack began to wonder at what was happening. It wasn't like when he masturbated with Dan, where what went on there was more a pre-sleep comfort, almost as if they were simply doing it to themselves and was never much more than being jerked off between friends with perhaps one or two fraternal kisses. What was happening now was different: his whole body was stiffened with excitement and when Tinker started caressing his buttocks with one finger in the cleft, it was like being strangled by feelings that grasped him from throat to the root of his penis. He was trembling wildly. He kissed Tinker on the neck. Tinker pulled back his head.

"What you do that for? We ain't faggots," he said uncertainly.

"Don't know. Jus' felt like it," stuttered Jack and he pulled Tinker closer and kissed his neck again. Tinker began trembling also as he moved to grip Jack's thighs, pulling him up and pushing his face into his chest.

With that Jack's strangling pleasure became unbearable. He pushed hard as it burst, pulsating low down in his belly and his sperm streamed across Tinker's stomach. Tinker gasped as his penis slipped between Jack's sweat-wet thighs and his orgasm also came, unexpectedly, suddenly, in throbbing spurts just behind Jack's scrotum. Unthinking, he kissed Jack: an act that was quickly returned. They shuddered together a long while occasionally exchanging kisses and with shivering breathlessness they lay still. Tinker clung to Jack and he to him. But Tinker had stopped returning his kisses.

After a few minutes, when all was calm, Tinker turned his head towards Jack. "That was good," he said, almost as good as with a girl," he added, needing to assert his manliness. "But then you're almost like girl to hold but with a bit harder body."

Jack blushed unseen and said, "An' you're very fanciful looking for a boy too. I've never had a girl, so I don't know about that." For a while they were silent again.

"Never had a girl. How's that?"

"I never had the opportunity. I ain't had a normal life. I don't remember much of my mother as I was still very small when she disappeared. I've always lived with my drunken father, in rags and smelly — a white trash kid. 'Til Dan and Bill Watson befriended me. So I was sort of adopted by the Misses Watson and her husband's ma, the widder Watson, who set about civilisin' me and was whipped by Pap 'cos I went to school now an' agen. Now, I've just escaped the Widder Williams and Pap's dead and I've run off with Dan who run off with me 'cos Miss Watson (mean cow) was gonna sell him down to New Orleans for eight hundred dollars. That's about it. There weren't no time for girls. The only sex I got was jerkin' off and my Pap and a pal tryin' ter bugger me when they was drunk. That was when he had me locked up so as to stop me bein' civilised — not that I particularly liked being civilised, always scrubbed down and in clothes to be kept clean."

"That's a sad tale," said Tinker, trying to make sense of Jack's not very explanatory reminiscences, "almost worthy of a slave. 'cept there seems to be a bit less whippin' and the buggerin', probably less systematic. I could have practically any girl on the estate and the buggerin' came from the Boss, who I think was my father. He'd get quite affectionate. He'd kiss me and call me his little Eefeeb or summat. That's when I was Tinker rather than, fucking nigger, wages of sin or nigger bastard. 'cept when he was drunk and then he'd call me them things as he fucked me 'cos he couldn't come. That's my tale."

"You don't look much like a nigger."

"That's why he preferred fucking me to any other boys on the farm. I'm an octoroon or summat — a high yaller."

"If he fancied you, why'd he send you off to be sold?"

"That's 'cos he thought I was after his daughter. But it were her that were after me."

"Did you have her?"

"Yeah, once I knew he planned to sell me. Fucked her long and hard. Reckon she'll be pregnant," he added with satisfaction.

"But she's your half-sister and that's... watchermecallit."

"Incest! Hadn't thought of that — and so what?"

"Could have a mad baby."

"They'll probably have her seen to anyway."

"I'll have to find a girl soon," said Jack after a while, "or I could get used to being faggot-like."

"We'll have to look one out for you."

"Thanks," said Jack and he hugged Tinker.

"What ya two bin upta?" called Washy from the darkness.

"Nuthin' you'd want to do," replied Tinker, "Go back to sleep."

With that Jack, once again, took Tinker's penis in hand and after a brief hesitation he did the same for Jack. Just before the moment of orgasm Jack again kissed Tinker's neck and then searched for his lips, but Tinker turned his head away even as he squirted his pleasure and Jack's orgasm felt a little lame. They said nothing and were still holding each other as they fell asleep.

The next morning, which was cool and calm after the storm, they loaded Dan into a cart accompanied by Salmon who was still weak and then set off for Prairie City where they hoped to find John Brown. Jack looked on and said he had to return the widow's horse but would find them afterwards. He rather liked the idea of seeing the Browns in battle with the Missouri people. Even if he had doubts as to which side was the good side. Dan's saviours, or the citizens protecting their right to slavery. Having spent his childhood in a climate where slavery was normal and niggers thought of as too stupid not to be exploited and cared for, the ideas and company of Abolitionists was threatening — and they didn't seem too friendly towards niggers either. And as for niggers being stupid, he was pretty sure they put it on to get some peace and not appear to be uppity. Dan certainly wasn't stupid even if he did have a few superstitions too many.

But in the sweet cool air of that morning with a high light sun in the sky and the smell of damp grass, he didn't want to trouble his conscience too much. He would have a word with Sam as he seemed to know how to think out things that were troublesome. The cart, accompanied by Jason, Tinker and Washy and two older blacks, rolled off up the hill towards the forest. Jack followed until, after a while, their paths divided. He waved energetically as he turned off towards Lawrence. Tinker waved back, but without too much enthusiasm, it seemed to Jack.

\*\*\*

On arriving in Lawrence he sought out the widow's house. There he found Sam and the widow getting down to a late lunch of ham and eggs. Gaining strength after their night's humping, thought Jack. He was invited to join them. They talked awhile of Jack's adventures. No one knew what to think of the strange Indians.

"So you've found Dan. What now?" asked Sam.

"I dunno exactly," said Jack, "but I reckon I've got to join the Browns and look after Dan. He's in a pretty bad state."

"Do you want me to come along? There's nothing doing here, what with the newspaper having been burnt down and I'm not due to join my boat 'til next month. Might get an article out of it I can sell in the North — Bleeding Kansas and stuff. The abolitionists eat up that sort of thing. But it's going to be difficult to be funny about that."

The widow looked sad. Was she again going to lose her nice young lover so soon?

"Won't it be dangerous?" she said, "Those Missouri folk, are a nasty load of ruffians."

"Oh, we'll stay out of trouble. Don't intend to go into battle either for cheating slavers or the murderous abolitionists of Pottawatomie."

"That'll be great," added Jack. "I reckon Dan will've most recovered in a week or two and we can continue our trip out west. I don't reckon he's safe with that John Brown."

"Oh dear," sighed the widow.

Sam kissed her cheek. "I'll come back and see you afore I go steam-boating."

The widow smiled.

"I'd like to go steam-boatin' with you," said Jack. Me and Dan could."

As Jack talked on Sam examined his beauty: his silky hair was almost the colour of a cockerel's tail feathers with their greenish reflections. Except in Jack's case the reflections were nearer blue. And his eyes, blue too, deep, but deep like a summer sky when a close heat darkened it and heralded a storm. Sam wanted to hug him, wanted to clasp that slim, lithe body to his. Wanted to kiss his lovely skin, honey burnt, but ivory white where the sun couldn't touch. It wasn't simple desire or for the most part not even sexual desire at all; those automatic, almost chemical feelings simply lingered as a possibility that could ignite if circumstances demanded it. He didn't want to hurt him or frighten him by demanding things he might not want. He wanted that his innocence should stay as it was. Not that his innocence had anything to do with not having sex as those brain-dead from the twisted, puritan hangover of religion felt. No, he was an untamed animal and no doubt with untamed desires, like a puppy who tried to rub itself off against your leg to express its affection. His sexuality would be part of his wild innocence. Sam had never felt an attraction like this with a woman. It was almost painful. He'd never met a boy who affected him like that either. He had to admit, though, that in general he found boys slightly more attractive than girls, though perhaps not as sexy. His widow was like the comforting aunt who had lightened the torments of his late adolescence. Jack was a moment of poetry — poetry in a foreign language that sung of its inner beauty with the music of word sounds only. He loved the boy and would take care of him.

*** 

Prairie City was in turmoil. John Brown, preaching free soil and abolition insisting upon the equality of all men and more fulsomely on the unfair economic competition of slavery, had managed to create a forty-odd band of volunteers ready to stop the Missouri slaver Pate from imposing the slaver's Constitution.

They also fancied a bit of vengeance too as Missouri attacks and murders had become more frequent after the fall of Lawrence.

Dan and Salmon were installed in a friendly house to rest. While Jason, Jack and Sam went off to see what was happening at Osawatomie and with Captain Pate and his militia near Black Jack Creek.

They found Frederick, another of Brown's sons, guarding the horses, as John Brown had thought his state of mind too unstable to join the surprise attack on Pate. They could hear sporadic firing in the distance.

"What's going on, Fred?" asked Jason.

"There ain't going to be nothing going on. Paw's only got twenty-five men, as all but seventeen of the volunteers got cold feet and slunk off. He's up there taking pot shots into Pate's camp which keeps 'em pinned down, that is until they realise how few men we've got and comes up to massacre us. Paw thinks I'm nuts, but I ain't so damn wild headed as him, insisting on attacking a force practically ten times his own."

"Sounds like a good moment to get us some cold feet," whispered Sam to Jack as Fred and Jason began arguing. Jack nodded.

"We can't just stand here doing nothing," Jason was saying.

"Who can't?" replied Fred.

"I'll go up and have a word with him," added Jason.

"Fat lot good that will do with that stubborn, old, religious nut. Now, I think I'll show him what it's really like to be completely mad." And he laughed as he jumped on his horse, drew his sabre and galloped away.

"Hey, wait for me, you barmy idiot," and turning towards Jack and Sam, "You two coming along?"

Jack looked at Sam and shrugged. He wasn't too keen about

getting into a gunfight but was very curious to see what was happening. Sam nodded and the two of them remounted their horses and followed Jason.

They found John Brown on the edge of a shallow cliff overlooking Pate's camp with eight men, by this time practically all that were left from his volunteers. Away to the left on the eastern slope above the camp a few others, no more than fifteen or twenty, continued desultory firing largely aimed at Pate's horses. Suddenly, a horseman appeared from behind the ridge. It was Frederick. He was standing in his stirrups and waving his sabre as he began galloping around the camp, shouting out confused encouragement to some unseen troops.

"We've got 'em surrounded, boys. They're cut off. Mass for the charge, etc." All this time Pate's men were firing ineffectual pot shots at the rapidly moving target. Then two men came out of the camp holding up a white handkerchief on a ramrod. Fred's mad ruse had worked. John Brown walked out alone to receive the surrender.

On reaching the two men, he addressed the one in the lead.

"Are you the Captain of the militia?" he asked.

"No, I'm not, nor him."

"Then go and fetch him, I can't negotiate with you."

They soon returned with Pate. And as they talked Brown's men began to expose themselves and descend to accept their surrender.

"I'm a Deputy United States Marshal representing the General Government in Washington." John Brown was unimpressed.

"If you've anything to say, say it now," Brown stated. "I'm demanding unconditional surrender," and shouting across the three men ordered the defending troops to lay down their arms.

He was not obeyed and Pate on seeing Brown's men was beginning to suspect the real strength of Brown's troops. Brown put his pistol to Pate's head. The frightened young man hesitated. Brown pushed the barrel into his ear.

"Lay down your arms," the young Marshal cried. Brown had won the battle and his men began loading the abandoned rifles into a cart as the other group moved forward their rifles at the ready to fire into the confused mass of prisoners.

"I reckon, there at least, I could write something amusing," muttered Sam and gave a laugh.

Jack simply nodded.

Once back in Prairie City, Jack and Sam joined the three at the friendly house, a large rambling building, partly an orphanage and often a refuge for those in misfortune. It was run by the Reverend Copley, his wife, his adult daughter and a young servant girl, Rosie, that Jack thought very pretty and caused a warm tightening of his lower belly. That evening they sat down to supper with the entire household that also included two young children orphaned in the Kansas conflicts and an ageing miner returning defeated from the goldfields. Jack and Tinker sat together. Jack was covertly scrutinising the servant, when Tinker dug him in the ribs and grinned.

"What you looking at?" he whispered. Jack ignored him.

"Reckon you could have her. Saw her eyeing you too."

"Naw! It were you she were fixing on."

"Don't reckon so. I'll have a word with her later. Tell her you've got the hots for her, or rather that you admire her greatly." Jack gave him a push.

"You boys," interrupted the Reverend, "we were saying Grace — a little respect for the Lord, if you please."

Jack blushed. Tinker looked solemn. "Sorry, sir," they said

in unison and steepled their hands. The servant girl grinned at them. She had never seen two such pretty boys before.

Grace ended and the meal began. It was simple fare but wholesome and plentiful.

Conversation could begin again.

"Where's Washy?" asked Jack.

"Oh, he's helpin' out in the kitchen."

"Why's that?"

"He said he didn't want to eat with the white folks as he didn't know how."

"That's ridiculous. Does he want to always be a slave?"

"No, he's just more comfortable there. They've got a black cook and Washy felt better along with him."

"He's gonna be difficult to rescue from himself."

Tinker laughed. "No, he just needs a while to get used to not being told what to do all the time."

"You've got a problem there."

Tinker pulled on Jack's sleeve. "See that," he said, nodding towards where the servant girl sat across the table. "I reckon you're made there."

Jack, who had noted another grin, was inclined to agree.

"You too probably, but ain't she a bit young?"

"Nah! Must be at least fourteen if not fifteen. Anyway, I'll give her the hint and let you have first go."

"How do I go about that?"

"Nothing to it. You just have to hang around the places she goes looking sort of gloomy and shy. An' if she looks at you, you say 'Hi!' and smile and let her think of what to say next."

"That sounds kinda easy. But what then? How do you get round to kissing and that?"

"Well, just touch her, as if sorta by accident. If she doesn't react negative, then after a bit you take her hand and squeeze it a bit. If she returns the squeeze you've made it. You could even try a kiss — a little peck on the cheek or something. If she stays positive, you're on home base. After that it's a matter of judging what speed she'll accept."

"How'd you know all this?"

"Trial and error, I've bin trying to bonk girls since I was twelve and with some success once I was thirteen and big enough to look as if I might have a dick."

"What are you two whispering about?" asked Sam.

"We're planning to have Jack lose his virginity."

"That sounds interesting. How are you going to do that?"

# CHAPTER EIGHT

Jack would like to lose his virginity, but wasn't sure that the servant girl, Rosie, was exactly where he wanted to lose it even if she was very sexy. But then it was a sort of dare that Tinker had imposed and so he felt obliged to try.

Rosie was pretty, even very pretty, and he could easily imagine taking a great pleasure in the operation. She was slim, blond and blue eyed, with a cute nose and quite well-formed little breasts. Indeed, a picture book model of the lovable girl. He was sure he wasn't an outright pansy, but at the same time wasn't very enthusiastic and would have been quite happy to just satisfy his needs with Tinker. However, that was more difficult in the Reverend's house as they no longer shared a bed or even a room. Tinker and Washy were in the stable and he shared a guest room with Sam. There was something else that troubled him. When he first saw Tinker and wanted to kiss his neck there occurred the "instant yearning", a desire not simply sexual but also a longing to be with him as if within him. It wasn't a matter of getting a hard on. He could do that thinking of Rosie very easily, perhaps more easily than with Tinker, but then that corporeal reflex, over which he didn't really have control, could come about at more or less any time of its own accord. Like at this instant and he didn't know if it was directed at Tinker or Rosie or simply a primal reaction to the idea of sex to come.

It was first thing in the morning three weeks into their stay with the Reverend Copley and Jack was standing at the bottom of the stairs leading to the attic where Rosie lived. Each day he had managed to encounter Rosie at least once. She had nodded to him and smiled several times. But he had been emotionally paralysed, dumbfounded — couldn't move, couldn't speak. Now here he was at the bottom of her stairs. A situation of compromise that meant he would have to explain himself if she appeared. He would be forced to act. But what was he going to say? What reason could he give for his presence other than he wanted to screw her? He was there under these strange stairs that were more like an overdeveloped ladder, very steep, with broad rungs and even a rope bannister. Somebody started down the ladder. He just saw legs coming down backwards. They wore trousers and had dark bare feet: thus, not Rosie. He backed away under the stair/ladder into a sort of alcove that held a heap of bed linen and some cleaning tools and saw Washy hurry away down the corridor. Well, thought Jack, what was Washy doing up there? Was she having it off with that little black nothing, who hardly knew how to speak? Was she fucking a nigger? What kind of girl was she? At that moment Rosie appeared at the end of the corridor down which Washy had run. So she hadn't been up there with Washy. So what was he up to?

"Hi, Jack," she said with what looked like a knowing grin, "what are you doing up here?"

"More important," he replied hotly, "what was Washy doin' up here?"

"Oh that," and she laughed. "He wanted me to mend his shirt, so I sent him fetch my sowing things, but he forgot the scissors. You jealous or something?"

Jack blushed and lied, "No, no I just thought it strange. I thought perhaps he was stealin'."

She touched his arm and smiled. More or less involuntarily he laid his hand across hers and moved a little nearer to her. She took his hand in both hers, raised one eyebrow and said, "Well now — why were YOU here?"

"I wanted to see you," he muttered.

"You see me every day, silly boy. I reckon you want to do more than just see me," and she giggled. "Tinker told me so."

He was somewhat disconcerted that his incipient conquest had been encouraged by Tinker. "Well, you holding my hand is very nice."

"Do you want to kiss me?" Jack nodded. "Come closer then."

Jack moved closer and put his hands to her waist and kissed her very gently on the lips. She smiled, pulled him against her and returned his kiss with her mouth half open. He wasn't sure what to do next and so he simply kissed her again and placed his tongue between her lips. He very quickly got very excited as she pushed against his belly, caressing his tongue with hers. The afternoon before he had chopped wood for the Reverend and so had fallen to sleep almost on touching his bed, with no thought for his usual little pleasure, and in the morning, he saved himself, just in case. She moved away.

"We'd better not stay here," she said. "Let's go upstairs."

He followed her up the ladder-staircase. He caught glimpses of her calves and thighs as she climbed. She didn't seem to be wearing any knickers. His erection became ever more rigid. In her room with its tent-like ceiling directly under the roof was a trestle bed, a small table and a chair. Her clothes were neatly arrayed against a wall. She closed the trapdoor entry and then once more pressed herself against him. With one hand she started undoing the buttons of his shirt, which she then pulled down from his shoulders, nuzzling and kissing at his nipples as she did so. Jack was helpless and out of control. His knees shook. He could hardly stand, and she began to work on his trousers and drawers and was just barely touching his penis, when he ejaculated into her hand. He clung to her as they fell onto the bed.

His breathing gradually returned to normal. "Sorry," he sobbed as tears sprung to his eyes. "I couldn't stop it. It just happened."

"Don't worry," she answered, now caressing the half-deflated member, with her warm and slippery hand. "A young boy like you will be ready again in five minutes." Jack smiled weakly and already felt his erection starting to return. He pulled up her dress. Indeed, she wore no knickers and soon they were both naked. Then with her help he entered her. He remembered having seen Beth make Bill move his buttocks up and down and so started gently to do the same. Rosie moved with him. He arched his back so as to kiss her breasts. The nipples were hard little rounded steeples. He licked them and she began giving little cries. His excitement grew, but he was more in control this time and held his sperm as long as he could. Finally, he could no more and with a last long, deep thrust ejaculated into her warm wetness. They lay together a long time, she trembling along with him, he still inside her half erect. His third orgasm came half an hour later.

Early that evening, he went to find Tinker to boast of his conquest. The stables were empty: no Tinker and no Washy. He waited a while for their return. Since that night in the farm Tinker had seemed to have become rather distant and to avoid situations which could become intimate. Perhaps Jack's passion had frightened him, and he didn't want a one-off bit of fun to become the start of a faggot "affair". This saddened Jack because the "instant yearning" had never left him. He didn't want just a friend even if it meant being a part-time faggot. He didn't care if anybody disapproved. He wanted to be himself and not a slave to the frustrating morals of others. The others and their morals had never done anything but despise him anyway and wish to rob him of things he enjoyed. He waited half an hour or so and no sign of Tinker. So he decided that perhaps another bout of sex with Rosie might not be a bad idea. It was still fairly early evening and Sam wouldn't yet be wondering what he was up to. And even if he did, did it matter? He liked and admired Sam for his gentleness and his understanding even if he was always in a book and trying to get Jack into it too — bit like the Widow Wilson but without her hatred of all that she considered a human failing, which meant any pleasure. The things from books were sometimes quite interesting, even so.

Jack climbed quietly up the stair/ladder and gently pushed open the trap door. He felt his approach should be timid rather than triumphant.

There were Tinker and Rosie naked and making vigorous love on the bed and perched on a chair in the corner was Washy intent on doing something similar for himself, but secretly and inside his trousers. Nobody noticed Jack's presence. Astonished, he watched for a moment and then shut the trap and slowly descended to the corridor. Desolately, even more slowly he made his way to his bedroom. Thus, he knew that Rosie's behaviour that morning had been a gesture of generosity encouraged by Tinker. They had felt sorry for him and helped him get rid of his virginity. While this meant that Tinker was still a friend it also meant that that was all. Jack with his instant and now permanent yearning would never have wanted Tinker to be with Rosie. Tinker had to be his. Rosie didn't mean much to him at all. He even felt guilty of the fact that he had enjoyed her and even a little disgusted with himself as if he had betrayed Tinker, the one he really wanted. And now Tinker was betraying him.

On entering his bedroom, he saw that Sam was already there and preparing to go to bed. He was sitting on his bed in his nightshirt and taking off his socks. Jack went quietly to his own bed and lay down on it. Silent tears began to flow.

Hearing no greeting, Sam looked across at him and saw the wetness of is cheeks.

"What's up, son?" Jack did not reply but began to cry more audibly. The note of sympathy in Sam's voice destroyed the last dam that had held back Jack's grief. He turned his back and buried his head in his pillow. He hated himself for being so weak and childish in front of Sam, who he had wanted to admire him for his bravery, like when they had been in the wagon. Then he had been brave, thinking of nothing but saving Dan. And his sobbing increased. He hadn't been to see Dan all day and not much at all these last two weeks, so taken up had he been with Tinker and the quest of losing his virginity.

"My gosh! This is serious," said Sam crossing to the other bed and seizing Jack by the shoulders pulled him towards him and into a hug. Jack struggled a moment and then relaxed into Sam's arms. It was as if he was with Dan the mother again. And the knot of ice inside him began to change and to resemble the flower — the very fragile ice flower, it's petals beginning to open. Sam waited a while before he asked. "Are you going to tell me about this?" Jack shook his head.

"I can wait," said Sam and began to stroke his head, pulling the dark locks away from the tear-stained cheeks. Jack's sobbing gradually quietened, and he looked up at Sam. His round, deep blue eyes, still shiny with tears and expressing a great emptiness hit Sam hard. Who was this boy, one minute a tough, world-wise adolescent and the next a desperate infant? He lowered his head and kissed the boy's forehead and, as Jack closed his eyes, on each of their lids. Jack took Sam's hand and kissed it too. They stayed in a silent and motionless caress for some while, until Sam reached for his tobacco.

"You want a pipe, son?" Jack nodded and pulled himself up until he was sitting pressed against Sam on the edge of the bed.

"Here, have a bit of this too," and he poured two generous portions of whisky into their bedside tin mugs. "It's good for conversation."

Jack sipped his whisky and did not know what to say. He did not feel talkative and was content with Sam's sympathy. This cuddle was a comfortable way to end a difficult day.

"Well, you ain't a kid anymore, so it's not despair because nobody loves you, and you're going to run away to find someone who does. So, it's got to be something serious." Jack found this analysis of childish reaction a trifle too real and could find no ready response but felt suddenly ashamed of his despair. He wanted to be brave and true while warm in Sam's arms.

"You're wrong, it's just like that. I think I'm really just a kid still." He sniffed.

"That simple?" Sam smiled in a slightly mocking way.

"It's not simple. It's very complicated. What do you think of pansies, you know, faggots?" Jack continued, almost fiercely.

"Where does that come from?" replied Sam with a rather astonished look. "I haven't thought about it much, 'though I don't like those terms. They're insulting and speak of moralistic nonsense, the sort of shit people go to church to hear, to be confirmed in their wish to despise others."

Jack looked up at him and nodded vigorously.

"The preacher's cant demands that you despise your body and its needs, that is, yourself, to save your soul, which is what? Let's say, what do I think of men loving men? In polite society women can sit around cuddling one another without disapproval. I don't see why men shouldn't if that's what they need. I've nothing against it; other than we'd stop having kids if everybody went for it. Perhaps it's not a bad idea," and he laughed. Jack did too but was not entirely reassured.

"But it ain't natural."

"To man there is nothing that is natural nor is there anything unnatural. Can't remember who said that. Some French philosopher, I think — maybe Pascal. Anyway, it makes sense. If you look at history, you'll find that in many societies faggoting was very well thought of. Among the ancient Greeks men loved boys and women were just for bearing his children. Not that that was much fun for women. But there you are — each set of moral rules has its failings, as they're created by faith or custom and not fact. The Greeks had one of the greatest civilisations ever — tops in everything: science, philosophy, art... But I'm going on a bit, becoming a boring old preacher from the other or hell side."

Jack laughed. "That's my side too." And surprised himself in giving Sam a little kiss on the cheek as he might have done Dan.

"Well, thank you." And he returned the kiss.

There was a long moment of silence while Jack digested this. "I think I'm becoming a man who loves men, 'though I quite like women too," confessed Jack suddenly.

"Congratulations. You can have more fun than most people."

"But it ain't fun, 'cause the one I want to love don't care."

"How do you know?"

"Because we had a cuddle once and since then he's being ignoring me and trying to pass me off onto a girl."

"How do you know you love him? How do you know you prefer men?"

Jack tried to describe the instant yearning that Tinker had inspired.

"Well, the first time I saw him, before we'd even spoken, I wanted to kiss his neck. He attracted me or more than attracted. It was like he was inside me. I instantly had this sort of ache in my chest and throat that said I really wanted to be with him and that's all and it's never gone away. I've never felt that about a girl."

"That sounds pretty convincing."

"It hurts," said Jack, his eyes suddenly wet again.

"It's probably not the news you want, but that nearly describes how I feel about you."

Jack looked at him with big, astonished eyes. "But you like women a lot?"

"Just so, so you don't have to worry, I'm not about to leap on you."

Having recovered from his surprise, Jack smiled. "I'm not afraid. I like you. After Dan, you're my best friend."

"That's nice to know," said Sam as afraid as he was pleased, "some more whisky?"

"Just a little one, I'm beginning to feel sleepy. I'll have to give up on blubbering. It wears me out. I'm sorry to have been such a silly kid."

"Not to worry, everybody needs to cry sometime. It helps heal wounds to the heart. Anyway, hop into bed when you've had your whisky and I'll tuck you in."

Jack laughed. "You sound like Bill's ma," he said, "'cept she'd've given me milk instead." He sipped away his whisky very quickly, doused his pipe and climbed into bed.

True to his word Sam tucked him in and gave him another little kiss on the cheek. He then sat down on his own bed and reflected on what had just happened. His relations with Jack had taken a leap. Evidently, he was no longer just a friend but a sort of mother and brother, anyway something closer than a simple friend, something more sensual, more intimate. He didn't know what would happen from there, but this extra closeness made him happy, if a little afraid. For a long moment he looked at Jack who was turning and moaning in his sleep. He was obviously amid dreams. Sam then got into bed and tried to sleep. Sleep wouldn't come. He started wondering about his future as an apprentice steamboat pilot on the Mississippi and how that would fit in with his new-found young friend — not all that young, about fifteen, maybe more, even if he looked younger.

Suddenly Jack gave a cry and sat up in bed. "Bad dream?" asked Sam.

"Yes," said Jack, "can I come in with you?" And without waiting for the reply that Sam was labouring to formulate, crossed over to Sam's bed, pulled back the covers and inserted himself. Sam moved over to make room. There wasn't much of it. He put his arm around Jack to make more space and Jack snuggled up against him and seemed to fall instantly back asleep.

Sam was in distress. With the boy's slim behind pressed against his belly, he was fighting hopelessly against desire. He didn't move, hoping the boy was unaware of his rigid member that he struggled to keep free of the boy's unconscious embrace and his little sleepy movements, but without success. Finally, as Jack wriggled even closer and without the least encouragement from Sam, it ejaculated into his nightshirt, reducing him to a mess of conflicting emotions.

He could no longer hear Jack breathing. Maybe he hadn't been asleep after all.

"I thought you might like that, if you feel about me as I feel about Tinker," murmured Jack and turning towards Sam, took his hand, put it on his own erection and a little while later really fell asleep. The boy's simplicity, his wild innocence, had again astonished Sam.

\*\*\*

The next morning Sam awoke before Jack, hurriedly dressed and went down to help with the horses. A little later, as he went in for breakfast, he saw Jack who gave him a little smile of complicity, which Sam returned. Jack was sitting next to Tinker, who was whispering to him animatedly. No doubt recounting his exploits with Rosic, thought Sam. Jack didn't seem to be paying all that much attention and often glanced towards Sam. And Sam was often looking at Jack too.

Watching the two boys, Sam decided he would have to have a talk with Jack to try and sort out what the exact nature of their relations were to be. The next time he caught Jack's eye he nodded his head and looked upwards towards their bedroom. Jack grinned and nodded his agreement. This exchange had not escaped Tinker, who immediately turned his head with a questioning look. Jack's grin probably indicated that he thinks I want my oats again, Sam decided. It wasn't that he wasn't still full of desire for the boy, but it wasn't satisfying that desire which was his immediate aim. In fact, he didn't know if he wanted to continue a sexual relationship. He felt uncomfortable with the idea as it seemed he would be exploiting an innocent — a savage little innocent, but an innocent, nonetheless. However, on the other hand Jack obviously needed his support and affection and seemed to feel that he had to pay for it with sex. Like Dan, he suspected that there was darkness inside Jack, a fear of love.

Jack left the table first and as he rose nodded upwards before heading for the door. Sam didn't follow immediately but waited until others had begun to move. On eventually arriving at the bedroom, he found Jack half naked, without his trousers and sitting on Sam's bed. He was weeping again. Sam went over to him and put an arm around his shoulder.

"What's wrong, Jack?" he asked.

"I thought you'd decided not to come," snivelled Jack as he put his arms round Sam and laid his head against his chest. Sam pulled him towards him and began stroking his hair. The boy stopped crying and pulling Sam's shirt loose from his trousers mopped his eyes and nose with it.

"Why'd you think that?"

"Because you were a long time getting here and last night you didn't want to fuck me."

Sam was somewhat taken aback by the directness of Jack's language. He kissed the top of his head several times.

"I didn't think you wanted me to do anything and you acted like you were asleep. Truly, I would have loved to love you."

"But I stuck my butt into your belly, surely that said I wanted to."

"I thought that that was an accidental movement in your sleep."

"Just as well I felt you come. Otherwise, I would've wanted to kill myself out of shame."

Sam didn't know how to continue from there. Was this a sort of confession or was it emotional blackmail? Was he with a little devil or a lost angel? Jack resumed the conversation:

"When my Pap tried to bugger me, mostly he just tried and then hit me instead as he was too drunk even to get a good boner. But when he did do it he was rough, and it hurt and I hated him and he'd hit me if I tried to pull away when he pressed his sores against me and he'd get very hot 'cause he couldn't come, being too drunk which was almost always. I don't think he ever came inside me 'cause when he was half sober it happened before he got in, me being a bit small there. Once he split my bottom hole but sewed it together the next morning. But sometimes he had a drinking partner who wanted to do it after Pap had passed out and he was very gentle and would want to pleasure me too, he would laugh and give me a kiss when I cried out and wriggled as I squirted a few drops and even more so later when I started to come properly — even those that Pap sold me to for ten dollars or a jug of whisky were often gentle and sometimes kissed me. So being fucked came to be one of my few happy moments — when it wasn't Pap, that is." All this was said in a cold matter of fact tone. Sam felt scored by the thorns of this ice flower and… battened down emotion. No wonder the boy weeps so easily, he thought and filled with pity, he struggled against tears himself.

"Was he drunk all the time?" he asked.

"Yes, mostly. He was often quite nuts, too. Raving, shouting he'd kill me, but I'd escape him — he was so clumsy. Sometimes he was like that for on and off several days. He'd be crying too as well as shouting and hitting. He said it was delirium tremens, 'cause he'd drunk too much. But he always seemed to drink the same as far as I could see."

"What sort of sores did he have?"

"Sort of weeping sores in his hair and a sort of shallow, red hole on his chest."

"All this sounds like syphilis to me."

"What's syphilis?"

"The great pox."

Jack gasped and looked frightened. "What if'n I've got it

155

and I've given it Tinker and Rosie?"

"No, you haven't. If you had been infected by him, you'd be very ill, mad or dead by now and if your mother had it, you would have been stillborn or at least a deformed idiot. No, I reckon if he gave it to your mother, she was cured before you were conceived. A 'spontaneous cure' they call it, happens all of itself in about a third of those infected."

"How d'you know all that?"

"It's the acquired wisdom necessary for a misspent youth."

"You got the pox?" cried Jack in horror.

"No, no, no. I ain't got the pox and never have had. My wisdom protected me and when in doubt 'I took her in armour', as Pepys said."

"Armour?" gasped Jack, with visions of a cumbersome iron-clad knight clambering onto his lady.

"I used a fine silk handkerchief, like the great man himself."

Sam had nothing more to say, distressed by Jack's revelations and filled with enormous pity for the boy. He simply hugged him more closely and when the boy once more took his hand and placed it on his penis he could only comply and caress him gently until the sperm flowed. He felt a deep excitement and a guilty reserve at the same time. This latter he put down to the difficult residues of a puritan morality.

Sam was completely at a loss before the desolation of the boy's wounded innocence: his total innocence that had nothing to do with puritan morality — a wild, sensual, woodland innocence coming from an absence of cynicism or even an awareness that such could exist. He could only try to supply the affection that Jack obviously craved while still distrusting it; but was that enough and how to express it other than by caresses? In order to clear his emotions a little he spoke again.

"I only know you as Jack," he said, "What's your full name?"

"Jackson Penn," Jack replied. "There was another name in the middle, but it was complicated, and I could never remember it. I think my mother told it me, but that was a long time ago and when I was very small. I don't really remember my mother 'cept one day I was lying on my front and she was stroking my bottom." He stopped and looked up at Sam who still had him cradled in his arms.

"You want to fuck me now?" he asked anxiously.

"Jackson, that's a very heroic sounding name," Sam replied, not able to deal with the last question. "Where'd that come from?"

"Dunno. Never heard of any other Jacksons and you ain't answered my question."

"There was a President Jackson not long ago, a heroic fellow. Don't like the word 'fuck' very much. It sounds too aggressive. How about 'do you want to love me'? It's gentler and more the way I feel about you. And my answer is, yes, very much. You've captured me, young Jackson, so now you'll have to put up with me. But what's that around your neck?"

"That's a coin from the treasure I found," replied Jack.

"Let's have a look." And Jack pulled the thong that held it over his head and handed it to him.

"This looks very old. Greek, I think. That owl is the symbol of Athena their goddess, the patron of Athens and that's her head on the other side."

"Is it worth much?" asked Jack.

"Don't know, but if it's genuine probably a small fortune. Could be more than two thousand years old," and handed it back to Jack. "Do you mind if I call you Jackson? Because you are my poetic hero, who goes around saving the Dans and Sams of this world and I just adore the sound of it. It's just you, as pretty as a girl and man handsome too, that is to say, you're very beautiful. You don't mind being adored, I hope."

"No," replied Jack. "I adore it." Sam laughed and Jack giggled. He finished adjusting the thong around his neck, then pulled Sam down on top of him and said, "Love me now."

"Like an Athenian," gasped Sam.

"If that means you put it in me, then 'yes'." And so he did, slowly and gently. Jackson sighed and pushed himself closer as Sam began to move. "And your dick ain't very big. Which is nice," whispered Jack after a while.

***

Two weeks later Dan had left his bed, as had Samson, and John Brown was planning to leave for the East to raise money for the Abolitionist cause and above all for that of a Free-Soil Kansas. It was also near the time when Sam had to join his boat. Jack was in a quandary. He wanted to be with Dan, and he wanted to be with Sam also.

Jack had been visiting Dan more frequently since he and Sam had started sleeping together and listened to him as he explained how he was going to help John Brown fight for the Abolitionists. John Brown had given him some books to help him understand what slavery meant and how all men were equal. One or two of them had even been translated from the French. Dan's reading skills had been rudimentary, nothing much more than enough to decipher Miss Watson's shopping lists and then reading her letters once her sight had started failing. With John

Brown and his sons' help he had made rapid progress. Even more so when Sam became among his visitors and could explain passages that had defeated him.

Sam had gone off the day before to say goodbye to the widow in Lawrence. Jack didn't go with him because he felt uncomfortable with the thought of listening to their love making from the room next door. He knew that Sam couldn't refuse her without being very impolite and so stayed in Prairie City doing his best to close his mind to thoughts of what might be happening in Lawrence and making up time with Dan.

"I'm beginning to know enough now," one day Dan said, "to be a really uppity nigger and from now on ah'm never again going to jump at whitey's biddin'. From now on he can shine his own fucking boots, metaphorically speaking." He gave a big grin of pride. "That's a word Sam taught me." Jack, who hadn't heard it used before, was impressed.

"I like Sam a lot!" exclaimed Jack.

"I can see that," replied Dan.

Jack then began explaining what had happened between him and Sam. Dan nodded his understanding as Jack arrived at confessing that he liked being buggered by Sam, in fact that he more than liked it.

"Do you think I've become a faggot?" he asked.

"Dunno what that might be rightly. But I've known black men who loved each other before and didn't act like pansies. If'n you don' act like a pansy, you ain't a faggot," he said with great finality and gave Jack a kiss. "You gonna go off with him?" he asked, trying not to show his anxiety.

"I'd like to go with him, but then I want to be with you too," he said despondently.

"Well, I'm gonna follow John Brown and Sam's gonna go

off on a boat. Looks like you gotta choose," and looked at Jack expectantly. Jack nodded unhappily.

Jack and Sam had arranged to meet in Lawrence, before Sam's boat carried him/them off, where they would spend three days together trying to decide their future. Jack left Dan promising to return and tell him what was to happen. He never arrived in Lawrence nor did he return to Prairie City.

Dan thought he'd stayed with Sam and hadn't had the courage to return and tell him; and also, as it was him who had insisted on following John Brown rather than do what Jack was doing, it was largely his fault. He despaired of seeing Jack again, who was, after all, something of a whitey and hardened his resolve to go out killing slavers along with John Brown and to hate and distrust all white folk, because even when they weren't slavers, they had no respect for blacks.

Sam thought Jack had simply stayed with Dan for shame. He thought that his explanation of the relations between a Greek warrior and the ephebe, his apprentice, hadn't really convinced Jack that he wasn't Sam's faggot, a simple joy boy of no account. He'd spent much time in the last weeks trying to demonstrate to Jack his love and respect but thought he could always detect a suspicion of doubt in Jack's eyes. But then, also, he recalled that there was "nothing less certain than a boy's love". He yearned a long time for Jack, but gradually the memory began to fade as his new duties filled his time and thoughts.

Thus, Jack's disappearance gave rise to no search.

# CHAPTER NINE

Jack had barely left Prairie City, when a sudden pain left him unconscious. When he came to it was night time and he was bound hand and foot, gagged, blindfolded and laid across the saddle of his horse. He heard voices of those around him and realised that he was once again the captive of the strange Indians. Before long they stopped and made camp.

Someone took off blindfold and gag. He saw that he was in a tent and sitting across from him was the Indian that had smiled at him on the previous occasion. This time he wore no bandage protecting his arm. Jack reckoned that he was in his late fifties, perhaps older. His hair was almost silver under its paint of red clay, but his whole posture, from the smile to his hands held open on his thighs, suggested wisdom and patience rather than age. As Jack tried to get into a sitting position despite his bound limbs, the Indian spoke.

"Sorry to have you tied up like that, but you have a tendency towards escape and we need you, because you are our Prince." Jack stared at him. Was he another bloody Bill Watson about to create an insane adventure of kings and princes and knights in armour in which Jack would be designated his appointed heir? The old man continued, "No I'm not mad, I'm just the Chief of what remains of the Mandan tribe and you, through your mother, are our Prince, that is to say Head Chief. I am thus Second Chief and my name is Mah-to-tow-pa, or in your language Four Bears." He rubbed his arm which still pained him.

"My mother!" exclaimed Jack. "Who was she then?" He had decided it was probably best to seem cooperative.

"She was the daughter of our then Prince, Ha-na-tah-nu-mauh or Wolf Chief and she was given to your father, a much-respected trader, as a wife, to comfort his days in our village. This was before he disintegrated into drunkenness."

"But that can't be," protested Jack. "My Pap was always an idiot."

"Not until he took to whisky. This was many years ago before our tribe was destroyed by smallpox and when those that remained of us joined other tribes to survive. My group, the bigger of the two large groups of survivors, joined the Sioux, who respected our customs, but now we have left them and are recreating our ancient tribe. The others joined the Crows, where they have almost been absorbed and a few individuals and couples found a home in other tribes. You were born after all this happened, when your father was already disintegrating. He beat your mother so often that he finally killed her. That death was avenged for us, not very long ago, when the Crow people eventually found him."

"But you tried to kill me too," said Jack heatedly.

"That wasn't us. That was the Crow group. They won't accept you as Prince as you descend from a woman and an enemy, the trader Penn. The trader Penn was once a respected man with our tribe. He was my friend, and I would often travel east with him. That's when I learnt to speak your tongue. But then he was ill with a great fever that he caught during his last visit to your people to sell his pelts. He came back to us when he was well again, if but physically; for when he returned, he was a different man, an aggressive, selfish drunk. We thought the fever had burnt his brain and that the Evil Spirit had entered with its cold darkness. It is also possible that he brought the smallpox with him as it was not very long after his return that the disease

162

appeared among us.

"There are no other descendants of the Prince; all his sons and other daughters died of the smallpox. You are the only hope of our traditions surviving. Trader Penn is hated for another reason too. He stole our treasure and part of that treasure was a very holy piece of gold, very ancient, that contained the Mystery Medicine of the Mandan spirit that was central to our rituals and the Buffalo Dance. It was always worn by the Great Chief in a little red sack hung from his neck on a golden chain. Your father cut it from him as he lay dying. And now we have found it around your neck, such an augury cannot be ignored. We forgive the hole you've pierced. You were not to know you were committing sacrilege. It is even perhaps a sign from our Great Spirit denoting you as the rightful bearer of our destiny. It perhaps makes the gold piece essentially yours and that of your children: a symbol of the rebirth of its power. So we must take you to join us where we are beginning to re-establish our tribe, to make you a great warrior like your grandfather and to give you a noble wife to bear your children. The last time we met there was no coin around your neck, so we had to let you escape."

"What if I don't want to be a Prince?" cried Jack, "Don't I have a say in this?"

"I'm sorry you can't have. Firstly, if we're not there to protect you, you will be killed by the Crow people. Your father had disappeared, but eventually the Crow people found him and killed him and then they heard about the treasure you had found. Now they hunt you. They knew most of the gold coins have disappeared into white man's banks and so are lost. But they also know that you had the great Mystery Medicine. We watched over you but they were getting too near and so it was time to act. You are now strong enough to learn quickly how to be a fighter and a hunter and to be initiated as a warrior worthy to be a Prince. It's a pity you have no weapons of your own. One's own weapons are stronger than those that come as a gift."

"But I do have weapons," said Jack suddenly coming to appreciate his new status and despite himself wishing to establish his worth.

"Where? We have not seen you with weapons in a long time."

"They're hidden on an island on the Missouri... not very far from here, I imagine?" and looked inquiringly at the old Indian, who smiled again.

"Indeed, probably not, shall I send for them?"

"Yes, I'd like that." To have his guns back opened up all sorts of prospects for the future and he instantly began to feel less insecure. Jack described in detail the whereabouts of the canoe and the old man relayed his description to the silent warrior sitting at the entry to the tent, who then left.

"So we will have the very noisy gun that shot me in the arm," said Four Bears and cackled. "Good medicine," he added.

Jack looked around him as the old man fell silent. There was just forest, deep and dark in the late twilight. There was no sound but the hoot of an owl and the sigh of an evening breeze high in the treetops. Seated around him were the Mandan warriors, their bodies gleaming redly in the light of the fire. He felt very alone among his silent hosts whose glances spoke more of hostility than welcome. He would like to have wept, but such behaviour would no doubt simply add derision to hostility. He would have liked to have his blindfold back on. Then his tears would be invisible. The old man was observing him, but he suddenly turned away and drew the attention of his companions to the need for another shelter as two more warriors had joined them and rain threatened.

Jack's tears flowed silently and just for a minute or two, after which and with some difficulty, he wiped his eyes on his sleeve as his hands were still tied. He thought of Four Bears, his kindness and understanding and concentrated hard on finding a princely composure. By the time a rough wigwam had been erected next to the tent he could even smile.

In the morning Jack was given food and his hands untied and later his feet when he wanted to go about his toilet. However, for this he was hobbled with a piece of rope and accompanied by two warriors. Afterwards, he was again blindfolded, his hands were re-tied, and he was put on his horse. His protests were met with no response. When they halted that evening it was already dark. They took off his blindfold and he saw his guns had arrived along with a little bag of coins that had been hidden with them. This latter was given him, but he was not allowed near the guns. He hadn't really expected to be given them immediately, but the situation was frustrating even so. He thought about escape; but escaping when you have no idea of where you are didn't seem a very good idea. He thought miserably of Dan and Sam and how they probably each thought he was with the other and so were not likely to be looking for him, as they probably felt abandoned or betrayed. Had he lost his best friends? His feelings for these two seemed very similar. They were more like big brothers than anything else, even with the sex; whereas Tinker was something else. Tinker was yearned for, much like food when you are hungry or, and he smiled to himself, like needing a shit. Shits could be very pleasurable: as one of Pap's friends had said, "A good shit is better than a bad fuck."

What was going to happen with these Indians? They seemed friendly, but what did they really want with him? The story of princes and stuff had not quite convinced Jack. Were they cannibals or something like that? Were they going to cut out his heart and eat it to gain the strength from his princely blood? Bill had said that there were tribes of savages that did that sort of thing; but then he was not very strong and only the descendant of a woman, so perhaps they wouldn't bother. He felt very lonely and again wanted to cry but didn't because then they would despise him as everybody else but Dan and Sam had done — though maybe not Tinker (but then he was a slave). But Sam was difficult to figure out as he was infected by that strange culture in the North, despite having been born not far from the Mississippi at Florida, a little town just a bit to the west of Hannibal.

One of the warriors gave a cry and shouted something which made the others laugh.

"What did he say?" Jack asked anxiously.

"You are like a white man as your medicine bag contains nothing but money," muttered Four Bears, worried that Jack was fast losing respect.

"Don't even want the money. No good to me now, is it?" then dropping this sudden sullenness, he said with a hopeful little smile. "Do you want to try the guns?"

"I know how to use the long rifle but I'm not sure about how to do it with a revolver pistol like that."

"You just pull the trigger. But you'll need to put some bullets in it. It's no use without bullets," Jack enthused; at least here he could be useful and then maybe they'd forget about eating his heart or whatever other evil thing they wanted.

The old man pulled a round from the revolver's belt and looked for somewhere to insert it.

"You have to release the cylinder from the barrel. Push that catch there," he added, pointing with his tied hands. The cylinder fell open, and the bullet was inserted. "Now turn the cylinder until the bullet is in the hole just next to the top. If the cylinder was fully loaded, the next bullet would automatically be in place when the first one was fired. Now, all you have to do is pull back the hammer, which puts the bullet behind the barrel, and then pull the trigger."

"Very ingenious," muttered Four Bears.

Four Bears took aim at a nearby tree, tugged back the hammer and fired. The pistol leapt from his hand as he hadn't expected the huge kick of the cavalry piece. Despite his tied hands, Jack picked it up and gave it to him.

"I think you should wear your princely revolver. But first we take the bullets out of the belt," he laughed as he nursed his bruised hand. "It has wounded me again."

Jack, his hands now untied, started extracting the bullets from the belt and handed them one by one to the old man, being as helpful as he could. Suddenly one of the warriors ran across to them, pointing behind him and spoke urgently to his Chief. Jack used this diversion to palm three bullets into his trouser pocket. The belt was now empty, and he handed it and the revolver to Four Bears and the old man threw the bullets into a small leather bag which he tucked into his belt. He then gave the revolver back to Jack, fastening it around his waist. He hoped this would bring respect. It certainly made Jack feel better. He could even swagger a bit while wearing his gun.

"Too heavy for me," Four Bears whispered. Jack was about to speak but Four Bears put his finger to his mouth and shook his head.

"The Crow people are coming," he hissed. A warrior undid Jack's hobble, and he was pushed hurriedly onto his horse. Then they were off. Four Bears nursed the long rifle the length of one arm as he ran alongside Jack and his warriors ran with their bows armed. The horse trotted obediently along with them. These are not horse Indians, thought Jack, even if they lived among the Sioux.

***

They ran for a good two hours, old Four Bears easily keeping up with them. They ran through forest that told Jack nothing of his whereabouts and had the same aspect mile after mile. Finally, he was brought down from his horse to be blindfolded again. Later that day they came to a river and Jack was seated in a canoe still blindfolded.

"My horse!" he cried.

"Sorry, but we have to leave it," replied Four Bears.

They went upstream a way and then turned against another slower current, evidently having joined another river. The journey continued mounting this new river for several days. Each morning, before full light, Jack was blindfolded again. The old man chatted to him about the nature of his new life as an Indian Prince. Jack began to like the old man even though he was his prisoner. He was being very gentle and even seemed fond of him. Maybe he would join the ranks of Dan and Sam — but perhaps without the sex as he was rather old and his beauty more spiritual than physical.

"We are a strange people. We are not like other Indians."

"I've noticed," said Jack.

"We are the people who arrived after the Flood, the descendants of the First or Only Man who had landed on a mountain in his Great Canoe and received the message that the Flood was finished from a dove carrying a willow branch full with leaves to show that the world had recovered. We still honour this bird and never touch it. Even our dogs know not to touch it."

That all sounds like the Widow Williams' Bible, Jack thought, but the bird should really have had an olive branch. These people don't look much like Indians. Maybe they are lost white folk from some early settlers. He reported his thoughts to Four Bears who nodded.

"The First or Only man is white and comes from the west. And our tradition has it that we have often changed places to escape the persecution of others, always heading west."

That night Jack secretly put a bullet in the revolver, turning the cylinder to hide it under the hammer. He now felt that he was beginning to be in control of things. In the morning and for many mornings after, the journey continued. Jack found that his troublesome penis that had lain quiet ever since his capture was now beginning to come to life again. This was reassuring if something of a nuisance as there was rarely if ever any privacy in which to deal with it. He resigned himself to awaiting wet dreams and a bit of surreptitious stroking when he thought nobody was looking. The old man, who noticed everything that passed, smiled to himself and pretended to be unaware.

After some days they had taken Jack's blindfold off but he recognised nothing of the bare hilly country surrounding them. But, observing the sun, he at least knew they were travelling north and west and that the river ran south and east.

The next day Four Bears came to him and said, "If you promise not to try and escape, we will untie your hands. You wouldn't get far anyway as you've no idea where you are." Jack nodded his promise, but his legs remained hobbled all the same.

It was perhaps a week later on a sunny morning with the leaves of the willows along the shore glimmering with the rain of the previous night and reflecting in the smooth slow water like so many hanging, soft, crystal necklaces when they saw at some distance, perhaps half a mile, a long war canoe approaching rapidly. With its many paddles it was gaining on them. They turned towards the shore, shot in under the willows and dragged the canoe along a while until they came to an overhanging bank under which they hid it. They cut off Jack's hobble and they all ran inshore. They could now hear the yells of their pursuers. Four Bears' warriors separated off in several directions, the old man taking Jack with him. Not a word had been spoken. There were distant sounds of confusion when the Crow people came to the spot where they had all separated. There was little cover, only the tall grass and the trees near the river. As the hunt continued the Crow people shouted to one another to keep in contact, Jack and Four Bears ran low through the grass, circling gradually back towards the river until they reached a little gully into which Four Bears led them. It looked like a trap as there did not seem to be an outlet at the other end. But on arriving there, Jack saw a sharp and narrow defile opening to the right.

As they turned into the defile, Four Bears said, "They can only come one at a time through here." Jack nodded. Thirty yards into the defile where it began to broaden, they waited behind a lone rock. Four Bears had left the long rifle in the canoe; the old man had his bow and arrows with him.

After twenty minutes they heard voices. There only seemed to be two of them, or maybe three. It was difficult to tell. The discussion in the gully ended when one of them gave a shout.

"They've discovered the defile," said Four Bears and Jack took out his revolver and pointed to the sack of bullets in the old man's belt. He smiled and shook his head.

"This will do," he muttered waving his bow and fitting an

arrow. "If you fire that thing, we'll have the whole crowd of them on us. They must be at least twenty." Jack grunted his dissatisfaction and crouched down beside Four Bears. Soon a figure appeared in the widening defile. Jack pulled at his companion's coat. The old man shook his head. Only after the enemy had carefully advanced ten yards did he release his arrow which pierced the man full in the chest. There was a second one five yards behind him who started to rush towards them, a hatchet raised high. Four Bears' second arrow caught him high in the belly and he tumbled over with a scream. A third man turned and ran back towards the gully. Four Bears' rather hurried third arrow just missed him and buried itself in the clay wall as the man disappeared from view.

"Shit," he muttered in his own language, "you clumsy old idiot." He looked at Jack. "Sorry about that," he said. "It looks as though we'll have to take on the lot of them, but we should have help soon." As he said this there was a rustle in the grass behind them and Jack swung round to look, his pistol raised and saw two of Four Bears' warriors approaching stealthily. The man with the arrow in his belly started screaming again. Four Bears ran across, picked up the abandoned hatchet and chopped into his throat. The screaming stopped. He returned to Jack and handed him the bloody hatchet. "Now you have a weapon you can use."

Jack took the hatchet astounded at the old man's agility and ferocity. Bill would still have been discussing what to do next and which of the alternatives offered was the noblest. His admiration for Bill, although still there, was fast waning. Here he was facing reality and not fantasy. He was a real Indian warrior and not a fantasy pirate. He again thought of Dan and Sam, as he often did and then of Tinker who was, however, gradually fading from his deepest yearnings. He wanted a corner in which to go and weep again. He looked up. Four Bears was watching him.

"Stay a warrior. You're no longer just a boy." Jack swallowed back the start of a sob and nodded. "Good," said the old man.

No enemy came, and one by one, Four Bears' other four warriors arrived. All this flight was premeditated, thought Jack, they knew the country. So we must be almost wherever it is we are going, he concluded. As dusk approached, they returned to the river and their canoe. There was still no sign of the Crow people. They went back downstream awhile to confuse the enemy and pulled in to make camp under the willows, well hidden from view. Under the cover of dark Jack inserted the other two bullets into his revolver. He was soon asleep but then woke suddenly, not knowing why.

He listened and waited. Four Bears was snoring gently next to him. He could see the warrior on watch leaning against a tree. There was no moon, but the night was bright with stars. He hugged his pistol against his chest and thought he saw a low movement near the standing warrior, who did not stir as it passed him. One of the others been for a piss, he thought. Then the shape reared up not three yards from him and Four Bears. It had a long knife in its hand, it looked familiar. Jack pointed his pistol and shot, and the shape went over backwards. Jack's brief glance at the man's face, in the glow of the exploding revolver confirmed recognition. It was the huge man that had killed his father. But then other shapes rose up around him with high screams. Jack shot again twice, each time hitting his targets, which would have been difficult to miss as they were so close. Four Bears and the other warriors were now awake, thrusting with knives and swinging hatchets as they struggled to their feet. Jack jumped up with his hatchet raised in time to fend off his next attacker and almost by accident buried its blade in the man's neck as he warded off a descending knife. Clutching at his throat the Indian dropped to his knees and Jack finished him with a blow to the head that split his skull. As Jack wrestled with yet another Indian, gradually being forced to the ground by the man's superior weight, four more attackers fell, under the hatchets and knives of Four Bears' warriors, and the rest ran off. Four Bears thrust an arrow into the back of Jack's opponent, who died instantly as the point entered his heart. The old man pulled Jack to his feet and then solemnly handed him his sack of bullets. The revolver was quickly reloaded. The sentry was still standing as before, pinned to the tree by an arrow through his neck.

Four Bears looked at Jack. "So, my big little man, you are a real warrior and cunning too, which is good, and what is more, we can trust you." He gave Jack a kiss on the forehead. The other warriors came and offered their congratulations. They gave little bows and touched their foreheads too as they made their respects to their Prince. Jack felt fulfilled. He had become a warrior Prince — or so it seemed. The fight had been so rapid that he hadn't had the time to be frightened. Only now did he start to tremble. Four Bears hugged him, and the warriors laughed. To hide his embarrassment, he walked with only a hint of swagger over to one of his victims and wiped clean his hatchet on the man's clothes. The warriors applauded.

They didn't see the Crow people again that night. The pistol shots had obviously made them wary and they had lost, dead or wounded, at least ten of their kind that day.

As Jack had surmised, they were not far from their destination and later the next day they arrived at the Mandan village. The canoe came to a halt on a narrow beach under a low clay cliff into which steps had been cut. All around them laughing, naked men and boys played in the water. Jack saw no girls. He learnt later that the girls had a separate beach from which to bathe. Having traversed the beach, they climbed up into the village. It was comprised of several large round huts partially sunk into the ground. There were Indians sitting on the roofs of many of them chatting under the late afternoon sun. The sun had begun to set, and a chill wind started which drove many from their roofs. Some stayed a little while longer, still laughing and talking but now wrapped in blankets. It was beginning to get late in the season. Four Bears pointed to a palisade made of heavy trunks sunk into the ground and bound to one another leaving gaps between them just wide enough to fire a gun or an arrow through. It cut across the peninsula which was formed by an acute bend in the river. Within the palisade was a trench.

"Why's the trench inside the wall?" Jack asked.

"To protect the defenders when they're shooting at the enemy," replied Four Bears. Jack wasn't convinced. Castles were defended from the top of their walls.

"Back along the Missouri," Four Bears continued, "there are the remains of the old palisade built when we had a big village of nearly five thousand people; that was before the smallpox killed them. Here we've built this smaller one because there are no longer enough of us to man such a long defence. We were impregnable then."

The old man shook his head sadly and led Jack to one of the larger huts, which they entered. In the centre, surrounded by a low stone wall, was a fire, its smoke escaping through a round hole in the roof which was about twenty feet high in its centre. The roof curved up from a low stone side wall of no more than four or five feet. All along the walls were oblong cubicles with decorated hide curtains that enclosed them. The occupants of the hut lounged around the fire on buffalo hide blankets continuing the conversations they had brought with them from the roof.

At Four Bears' entry they stood up and greeted him with great respect. He pointed to Jack and gave a little speech. They all greeted Jack with the same respect. They regarded his holster with equal respect and laid a hand over their eyes when they saw his Athenian coin. Jack was then led to the fire and given food. Nobody else ate; they just watched him with bowed heads and offered him food from the stew pot suspended over the fire if ever his wooden platter looked like being emptied or drink from a gourd if his cup was not overflowing. When he was sated, he was offered a pipe. He puffed at it a couple of times. It wasn't like his tobacco but had a curiously wooden taste. Four Bears touched him, nodded towards the man next to him, who was looking expectant. Jack passed on the long pipe with its decoration of coloured feathers. It then continued and made the round of the fire. All this occurred in silence. Jack was beginning to find the ceremonial of being a Prince rather tedious. He was also very uncomfortable from a distended bladder. He turned and whispered to Four Bears.

"Sorry, but I need a pee."

Four Bears stood up and pulled Jack up with him. He said a few words and made a brief sign with his hand. This was obviously the signal that ended the ceremony, and the assembled Indians began to move and to serve themselves from the communal pot. Jack was led outside and was shown where to pee or do other things. Four Bears waited with averted head. His business done, Jack was taken back into the hut where he was led to one of the oblong shelters. It was to be his bedroom. Outside, around the fire, conversation and hilarity continued and he and Four Bears re-joined the throng. Over the weeks of his journey,

Jack had begun to understand a little of the language of these Indians and found that conversation mainly consisted of jokes, stories of battles and loves. He had the impression that the majority of those present were Four Bears' children. Jack then realised Four Bears was relating the story of the battle under the willows all the while either patting the revolver or thumping Jack's shoulders. The company seemed impressed and Jack tried to find a response: should he be smiling modestly or thumping his chest? He tried to do both at the same time which added to the merriment. As this was a grand moment Four Bears brought out a jug of whisky that he had brought with him from Kansas. This was a very popular gesture and soon many became more than a little drunk, including Jack who was holding an inner celebration: he was no longer afraid, and he was admired. His happy drunkenness seemed to add to his reputation.

He awoke later in his bed with a thumping headache. He couldn't remember how he had got there. He crept out of his bed cubicle in search of water. It was very quiet. Most of the crowd had gone or were in their miniscule bedrooms, but one or two were asleep round the fire wrapped in their blankets. Jack found a gourd of water, satisfied his thirst and went out to urinate. It was intensely cold, and he sensed the coming winter snows. He realised that he was very much further north than Kansas. He thus put away his thoughts of immediate escape: he didn't want to be frozen to death, lost in a blizzard. It would have to await the spring. This was not an unpleasant thought. He liked Four Bears and his people and their happy if fierce natures and above all he loved being admired. He was no longer white trash, but a princely warrior half-breed who had found his people.

# CHAPTER TEN

On the morning of Jack's first day with the Mandan Four Bears had decided that his hungover young warrior should visit the Sweat Lodge.

Jack was stripped naked, wrapped in a buffalo skin cloak and led up to the lodge. Then, having taken off his buffalo skin, he was seated in a crib on a bed of herbs and a squaw entered holding a heated stone between two sticks lashed together as tongs. This was placed on the hearth under the crib and she immediately threw copious amounts of cold water on it. Once the lodge was filled with steam, she left to tend to the other stones firmly closing the lodge behind her, while a child that had accompanied her, to carry the water, stayed and continued to throw it on the stones thus constantly increasing the steam.

At first Jack felt he was going to suffocate, but then the hot, fragrant, herbal vapours filled his lungs attacking the toxins of the night before. He sweated copiously, which rid him of the accumulated filth of his journey north. He felt drugged and then exhilarated. Having finally benefited from the steam of three or four consecutive stones, he followed Four Bears' instructions: climbed out of the crib and ran from the lodge to throw himself in the river. Then, after but a moment, he rapidly got out again and ran to the squaw who rewrapped him in his buffalo cloak and led him back to the round hut and Four Bears, who laid him with his feet towards the fire under two more buffalo pelts. He slept a while and awoke with all signs of his hangover evaporated. Four Bears was sitting beside him.

"Now you are fit to meet your mentor," he said. "But first

we must dress you." He then uncovered a bundle that lay beside him and began to hand Jack his new clothes. His European ones had disappeared. First a loincloth and belt, then some leggings in soft deer hide, a shirt of the same and finally a heavy, long over-vest of buffalo hide. The long vest, leggings and the shirt were all beautifully decorated with intricate symbols, some of them depicting animals or plants and others totally abstract. All was completed with a simple headdress of feathers. Jack rather wished there was a mirror he could look into. He felt he must be very handsome.

Four Bears regarded him. "That will do," he said. "This is your formal dress; your everyday dress will be simpler. You're very beautiful like that," he added, confirming Jack's surmise, "but you must wear your Medicine — your revolver and your coin." He handed Jack the coin and then the revolver with its holster and belt: these latter objects had been cleaned and polished and elaborately decorated with ribbons and feathers. Jack didn't think this was very practical. A Bill Watson addition, he thought, but accepted it as it was obviously important for Four Bears, who caressed the feathers lovingly as he handed him the revolver in its decorated holster.

"Don't worry," the old man said, smiling as he saw the dismay on Jack's face. "If you have to fight you can take the feathers off. And now we must go and meet your mentor. He is quite young but already a famous warrior. He is to ensure that you will become like him: strong, swift and brave."

"I'd like to be," said Jack, hoping that this mentor was not a disciplinarian of the Wilson temperament. He did not want to be de-civilised any more than he had wanted to be civilised. There were too many people who wanted him to be someone else. Warrior or no, Prince or no, he was going to stay the essential

Jackson Penn, warts and all.

He was led to another hut, not as big as that of Four Bears, but still one of the larger ones. Four Bears stopped at the entry, tapped on the doorway to announce their presence. The door curtain was pulled back to reveal a very handsome young man, he also in formal regalia. He ushered them into his hut.

"This is Six Shot Revolver," Four Bears said to introduce Jack, and turning towards Jack added "and your tutor is Black Crow Killer, and like me he speaks a little English and will help you to quickly learn our language."

Jack looked a long look at his mentor and instantly liked him. Was there even a bit of an "instant yearning"?

"Pleased to meet you, Black Crow Killer," Jack said politely.

"And I like you too," the handsome warrior replied. "You will come to live here now," and added, "Your bed is over there." He indicated a small bed chamber similar to those in Four Bears' hut.

After a little more ceremonial conversation in Mandan, Four Bears got up to leave. He kissed Jack on the head saying, "Be brave, be strong, be swift." Then with a final pat on his shoulder turned and left. Jack was sad to see him go. He had got used to having this surrogate father looking after him, softening his anxious fears of an alien future. The young warrior turned and drew closer and Jack saw that despite his youth his hair was silver grey. This was something that occurred quite often among the Mandan, as he was to learn.

Black Crow Killer then spoke a few words in Mandan and repeated them in English.

"Come, I'll show you your things. You can take off these clothes and put on your working clothes." They entered Jack's little bed cabin, where he found some simpler things laid out.

There were also his European clothes now all clean. Jack tucked these away under the bed and climbed into his simpler outfit and became a workaday warrior. For the rest of the day his mentor showed him how to aim and fire a bow, in a way very different to that of his childhood games, took him swimming and running. Then there was more bow practice. By evening he was very tired and even more hungry but said nothing of this. He had to be strong. Black Crow Killer took him back to the hut where they ate with the other inhabitants without ceremony. Their relations had obviously become informal. Very soon Jack asked if he might go to bed and the young warrior made no objection. He too was feeling tired.

Jack closed the cabin's curtains, stripped naked and climbed under the bed covers and was soon asleep.

The next morning, when he awoke, he found Black Crow Killer sharing his bed. His thoughts went once more to Sam and his lessons on the ephebes of Ancient Greece, on squires and their knights and pages in the courts of kings or, again, acolytes in the arms of Jesuits. Here he was the disciple of a great warrior and that warrior was in bed with him. There seemed to be only one conclusion, that the contract included sex. His warrior was on his back and still asleep. He felt under the blankets and found that he too was naked. He laid his hand on the young man's thigh and waited. He didn't need to wait long. Black Crow Killer slowly turned towards him until they were face to face. Jack's hand slipped round with the turn up in between Black Crow Killer's legs.

"Four Bears said that he didn't think you knew about this and that white men have funny ideas about it," and he stroked Jack's smooth cheek. "But I thought I'd see if you wanted it. If you'd leapt out of bed with a scream that would have been difficult, as it's impossible to teach without that you have my spirit within you."

I suppose that means your warrior dick up my apprentice butt, thought Jack with a little smile of complicity.

"And as you're very beautiful too, you would have destroyed me had you refused me." Jack took the hand from his cheek and kissed the palm; whereupon they moved together into a long embrace. Jack wondered how a Mandan warrior made love to his boy. He discovered it was much the same as anyone else did. They quickly had an almost simultaneous orgasm and then continued their caresses far into the morning.

The days of training followed one another until the snows came as did the nights of spiritual union. The young warrior's wife was somewhat neglected, but then she had not expected otherwise. Mandan women were little short of slaves and like the wives of Greek warriors, the simple bearers of children. In the dark winter days, the training continued as much in language and customs as in knife fighting and the wielding of a tomahawk or hatchet. Very often it was Indian wrestling, which almost as often became daytime sex. Spears and bows and arrows were more outdoors and were largely reserved for the following spring: however, there were long hikes for hunting deer in snowshoes, which kept these things to hand. Black Crow Killer also learnt about the revolver; but fired very few shots as Jack wished to conserve his ammunition. He was down to about thirty shells.

***

Come the spring and a long, slow thaw, Four Bears decided that Jack should take a wife as he was almost a man and, Black Crow Killer assured him, sexually competent. Also, the old man was anxious for princely descendants. He chose one of his prettiest daughters, a girl a year or two older than Jack as she had to be well grown enough to bear a child without difficulty. The ceremony was very simple. Jack was simply asked, accompanied by a few ritual gestures and the waving of a pipe with elaborate feather decoration, if he would accept the gift of this woman to be his wife. Jack felt a certain reluctance as this was going to make life with his warrior less simple and could bring long-term complications — although the girl was pretty, he yearned not. Life with Black Crow Killer had come to please him greatly and he was almost persuaded that perhaps his Mandan blood and faggotism were dominant and that this was to be his future life. Dan, Sam and Tinker were beginning to become shadowy figures from a distant world full of intimate hate, anger and violence. The Mandan were gentle and affectionate, except when fighting their enemies when they became cold, fierce and murderous.

His wife, Meadow of Spring Flowers, came to his bed that night. He was back in the hut of Four Bears as was the custom. By tradition, once man enough to have a wife he should not continue to be a warrior's boy. This saddened Black Crow Killer almost as much as Six Bullet Revolver. But now he lay beside his wife wondering where to begin. As he didn't move, she took the initiative, grasping his somewhat flaccid penis and after encouraging it to a satisfactory size, she straddled him. This is all rather business-like, thought Jack. However, once he had ejaculated and her duty done, she calmed down and became tender. He caressed her, as he thought he should and exhorted his member to remain awake and be polite to the girl, which it did, after a little sulk. Jack wondered why he found this less exciting than his experience with Rosie; but then, that morning with Rosie, his sex had been famished after nearly twenty-four hours without activity. He wondered if his nights were not to become rather boring, governed by duty rather than frank desire. The images of Dan, Sam and Tinker began to re-affirm form and the gentle life of the Mandan became less attractive, circumscribed, as it was, by duty. Jack began to feel a loss of freedom and sometimes longed for his life where he had escaped his father in the company of Dan, Bill and the other boys.

The next day Jack talked with Four Bears and suggested he should continue his training, to which the old man agreed.

"You should perhaps try Raging Bear," he suggested. "He's brilliant at in-fighting."

"I would prefer to rest with Black Crow Killer, I have still much to learn from him." Four Bears gave his knowing smile and nodded consent. No need to contrary the boy unnecessarily if we want to keep him, he mused.

That afternoon Jack went running with his warrior, as was their custom. They ran across the prairie, the long grass swishing against their legs while insects whirred and chirped their songs encouraging them as they passed. After two hours Black Crow Killer raised his hand and stopped.

"We shall do some wrestling," he said.

"Your Spirit needs to enter me," Jack added, trying to make his face as serious and as expressionless as possible. The warrior laughed and Jack too. They fell to the ground as they undid their loin cloths. The insect song rose to a crescendo of approval, with the exception one or two buzzes of irritation from disturbed pollen seekers whose flowers were crushed under the two falling bodies; and the cool spring sun stroked them as they quickly re-found and re-shared their pleasure.

Life resumed a pattern and Jack didn't find it too difficult to divide his life between Meadow of Spring Flowers and Black

Crow Killer. The latter receiving a major part of his attentions. Spring moved into summer and the annual Festival of the Buffalo approached. It was during this festival, which lasted four days and was designed to make the buffalo come to feed the tribe, that the young men were initiated into full warrior manhood. The festival was divided into two parts: in the open was the ritual Bull Dance and in the Lodge of Holies were held the painful rites of initiation. The Lodge was only ever used on these occasions for in it was stored the Great Canoe, in which the Mandan had escaped the flood, that would be taken out for the Bull Dance. Finally, at the end of the four days the dance and the initiation rites came together.

Normally, only the initiates and the old medicine men performing the rites were allowed into the Lodge. However, Four Bears, the most respected of the Chiefs, decided that Jack, as a Prince of Great Medicine, should see the entire event. Jack was not very keen, having heard about the torture that went on in the Lodge of Holies from other youngsters and the boasts of older men who liked showing their scars and missing fingers, but as usual he submitted to Four Bears' decision. There was no choice.

Jack watched the initiates, painted red, yellow or white with clay and bear grease, being led into the hut. They were naked but for their feathers, medicine bags and weapons. They sat down around the walls with their weapons hung above them, cross-legged, hands on knees, backs very straight and heads held high in an anxious semblance of courage. Even if some of them were very beautiful, Jack thought they looked rather pathetic in their paint and feathers. He felt the fear and anxiety of these fragile boys trying to be men. Jack knew they were going to pass four days without food, drink, or sleep and he pitied them. He could see hidden emotions in their eyes, little flickers of fear, uncertainty, tremors of childhood. Despite this, they were still beautiful, and Jack would have liked to give them all a reassuring hug. Well, not quite all: there were two who inspired in him no pathos — two Bills — implacably sure of themselves, predators, and whose despising glances at their anxious companions betrayed their conviction that they were the future Chiefs. Jack hoped not. They were not like Four Bears whose simple presence breathed of wisdom and forbearance.

Then an old Indian, representing the First or Only Man, entered and passed among the initiates smoking his medicine-pipe. He was painted white as the tradition held him to be. He greeted the initiates, blessed them with his many-feathered pipe and called upon them to trust in the Great Spirit who would help and protect them throughout their ordeal. He then called an old Medicine or Mystery Man into the Lodge whom he appointed Conductor of Ceremonies and to whom he handed his pipe, thus giving him the holy authority to direct the ceremonies. Afterwards, he left and was not seen again. It seemed to Jack that the boys took courage from the old man's words.

In the centre of the hut were other old medicine men that now began drumming on large gourds of water and some others that began chanting and waving rattles, all creating a great cacophony. At the very centre was the Holy Mystery Medicine bag of which nobody was allowed to see the contents, for it held the Spirit of the Nation, but Jack knew that it contained his coin. It was surrounded by buffalo skulls and other medicine objects. This ritual of rattles and chants was to continue for four days and nights. It ensured that the candidates could not sleep. Jack would have liked to block his ears; but feared that Four Bears might not approve and so, instead, he adjusted his posture to match that of the initiates. This caused the old man to smile.

To Jack's relief, after a while the Conductor of Ceremonies and the gourd drummers left the Lodge to join the Bull Dance, followed by Jack and Four Bears who, having shown Jack to his seat, went to join the other Chiefs. The Bull Dance, held in the open air, was led by the Conductor of Ceremonies who sung and howled a long lament as he danced. The dance was made four times: a separate dance at each of the cardinal points around the Great Canoe, which had been placed in the middle of the ceremonial area. The cardinal points were indicated by pairs of young warriors, one of whom was painted black with white spots and the other bright vermillion red with white stripes. All waved wands and rattles. Jack, who by now had some grasp of the language, turned to his neighbour.

"Who are they? The red and black ones," he asked.

"Night and day," was the reply. "You see that one has stars and the others the rays of the sun." Jack nodded.

At each halt before a cardinal point the medicine pipe was ritually waved. Jack discovered that every day it followed exactly the same pattern, but was also repeated an extra time each day, so that on the fourth day the tour of the cardinal points was repeated four times making sixteen dances in all. On the last day the dances ended as two other characters entered on the scene, who Jack thought were like the clowns in a circus as they created laughter among all the ritual seriousness. They were covered in bearskins and the bears' heads were masks with eyeholes to look through. These two rushed about growling and shouting threats and to whom women brought plates of food to appease them; however, two other characters entered painted black with their heads white, who rushed about and grabbed the food from the bears, with which they fled from the village chased by small naked boys, painted yellow, again with white heads, who stole back the plates of food and ate them. Jack laughed along with the crowd at these antics and tried to make sense of the symbolism. There didn't seem to be any direct meaning other than a sort of dispute between good and evil, but then he wasn't quite sure which group represented what other than a hilarious confusion. He was lost in these thoughts when a sudden and horrifying scream brought his attention back to the scene. He saw a strange creature enter the dance. He was a big man, completely naked and painted black from head to toe, with great white fangs on his face and white rings painted here and there on his body. In his hand was a thick nine-foot wand with a red ball at the end of it. The crowd fell silent. The creature at first ran without direction, flitting here and there screaming and pushing his red ball before him, until finally he charged, gesturing violently with his thick wand, at a group of women who fled in all directions. A Dick, thought Jack, an evil one. All but those doing the ritual dance were watching the intruder. The women screamed for protection. Then there was sudden silence. The old medicine man, the Conductor of Ceremonies, had come away from his station by the Great Canoe and holding his medicine pipe before him confronted the horror with his wand that froze it to instant immobility, his limbs contorted.

"Who's that horrid thing in black?" Jack once more asked.

"The Satanic Majesty, the creator and master of all evil, who has come from his icy hell," the neighbour replied. Hell for the Mandan was cold rather than hot, Jack had learnt.

The crowd, having recovered its previous good spirits, started mocking Satan who was momentarily frozen into a ridiculous posture. He then made several other attempts to interrupt the ritual but was always defeated by the spell of the pipe and reduced to ridicule. Finally, on brushing against a dancer in a buffalo skin, he took on the posture of a buffalo bull himself. Everybody cheered. The buffalo would come. Finally, the women, having overcome their fear, approached him and mocked him, until one seized his wand and broke it over her knee. Others seized the two bits and broke them into several pieces and kicked the red ball away. Then a woman threw a handful of yellow powdered clay at him which stuck to the bear grease of his paint and changed his colouring. He started crying as the power of his wand left him and fled from the village into the hills, the hoots of the women following him. Here the morality play ended; the ritual dance was complete.

Finally, as the general hilarity continued, Jack was once more led into the Holy Lodge to witness the finale of the initiation trials. He saw each youngster led in turn to the centre of the Lodge where strong leather thongs hung down from the smoke hole of the roof. The boy was then seized by the old medicine men who proceeded to cut twice into his pectorals and twice into the flesh of his shoulders and into which wounds they inserted thick wooden skewers. The boy stood unflinching. They then did the same to his arms and legs there inserting thinner skewers. To these latter were attached, by leather thongs, his medicine bag, his weapons and gourds or skulls from the collection around them.

Finally, the large skewers on his chest and shoulders were attached to the thongs hanging from the hole in the roof. Jack watched the unmoving and silent initiate hauled up by the men hidden on the roof until he was five or six feet from the ground. Then the old medicine men seized long poles and started turning him round, thus causing the thongs to twist around each other until under high tension they began to spin undone. The victim then started shouting and screaming incantations to the Great

Spirit as he whirled around squirting blood about him and with his weights, medicine bag, arms and skulls, flying out like the swings of a roundabout. This process was repeated several times, with the screams of the youngster pitching hysterically higher and higher until there was a sudden silence as he fell unconscious. Jack couldn't hold back his tears at the sight of these beautiful youngsters being disfigured by pain and hysteria and he buried his face in his hands. Four Bears put an arm around him, but whispered, "No tears and watch." The next victim was then brought forward, and the ritual began again until there were five of them on the floor. They were left to recover their strength and crawl away to the wall. When all fifteen had suffered this ritual, they formed a queue and one by one approached a man with a hatchet and a skull and one by one they knelt before him and raised the little finger of their left hand and asked the Great Spirit to accept their sacrifice; whereupon they laid the finger on the skull and the hatchet man chopped it off close to the hand. All this last ritual was in silence, with not a whimper.

Then they were all led outside to be observed by the villagers who had long waited in silence once the screams of the initiates had called a halt to the clowning. The stumbling boys were given no help and no wounds were dressed. Each was seized by a warrior who pulled them into a run around and around the Great Canoe with their weights still attached and trailing behind them and the gourd drummers beating an increasing rhythm. They were forced to go faster and faster until one by one the weights fell, the skewers being torn from the skin. Finally, those things that had been too firmly attached were stamped on by spectators, which tore them away too. All the while the crowd shouted and cheered their encouragement.

From the insertion of the skewers to the fall of the last weight the initiates had been watched by the Chieftains of the tribe who were judging which were the bravest and would make the best leaders: which had spun and screamed the longest before falling unconscious; which had run the fastest and by his own speed lost his weights. Finally, the initiates were given water to drink and gently led away to have their wounds dressed.

Jack didn't want to see or hear anymore. He was exhausted by living through his own empathetic torture and wanted to crawl away to weep and sleep. Once the ceremonies finished, he bad Four Bears goodbye and went to his sleeping cabin. But sleep would not come. How had these youths had been able to suffer all this and still be sane and alive? Jack thought that perhaps the four days of sleepless fasting had probably left them benumbed as if drugged. After a while, he dozed, but each little drop into unconsciousness was swept away by visions of the screaming boys and their tearing flesh in the whirling roundabout of their suffering.

\*\*\*

Not long after the Buffalo Festival winter was again upon them. The life of exercise and training continued, and Jack began to have great affection for his pretty wife, who each night put him to sleep so ably.

The snowshoe hunting expeditions began again, but now they often came across marauding bands of Crow people, the renegade Mandan and sometimes, unable to hide, had to fight their way back to the village. They lost half a dozen warriors over the winter months.

In the spring, to the great joy of Four Bears, Jack's son was born and very soon Meadow of Spring Flowers was pregnant again. Four Bears decided that he had chosen well in making Jack his son-in-law. Four Bears wanted to call the baby Long Rifle; however, Jack decided the Sharpe's Repeater was more appropriate as it was very much more effective weapon.

As spring progressed the skirmishes with the Crow people increased as did the resulting casualties. As the Mandan amounted to no more than a few hundred people this threatened to be a demographic disaster. Jack felt a growing resentment towards him, as all knew that it was his presence that enraged the Crow people, his presence and that of the Holy Mystery. Thus, the resentment spread also to Four Bears and his continued insistence on keeping these two motives for revenge. Some even began to mutter that Jack should be given to the Crow People even if they kept the Holy Mystery. And then, even that the Holy Mystery was not essential to their well-being and that Four Bears was a poor Chief.

As these feelings developed Jack began to fear for himself, his wife and the old man. Even the ardour of Black Crow Killer seemed to be lessening. He appeared less often to replace Meadow of Spring Flowers in Jack's bed and stopped wishing to wrestle in the long prairie grass. Then, a week before the Buffalo Festival, Jack caught his foot in a prairie dog's hole while running and badly twisted his ankle. He was secretly pleased as this could present an excuse for avoiding the initiation tortures that year. Four Bears became worried. It was not a good time for Jack to appear to be cowardly. The dilemma was resolved three days later when Black Crow Killer and two of his followers failed to reappear from a hunting expedition. The loss of this Great Warrior pushed the growing hysteria of the villagers to crisis point. It had become impossible that Jack should not be initiated with the other young men of his age.

Come the first day of the festival Jack, trying to look brave, limped miserably to the Great Lodge to begin the four days of sleepless fasting that led up to the torture of the thongs. In the afternoon of the second day when hunger and thirst began their own torture, over and above the sound of rattles, chanting and the Bull Dance ritual and the laughter of the crowd, came the sound of a fierce outburst of gunfire, followed by screams of fear and of war cries. The youngsters round the walls started getting up, but the old men, their keepers, insisted they sat down again. One old man went to the door and looked out and then hurried back and whispered to the others. The unexpected noises increased, while the ancients argued amongst themselves. Suddenly the doors burst open and a warrior, his chest pierced by a spear, fell in. The youngsters jumped up, and seizing their weapons rushed out into the village ignoring the feeble protests of a few of the old men.

As Jack limped into the open, he saw a crowd of warriors fighting at the entry to the village and the naked initiates were running to join in this battle; but also, dispersed here and there other smaller groups were fighting and some huts appeared to be on fire. Forgetting the pain of his ankle, Jack rushed to Four Bears' hut. On entering he froze. Meadow of Spring Flowers, Sharpe's Repeater and Four Bears lay in a pool of blood. All were dead. Their bodies were twisted and broken, slashed and bloody. The baby was almost cut in two. His intestines were seeping through the wide stomach wound and his mother had her head split open. As for Four Bears, he was only recognisable by his fallen headdress. He had obviously fought fiercely and enraged them. About them three Crow warriors lay dead too, two of them pierced by arrows. So, the real Crows had joined with the Mandan Crow people. They must be thousands, thought Jack, no longer in shock and filled with cold, angry fear. His mind went blank and he became a warrior. Like an automaton he took his old clothes and his little sack of money from under his bed. There was no sign of his long rifle. He ran from the hut back to the Great Lodge and once there snatched up the Holy Mystery and his revolver, unnoticed in the confusion, and while the Mandan warriors were being overwhelmed and massacred by ten times their number, he ran to the Sweat Lodge and crept inside.

It was evident that the Crows had taken advantage of the lack of surveillance created by the Bull Dance and the open gates to let out the fleeing bears and small boys chasing them, to launch an attack.

In order to escape, Jack knew he had to get to the river and find a canoe; running out across the prairie would be a simple suicide. There were canoes at the men and boys' swimming beach; but that was some three hundred yards across the village now peopled by Crows seeking the blood of the last of the Mandan warriors and screaming their victory cries at the sky. Suddenly the door flap opened and a painted face stared in. Jack raised his revolver and fired. The face became a mask of blood and the man fell in. Jack pulled him further in to thus clear the doorway. He then cautiously parted the flap a little and looked out. In the distance noisy fighting was still going on, but there did not appear to be anyone nearby — the noise of his pistol shot had been lost in the general din of battle. He waited in the darkness of the Sweat Lodge trying to discern any foot falls through the gradually lessening noises of the clamour outside. But nobody came. The lodge was isolated, its purpose known and thus of little interest for those seeking loot or glory.

Finally dusk came and night fell. Jack got into his white man's clothing, as he was still naked and beginning to feel the night chill. He then pulled open the door flap. In the village, or what was left of it, several fires were burning. The way to the beach and canoes was blocked by a party of Crow warriors enjoying a cache of whisky they had found. Other groups were scattered about with little space between them and the light of their fires ready to reveal anyone trying to pass. He would have to make a circuit of the village. He set off using the belly crawl, a snake-like movement Black Crow Killer had taught him. As behind him there was a high clay cliff, smooth and impossible to climb down, it meant crawling several hundred yards down one side of the village, then along the now broken palisade and up the other side of the village to where the steps down a lower part of the cliff led to the beach and canoes. He set off pulling his gun belt and bag of coins along behind him. After half an hour's effort he reached the palisade. There the going was easier as he could run crouched along the inside ditch.

However, in the middle where once had been the entry there was a small group of warriors. Jack waited, hoping they would move away; but ridiculous as it seemed, with the palisade broken in several places, they were performing some sort of sentry duty. Finally, Jack went through the palisade and crawled out into the darkness. When he thought he was far enough away not to be seen or heard, he returned towards the village on the far side of the sentries, but his trousers snagged on a dead branch and as he pulled himself free part of it snapped away with a loud crack. The sentries stopped chatting and two of them began to walk towards the noise. Jack then hurled the broken branch as far as he could behind him, where it landed with a quiet thud and another crack. The two men changed direction. Jack then wriggled hurriedly back towards the palisade. As, finally, he fell into the ditch he was confronted by another figure also crouched there — a Crow come to relieve himself. Jack swung his gun belt and the butt of the revolver crashed into the warrior's head. He rolled over semi-conscious into his own mess. Jack relieved him of his knife and then stabbed him violently in the chest and stomach eight times: twice for Sharpe's Repeater; twice for Meadow of Spring Flowers; and, finally four for Four Bears as his name demanded. He then wiped the bloody instrument on the man's loincloth. Breathing heavily, silent tears running down his cheeks, he contemplated his work, spat in the man's contorted face and finally stuck the knife in his belt. It would come in useful if again he had to kill silently.

He came to the end of the palisade and started crawling up the riverbank, descending below it where possible. He reached the clay steps on the cliff above the canoes and saw that there were two warriors guarding them. He decided to abandon all caution as there seemed no other way of getting down to the river. He approached to within ten feet of the guards before they noticed him. He shot twice and both men fell. He then rushed for the steps, but one of the Crows was only wounded and he grabbed at Jack's foot as he passed. Jack fell and his revolver went tumbling down to the beach. Jack turned and pulling the knife from his belt slit the man's throat, but not before he could yell out a scream. Two shots and a scream were more than enough to alert the whole village and Jack hurried down the steps, quickly found his revolver and ran over to the canoes. He soon found a small, light canoe and pushed it out into the river just as shouts came from the cliff above. He jumped in and paddled frantically away from the village. As he reached the main current on the far side of the river, arrows and the occasional bullet began to plop into the water around him. He then let the canoe ride with the current as he shot four times at the crowd on the beach. They hurriedly fell to the sand. He then took the holy coin from his pocket and its ritual wrapping, he placed it around his neck, the original thong still being there. I was not going to let those murdering bastards have that, he thought, as he once more seized his paddle and began to guide the flying canoe away from any rocks or snags as they appeared. An inner mist began to cover the sight of his dead family. His mind refused to dwell on it — his little son lying in his own blood and torn open so that his intestines were visible and starting from his tiny stomach and the gentle loving Meadow of Spring Flowers with her head split open, the grey matter of her brain still pulsating and kind old Four Bears unrecognisable. Tears continued to stream down his face as he sought an oblivion where only the river and its rocks held his attention.

By nightfall, he was still in the tributary (the Niobrara, he later learnt) and was some miles from the Missouri. He recognised the spot where Four Bears and his warriors had hidden their canoe under an overhanging bank sheltered by willows. He manoeuvred his canoe beneath it. Then he stripped his gun belt of its feathery decoration and lay down to sleep. The canoe was not very comfortable but safer than sleeping under the trees. The sleep of exhaustion came, but he was not still. His limbs jerked at the bid of his dreams. The sound of his whimpering rose and was lost among the rustle of the weeping leaves of the willow.

It took him five weeks to reach Hannibal: at first down the Niobrara to the Missouri and then on down to the Mississippi and finally northwards against the current, hugging the banks for dead water. Most of the time hungry as a revolver was not really a hunting weapon and he had soon used almost all his bullets. He much regretted having abandoned his bow and arrows. His little sack of money saved him from starvation each time he hit a bit of civilisation; first of all, in the newly founded Sioux City, a sprawl of half-built huts, nowhere to sleep but at least there was food. As he progressed, and once he was beyond Omaha, he found villages more and more frequently. To his great relief, he never once saw sign of Crow or the Mandan Crow People.

Early one evening, several months over two years since he had been captured by the Mandan, he knocked at the Reverend Doctor Winston's door.

# CHAPTER ELEVEN

Bill Watson opened the door and stared in disbelief. Jack was also rather surprised to find Bill there.

\*\*\*

One afternoon, a few months after their first coupling in the schoolhouse, Bill and Beth were in Beth's bedroom. Her father was downstairs engrossed in the writing of a monumental work on the ill effects of Puritanism on the development of American society and thus unlikely to move within the next three or four hours. They were both naked and Bill was anxiously examining the now slightly bulging appearance of Beth's belly.

"Does it move?" he asked anxiously. Beth nodded.

"What we going to do?"

"We'll have to tell Pap."

"He'll shoot me."

"No, he won't. He's a gentle man." With that she pulled him close. Bill hugged her and became, as ever, filled with desire. She felt him growing against her and led him to the bed, where they entered temporary forgetfulness as they began a second love making.

Downstairs, the Reverend Doctor was seeking a small piece of paper on which he had made notes that morning, which he had later jammed into a waistcoat pocket as he realised, he was late for lunch. The gong of summons had sounded several minutes before and Misses Hardly, his cook, was not one to be kept waiting. He had eaten hurriedly, barely remarking the presence of his daughter, his head was buzzing with the construction of new sentences to be written. Beth had been equally preoccupied as Bill had come by just before she and her father had sat down to eat. When Beth had invited him to join them, he declined, protesting that he had already eaten and that would wait for Beth in the garden. When they finished eating Beth left to find Bill and led him quickly and silently to her bedroom where their embraces led rapidly to a hurried love making. The Reverend Doctor got to his feet and hurried off to his study. An hour later he felt in his waistcoat pocket for the notes he had stuffed there. But now, there was nothing in his pocket. He left his study to search for it. The two lovers, totally absorbed in their activity, heard nothing of his mounting the stairs. He had not found it downstairs, and so he was seeking his bedroom where he had briefly passed after lunch to take a clean handkerchief. His bedroom was next to Beth's, and searching the floor as he walked, he absentmindedly turned the handle of her bedroom door and entered. He then noticed that he was treading the wrong carpet and looked up.

Beth and Bill, having completed the more energetic moments of their lovemaking, were lying entwined in each other's arms. The bed covers had fallen half off and exposed the most part of their naked bodies.

The Reverend Doctor stood quite still, not sure what to do or say — the two children looked so beautiful. Finally, he coughed politely.

"Sorry for the intrusion, I mistook the door," he said.

Bill and Beth looked up and froze. Then Beth pulled the bed clothes up to her chin, which left Bill completely naked. His hand shot to cover his not very dormant sex.

"Well, well!" said the Reverend Doctor, quite mildly. "What

have we here?"

"I love your daughter, sir," stuttered Bill, clambering from the bed and standing protectively in front of Beth, his arms spread.

"And I imagine she returns your affection?"

"Yes, sir."

"Come here, Beth," added the Reverend Doctor. And Bill took a step back, raising more stiffly his protective arms.

"Don't you worry, Bill Watson, I'm not a violent man."

Beth came from the bed, and pushing down one of Bill's arms, which went back to its cloaking duties, she walked, head bowed, to her father, who examined her, his glance resting awhile on her belly. He smiled a trifle sadly.

"This is all rather premature," he said, "but then I suppose these things happen. I think, young man, that you had better come and live here and take up those responsibilities that go along with the joys of love." Bill stared at him wide eyed.

"I would like that, sir. Thank you very much." He walked forward to shake hands. The one offered was somewhat sticky, but then the other one was hugging Beth. The Reverend Doctor left them to continue their joy and descended the stairs to his study, all the while muttering, "a fine boy, a fine boy" in reassurance.

\*\*\*

"Jack Penn," he declared, "where have you been all this time? Sir, Beth, come here, see what the cat's brought in." He then seized Jack in a big hug. Beth arrived carrying her second child and Judge Thatcher came leading the first. The Reverend Doctor hadn't been much disturbed by his daughter's premature parenthood. He thought Bill was a fine boy and fine boys got their way. He had been one himself.

"I was captured by Indians," Jack said. "It's a long, strange story."

"I bet," said Bill grudgingly. Adventures, strange or otherwise, were his territory.

"Come in, boy," cried the Reverend Doctor. "Never thought to see you again! Thought you must be drowned or shot in the Kansas troubles. Come in, come in, have a seat. Beth, fetch the boy some lemonade."

"Sure, he wouldn't like something stronger?" said Bill.

The judge looked momentarily surprised. "Suppose he might. How old are you now, Jackson?"

"Getting on sixteen, maybe seventeen even, I reckon."

"Old enough then!" exclaimed the judge. "Cancel that order, Beth, and fetch some glasses."

"What's your poison?" asked Bill, moving towards the drinks' cabinet.

"I reckon I could murder a whisky," was the reply. Again, the Reverend Doctor looked mildly surprised, having had beer in mind for the boys.

Once they were all seated, glass in hand. "Well, fill us in," urged Bill.

Jack began his story from his first encounter with the two groups of Mandan Indians on the riverbank while waiting for Dan, (he felt sudden guilt on mentioning the escaped slave and faltered momentarily, but nobody else reacted — maybe they had not connected Dan's disappearance with his, and so he continued) and how odd their appearance was, later to be confirmed by the curious colouring of the Mandan villagers: their skins varied from white, through pink to a dark honey colour and their hair of all the shades to be found in any European village, except ginger or auburn. Some had silver grey hair, even the youngsters.

"How's Dan, by the way?" interrupted the Reverend Doctor.

"Don't know," replied Jack before continuing with his story. "I've gotta go and find him. Reckon he could be in trouble. He was getting rather Abolitionist last I saw him." The Reverend Doctor nodded, and Bill frowned and shook his head sadly.

"You probably don't know, but the Widow Wilson has passed on and she freed Dan in her will. A case of bad conscience, I think."

"I think Dan needs a bit of a lesson. Running away is not on," Bill added.

"I see it as self-defence," said Jack. "Selling him down south was as good as shooting him." All but Bill nodded. He simply shrugged.

By dinnertime the story was half told, and Jack continued it sporadically while eating.

"Fascinating," said the Reverend Doctor. "So you've got a child too."

"No," replied Jack. "He's been killed and my woman too — and Four Bears," and tears started to his eyes. The Reverend Doctor could make no reply, he just blinked. They poured him another whisky.

"You know," Jack said apropos of nothing in particular. "The guy that killed Pap must've been one of them Crow People."

"As you described him, he didn't look much like an ordinary Indian," said Bill.

"You're right there. I reckon he was looking for the coin," added Jack thoughtfully. "I think I killed him later. You know — the fight under the tree."

"What a load of violence for a stupid superstition!"

"A bit like the sacred bit of bread kept in a chalice or worshipping bits of wood from the Holy Cross — at least it's gold!"

Bill looked at the Reverend Doctor with a raising of eyebrows, but he simply nodded and smiled.

"You're a right little Martin Luther," he said.

"Anyway, get on with the story. How'd you get away?" urged Bill.

"Well, it's all to do with the Buffalo Festival, the Bull Dance and the torturing of the young warriors to see how brave and strong they are." He described how Four Bears had wanted him to see the initiation ritual and how there were the four days of fasting and how thongs and weights were attached to the youngsters before they were hoisted up and spun round.

"But didn't the skewers get torn out when they were hoisted in the air?" interrupted Bill.

"No, because unlike the weights whose skewers just went through the skin, the thick ones cut through muscle and the sinews were too strong to do more than tear a bit. There were lots of blood. It spattered all over the place as they spun round." Beth was looking pale.

"I don't think we want to hear any more about that," said the Reverend Doctor, firmly. Jack nodded, but Bill looked a bit disappointed.

Jack took another sip of his after-dinner whisky and continued his story with the two days of fasting in the Great Lodge before the Crow attack.

As he was describing the attack itself Bill interrupted. "How'd the Crows get past the palisade," he asked, "what with the shooting holes and the ditch which must have acted like the walk behind the battlements of a castle?"

"Difficult to pour boiling oil upwards," said Jack with a tinge of sarcasm.

"Don't bullshit me." Bill smiled.

"They took advantage of the Buffalo Festival — everybody was looking the wrong way and the gates were open."

When the story was finished and a last whisky drunk they all went off to bed. Jack was a bit drunk, but despite that he treated himself to a little autonomous sex. He hadn't had any for nearly ten days, if one didn't count the rather shallow nocturnal emissions that sometimes accompanied his dreams. He didn't know who to think of most: Black Crow Killer whose recent reticence left his memory less warm; Sam, who was a very fond memory: Tinker the most exciting, but somewhat faded; or, finally Dan, but there it was more simple and warm friendship. He decided to mix Sam and Tinker. He achieved a quite satisfactory level of pleasure imagining the gentle strokes of a trembling Sam, but the moment that caused this pleasure to defeat whisky and burst into orgasm was an image of Tinker fucking Rosie: his glorious, tight, round arse pumping and his swollen piston thrusting until, deep within her wet warmth, it stopped and squirted and squirted. He fell asleep still dribbling pleasure as he realised that, at the end, it was he and not Tinker that was in Rosie. He awoke the next morning as the sun reached his window and with only a slight headache, whereupon he repeated his good-night exercise. Things were back to normal.

***

As nobody in the Winston household had heard anything of Dan, Jack decided to backtrack to Kansas to seek news of John Brown's whereabouts even though it would probably mean several days, of first a luxury steamboat down to St Louis and thereafter whatever smaller craft was going up the Missouri. But then money was no problem as he had learnt that his bank had not failed and that had been a story put about, with the unconscious aid of the town gossips, to put off the various doubtful claimants to Jack's inheritance on the basis of the imagined debts of Joshua Penn. The Reverend Doctor had remained convinced that one day, this rascally Jack, who he had long suspected had stolen the Widow Wilson's Dan, would be back as he had the makings of a survivor, moulded by the violent rhythms of his infancy.

Jack had also thought of going east with Bill who was on leave from West Point: which had meant that he was not yet officially married to Beth as they didn't accept married cadets. Once Bill had been co-opted into the Winston family, he had been sent to a Military Academy as the Reverend Doctor had decided that his future son-in-law should have a career. And a fine, brave and adventurous boy like Bill was evidently to be a soldier. Going to boarding school had not greatly interfered with his procreative activities as the holidays were long and often, as suited a rural community.

Going east with Bill could have been fun but didn't seem particularly suited to finding Dan. Jack finally decided that a visit to Kansas was likely to be more fruitful if less enjoyable. And so, with a pocket bulging with easy dollars, he set out with hopes of finding his friend and with thoughts of adventure consoling the threat of loneliness in his mind.

Bill had also given him the missing fifty dollars that he had kept back to add reality to the bankruptcy story and to make Jack's voyage west tougher and more adventurous, while also adding the pleasure of surprising Jack with it on his return. Dan, to whom he had related his story of a failing bank, never questioned it, being too concerned with his own plans to snatch his freedom. Jack was unmoved too. Money was something hard and round in his hand. Money in the bank had no reality and thus the hundred dollars donated by the Reverend Doctor was riches beyond his adolescent dreams. The inheritance hadn't meant much to him anyway. It was something nebulous, not really his, lost in a bank. The same went for the coins. They didn't even look like real money, nothing like the dimes and nickels or the occasional dollar he had owned. The Reverend Doctor had said it was all invested in railroads and was multiplying fast, whatever that meant. But now, nearly two and a half years later, he began to appreciate the presence of his nebulous fortune.

The journey was uneventful. He made stops at St Louis and Jefferson City, where he feasted, drank and made enquiries, then up the river Kansas to Lawrence and then Topeka. There, finally, he had news of Brown, who was ensconced nearby with a few disciples. Jack went in search of Dan and found him without difficulty. He was living with John Brown himself and Jack came across him one afternoon in the garden of Brown's lodgings. He was sitting in the shade, under a great oak, stripped to the waist and dappled with spots of sunlight that made his brown skin turn golden where it hit. For the first time Jack thought of him as beautiful rather than simply dear and familiar. He was reading a serious looking book.

"Hi, Dan," cried Jack as he caught sight of him.

Dan stared dumbfounded for a moment, then jumped to his feet "Ain't you dead? Where's Sam? You abandoned the river boats?" he asked with just a suspicion of resentment in his voice.

"Never been with Sam," replied Jack and began his story of abduction. Dan was quickly with him, remembering with satisfaction the incident on the riverbank when he had shot his first white man, who now turned out to be an Indian, which diminished the satisfaction somewhat. He was given a shorter and less elaborate story than that given the Winston family, but all the same took the rest of the afternoon, at which point they were joined by John Brown and all had to be partially repeated.

"The Indians are treated like the blacks, only worse; it's not just a matter of denied equality and humanity. It's a genocide, we're massacring them, wiping them out, with disease, with stealing their lands and pushing them to the deserts," thundered John Brown. "Not the Lord's work that. Doubt if there'll be any left by the end of the century." He was almost shouting.

"The ones I saw were busy killing each other," muttered Jack.

Dan chuckled. "You're missin' the point," he said. Jack remarked that there was no longer much nigger/slave argot or accent in his speech, except when he got excited and slipped. "They have their warrior and hunter traditions; with which, in the wide-open territory and with their rules of bravery and honour, they live in their own wild harmony. They have a natural existence. They are married to nature and its rhythms. They fit into nature like the birds and the buffalo. In fact, they and the buffalo are inter-dependent as neither could exist without the other: the buffalos feed the Indians and the Indians cull the buffalos eliminating the weak and keeping their number within that which the territory can support. While whitey tries to simply dominate nature. He's against nature. He wants to kill it for his profit." He stopped to gather breath and thoughts. "Yeah, but the Mandan's acquaintance with the white man and his maladies, the pox and avarice, seems to have created new criteria, fear and greed, that didn't exist before and which is finally destroying them."

Jack just nodded. He and John Brown were impressed, even startled by Dan's command of his new language.

John Brown bent down and picked up the book. "Walden!" he exclaimed. "Young Dan here is becoming a learned man, if a rather fierce one. But, rather like myself, not so very Thoreau in the matter of violence."

"Thoreau's jus' developin' Emerson," interjected Dan hurriedly. "He's makin' a natural philosophy of Emerson's analysis of an unnecessary dependence on European culture. He's against violence <u>and</u> against slavery," added Dan with an expression that doubted the consanguinity of two such positions.

"You'll have to explain all that to me later," said Jack. "I'm just a simple half-breed."

"You'se mockin' me, Jackson Penn, chile?" smiled Dan, returning affectionately to his past language.

"No, he ain't mocking you, Dan. It's just that what you said was a bit too concentrated for one not familiar with philosophising and that." Dan didn't look entirely convinced. He knew the teasing Jack of old. Jack just grinned.

"Have to be off," said John Brown taking out his pocket watch. "See you boys later. You'll stay to eat?" he added looking towards Jack.

"Yes, sir, pleased to."

As Brown walked off Jack turned towards Dan. "So what's going on, he being back in Kansas and all?"

"Nothing much at the moment," answered Dan. "He's stymied, as he can't get at the money his rich friends in the East promised him. He's sittin' on a load of arms he's stashed away at Tabor that they've paid for and that he's supposed to use or distribute for imposin' the Free State, which means harassin' the slavers with the raidin' and rustlin'. He's usually up to that. But he seems to have other plans now that things are calmin' down here. Also, the Federal Army's movin' in to keep the peace while Washington sorts things out and all these Constitutions people keep creatin'. There's the Slave State one that nobody but heated slavers want, a Free-Soil one that the eastern politicians found too radical — forbiddin' slavery and the arrestin' of runaway slaves, plus equal rights for blacks, votin' etc." and he laughed, "even equal rights for women."

Jack sniffed, "I've known women more sensible than most men, even black ones." He grinned again and Dan chose not to react.

"And there's a third one now — created by this moderate called Wyandothe, I think; but what's really done for Brown's raidin' and that was the referendum which proved, at six to one, that Kansas folk, mainly Free Soilers, didn't want no slavery. When Buchanan and the Senate tried to push through the Slave Constitution, Congress demanded a referendum before they would vote for it — the result was that the slavers were blocked, and Mister Brown left with not much of a cause as no one wants slaves or any niggers at all for that matter."

"You're very up on things," said Jack. "You've obviously not wasted this last two years. Me, I've only learnt how to be an Indian. Which ain't a lot of use."

"At least you've become warrior. We can use that."

"I don't see how: can bows and arrows match up against Sharpe's Repeater?"

"Rifles are quick to learn about."

"Not sure what the fight's about anyway." Jack waved his hand about and stared blankly at Dan.

"It's about getting rid of slavery and admittin' blacks into the human race, lettin' 'em have the same rights as white men: the vote, liberty and property," said Dan angrily.

"Okay, I see you as a real human being, but all them dumb, ignorant niggers running scared and afeared of everything, what are they gonna do with liberty and the vote, let alone property?"

"At first maybe, they'll be like white trash, voting for the first that gives 'em a dollar or a pot of whisky, but that don't mean they can't learn given the chance. It's the fuckin' principle, clearly stated in the Constitution: 'All men are born free and equal.' All Free Men, contributin' to the democracy and submittin' their particular interests to the general will and not to that of the crooks with the money to buy an election."

"You believe that can happen?" asked Jack shaking his head.

"I believe it should happen and that I should fight for it. As Mister Brown says, it's no good waiting for the crooks to give up their power and wealth. They never will. You've gotta shoot the bastards and take it back. That's the only way things will change."

"You'll end up getting hanged. The Browns of this world might go around shooting slavers and stuff and get away with it in the confusion, but a black touch a white man, then both slaver and Free-Soil folk will be after him with a rope."

"Don't think I don't know. But we ain't goin' nowhere by bein' Uncle Toms. That's jus' aidin' and abettin' the system. Yes massah, no massah, three bags fuckin' full massah. Ain't I a lovely nigger. Yah can kick my arse and I'll come back fo' more. No, Jack, we's gotta fight." He regathered his breath and his new-found speech. "Soon we're movin' off. Brown's going to train an army at Ashtabula and then raise a rebellion. He's planning to conquer the South for Freedom."

"That's all crazy. The slaves ain't going to rebel, at least not many and not all whites are all wicked."

"You coming along or not?" muttered Dan impatiently.

"Don't rightly know. I've had enough fighting and killing for the moment... Okay, I'll come, just to keep an eye on you, but don't rely on me for any fighting. I want to know what the new Dan's like and, this last two years, I've certainly missed the old one."

"Okay, whitey, and keep that eye wide open. 'cos I'm goin' to fill it with surprises."

That evening Jack ate with John Brown and his companions. The talk was very heated: all fine principles and strategy, from Montesquieu to Proudhon via Plato (but there they had difficulty with a philosopher king, all except John Brown, that is) and from Caesar to Napoleon. Dan joined in with quotes from Emerson and bits of translated Rousseau when defining the nature of American culture from the Afro-American point of view, all with great applause from the others. Jack could see how Dan had been seduced by these youngsters, part intellectuals, part simple adventurers, how he bathed in their praise, was flattered by their interest or so it seemed.

That night he passed in the stables with Dan, but not beside Dan, who had a servant girl from the house to comfort him. Jack was much troubled by the new Dan; even though he could see his old friend beneath the skin of learning and see he had grown in the company of John Brown; grown from having been to the eastern states and met with the likes of Emerson, Thoreau, Whitman, the cultured society of Washington and New York; grown to be gratified by their interest. The sensible, kind Dan of old was confused and wonderstruck by the fire of ideas. His once humility before the everyday white man had been transformed into open distrust and even simple hatred when it came to the southerner. He sensed that even he, good old Jack, was seen through colder eyes. But then after two years of separation, two years of dramatically opposed experience what could he expect — two years in which Dan had felt abandoned by his greatest friend, the happy go lucky, worldly wise Jack, his white trash friend? This Jack who was now a rich man, whose money was invested in railways, but who was intellectually somewhat underdeveloped.

Dan, who had educated himself far beyond the simple, ingenuous if guileful thinking of Jack and who had yet to find himself in his new world, where each proposition was disproved or threatened by the next, where nothing was sure and everything just a theory to be subjected to doubt. Dan's new reality eluded Jack and, quite often, even himself. When excited, showing off he would quote his favourite lines from Whitman:

*Do I contradict myself?*
*Very well then, I contradict myself*
*(I am large, I contain multitudes).*

\*\*\*

The next morning John Brown started his preparations. His decision to leave Kansas and pursue more ambitious plans elsewhere had met with some opposition, but in the end his enthusiasm and persuasion had encouraged most of his group to go with him and become soldiers for the cause. The fact that he had deceived the Eastern friends who were unknowingly to finance his venture was put aside as irrelevant before the greater task that John Brown had now assigned himself.

The day after, they set off for Tabor where the arms were stocked and then started the trek north to Ashtabula, where his army was to be trained. The Ashtabula was famed as a rallying point for runaway slaves on their way to Canada.

However, John Brown's party never reached Ashtabula. They fought their way through cold and snow for several weeks, often sleeping in the open until lack of funds enforced a halt.

Jack and Dan suffered with the rest. For Jack living rough was no new experience. In fact, he rather preferred it to sitting around in relative comfort awaiting the decisions of John Brown; whereas for Dan, taken up with his enthusiasm for his crusade against slavery, if it meant discomfort, it had the puritan appeal of suffering, of mild martyrdom. At the same time, they both appreciated the gradual renewal of their old friendship. Jack had almost immediately noticed a change in their roles. In the past, before his two-year absence with the Mandan, he had been the leader, encouraging Dan towards a rather limited kind of freedom and equality — limited to themselves. Now, it was more often Dan who led; who created their means of renewal; who was the educated one introducing Jack to the world of politics and theory. He was no longer the simple and fearful soul following the worldly-wise child. Jack still had his great affection for his friend and Dan his motherly protectiveness, but both had much changed. Jack had experienced being a Prince, protected by a long tradition of innate worthiness: he was no longer white trash. Dan had been the doyen of white intellectual society: he was no longer nigger. Both had gathered confidence in their personal value even if it remained fragile.

When they huddled together, fully clothed and under shared blankets in the freezing winter nights under a wagon, the frost biting their ears and noses, it was Dan who warmed his friend and instigated a fumbling search for affection. He talked of Walt Whitman and his admiration for him and how he had told him of Jack and their shared life. Then he burrowed beneath layers of cloth to finally caress his friend to pleasure and Jack did the same for him. This exercise left them both a trifle wet and uncomfortable for a while, but finally re-established their simple loving of long before. Jack wept just a little with happiness as he snuggled close in the arms of Dan. Dan momentarily forgot his mission as he mothered Jack and remembered the poet.

\*\*\*

John Brown's expeditionary force had run out of money with Ashtabula still some weeks of travel distant and under the banner of Abolition settled for the charity of a Quaker settlement in Ohio, where they set up camp and started their training. The excitable young men of the company soon took on soldierly habits and prerogatives: arms drill and waving their wooden sabres was not enough and they had subjected a few not unwilling girls to their military will. This latter activity did not increase their popularity with the local population. Finally, they left the Quakers having made an agreement with a farmer who gave them food and rudimentary lodgings in exchange for carts and horses.

As time wore on John Brown went east again to raise funds, but without a great deal of success as his supporters were expecting him to be in Kansas and not wandering about Ohio or making plans for adventures that had little to do with creating a slave-free state. Another trip north to Ashtabula to visit the black enclaves along the Canadian border met with more success. He took Dan with him to prove his Abolitionist credentials, whose education greatly impressed certain blacks that had grown rich and were willing to part with money for the cause. However, his hopes of getting recruits for his planned campaign in Virginia had but little success. Those that had escaped slavery and even those that had not known it were rarely inclined to risk their freedom in such a venture.

On his return, John Brown decided to go back to Kansas and Topeka: firstly, to re-enforce his credibility with the Eastern Free-Soilers and, secondly, in the hope of creating a little "business" for his boys. This latter motive turned out to be a raid into the Missouri Territory, where he freed ten slaves and plundered a little — just to defray his expenses. This venture raised a storm of protest and a posse was sent to arrest Brown and his followers. Mr Wood, the Marshal commanding the posse, awaited Brown at Muddy Creek. When Brown arrived, Wood demanded his surrender and was astonished to see Brown's tiny army form up and charge him. The posse, which had not expected to fight and had yet to receive promised Federal reinforcements, thereupon turned their horses and fled with Mr Wood spurring furiously very much in the lead. This incident became known as the "Battle of the Spurs". Thus, the heroes continued north on their way to Ohio unmolested. The further they went north and east, the more popular they became. In Kansas John Brown was a bandit, a criminal who used abolition as a pretext for robbery; in the eastern states a heroic crusader who had freed eleven slaves (a baby had been born shortly after they had been freed).

He had returned to Ohio from the Missouri with a suspiciously large amount of money, very much more than could be explained by the sale of a few rustled horses to defray expenses. No explanation was demanded. At first, Dan had been rather disappointed at being left behind despite being suspicious of the nature of Brown's real motives, but Jack had been content to remain a student soldier. When not marching and double marching or learning how to wield the bayonet, they walked about the countryside admiring nature burgeoning butter green beneath the late spring sun and discussing and redressing the world at large. Jack was beginning his education. He even read a book or two.

One evening, seated by a rustling stream that twinkled its way between low banks of sun-spotted willow branches, Jack looked closely at Dan and fixed his eye as he demanded, "What do you really think of John Brown?" He had begun to suspect that Dan's idealisation of his hero, based on the fact of his having been saved by him when brought down by the slavers and their dogs, had begun to falter before reality. Jack himself was convinced the old man was not a little mad if full of good intentions that stumbled about among baser ambitions.

"Dunno," answered Dan, looking away. "I can't really figure him out. I owe him a lot and I think his mission is just. However, what he says and what he does don't often really fit together. If he could get rid of religion, he would make more sense. He hides behind it, shoves his responsibility behind it, so that whatever he does is God's will, especially the doubtful bits, like stealin' and stuff, which is a contradiction because the good bits he attributes to himself even if admitting to a bit of divine inspiration."

"Whether his mission is just or not, I think he's nuts," commented Jack.

"It's his religion that makes him nutty. It means that he doesn't have to make sense by human standards. His puritanical notions, like his violence, don't have to be explained, don't have to have logic. Like those grim old ladies who go to church thinking that they're good Christians on the side of peace and love while hating others and acting spiteful. Or like them good Christians who hold slaves and who believe all men equal, but some, white men that is, are more equal than others. It's all done by faith. If we could get rid of God and blind faith, then the world might start to make sense. That's what Spinoza says, at least."

Jack shook his head. "That would leave a lot of people without hope as they've only got religion as a comfort in the horrible lives they live."

"Then they should become revolutionaries and attack their oppressors rather than cower behind religion."

"Not so sure," said Jack. "I've known non-believers among the poor who just accept their misery, even think their inferiority justified, who sit in their shit and no longer notice the smell."

Dan laughed. "You gotta point there. A lot of slaves are like that — beyond despair. That's why I think that John Brown's idea of spontaneous rebellion among the slaves when he strikes is just wishful thinkin'. First of all, they'd have to be educated, so that they understood freedom rather than simply acceptin' misery as their just lot."

The next day John Brown arrived and started his final preparations for the conquest of the South and a week later he set out to reconnoitre the site of his uprising.

# CHAPTER TWELVE

John Brown arrived at Harper's Ferry accompanied by three of his young men. He was looking for a headquarters from which to launch his conquest of the South. They rode about the foothills of the Maryland Heights above Harper's Ferry — a small town, home to a Federal Arsenal, situated at the confluence of the Potomac and Shenandoah rivers. He was seeking somewhere discreet to rent, preferably an isolated farm where arms could be stored and his army gathered. From the foothills above the town, there was a fine view. Below, the two rivers glittered in the sunlight as they rippled around sandy spits and fallen trunks and reflected the rich green of the surrounding countryside. Beyond the rivers rose the rocky Loudon Heights, well covered in thick woodland. The town itself lay in the peninsula created by the joining of the two rivers, its outer suburbs drifting up further foothills beyond the peninsula towards the Bolivar Heights. It was just the sort of semi-mountainous country that John Brown had wished for, largely insulating the town from any rapid outside intervention. However, this geographical situation made it an unlikely centre for a slave revolt. There were no plantations, just, for the most part, small holdings devoted to subsistence farming.

On the second day of their search, they came across a certain Mr Unsfeld, a friendly man who greeted the strangers warmly. Having exchanged greetings and introduced themselves as a Mr Smith and his two sons Oliver and Watson accompanied by a friend called Anderson, they went on to inquire if there were any farms for sale in the neighbourhood. It turned out that the farm of the recently deceased Dr Kennedy was for sale. John Brown evoked an interest.

The matter was negotiated with the Kennedy heirs and it was decided that he would initially rent it for a year and thereafter decide if he was to make the purchase. The farm was a little further into the Maryland Heights and about five miles from Harper's Ferry, which assured that their preparations would not be too easily observed. John Brown wrote to his wife asking her that she and his daughter Anne, accompanied by his son Oliver, come and join him. The presence of women would give an air of normality to the headquarters. His wife, however, declined and sent instead daughter Anne, accompanied by his daughter-in-law Martha. They were soon established as part of the household with Martha taking care of domestic arrangements and Anne more or less permanently seated on the porch to forestall the good-natured curiosity of neighbours.

He started to gather his troops. This task was visited with a measure of disappointment. Much of the original enthusiasm of the months before had evaporated and very few answered the call. His sons Jason and Salmon also defected. Nevertheless, Brown did not despair as he felt he had enough trained men to organise and officer the slave uprising he was going to create which would be the bulk of his invading force. As his troops dribbled in and numbers rose, neighbourly curiosity became more difficult to assuage.

"Your men have got a smart load of shirts," commented a neighbour, Mrs Crawley, looking at the washing line, who also demanded why much of the furniture was still in crates.

"Mother is very particular," explained Anne. "She wants to sort everything out herself when she comes."

It was also noticed that there was a constant coming and

going of a small cart loaded with boxes. As a precaution all the blacks were kept to the first floor of the building in daytime and only allowed down at night. However, despite mild curiosity about the activities of the "old man", nothing occurred to arouse less friendly suspicions.

Even two anonymous letters, coming from different sources, addressed to the Secretary for War and explaining Brown's plans, were ignored. They had been written by two of his supporters grown frightened by the treasonous nature of Brown's intentions, now that his activities were no longer limited to inner-state quarrels and had become of Federal importance. These letters were thought to be the ravings of overheated abolitionist enthusiasts, the supposed attack on Harper's Ferry lacking any practical sense.

When Jack and Dan arrived at the Kennedy farm preparations were far advanced. There was heated discussion as to the wisdom of Brown's plan to attack and take the Harper's Ferry arsenal, but he argued against all. He had already been told by Frederick Douglass, ex-slave and abolitionist intellectual, on August 19th that his plan was sheer folly. He would be trapped, and it made no difference also to be told of his idea of taking hostages and thus being able to negotiate a retreat in the event of failure. It was all unrealistic, as the Federal Army would blow him and his hostages to smithereens if they thought he could hold the arsenal for even one hour. To which Brown answered, thrusting his new-grown beard in Douglass's face, "Then I would cut my way out!"

It was not only Douglass that attempted to dissuade him from the occupation of Harper's Ferry, but his sons and some of his staunchest followers. Some, like Douglass, left but most of them stayed to see what would happen, or went off in a fury at the old man's stubbornness to return a few days later. Another problem was the dilatoriness of John Brown junior whose task it was to raise funds, forward supplies and find reinforcements. Like his brother Frederick, shot down in Kansas the year before, he was psychologically unstable, as was indeed his father, and not too well organised.

Jack and Dan found life in a small farmhouse with nearly thirty others rather claustrophobic and would go and hide and often sleep in a small log cabin on the other side of the track which came with the house and was used for storage. That was when others of an asocial turn of mind did not get there before them. It was a good place to read by its small window, far from the barking exhortations of John Brown and also, once night had fallen, a good place for a little calm and friendly sex as Dan's woman had not been able to come with them. Dan also wished to please and comfort Jack, who became more and more disturbed by the hazardous nature of the Brown enterprise. He didn't want to kill anybody, much less, the peaceable, if perhaps misguided, folk who lived and thought in the normality of slave society, as he had once done and as did all the people he had ever known — other than Indians, that is. For these homely people it was simply how life was and had always been — the unquestioned model of the hierarchy of existence.

Jack and Dan had been assigned the task of sounding out the slave population and persuading them to take up arms. The response was very limited. In this western part of Virginia there were a minority of field slaves as the terrain did not give itself to vast farms. Thus, great numbers of hard-driven, discontented slaves with hatred in their hearts did not exist here as they did in the southern plantations. The majority of slaves around Harper's Ferry were house slaves that were treated, if not always with kindness, then with a certain respect for their comfort arising from the need for trustworthiness and a constant proximity without conflict. These trusted slaves quite often had much freedom of movement and even responsibility and in certain cases were treated almost as one of the family — often the case with those who had been with that family for more than a generation. Thus, they did not wish to risk their quiet comfortable lives for principles that were largely meaningless for them. When Jack or Dan questioned slaves and hinted of revolt they were often received with hostility; so often that they decided to pretend they had made a bet and needed to make a survey and count those either contented or discontented. They even acted like a good-hearted slaver accompanied by his pet slave, among other ruses.

On one such occasion, they came across a large farmhouse where the farmer was sitting peaceably on his porch with his pipe accompanied by a slave woman serving him coffee. Jack approached and at a respectful distance raised his hat (Dan did the same) and addressed the man.

"Good morning, sir, might I have a word with you?"

"By all means, young man, what can I do for you?"

"I represent the 'Virginia Society for a Just Slavery'. We are making an enquiry as to the condition of slaves in this county." He paused.

"You an Abolitionist or something?" said the farmer, looking a little less welcoming.

"Certainly not, sir, quite the contrary," replied Jack. "We are making this enquiry to establish the fact that the vast majority of slaves are well treated and have nothing against their masters." The woman slave nodded with the look of one defending a known truth.

"The purpose of this is to publish a document, based on

sound facts that will confound the lying attacks of Abolitionist fanatics. Therefore, sir, we would wish to meet your negroes and question them. Mr Browne here, a freed man, is to help me as a sort of interpreter to be assured that I have rightly understood their words that are at times a trifle confused and ungrammatical." Dan gave slight bow.

"Browne with an 'e'," he interjected. The farmer looked at him with raised eyebrow, not quite sure if this interruption of white conversation was not a moment of freed man impertinence.

Dan had received his surname when John Brown decided he needed a few sergeants among the blacks under his command to help maintain discipline and a sergeant needed a surname to be respected. Dan had chosen Browne in recognition of John Brown's part in his rescue. He added the "e" to distinguish him from all the other Browns and because he thought it gave the name a certain distinction that plain Brown did not have.

"So you want to meet my niggers," and the farmer smiled, reassured by the fact that Dan had quickly reassumed his humble pose of hands clasped before him and his eyes on his feet.

"That is correct, sir." Jack made another little bow.

"In that case, you'll have to do what I have to do when I need 'em."

"And what is that, sir?"

The farmer laughed. "Go and hunt for them."

"Too right there," interjected the woman. "Wen dem idle boys is not up to mischief, they's jus lazyin' aroun' sum'eres outa sight." And she laughed too.

"There you have it in a nutshell. Can I offer you some coffee, young man?" Jack declined the offer as Dan was obviously not included. Then, having excused themselves for any inconvenience caused, they left.

They had not gone far when the still audible voice of the farmer said, "Ain't them folk from among them strangers up the hill. Now we know what they're up to. I'll have to tell Mrs Crawley. She's itching to know, the ole gossip."

Thus, in a day they wouldn't come across more than two or three slaves with even a small measure of discontent and the least interest in rebellion.

"I can't see this going anywhere much," said Jack on the third day. "It just ain't the territory for it."

"I gotta agree there," Dan replied. "The old man's got it all wrong, he seems to think every nigger's only waiting for the opportunity to cut master's throat and create hell, while most of 'em want a quiet life, are mostly quite humane and not at all of the murderous kind. Now if they were all like me, then we could have fine war."

"I don't believe you're murderous, Dan," said Jack smiling.

"Jus' you wait and see," was the earnest reply and Jack's smile faded a little.

The next day as with all those that followed, they made a few desultory enquiries, but spent the best part of the time drinking beer in town or reading a book. They bought peppermints to hide the smell of beery breaths as John Brown forbad drinking as the devil's work.

In the end a sort of fatalistic loyalty set in and Brown's son Owen proffered that one bad plan was no doubt better than the confusion of too many good ones; and perhaps all might have concurred with the ex-slave "Emperor" Green who said, when Douglass tried to persuade him to go with him and leave Brown to his fate, "I b'lieve I go wid de ole man."

Little by little the days passed; August and then September 1859 came and went. All the time John Brown was harassing his son John to raise the money needed to feed his horde and supply them until the march south had started. There were also rifles still to be sent and the pike heads he had ordered in Collinsville, Connecticut, that needed to be fixed to stout staves, to be handed out to the liberated slaves. There had been a good harvest, so feeding his army once on the march would not be too great a problem. Finally, all but for a supply of money everything was more or less ready.

At last, the pike heads had arrived and most of the rifles too and Brown's army was becoming restless having little activity and having to stay hidden for the best part of the time. Then on the 15th October young Francis Meriam, the son of one of Brown's supporters, arrived and handed Brown his life's savings, six hundred dollars, offering to help in any capacity Brown might think worthy of him. This sudden addition to his finances resolved his immediate problem of feeding his men and recent news of slave resentment, when a well-liked and respected slave committed suicide after his wife and seven children had been sold away from him to a southern plantation, caused John Brown to decide that the moment to act had come.

# CHAPTER THIRTEEN

On the 16<sup>th</sup> October 1859 John Brown marshalled his troops in the large living room of the farmhouse. He wanted to address them to give them their orders for the attack and to inform certain lesser members, up to then innocent of knowing exactly what was planned, of the Conquest of the South and their role in Brown's Provisional Army. This late introduction of the conspiratorial facts had been a measure of precaution, to ensure the secret remained safe and away from the garrulous elements and that certain weaker spirits might not acquire cold feet.

John Brown stood legs slightly astride, his arms crossed and with the expression of one about to talk of things practical and serious that brooked no interruption. He explained their action that day and the details of his plan, exactly where each of them was to be stationed and when. He also covered mealtimes, sleeping arrangements and sentry duties. In all he spoke for over an hour.

In the silence that followed he picked up the Old Testament from the table beside him and sat down with the holy book open across his knees. He leant slightly forward. He looked or rather glared at his disciples, his expression that of a prophet about to impart an undeniable truth, the words coming directly from the Lord. His voice, at first calm, gradually became harsher until it mounted to a crescendo with the final phrase:

"I hate vain thoughts, but your Laws I do love; Except the Lord build the house, they labour in vain that build it; Except the Lord keepeth the city, the watchman waketh in vain; Remember those that are in bonds as bound with them" and finally "And almost all things are by the law purged with blood; and without shedding of blood is no remission."

He rose to his feet, once more the practical man of action, "Men, get to your arms; we will proceed to the Ferry." Upon which he left the room, beckoning the others to follow, which they meekly did.

\*\*\*

Outside, there was a wagon already harnessed and loaded with guns, ammunition and pikes. Brown mounted on this and set it moving. The men of the Provisional Army fell into ranks of two and marched behind it, their arms held under their cloaks.

His son, Captain Owen Brown, with Copoc and Meriam, was left behind to keep watch over the rest of the arms and to distribute them to slaves as they arrived. They had been selected for this work as weaker elements not thought to be very useful or stalwart when it came to real fighting. This was particularly the case of Meriam, a slim and frail youth who, while having charm lacked the stature of a soldier. He was very much still a child despite his sixteen years. Jack rather liked him, even felt a vestige of the "instant yearning" in his presence.

A while before reaching the covered bridge that straddled the Potomac, joining Virginia with Maryland, two of Brown's men went ahead to cut the telegraph wires. Then once hidden under the roof of the covered bridge the column halted and the men threw back their cloaks revealing their rifles and the heavy ammunition boxes that contained their forty rounds apiece. Captains Kagi and Stevens went ahead to neutralise the bridge watchman. This poor man was taken totally by surprise. Told he was a prisoner, he thought it a good joke as he recognised Cook, a lock keeper, among the men who had joined his captors. Then seeing the guns levelled at him realised that it was no joke and was later informed that Cook had come to Harper's Ferry some weeks before simply to spy out the land and its people. Captain Watson Brown and Stewart Taylor were detailed to guard the bridge.

The Provisional Army then continued past the railway hotel and station, known as the Wager House, to the Federal Armory, whereupon, being refused entry by the watchman, broke open the gates with a crowbar and made the watchman prisoner. Brown then sent off his men to their various posts, remaining himself with the bulk of his troops in the armoury yard to guard the two watchmen and other prisoners — a few aimless youths found wandering the streets and rather drunk.

Captain Stevens and three others, two of whom were Jack and Dan, then went off to capture the Colonel Lewis Washington, great-grandnephew of the great man himself and aide to the Governor of Virginia. Arriving at his home they knocked loudly on his door. Washington himself came to open it, dressed in a nightshirt, dressing gown and slippers. He was astonished to find himself confronted by five armed men. Summoning as much dignity as the circumstances allowed, he stroked his long drooping moustache and said:

"Possibly you will have the courtesy to tell me what all this means."

Stevens, somewhat abashed to find the Colonel less cowered than he had expected, endeavoured to assume a dignified attitude himself, but didn't arrive at anything more than a rather confused pomposity.

"We have come here, sir, from Kansas. We want to free all the negroes. We have possession of the US Armory, and if the citizens interfere, we must only burn the town and have blood." Having said that, he pushed past Washington and entered the house, strutted forward and found himself to be in the main salon. There, he immediately espied, above the fireplace, the second reason for his visit: the pair of pistols given George Washington by Lafayette accompanied by the sword thought to have been presented him by Frederick the Great. In Stevens's eyes these great symbols of liberty and revolution were like a Holy Grail, to be held high to strike fear and submission in the cowardly hearts of the slavers. He mounted on a chair and took them down. He then handed them to Jack to carry, who looked at the Colonel with a little shrug and grimace of apology. Stevens brushed his hands with satisfaction and turning to his prisoner told him to get dressed. A house slave, who had been standing by the door with the Colonel's clothes in anticipation, hurriedly entered and handed them to him. During the process of dressing Stevens asked Washington to hand over his watch and any money he had. These requests were firmly refused.

"Take care, sir," Stevens repeated twice, putting his hand to the revolver in his belt. Then as Washington did up the final button of his breeches, thus assuring total dignity and a good measure of courage, he addressed Stevens:

"I'm going to speak plainly," he said. "You told me your purpose was philanthropic, but you did not mention at the same time it was robbery and rascality. I do not choose to surrender my watch. There are five of you here with guns, and you may take it and my money, but I will not surrender it."

Jack blushed with shame, lowered his eyes and hurriedly placed the historical arms on the table. Dan remained impassive.

"Pick those damned things up," shouted Stevens. Jack hurriedly obeyed.

"I see there is at least one gentleman among you," added the Colonel turning his back on Stevens as he retrieved his hat. Stevens wanted to give Jack a great cuff but saw Dan's eyes upon him and resisted the temptation. Meanwhile, Washington's coach had been prepared and the household were sent out into the street, with the exception of his young daughter Eliza who was allowed to remain with her elderly black maid. Jack thought she was very lovely and quickly felt unexpected desire. She was much like Rosie, only rather more slender, and finer of feature — breeding, he thought. Having once again the historical arms to carry he used them to hide the evidence of his desire.

"I am now to take you to the chief, Osawatomie Brown. No doubt you've heard of him," declared Stevens.

"No, not at all," replied the Colonel, unimpressed.

"Then you have not paid much attention to Kansas matters."

"I have become so disgusted with Kansas and everything connected with it, that whenever I see a paper with 'Kansas' at the head of it, I turn it over and do not read it."

"You will see him this morning," and taking on a sarcastic air of ceremony, Stevens gave a bow and said, "Your carriage awaits you at the door."

The four-horse carriage and a wagon containing other prisoners and Washington's slaves then proceeded towards town.

As they marched, Jack looked sideways at Dan.

"You're wasted here," he hissed. "With your education and the folk you know, you could find a good situation in the North. These are just a band of rascals and thieves. Their only saving grace is they don't hate niggers, but they ain't all that friendly with 'em neither, 'cept perhaps Brown, but then he's a nutter." He gave Dan a little punch in the ribs.

"Hold on, Jack chile," and he smiled. "I'm not about to eat

the white man's cake. I didn't learn all that stuff about freedom and that, just to have a comfortable life circumscribed (he paused here a moment that Jack should notice the high tone of his vocabulary) by whitey's rules. No sir, I'm here to do something about it. I reckon Brown's plan is a load o' shit, but it'll accomplish one important thing. It'll raise the ire of the South and create martyrs for the North."

"But you're gonna be killed, probably hung or burnt alive when they capture you."

"They ain't gonna capture me, my dear friend. When all this fiasco burns out, I'll either be escaped or dead. No, I've got a mission and it's bigger 'en Brown's: I'm subject to a natural philosophical law of higher things that don't take no account of the details of circumstance. What happens to me now don't matter; in 'goin wid de ole man' as Green said, I'm forwardin' history, creatin' another culture. This ain't fatalism, it's makin' another age. It's a purpose much greater than either me or Brown, even though we're its actors. We're two small cogs of a huge machine that we're pushing into life. I reckon we are lightin' the fuse of an enormous bomb that's goin' to blow America apart." He stopped. Jack could see tears of emotion starting from Dan's eyes. He wanted to kiss him, but that was impossible, so under the cover of their cloaks he took Dan's hand and squeezed it. Dan squeezed him back.

On arriving at the armoury, Colonel Washington was introduced to Osawatomie Brown, who took on the role of one being host to an eminent guest.

"It's rather chilly this morning," he said jovially. "But you'll find a fire over there," indicating the watchhouse. "I'd like to have a parley with you later if you'll oblige me," and so saying he left the bewildered Colonel to give further instructions to his men and to arm the slaves so far gathered.

A little later he returned to find Washington warming himself by the watchhouse fire and addressed him in a formal manner, firstly, on a matter of his ransom: he was to write to his friends to demand a "stout negro" from each of them. Then becoming more meditative, softened his voice.

"I shall be very attentive to you, sir, for I may get the worst of it in my first encounter, and if so, your life is worth as much as mine. I shall be very particular to pay attention to you. My particular reason for taking you was first that, as the aide to the Governor of Virginia, I knew you would endeavour to perform your duty, and perhaps you would have become a troublesome customer to me; and apart from that, I wanted you particularly for the moral effect it would give our cause, having one of your name as a prisoner." With that he left Washington and the other prisoners to their own devices, free to wander about the yard or to profit from the fire; where, from time to time, small groups of negroes came to warm themselves, diffidently dragging their pikes behind them, as if they didn't really belong to them, but somehow got attached to their hands by accident.

Meanwhile, blood began to be spilt: the watchman who came to take his turn on the bridge was apprehended. Again, at first, he also thought this was a joke, as he recognised Cook. On realising his mistake, he punched Captain Owen Brown and broke away to run to the Wager House station and hotel. As he passed through the door a bullet grazed his scalp. Less lucky was the baggage-master, a freed man, who was shot and mortally wounded as he walked towards the bridge in search of the watchman. A train that arrived was hurriedly backed away out of danger when rifle shots came from the bridge. Another victim was an Irishman of the town who went out into the street to see what the excitement was all about and was shot dead without summons. Cook and two others with pikes and another two with rifles went across the bridge to collect and arm rebellious slaves.

Very soon, town began to organise resistance, the bells of the Lutheran church were tolling, and its citizens began to gather with what arms they could find: a motley collection of shotguns, squirrel rifles, hunting guns and even old flintlocks, which were not very effective when faced with Sharpe's rifles. By train, from the nearby town of Jefferson came the Jefferson Guards, a poorly trained but well-armed militia, who saw themselves as soldiers, even if they had no uniforms. They were accompanied by ranks of local men and boys armed, in much the same way, as the citizens of Harper's Ferry. Church bells pealed out endlessly in both towns announcing insurrection and civil war. The Governor was alerted and Buchanan, the President, received a telegram to inform him. General George H. Stewart prepared the First Light Division, Maryland Volunteers to intervene.

John Brown was still convinced that there would soon be overwhelming numbers of rebellious slaves come to help and so ignored the pleas of Cook, in his isolated position in the Rifle House, to evacuate the town. The citizens of Harper's Ferry were now better armed as a store of rifles had been released to them, they were disorganised and largely leaderless and poured fire into the armoury despite the danger this created for the prisoners kept in the watchhouse. Things suddenly changed for the worse for Brown when the Jefferson Guards made a sudden attack, took the bridge and then the Wager House, little affected by the sporadic fire from the few men in the armoury. Then two of the men that had been holding the bridge retreated to the Engine House where John Brown was installed. Dangerfield Newby, the third man, was shot in the back as he ran across the yard. His body was left there to be riddled with bullets by the undisciplined townsfolk.

Colonel Gibson of the Jefferson Guards was well pleased with his attack. At a stroke, in taking the bridge and the Wager House, he had cut off all possibility of escape from the armoury and also cut Brown off from Kagi's men at the rifle works. Brown's division of his forces was proving to be fatal. His only hope was the slave revolt which seemed very long in coming. The Second Volunteer Company from Charlestown had then arrived in Harper's Ferry, occupied the Shenandoah Bridge and the Galt House, a saloon on the banks of this river. Also, several houses between the hill and arsenal were occupied from which they could fire down into the armoury yard. It was from there that had come the bullet that felled Newby — the first of John Brown's men to go.

John Brown began to recognise the difficulty of his position and ran to the watchhouse, which was adjacent to the Engine House but with no connecting door. He selected eleven of the more important men amongst his forty prisoners, including Colonel Washington, and brought them round to the Engine House to serve as hostages. It was growing dark and the Provisional Army and their newly gathered hostages settled down for the night, besieged in the dank building and listening to the rain pattering down outside. Brown's little army hoped that by morning the slaves would have been gathered for the revolt while the hostages longed for inevitable arrival of Federal forces.

Dan and Jack lay huddled together, their proximity, as black and white, no longer presenting a problem in the crowded conditions; it also forbad more intimate relations, but then the circumstances were not exactly conducive to inciting desire.

"This is a right mess," Jack whispered.

"No more than was to be expected," replied Dan.

"Nonetheless, the old man has created a situation that all America will hear of and no doubt will cause a violent reaction and demands for action impossible to refuse. I think we have started the civil war."

"We could all be dead by morning and won't know about it. There's no escape from this trap."

"They say that bein' shot dead don't hurt too much and dyin' for a cause is better than endin' up juss suckin' eggs and pissin' yerself." Dan's language was degenerating in his excitement.

"However," muttered Jack, "I'm not sure I've got a cause to die for and between now and being a senile old git, I could still have had a lotta fun."

"Maybe you will yet," and Dan gave him a furtive kiss. "They won't want to kill anyone as pretty as you." Jack was little reassured but moved closer to Dan and again squeezed his hand.

They fell silent and listened to the sleepless breathing around them filled with whispers.

Dan spoke again: "The trouble with old Brown is that he has no political understandin'. He thinks in headlines and battle cries. So it's probably best if he dies now."

"I thought you believed in him."

"I believe in his hatred of slavery, but that's about it. He'll just create chaos. Which might be a good thing to start with, but afterwards things'll need thinking out and he don't think."

In the morning, Brown sent William Thompson out with a prisoner to negotiate a ceasefire. The town citizens had no notion to negotiate and promptly locked Thompson up in the Wager House. Time was all important and Brown wished to delay things as long as possible, hoping that later on the slaves would come under the cover of the darkness of the following night. Therefore, despite the disappearance of Thompson, he later sent out his son

Captain Watson and Stevens under a white flag and the protection of a prisoner. As they walked out into the yard there was immediate gunfire and both men fell. Watson, mortally wounded, crept back into the Engine House while the more lightly wounded Stevens was led back among Brown's prisoners at the watchhouse by his hostage, strangely unmolested.

When, that evening, a Captain Sims came to the Engine House for a parley Brown protested vehemently about the fact of his men having been shot down like dogs under a flag of truce. The response of Sims, nevertheless an honourable gentleman, brooked no reply:

"Men who take up arms that way can only expect to be shot down like dogs."

The mob of townsmen continued to howl for revenge and the firing went on non-stop. But like most mobs it lacked courage and no concerted attack was launched on the armoury. Later, a boy, Leman, tried to escape the armoury, by fording the Potomac. With shots splashing up the water all around him he took refuge on a small island. A townsman came wading after him and demanded his surrender and, on receiving no reply from the terrified boy, shot him dead. The body of the boy, spread-eagled across the rocks, served for target practice for the rest of the afternoon. Not long after two more townsmen met their deaths, one being the much-loved mayor, Beckham. Beckham's grandnephew and a friend went to the Wager House and dragged the prisoner Thompson out into the street by his throat and executed him with their pistols. His body was thrown from the bridge into the Potomac.

Later in the afternoon an assault on the rifle works was organised and Kagi and his men attempted to escape from the rear of the building by wading across the shallow Shenandoah, but on the opposite bank were other attackers who drove them back. Kagi died in the river, his body drifting slowly downstream to join that of Thompson snagged on a dead tree on the Potomac. The collision broke him loose, whereupon they floated away enlaced like lovers on pink, silk sheets — the water stained by their blood. A rebel called Leary was shot also, as he struggled across the river from the armoury under a hail of bullets. Later he died from his wounds. A townsman called Hunt waded after the last man that tried to escape, Copeland, a mulatto; when both their guns misfired because of the damp and seeing how hopeless his situation was, Copeland surrendered. He was, with difficulty, saved from lynching by a Doctor Starry who put his horse between him and the mob. The mob had been already knotting their handkerchiefs to make a rope as he was taken. Finally, he was led away by a policeman. For some unknown reason other than the fickle humours of men and the shifting emotions of a mob where vengeance, cruelty and pity took their turns to rule, Stevens was spared to be later tried and hanged.

At the schoolhouse, commandeered by Cook and his men, they awaited events, still confident that the firing they could hear was the victory of John Brown about to be completed. Of this, they informed the schoolmaster who was released under oath to relate nothing he had seen. Cook then went to reconnoitre the situation in Harper's Ferry.

He saw the desperate situation of the men in the Engine House and from the cover of the rocky hillside took one shot at a careless townsman and retreated to the schoolhouse. Meanwhile, all the slaves they had armed earlier had one by one dropped their arms and slipped away to their masters. The five men decided that it was simple suicide to try and rescue Brown and fled away into the woods, where they tried to sleep huddled under a tree in the rain. Meriam, who had an uncle living not far off, left the others on the pretext of going to relieve his bladder and never returned.

*\*\**

In Harper's Ferry the drama was hurrying to its climax. The Federal Army had arrived with a regiment of marines under Colonel Robert E. Lee. It was already after midnight and Lee, fearing a night attack might endanger the hostages and other prisoners, determined to wait for morning before making a no-nonsense assault with fixed bayonets. He had real soldiers; his was not a timorous mob.

In the Engine House, Watson and another man lay dying on the floor with John Brown exhorting them to courage. The hostages were crowded to the rear of the room, more or less unthreatened by bullets that hailed upon the doors and the loopholes made by the besieged. The men still fit enough to fight made a desultory fire on their attackers, dodging backwards and forwards to their firing slits. Jack sat on the floor behind Dan whose activity showed more enthusiasm than that of the others.

For Jack it was a scene of dark horror. Tears streamed down his face as he tried to take a comforting hold on one of Dan's legs as he came and went, but to no avail. Dan was too intent on killing in cold rage, avenging the life where all had been stolen from him. "Property is theft", he knew, and he knew that he had been stolen from himself. That throughout his life he had been only half a person, the half that ate, slept, shat and fucked, like any animal. All he felt to be noble had been stolen away. Even these last few months, since he had been "freed" were only a partial freedom. There was nothing that was really him; he had simply been lent bits of white culture and upon acquiring these he was praised and patronised, a part person with a part culture, an incomplete facsimile copy of his white hosts. Even Douglass was just that — a black ghost in a white sheet. That woman, Beecher something or the other, had been just when she created Uncle Tom. They were all Uncle Toms. Dan was weeping as he fired.

Then suddenly Dan fell, a lucky shot from the hail of bullets sent by the townsmen entered by his loophole and smashed into his chest. He fell into Jack's lap, his breath whistling up through battered lungs. Blood soaked his shirt front. He lay there a long moment without moving, Jack caressing his head. Every now and again he would mutter something that Jack couldn't distinguish. Then with a little smile, he gathered his strength and beckoned Jack to his lips. Jack put his ear to his mouth.

"Love you, Jackson Penn," he murmured and then added, "You know, I don't think Brown will ever appreciate the necessity for the separation powers in a democracy — or even a democracy," with which he closed his eyes and fell silent.

Jack shook him gently, but there was no response and then through the harsh background noise of gunfire he heard a voice. He turned his head. There was Lewis Washington beckoning to him.

"Come here, boy," he shouted. Jack shook his head and clung to Dan. Then two hands grasped his arms and pulled him away.

"You can't do anything for him, he's gone," cried Washington above a loud volley of shots. Jack struggled a moment, then gave in. He was right; there was nothing more that he could do for his greatest friend. He even stopped weeping, he had been weeping for himself and not Dan. He felt ashamed as he now followed Washington back to the group of prisoners. What he felt for Dan was beyond weeping. He would never weep again, he resolved.

"Now, boy, you just stay with us, you are one of us hostages now. I don't think you were ever really one of those people." Jack shook his head, whether in affirmation or negation he left uncertain. "I never saw you shoot at anyone, nor did you seem to agree with what was happening."

Washington then turned to the group and said, "This boy is one of us now." A young man started to expostulate. Washington turned on him.

"Do you want to see this child hung in the morning? Do you? If so, you might as well strangle him now." With which he pulled Jack round and pushed him up against the young man, who shook his head and backed away. The others agreed without a problem, whether it was because he was, despite the dirt and dark tear stains, still a beautiful boy, or because they had silly wilful adolescent children themselves, whom they loved, or because simply they didn't like killing large children, they didn't bother to question: Jack looked all right, and Washington was a sound man.

"Who was that negro you were with?" Washington asked.

"My best friend, Dan: he's always looked after me. He was a very good man," Jack added, almost aggressively.

"If such a good man, why was he here?"

"'Cos he'd been a slave and was sold away from his mother when he was seven, and his wife and children were sold away from him when he was eighteen, and then old Widder Wilson wanted to sell him down to the plantations and he ran off and me with him 'cos I was fed up with bein' civilised by the Widder Wilson and Misses Watson. I suppose the Widder wasn't all mean as she freed him in her will while he was away."

"Just so," murmured Washington at the end of this tirade and ruffled Jack's hair.

A doctor came and went. There was nothing he could do for the wounded Watson or his brother Oliver, Brown's two sons. Soon they were both dead. Later they heard the arrival of the Marines. They knew that their adventure was nearing its end and sat patiently with their arms beside them to await the inevitable attack. Next to John Brown were Lafayette's pistols and Frederick's sword, the symbols of a revolution that had succeeded.

At first light a Lieutenant Stuart approached the Engine House to make a final demand for surrender. John Brown simply reiterated his terms: to cross the bridge with his arms, horses and hostages, after which these latter would be released. Stuart reiterated the refusal of these terms and signalled to Lieutenant Green, in command of the attacking force, to come with his twelve picked men and their fixed bayonets. They rushed the doors of the Engine House without problem and started to attack them with sledgehammers. But the old doors resisted well as they were heavy, well bolted and with a fire engine backed up against them. Then there was a brief pause. The marines were in shelter while they stood against the doors as there were no loopholes angled against them. All this while, Brown's men kept up a continuous, futile, if discouraging fire on the doors. Suddenly there was a huge crash as the marines assaulted the doors with a heavy ladder as a battering ram. A hole appeared in the top of the left-hand door above the fire engine, then another crash, and the right-hand door caved in. Lieutenant Green raced in followed by two marines. These latter were shot down. Green found Brown, indicated to him by Washington, and thrust at him with his light dress sword. Brown was lifted in the air, but the sword buckled having caught on a bone or thick clothing, and he fell to his knees. Green then seized his sword by the middle and beat Brown several times over the head with the hilt. Brown fell flat on the floor, his head streaming blood. In the meantime, the other marines had entered the room and bayoneted one of the defendants and accepted the surrender of the rest. It was all over in two minutes.

# CHAPTER FOURTEEN

The hostages filed out of the Engine House along with Jack, again carrying the historic arms this time for Colonel Washington. They were all given blankets and hot soup, and a jug of whisky also appeared. Nobody questioned the presence of Jack; everything was still very disorganised and enquiries had not yet started as to the composition of John Brown's little army and so finally he was led away by Washington unmolested. Jack began to feel very cold and feeble as they arrived at the Colonel's home and he was given into the care of Eliza's maid who was used to dealing with the young. For all his maybe seventeen years Jack could have easily passed for fifteen or even fourteen. He was, finally, to rapidly sprout up a few months later.

The next few days passed hazily for Jack as he had a fever and was kept to bed, where he was nursed by the maid and Eliza, who would read to him to pass the time once he had become aware of the world about him. She had already noticed this beautiful youth, seemingly not really old enough to be called a man yet. She had remarked him when he came to the house with Brown's men and had noticed the way he had looked at her. She knew she had fallen in love.

She was to be sixteen in two weeks' time, after which she was to be sent to Boston to be married to her betrothed. He was the son of a very respectable and wealthy Eastern family. She had met him twice. He was thirty-two years old, exactly twice her age and looked nothing like this adorable elf called Jack. He was big, russet blond and beginning to thicken at the waist. She didn't dislike him — he seemed kind and gentle, but she certainly had no passion for him. She thought she might be bored for the rest of her life.

Jack quickly recovered his health despite having Dan's death weighing numbly in his mind. Eliza's presence helped a lot as did the constant flood of desire she created that he had to rid himself of before he could sleep at night. Soon, after finally leaving his bed, he found himself walking the garden with Eliza after she had taken him to see her horses. She loved riding.

"Do you ride?" she asked Jack.

"Have done in the past," he replied thinking of his days before he was a Mandan.

"Then tomorrow you must come riding with me." He nodded his assent and without thinking he took her hand. She didn't withdraw it. He held it a while and gave her a smile as he reluctantly let it drop. She smiled warmly back.

That night he had to calm his desires twice before he could sleep.

The next day, despite the late autumn or maybe because of it, was one made for young lovers. When they set off that morning the sun was not very high and only a little hot. The air was still and scented by the morning dew and a light mist disguised the further trees as mountains of red and golden flowers. The grass glistened with the dew that reflected not only the warm light of the sun, but also the brilliant colours of the surrounding trees. A normally rather ordinary woodland scene had taken on fairylike qualities, covered with a magic cloak scattered with jewels. Jack and Eliza smiled at each other breathing in happiness from the limpid air. They rode a while: galloping; then trotting; and finally walking to a halt by a narrow stream. They dismounted and attached their horses to a sapling. Then hand in hand they walked along the bank of the sparkling rivulet. Under a fine maple in full autumn colour, they stopped and faced one another. He put his hands on her shoulders and she hers on his waist. They were more or less exactly the same height. There was no need to stoop as he kissed her. At which Eliza's hands moved around him and pulled him against her. He thought of Rosie as he began to tremble. She trembled also and gave a sigh as his penis, already stiff against her belly, grew a little bigger. She still wore light summer clothes and through that and Jack's thin cotton trousers she could feel the urgent throbbing of Jack's penis in its final paroxysm. Something inside her convulsed along with it as she crushed him to her. Jack gave a little cry when the semen began to spurt that afterwards dribbled down his leg. Eliza felt his warm wetness seeping through her dress.

That night as Jack lay in bed, thinking of the events of the day, how they had walked hand in hand practically all the way home exchanging little kisses, neither of them mentioning the damp patch on his trousers or that of her dress. Then as his hand moved down with the intention of calming his troublesome penis, he heard a little scratching at his door. He threw back the covers and sat up. The scratching re-occurred but more urgently. He went to the door feeling anxious, almost fearful: had his feelings for Eliza been too apparent; was he about to be sent away? But then scratchings were not an authoritative summons.

"Yes," he whispered.

"It's me," came Eliza's voice.

He quickly let her in and looked at her in surprise.

"Won't Polly know?" he asked, already aware that her ex-nurse and now-maid had always shared her bedroom.

"She does. It was even mostly her idea. I was telling her how I longed to be with you and how I loved you and she said, 'Why not do something about it?' She said that as I was being sold into a loveless marriage, almost like a slave, in order to join up two family fortunes, I should seek love where I found it."

And she pulled Jack to her and kissed him. Jack returned the kiss hungrily. Then she took his hands and moved him towards the bed, pulled his nightshirt over his head and dropped her dressing gown. He helped her off with her nightdress. They were now both naked. They clung together a while and as they began once more to tremble, they reluctantly parted to climb into bed. Almost immediately she helped him enter her, giving a little hiss of pain as the hymen parted. He didn't move. He didn't want to hurt her more. But it didn't matter. Almost without movement their pleasure grew and grew until the vibrant pumping of his ejaculation created her orgasm too. They coupled twice more that night, but rather more elaborately, she giving him a helping hand for the erection that led Jack to a final tearing orgasm as near pain as pleasure as it pumped at the vacuum of his prostate, while Eliza trembled and shook into a deep transport. She felt as if the whole of Jack was absorbed and pulsating inside her. Polly's tales of love had not prepared her for that.

They lay there recovering their breaths for a long while and then, rather belatedly, Jack anxiously enquired: "But won't you get pregnant?"

She looked at him, smiled and gave him a little kiss on the nose. "Maybe, but Polly says she has herbs that can counter that, besides which, if it happens, my poor husband will think the child his." And she gave a little laugh.

They went riding again the next day and every day after, just as every night she scratched at his door. Then one night, not long before she was due to go east to join her husband to be, she pushed him from her once they were in bed and made him lie on his back. He complied with a questioning look.

"I want to see in detail how the child-getting liquid comes; how this love juice will enter me and create new life," she whispered and, on her knees beside him, she started caressing his member which was already well erect across his belly. With her attentions it rose to an angle of forty-five degrees and then started giving little anticipative jerks.

Jack, pushing himself up a bit on his elbows, looked on. He remembered Bill and Beth in the schoolhouse and decided that all girls must have this avid curiosity about the workings of boy's dicks. Eliza took hold gently of his scrotum.

"What's this for?" she asked.

"I think it's where my half of any baby is stored." She nodded and let it drop. This had further excited Jack and he held his breath to hold back his semen.

"There you are, my blue-eyed, black-haired elf. You're just like Cupid observed by Psyche. You are very, very beautiful and your wand of love strikingly handsome!" she exclaimed bending closer with her candle to examine this wonder. She took it between two fingers, raised it to ninety degrees, and then started moving her hand slowly up and down. Jack began groaning.

"Shush, you'll wake everybody up," she murmured and kissed the gland, which suddenly increased a little more in size, the skin being drawn so tight it glistened in the candlelight, just as had Bill's, Jack thought. Then as she pulled her head back a spurt of semen leapt three feet into the air followed by another a little less high and then several more each of diminishing height. Eliza forgot her candle for a moment and a drop of hot wax fell on Jack's thigh.

"Ouch!" he whispered.

"Thus, my Cupid has awakened. That was very impressive,"

she added. "Just like a firework, a Roman Candle; but spurting life instead of fire."

"Better than a damp squib," said Jack giggling.

"But a rather messy firework," she said and taking Jack's handkerchief from the chair beside the bed began scrubbing at the bespattered sheet and then wiped his belly.

"What's that thing around your neck?" He had forgotten to take off his coin.

"That's a souvenir from the past. It's very old, I'm told. It comes from Ancient Greece."

"It's a bit crude, rather lopsided. We do better today. Is it gold?"

"Yes, I had it tested. Very pure gold, they said." She gave his belly a last little wipe and put the handkerchief back on the chair.

"However, back to the business in hand," and she giggled, "I can't let Cupid the elf, with his fairy gold amulet, flee yet. He still has his godly duty to perform." And so saying she knelt astride him and once more began caressing the magic wand which once more rose in response. She then lowered herself upon it and moved slowly and gently up and down, gradually a little more rapidly, thus causing a second flood of semen that shot directly into her welcoming womb.

"There that's done, my godling," she said, falling against him trembling with silent laughter and spent desire. "I imagine that's made a baby — it squirted so deep inside me."

Two days later, Jack stood next to Colonel Washington as Eliza, silent tears running down her cheeks, climbed into her carriage and sought the comforting arms of Polly. Jack tried not to look too unhappy as he, the Colonel and the rest of the household waved goodbye to an empty carriage window.

Washington had soon remarked Eliza's infatuation with Jack

and saw the signs that it was reciprocated and was therefore glad that his arrangements for her departure were to come about so quickly, before any disaster, or the evidently too attractive Mr Penn, could strike. He recognised and from personal experience, that the passions of youth respected few limits. If disaster had occurred, he couldn't have blamed them: what ardent youth could resist the beauty of his daughter and what sixteen-year-old affectionate girl could resist the allure of this boy with his elfin looks of a fairy story prince? There was little he could have done, other than locking them both up, but wait and hope. There was no trusting that Polly to keep guard and resist the designs of lovers as she loved her mistress too much and ever spoilt her. She was more likely to be an accomplice.

Jack was a charming boy, with even a little money; but what was important for the Colonel he had no family and, to say the least, a rather chequered past that even included his best friend being a rebel negro. Thus, it was with great relief he saw his daughter taken away to her well-chosen husband; so that even if disaster had struck, it wouldn't become evident until circumstances rendered it invisible.

Some years later he observed, without astonishment, the presence a black-haired, blue-eyed, slender elf leading his otherwise blond and russet, rumbustious grandsons.

*\*\**

Eliza was married two weeks later and allowed her kind and gentle, if slightly fleshy, husband to couple with her while she thought of Jack and took but little pleasure. He was a very gentle but also very timid partner: thus, after kissing her chastely a few times, barely lifted her nightdress and supported his weight on his elbows, as he slowly and shyly pushed his penis between her labia or slid it in quickly if he was wet enough, as if hoping she wouldn't notice. It wasn't as if he had no desire. His desire was even strong, hence enough pre-seminal fluid to aid his entry and quickly bring him to a shallow orgasm once he was there. He was simply ashamed to show his desire — as if he was going to soil her, a bit like going to the toilet in front of her.

Every morning he dutifully went riding with her and every night came dutifully to her bed. At first his timidity irritated her, but then she began to feel sorry for him; he seemed so unloved, so she would help him with little caresses to his head and shoulders, then putting her hand under his nightshirt stroked his back and finally, after a few days, his buttocks. This last, more adventurous stroking gave results, as he lost control of his breathing and even gave a few thrusts before having a slightly noisy orgasm. She enjoyed that a little more too. He was also losing weight with riding each morning accompanied by increasingly feverish sex each night; and so, after a few weeks, he became quite lithe and muscular, his waist almost regaining the slenderness of his adolescence. This pleased Eliza greatly and helped her to love him with increasing enthusiasm as his shyness began to drop away. Very soon she could touch his member without him shying off and she began to teach him about all sorts of pleasures, beyond simple coupling. (Polly, her nurse and maid, was very informative.) Soon his dutiful attempts at coitus became more and more prolonged, until finally, he was actually making love. The educative efforts of his puritanical nurse and governess were being undone.

He talked more, he laughed more, and his complexion took on colour. The family thought they had chosen well with this child wife, who made her husband happy and was quickly pregnant. Her duty was accomplished.

One evening, just over two years later, this transformed husband sat nursing a dark-haired, blue-eyed, sleeping eighteen-month-old little boy. Next to him on the sofa sat Eliza suckling her second son, just two months old. They had been sitting in a comfortable silence for a little while. When, coming out of his reflections, he turned towards her and said composedly:

"This beautiful, little elf is not my son. Who did you know just before you knew me? You no longer had a hymen when you came to my bed and he did arrive a little too soon and we're both sort of blond." She gave him a startled, frightened look. She had no idea that, all the while, he had been making these calculations.

He smiled at her. The baby, sensing her emotion then her relief, stopped suckling, stiffened, then relaxed and smiled at her too.

"Jackson, my father had rescued him at Harper's Ferry," she whispered, knowing that lies or explanations would serve no purpose. "He was very beautiful," she added after a pause as a sort of excuse.

"Well, there's a nice presidential name, for the beautiful father of this mysterious elfin child that I love so much, just as I love his mother." Then laying the little boy down with a kiss, he turned to her again, took her head in his hands, kissed her eyelids, then her nose and afterwards her chin, her cheeks, her ears, then nuzzled her neck and finally gave her the long, lips parted kiss she had taught him to do.

"Sorry I waited so long to clear the air, but I wanted you to have had one of mine too before I could entirely relax. Let's go to bed," he said.

The two children were given to Polly and they went upstairs. He never again mentioned the origins of this elfin son.

Their future lovemaking was unlike any they had had before. Eliza's husband had become a boisterous loving puppy, wagging his tail and leaping about. He had absorbed all Eliza's lessons in love and now took command and practised them without inhibition. They often climaxed together, and Eliza sometimes wept in happiness on finding this new-born husband who had burst from his chrysalis of timidity, shame, secrecy and respectability. She now took as much pleasure from her robust lover as she had from Jack: a different pleasure, lustier and more outright, if less poetic and mysterious. Jack remained with her in his child who had a special place in her heart; but she loved equally her other ten children as they came along — the boys strapping open-hearted lads and the girls as forthright as their mother in later teaching their lovers to love. For the long years of her married life Eliza was rarely bored.

# CHAPTER FIFTEEN

The day after Eliza left Jack took his leave of Colonel Washington. He had written to Judge Thatcher that he forwarded him some money. A thousand dollars had arrived in the form of a credit note to be cashed at a local bank. He tried to persuade the Colonel to let him pay for his board, but he would not hear of it. He did, however, accept to be reimbursed for the clothes and revolver he had bought Jack as his belongings, at the farmhouse, were irretrievable.

"Well, you no longer have young company, so I understand your wish to get on with life and wish you well of it," and he kissed Jack's forehead. Why do they always kiss my forehead, thought Jack? Maybe it's because it's the part of me furthest from my dick.

The next day Jack took the train to Charlestown. His plan was to go and see if there was anything he could do for John Brown, whom, he felt, he owed a debt of gratitude, above all for rescuing Dan. He couldn't blame him for Dan's death. Dan had chosen his path and was given plenty of opportunities to avoid the end that seemed inevitable. Gentle and kind as he had been to Jack, there had been a bleak melancholy and hate within him that no love could get to and heal.

After John Brown's capture, the Virginian authorities decided to bring him quickly to trial allowing no time for the development of any rescue conspiracy. The Special Prosecutor Andrew Hunter wrote to the Governor: *"The judge is for observing all the judicial decencies; but so am I, but in double quick time. "*

Brown protested that they gave him no time to prepare his defence. But most people felt he was so evidently guilty that there was nothing left him but the gallows or lunacy. But Brown persistently refused the defence of "insanity". Such a defence would deny all he had created, all he stood for. He preferred to die and let the hand of Divine Providence see to his legend.

John Brown was tried between the 27th and 30th October 1859 and found guilty of treason (papers found at Jackson's Farm relating to the creation of a Provisional Government with a Provisional Army were fatal) and of inciting slave rebellion (the fact that he had armed slaves with guns and lances was sufficient). He was sentenced to death by hanging on the two accounts: the joint sentences to be carried out on the 2nd December. Rescue attempts were feared, even though his prison was surrounded by militia and a regiment of regular soldiers. Their fears were well grounded: even though many of the original conspirators who took no part in the attack on Harper's Ferry had already fled abroad, including Frederick Douglass who went to Canada and then on to England, there were many supporters who felt "someone" should act and a few of the more secret conspirators, who simply allowed that John Brown was being abandoned. Many felt guilty that they had not had the courage to take an active part in his venture. Others felt that justice should take its expeditious course and create a martyr for the Abolitionist cause, like Henry Ward Beecher who at the time of the trial expressed his sentiments:

*"Let no man pray that Brown be spared. Let Virginia make him a martyr. Now, he has only blundered. His soul was noble; his work miserable. But a cord and a gibbet would redeem all that, and round up Brown's failure with a heroic success."*

Jack hoped he would not be too late to help in some way. He felt more than a little guilty that he had allowed his passion for Eliza to so delay him. But there was nothing that could have deflected him from that particular destiny. It had been too beautiful, too pleasurable; but he had begun to wonder why, after three days, the sorrow of his loss no longer strangled him and why he had made no attempt to take her for himself but simply accepted fatalistically that the moment of their fairy love was to be cut short. He felt intimations of his cold void, his "ice flower soul" as Dan had called it.

There was little he could do. He sounded out some sympathisers but that led to nothing. John Brown himself was more or less unvisitable for the moment; there was too much hatred in the air and the visitors he had from the North were treated with contempt and suspicion. He could only wait for the hanging.

One day in mid-November, Jack was sitting in the lobby of his hotel, when he espied a familiar frail figure accompanied by a much burlier and stouter, late middle-aged man. They were part of a larger group talking loudly amongst themselves on the irresponsible and undisciplined nature of slaves. The frail figure was that of Francis Meriam, the boy who had arrived at the farm the day before Brown had launched his attack. He had seemed to have had a crush on John Brown. Jack had felt the beginnings of an "instant yearning" the last time he saw him and now it was repeated, but a little more strongly. If frail and slight, his body was well formed: narrow hips, a tight little behind, slender legs and wide enough shoulders to give off a certain fragile masculinity as he moved. His pale face was perhaps a little too long, a nose to match, which increased the general air of fragility set between large, dark brown eyes and, below, astonishingly cherry red lips; however, all in all, Jack found him very attractive.

Jack walked towards the group, and as he did so, dropped the book he was carrying causing a sharp bang as it hit the wooden floor. Several heads turned and then all but one looked away again. This was the startled face of Francis Meriam. Jack smiled and put a finger to his lips and then gestured in the direction of the hotel bar. He went into the bar, installed himself at the counter and ordered a whisky. He did not have long to wait before Meriam appeared beside him.

"I can't stay long," he said in a hushed tone as he warmly shook Jack's hand with both of his. "I'm with my uncle and some of his friends."

"Can you come back later? This evening, say? We can have a drink together," asked Jack.

"Not today. How about tomorrow? I'll be free after five."

Jack nodded. "Six o'clock then," he said. Meriam agreed, took his hand again and Jack thought he gave it a little squeeze, which Jack returned and then the boy hurried away. Well, thought Jack, maybe he has developed a little yearning too.

\*\*\*

The next evening Jack was once again on his stool at the bar. It was a quarter to six. So far there was no sign of Meriam. He bought himself a second whisky, for Dutch courage. He was going to sound out Meriam very quickly. The hanging was just a week off after which he planned to be away to the Mississippi to find Sam, which left little time for a prolonged courtship. He wondered why, so soon after losing Eliza, he felt this need that had nothing in common with what he felt for her. He pondered over the difference, the different physical sensations that heralded desire: with Eliza there had been an immediate clenching in his lower belly and the root of his penis, causing his anus to contract a little and an erection to commence; whereas with Meriam, as with Tinker, the sensation began as a tension in the throat, then chest and upper stomach, which only gradually, as if reluctantly, descended to his genitalia where it hesitantly started an excitement.

With Eliza it had been instant desire followed by love; but with Meriam and also Tinker, there was this instant yearning. Was it love, he demanded, even before you knew somebody? Love at first sight, based upon an attraction that flowed from its object's body language (not that Jack could have put it that way) that was followed by a deepening desire. Dan and Sam were somewhat different. He had constructed a yearning about them, led by their affection. While he was thus reflecting on his emotions a hand took him by the shoulder. It was Meriam.

"What are you having?" Jack demanded almost brusquely, having been startled from his reverie.

"Oh, perhaps a beer," was the diffident reply. Jack ordered a beer with a whisky chaser and the same for himself.

"We might as well start as we mean to go on," he said. Meriam, slightly taken aback, nodded.

"I'm sorry I'm a bit late," he said. "Uncle wanted me to finish doing his books for him as I wasn't sure when I'd be back. Going fishing, I told him," and he gave a little giggle. Jack replied with a smile of connivance. He wondered how Meriam had thought that this was a tryst — but then perhaps he had seen him go off with Dan to the cabin on the last night at the farm or had heard gossip from the others. He doubted if their relationship had gone entirely unnoticed.

"Well, we'll have to see what fishes turn up this evening,"

laughed Jack.

"I was awfully glad to see you yesterday. Living with Uncle can be a bit of a bore." Jack smiled again.

"Me too: to see you. I don't really know anybody in this town. And those that I do, that were connected with Brown, are keeping themselves very much to themselves at the moment." At this he put an experimental hand on Meriam's knee under the cover of the bar counter's overhang. For a moment the boy didn't move and then, after ten seconds perhaps, drew his knees together to trap Jack's fingers. This was signal enough. Jack called over the barman and asked for a bottle of whisky and two glasses. Then he said:

"Let's go upstairs."

As they passed the desk he called out to the receptionist, "We'll be two for dinner this evening." The man waved his hand and nodded.

As soon as they entered his room, Jack took Meriam in his arms and gave him a big hug. Meriam responded in kind. Wordlessly, Jack took off Meriam's jacket and his own. He then started unbuttoning the boy's shirt and as they began to appear gave little kisses to his hairless chest and rosy nipples. All this time Meriam stood in a frozen immobility, his hands gripping just the shoulder' pads of Jack's jacket and then suddenly, as if having finally arrived at a difficult decision, he reached down and grasped at Jack's erect penis. Jack did the same for him and for a while they stood slowly massaging each other through the cloth of their trousers. Meriam was arriving dangerously near ejaculation when he stood back a little and undid Jack's belt and fly and swiftly sought the stiff member. Jack simply continued his massage and very quickly Meriam did ejaculate.

"Sorry," he said. "It was just too hungry."

"No, it's me that's clumsy," grunted Jack, "too much whisky." He stood looking rather disappointed and peered around to find the glass of consolation, until Meriam bent down, lowered Jack's trousers and dropped to his knees. Pulling down the loose, already slightly damp underdrawers, Meriam took up the now almost deflated penis. Rubbed it once or twice and put it in his mouth. Almost instantly, it resumed its full erection and encouraged by Meriam's hands on his buttocks, Jack began giving little thrusts, he had to grasp onto the nearby table with one hand as he guided Meriam's head with the other. His legs began to wobble. The boy took hold of the jerking penis and thrust it deeper into his mouth. He felt the shock of the spurting semen against his throat and palette and his own erection began to return.

Jack staggered to the bed and fell on it and as his breathing became more controlled, said: "Where did you learn that?"

"At the military academy. The bigger boys made us do it."

"Let's have a drink," Jack gasped. And taking up the bottle poured two generous measures. "So you're a funny bugger, like me," he added.

"Not full time," said Meriam.

"Snap," was Jack's reply. "In fact, I've just finished a very delicious little affair with a girl."

"Me — not so lucky." Jack gave him a commiserating smile, a little kiss and ruffled his thick curly auburn hair that had just been caught by the setting sun suddenly shining in through the window. In movement, his hair took on several autumnal shades from orange through red to a brown that was almost purple. Jack kissed this thick colourful hair.

"It's Francis, your first name?"

"Yes, that's right."

"Hmm, don't like that much — too sharp, serpentine. It hisses. You need something smoother, rounder. That's why I think of you as Meriam."

Meriam frowned. "A bit like at school — the Military Academy — 'Meriam, suck my cock, will you.'" Jack shook his head.

"I've got it. You'll have a special name, just for me. I'll call you Merry. That's a nice, warm, friendly name."

Merry was smiling again. "I like it too," he said and gave Jack a hug. Jack picked up the two glasses and handed him one. They clinked glasses and drank a silent toast.

It began to occur to Jack that his sexual role was changing. With Dan and Sam and even, but to a lesser extent, with Tinker he had been the receiver, the object of love. This time it was he, that was taking the initiative, being the lover creating the beloved. Was he growing up or simply becoming the full-time faggot? However lovely the experience with Eliza was, it was perhaps superficial in comparison to the emotions he was experiencing now and especially with memories of Tinker, that constantly returned as his great moment of "instant yearning". He wondered why he had never fancied Bill Watson.

They went down to dinner, which was a rather ordinary affair, but in Jack's heart celebratory. They drank French wine and brandy. They talked of everyday things and John Brown. Merry explained how he came to be in Charlestown: his father had sent him to explore the ground with the idea in mind of rescuing Brown. He had come with another youngster, a lawyer called Hoyt, who could make contact with Brown as an extra defending counsel in his appeals against the sentence. Merry was still in his teens, like Jack, indeed probably a bit younger than Jack and Hoyt but twenty-one. This was expressly chosen so that their youth would excite no suspicions. They had found the situation impossible: Brown sought to seek his death as giving, at last, some meaning to his life; so that he was no longer in the ambivalence of being between bandit and revolutionary, but a martyr to the Abolitionist cause; whereas it also became apparent that any attempt at physical rescue was doomed by the rigour of Brown's imprisonment and the numberless soldiers ensuring it. They finished dinner and went back upstairs.

They quickly undressed again and got into bed. Jack, emboldened by his wine and brandy, pulled Merry to him and whispered in his ear:

"Have you ever been entered?"

The reply was a questioning, "What?"

"Have you ever been fucked?" asked Jack more baldly.

Merry nodded, "By one boy at school."

"Can I do it now?" There was a pause.

"Well... Okay, but don't be rough."

Jack added spittle to the pre-seminal liquid already present and gently pushed into the behind Merry had hesitantly presented. Despite the effects of alcohol Jack ejaculated almost immediately and then brought Merry to his own wet pleasure. Jack's still inserted penis felt Merry's throbbing. They lay together silent, joined at the hips for a long while. Jack thought he heard a little sob, the start of a sob as if Merry was trying hard not to cry.

"That was better done than that boy at school did it," eventually commented Merry, with an uncertain voice and gave Jack an additional kiss.

"In what way?" muttered Jack, feeling somewhat flattered.

"That boy was too dominating, too rough. It mostly hurt. He reckoned men did it like gods. Real men he reckoned could fuck boys but then had to move on to women only. For him, having his cock sucked like the other senior boys was sissy, not manly enough. He'd read some Greek stuff — mythology and that — where the gods were always carting off people and fucking them. He said that as I wasn't a girl, I couldn't be Europa, so I had to be Ganymede carried off to be his cupbearer etc."

"Mainly the etc., I imagine," interrupted Jack with a little laugh.

"So it was. I had to bring him an imaginary cup of wine — sarsaparilla it was, actually, in a tin mug. Which he'd quaff back dramatically and then he would tear off my clothes (which were already unbuttoned, so as they weren't spoilt). Then he'd carry me round the room acting as he thought an eagle would. He'd then throw me across his bed with a screech, which I imagine he thought represented the Holy Lust of a god as an eagle and raped me. That is, he tried to, but as he wanted to tread me like a cock eagle on its hen there was difficulty getting his prick in at the same time. Then finally he would stick his prick in rather roughly, me on hands and knees, doggy fashion, while he held my head into the pillows by the hair. He did use a bit of spittle."

"Very considerate of him."

"… probably for his own comfort — no kisses or anything. He never wanted to bring me off as that was below the dignity of an Eagle God, so he said I had to do it myself. He didn't mind watching and giving advice and would even hold it once or twice to show what he meant… but he got that rape business wrong, because when I looked in his book, raping simply meant carrying off somebody and then maybe having sex. He forced me to do all that and then wouldn't look at me. I had difficulty looking at myself too as he said it was sodomy to be fucked. He didn't seem to think his fucking someone's behind was the same thing."

"What was his name?"

"I don't remember, something very ordinary. It's not something I've ever wanted to think about again... Hold on... Bill, I think, yes Bill."

Jack laughed. "Where was he from?"

Merry thought a little. "Somewhere small on the Mississippi, just above the Missouri."

"Hannibal?"

"Yeah, that's it."

"Bill bloody Watson," almost shouted Jack with a great laugh.

"Yeah, that's him. You know him?"

"You bet. He always made things complicated, trying to improve on reality, but in fact spoiling it, making it ridiculous. But I'd have thought he was a straight up and down girls only type, perhaps, using his right hand in a famine."

"I reckon so. But when you're locked away with two hundred other boys, some of them quite pretty and not a girl in sight, you can get very randy, then you make do with what's available. Just your right hand is rather boring after a while."

"Reckon you've got something there, but he could've been less selfish about it."

"That's so. He was so taken up with his role of God. I don't think it even occurred to him that I mightn't find that too satisfactory. He thought everybody wanted to join in his games."

"He always did," and they laughed together.

Jack's penis encouraged by the internal warmth of Merry hardly deflated during this conversation and after a while came back to its full dimensions. Merry had felt Jack's ejaculation, then the slight deflation and now his increasing size. This created a new sensation; his rising pleasure no longer centred on the gland but deep at the root of his penis where it sprang from the prostate; and as Jack began to move again this pleasure became a guilty pleasure, but still increased and stayed deep inside him, his anus gripping at Jack. The inhibiting guilt even became part of and prolonged the pleasure. When it exploded, almost at the same time as Jack did, it filled his member from root to gland as his semen burst through into Jack's hand. He sobbed with ecstasy and remorse — and Jack also gave off little cries.

This time Jack went limp and slid out of Merry. Once more they lay still a long while and then Merry murmured, "I liked being Ganymede this time, but I'm not sure I should."

"Why not?" whispered Jack.

"It's supposed to be disgusting. Someone who lets himself be buggered is not a real man, like Bill said, he's someone to despise, a sodomite."

"You believe all that nonsense?" asked Jack, his voice rising.

"Don't know. It just felt wrong, because I was liking it. When Bill forced me it was different. It wasn't my fault. This time I chose, and I really enjoyed it."

Jack pulled him close and kissed him. "Forget all that, it's simply nonsense thought up by preachers — just be Merry with me." Merry looked into Jack's eyes as if the truth might be written there and gave a little nod.

"I'll try."

They lay still and silent again until Merry suddenly sat up and seized his watch from the bedside table.

"Oh gosh," he cried. "It's already five o'clock. I'll have to go. I must be back before Uncle wakes, so that he won't know I've slept elsewhere. Well, sort of slept." And he giggled.

Jack looked up, smiled and nodded. Then he watched Merry hurriedly dressing.

"Will I see you tomorrow?" he asked with a rather flat voice.

"Yes, I think so," replied Merry.

"Same time?" Merry nodded. For a reason Jack could not yet fathom, Merry's guilty little remorse had brought him close to tears and he couldn't reply to his final farewell. He couldn't speak. The door closed and he was weeping.

There in his arms was the warm dead body of Dan, and he clutching to it, as in the armoury. His sobbing was hard and painful. Suddenly, his new love for Merry, and Merry's hesitations, had released the mourning bottled up inside him. By loving this fragile boy his hidden grief that his unconscious had withheld from his reality for more than a month, had just burst open, like a cracked dam hit by storm water. How could he have had those blithe days with Eliza while Dan lay lifeless, thrown upon a heap of other dead niggers, to await mass burial, to stink in the heat, treated as an animal and not, at least minimally respected, as were white criminals? How could he have forgotten the man that had been the most loving person in his life for so long? Why hadn't he invited Dan into his body as he had Sam? The dreadful and chill realisation of his inhibited feelings for Dan fell into his memories as a heavy cloud, a dreadful betrayal, a very treason against the nature of love. He hadn't wanted Dan to fuck him because he was a despised nigger who couldn't be given the opportunity to despise him, the white man. It was as simple as that. He saw how he had first masturbated Dan as a joke as an insult to his ingenuous love: a Bill Watson pleasantry for mocking the simple black. He saw how he accepted Dan's wish to pleasure him, Jack, as the ministrations of a likeable servant rather than those of a lover. He fought against these thoughts and searched for an untainted love of Dan. He saw that he had romped naked with Dan in the river, played games with him in which they held equal parts. He had helped Dan the runaway, which was a dreadful crime, but about which he had felt guilty. But he had also helped Bill exploit him, thinking that complying with the follies of a "well-brought up" white boy out-measured the loss of dignity and self-respect for a black. His whole relationship with Dan was one of ambivalence, one of half love and half betrayal. He realised that he had always withheld his full love and partially refused that of Dan — the part that requested equality. He had given more to Merry in a day than he had given to Dan in a decade. He could see now that Dan must have recognised this and forgiven him his weakness. His sobbing was renewed and continued until he fell into an exhausted sleep. He dreamt of a loving Dan and wept silently through the dawn.

The next day they made love again as Merry could once more get free for the evening. Their love making was sometimes calm and reassuring, sometimes passionate and guilty. Merry cowed by thoughts of sodomy, Jack by thoughts of Dan. Jack suggested they changed roles for penetration, so that Merry could feel manly. It helped him a little. He stopped wondering if he was not being simply being played with, the despised toy boy, like at school and felt loved. They talked about John Brown and decided to visit him in prison, despite the unease local opinion and despising looks of the townspeople might cause them.

As the days passed, since Brown's imprisonment, the nights were often lit up by burning barns and haystacks. It could have been the work of slaves, but most people thought it was part of some Northern conspiracy to destabilise the town and disperse its soldiers as they sought the arsonists in preparation for an attempt to rescue Brown. Nevertheless, two days later when Merry managed to free himself once more, they forwent their pleasures and set off to the prison and after being searched and interrogated, by the soldier guards, were let in without further difficulty. No doubt their youthful looks had helped.

They found John Brown sitting in a comfortable cell with his Bible on his knee and seemingly rather pleased with himself.

He greeted the boys enthusiastically and upon their first words of commiseration raised his hands to stop them.

"Don't criticise the work of the Lord," he cried. "Divine Providence has decided to make me its weapon. I no longer fight with the sword but with the holy weapon of my faith. My martyrdom will free the slaves and save the world. John Brown will be the legend that leads the righteous to their duty."

"I shall be among the righteous," said Merry enthusiastically. Jack looked on in silence. When things became sanctified he was always suspicious.

Merry continued. "Like you, sir, I think slavery to be an abomination."

Jack intervened. "I think slavery is bad too, but I don't think you should go around killing folk for something they were just brought up to. You need to convert 'em."

"No good ever came about in this sad world other than that blood was shed," was the sanctimonious reply. "Also, those that have money, as do you, I believe, could do a lot more to destroy slavery. A contribution to the Abolitionist cause would please the Lord almost as much as physically fighting the propagators of this injustice. Are you a righteous man, Mister Penn?

"I believe so, but not religious. Religion nourishes hypocrisy and irresponsibility. If I were to contribute to any cause, it would be that of peace and not of war. Whether a cause be just or not does not excuse killing the simply ignorant."

"Those words are unjust and go nowhere," said Brown. "Now my foundation, founded to recompense those that have suffered in the cause—"

"Like your family?" interrupted Jack. "And I don't see that horse stealing in Kansas needs a reward."

"With your blasphemy, atheism and selfish hoarding of your riches," shouted Brown, "you'll end up deep in the fires of hell."

The door opened and a guard looked in. "Everything all right here?" he asked. Brown waved him away but did lower the volume of his voice.

"You and your nigger were never really with us. After all I did for him, he denied the Lord just as you do. I doubt if his death saved his soul."

Merry looked close to tears. "But, Mr Brown, he died for the cause. I'm sure God won't damn him just for not believing and I think Jack is a good man too, even if he doesn't share our beliefs."

Jack was dumbfounded. He looked hard at Merry, trying to read his inner thoughts.

"Maybe you're right, Meriam," added Brown. "I was carried away by my emotions and my love of the Lord."

"I'm sure that if it comes to a battle Jack would be with us," said Merry excitedly, even if he does come from a slave county." Jack shook his head in disbelief. Was this his Merry?

"I don't think so. I've seen enough bloodshed," Jack added.

"But you can't just let slavery continue and do nothing."

"And I can't fight either or give money for others to do killing for me."

"I don't believe you," cried Merry. "You will help whether you believe in the Lord or not."

"I would ensure that your money was not spent on guns and ammunition, but in helping the helpless," added Brown.

"You see, it's not all violence, it's for love and freedom too," continued Merry.

"You're right, my son. I knew your father and he was a righteous and generous man. Let not the pleasures of this sinful world distract you from your duty, dear Francis. Put aside sloth and lust and pray for the freedom of all men and your salvation."

Merry looked rather startled and started blushing. Jack wondered if Brown hadn't remarked something in his relations with Dan or with Sam, having met the latter once or twice in Jack's company. The old man continued as is if oblivious of the effect of his words.

"We all know how the Lord destroyed Sodom and Gomorrah. For there they had cultivated that heinous sin named after that benighted city." He then laid his hand on Merry's head, looked skyward and muttered a silent prayer. Merry stood petrified. A minute passed and then he spoke again.

"Take this thy son, O Lord and put him on the good path, that he might do his duty by God and man. Lead him to the good fight. Let him not seek evil counsel, let him be pure in the sight of the Lord." He looked down at Merry who had started to tremble and smiled in a fatherly manner. He then turned to Jack. His eyes stared fixedly and addressed him in a loud cold voice:

"Do your duty too, young man. Help this lamb not to stray into sin and depravity. Help him in his sacred mission. Let him free the enslaved with the sword of innocence." Jack just returned his stare and then turning towards Merry he indicated the door with his eyes.

John Brown went down on one knee, his head in his hands, muttering prayerfully. Merry stood as though transfixed. Jack again indicated the door, this time with a jerk of his thumb.

"I think we should leave you, sir, to prepare for your coming ordeal. I think… " and he broke off as Jack took his hand and led him to the door. Brown seemed not to notice their departure. Jack, as he closed the door, mustered a sanctimonious voice and said, "We'll pray for you." Once outside he couldn't help giggling. Merry did not look at all merry.

Back at the hotel, Merry sat on the bed seemingly anxious, even frightened. He looked questioningly at Jack. "What if he writes to my father?"

"About what?" replied Jack. "He's just trying to frighten you with his ridiculous puritan morals and the ridiculous god who doesn't seem to do anything but hurt people and act the killjoy. Maybe he thought there was something going on with Dan and me and simply wants to stop you having any fun, wants you to be as miserable as himself who can only take joy in his own death. I even think he's probably jealous. He did a lot of laying on of hands etc. But most of all, I think he wants my money."

"I don't know. I used to admire him a lot. Now he's made me feel bad for us. I feel sort of ill about what we do — especially the sodomy bit." Jack sat down next to him, took his hand and gave him a kiss.

"Forget it. What harm do we do, except to contradict the notions of this ridiculous, vengeful god we've invented? We harm nobody." He pushed Merry gently down, then started unbuttoning his clothes. He kissed his chest and then his belly and finally his penis that was not yet beginning to stiffen. He finished undressing Merry, as he still lay on the bed in unmoving, unhelpful sadness. Jack then undressed himself and joined him under the covers. He started making love with a childlike, gentle masturbation. He did for another, what the great majority of lonely but hungry adolescents were doing for themselves that same night — all of those, that is, he thought, whose souls had not been scarred by the claws of religion. Sex with two he knew was more companionable and as Tinker said, more fun. This simple lovemaking seemed to reassure Merry and he gradually joined in as he relaxed into desire.

In the calm that followed Jack posed a question: "Do you believe in all that stuff you were saying about religion and that?"

"I don't know. It's what I was brought up to — like you were brought up to slavery."

# CHAPTER SIXTEEN

Jack and Merry left the hotel together, well wrapped up against the December cold. They walked unhurriedly to the prison where John Brown was being held. Waiting at the prison gates was a simple cart harnessed to two white horses. Drawn up in marching order in front of the cart were four companies of soldiers.

"Are they expectin' a war?" said Jack, as they approached the assemblage. Merry said nothing but shivered in the chill breeze despite his heavy overcoat. Jack started rubbing his arms and shoulders to warm him. Merry shook his head and stepped away, looking with alarm at those about him.

"Okay, stay cold then," muttered Jack and thrust his hands deep into his pockets. They stood silently watching the cart and the soldiers for a good twenty minutes before there was activity at the doors to the prison. Then they were pulled wide open and John Brown shuffled out, his shorn head bent under a narrow-brimmed hat and his grizzled beard catching the feeble sunlight. He walked between two soldiers and was preceded by a preacher, a prison officer and the hangman. Brown mounted from the back of the cart helped by the soldiers and seated himself on the coffin. The other three took the seating at the front where the driver was already in place. The column moved slowly off through the grey landscape of scattered buildings and bare trees whose long winter shadows created cold, linear patterns across the road.

Jack and Merry and a few other spectators followed the column along the road toward the execution ground where a gibbet had been constructed on a low knoll. Around the gibbet, in a large open square, were deployed fifteen hundred marines and militia. There were also cannons trained on the centre of the square and every few yards an officer sat on his horse. The cart drove into the square. John Brown got down and without the least hesitation mounted onto the gibbet. He was followed by the hangman, the prison officer and the preacher. This latter approached Brown and said a few words, inaudible from where Jack and Merry stood. Brown replied something of no more than two or three sentences and then the hangman covered his head with a black hood and placed the noose. There was a moment when the hangman seemed to consult with the others before he moved over to the releasing mechanism of the trapdoor. He pulled the handle and John Brown shot through the hole and jolted to a stop. Jack thought he heard a crack. Brown made no movement and swung slightly in the winter breeze. The whole ceremony had taken no more than five minutes and Virginia was avenged.

Jack and Merry walked back to the hotel, still in silence. "Coming in for a drink?" Jack asked. Merry looked sadly at him and shook his head, briefly took Jack's hand and then walked off in the direction of his uncle's house. Jack wasn't sure what to think. He went to the bar and ordered a whisky. This, despite the earliness of the hour was followed by another. He thought that perhaps he should get drunk and then find a prostitute. This was not something he had ever done before, but it seemed like the sort of gesture Bill might have approved of: a dramatic statement that was just a dramatic statement. He changed his mind. He didn't want to risk the pox. He didn't even really want to get drunk. What he wanted was Merry. He decided to call on the uncle that he had already met once, pay his respects, as someone about to leave town and ask for Merry.

The uncle was very welcoming, even offered coffee, but

didn't think Merry was available.

"I'll go and see, if you like," he said. "But when he came in this morning after the hanging, he didn't seem very well, feverish even. You know, he's a fragile boy and I think he got badly chilled. I had asked him not to go, but he insisted. Said he wanted to say farewell to the old fool — seemed to like him for some reason."

"It would be very kind of you if you could pass a message in the case that he can't come down."

"Yes, certainly, young man."

"Tell him that I should dearly like to have a farewell dinner with him at the hotel, if and when he might be feeling well enough, I shall still be around for three or four days."

"No problem. I'll go and see him now." So saying he mounted the stairs to return alone three minutes later.

"Sorry, but he's asleep. But no matter, I'll give him your message when he awakes."

"Thank you, sir," said Jack and took his leave. He went back to the hotel, drank two more whiskies and went back to bed.

The next morning, he went down early for his breakfast of bacon, pancakes and two pints of coffee. He then read the local paper the *Charlestown Recorder* that told him about everything he had seen the day before plus a lot on the Southern way of life, the need for slavery and how the negroes were well treated and content, as the events at Harper's Ferry had demonstrated; which also demonstrated the slaves' lack of initiative and in general the low level of intelligence of an inferior life form. Jack started feeling angry. Dan was twice as bright as the majority of these self-satisfied Virginians. Dan "had been", he corrected himself, and held the paper in front of him to hide the tears that were beginning to fill his eyes. Just then a small boy ran in from the street and spoke to the receptionist who indicated Jack with a small gesture. The boy ran over:

"Mistah Penn sah," he said breathlessly, full of the importance of his mission. Jack, who had quickly wiped his eyes, smiled at the boy and nodded. "Got a note for you, sah," and he handed Jack a sealed envelope.

"Thank you, son," said Jack, searched in his waistcoat pocket and handed the boy a dollar. The boy's eyes opened wide.

"Gee, gosh! Thanks ever so, mistah," and he turned and ran, his hand clutching hungrily at the precious coin already translated in his mind into a heap of bright coloured candy.

Jack looked at the envelope. It gave off the glow of family money, where expensive stationery let one know of their status. He hesitated momentarily and then tore it open.

*Dear Jack,*

*Just to let you know that I can come to see you this evening at six o'clock as before. I forewarn you that I shall not be very Merry as this could be a farewell visit.*

*All my love, Francis*

"Could be a farewell visit," mused Jack. And the biting hiss of "Francis" was like a clenched fist in his chest, in the seat of the ice flower. Jack fetched his overcoat and went walking. He hardly saw his surroundings other than to guide his feet. The fitful sunlight gave him no warmth and the chatter of the town went unheard. As he left the town he was enveloped by the gaunt forest, where frost glinted warily from the icebound trees which were barely visible as separate shapes through a freezing mist. Jack was enveloped in a same icy confusion. His thoughts wouldn't come together and make a single idea but leapt here and there seeking escape from his distress. There was no escape. He sat down under a tree, not feeling the cold wetness of the melting frost as it seeped into his trousers. He sobbed as he had often sobbed before.

An hour or so later the sobbing stopped. He stood up and was suddenly aware of the freezing air and the wet seat of his trousers. He shivered and began to walk briskly into town. His head was now cold and clear, a dismal clarity of total misery. Now he was beyond weeping and thought how quick had been John Brown's end. It was the drop. If he was to hang himself there had to be a sudden drop. He could tie a rope round his neck and jump out of the hotel window. How happy he had been just two days ago, and he very nearly started sobbing again. On entering the hotel, he went straight to his room to change his clothes. It was soon time for the midday meal and so he went down to the bar for a few pre-lunch whiskies. His lunch was also accompanied by whisky. The meal finished, he went up to his room and lay on the bed to have a think about quick suicides. He fell asleep.

He awoke blearily with a hand pulling at his shoulder. It was Merry, or rather Francis-is-iss-hiss. Jack sat up, surprised that he only had a rather mild headache. Merry bent down and kissed him.

"Are you all right?" he asked anxiously. A kiss — a ray of warmth entered Jack's spirit and softened; then perhaps all was not lost. The ice flower opened a little.

"They said at the reception you were up here… You should have locked your door. Anyone could have come in."

"But then you couldn't have," implying that the unlocked door was on purpose.

"I'd have banged until you answered. I hope my silly note didn't worry you. I was feeling dramatic."

"No, I went for walk, ate, drank a few too many whiskies

and waited for you. I shouldn't have fallen asleep."

"Do you want a cuddle before dinner?"

"We might miss dinner... I want you so very much. I'm glad you got my message."

"What message?" said Merry with a puzzled frown.

"The one I gave your uncle."

"He said nothing about that to me — the old sod."

"We'll think about that later," and he took Merry in his arms almost crushing him. "I really do want you so very, very much." Jack started trembling.

"I want you too. I really need you... but I don't know what to do."

"What do you mean?"

"I don't want to sin."

"Oh no, not again!" Jack's trembling ceased, replaced by irritation. Even so his underwear was already damp.

"When I say sin, it's not in a religious sense, but as an offence against my family, my origins and everything," whispered Merry. "I'm sure Uncle thinks I'm a pansy."

"We'll talk about it, but let's go to dinner first," Jack replied and gave him a cool kiss which was reciprocated a little more warmly.

They went first to the bar, while their table was being prepared, where they quickly downed a couple of whiskies. First, they talked of John Brown. Was he just an old crook, with little in mind but the unscrupulous acquisition of the money of others and Jack's in particular? But then again, he had seemed convinced of the abolitionist cause and had got himself killed because of it. Advocate of a just cause or not, he was obviously a megalomaniac, they decided, that created his own reality while seeking to appropriate to it all those about him, brooking no reticence.

Merry told Jack that in Boston Brown's reputation had grown quickly. The Abolitionists took little heed of the murderous events in Kansas and talked only of Brown's self-sacrifice and his freeing of slaves. And thus Merry had become infatuated by his legend and on meeting him fell under the spell of his enormous ego. Even in the prison cell, where Brown's avarice and cruel manipulation was apparent, he couldn't quite rid himself of admiration and submission. However, a day's reflection at his uncle's house had finally rid him of these last traces of hero worship and he wrote his dramatic note to Jack. But being a pansy still worried him.

They went to table and as Jack was unfolding his napkin and tucking it under his chin he said, "So why do you imagine your uncle thinks you're a pansy?"

"I don't know really. Just things he says or hints at that show he dislikes what he calls 'soft men' and his constant exhortations to be tough and manly. There is also the fact that I was thrown out of the Military Academy after being found in bed with a senior boy. He was thrown out too despite his being a Captain of something or other — and now, he didn't pass your message."

"But most, maybe all, boys get up to that sort of thing, as everyone knows but pretend otherwise. Most parents, even uncles, might briefly create hell, but then forget about it, having sent the appropriate lying moral message. It's like jerking off — everybody does it, but nobody admits to it. As to my message, maybe he simply forgot."

"I don't think so. He's not that old. No, it was deliberate. I think he also rather despises me because I'm physically frail and, I suppose, a bit pretty. More like a girl than the ideal rumbustious boy he would like, rushing round fighting and stuff."

"Nothing there to be ashamed of," asserted Jack. "Can't stand those boisterous boys, though I suppose I admired them when I was younger — people like that, people like Bill Watson."

"Which brings me to why this is a sort of preliminary farewell."

Jack stiffened and tried to smile encouragingly. His stomach clenched. "When I get to Boston and I hope you'll come with me, I will receive notification as to whether or not I've been accepted at West Point. I'm worried that I might have failed the physicals. I've got one eye that doesn't work very well, but it's not my shooting eye. You see, I think there is about to be a war and I wish to fight slavery. Despite appearances, I'm not a peaceful fellow and I need to demonstrate to my family that I'm a man. I'll come and join you whenever I can get leave." He stopped and gave a silent Jack a questioning look.

"Well!" exclaimed Jack, "When do we leave for Boston?" He put off thinking about the moment when Merry would abandon him. It was still far enough away.

They climbed the stairs to Jack's room. "We'll have to do something about your social sin complex," muttered Jack as they climbed. "The best cure, I think, is to keep sinning and as often as possible until the sin gets tired and gives over. That's what happened to me when I helped Dan run away. So you're going to fuck and be fucked several times a day until the day you wake up and re-find your natural innocence and the courage to be a man on your own terms. John Brown is dead, and sin is going to die with him."

Merry laughed and gave Jack a hug. The receptionist, watching them ascend the staircase, was taken aback. Were they two pansies? In those times there was nothing unusual in men sharing a bed. It was regarded as a normal economy. He decided it was just friendship as neither of them lisped or had hands that waved about on floppy wrists.

They got into bed and rapidly started on Merry's cure.

# CHAPTER SEVENTEEN

A week later Jack and Merry left for Boston. The journey was long, a week or so in various trains and their various gauges, but not arduous, for as they climbed north and east, the countryside was increasingly domesticated and the towns increasingly civilised with all the comforts necessary for well-off travellers. Jack was becoming very used to being well off. His pistol which he wore often in Kansas, Missouri and even occasionally in Virginia was packed away in his suitcase. He bought himself smart clothes, elegant boots and a tall shiny silk hat. With Sam's past aid and now that of Merry, he was becoming a gentleman. Every day he had his boots polished and he also tried to polish his language.

By the time they arrived at Merry's family home nobody could have guessed that he had been "white trash" and the half-breed son of the town drunk. He was the new Jackson Penn (Jack was a trifle too familiar for all but those close to him). The family had been forewarned of his coming and greeted him with great friendliness. Perhaps this wealthy gentleman, of whom they knew nothing, might find one of their daughters attractive enough to marry.

However, living in this house with its eight other children and a crowd of domestics rendered the continuing of Merry's cure rather difficult. As soon as politeness allowed, Jack moved to a hotel in the town centre, where Merry was a daily visitor. It was at this point that Merry learnt of his acceptance by West Point. As war was looming, the army was getting less choosy and Merry's family and money did the rest for him. Merry's cure seemed to have worked and he grew more and more enthusiastic about the joys of penetration. He even began to prefer being served rather than serving, as he found it less tiring as well as more fulfilling. They experimented more, returning from time to time to fellatio and some more elaborate forms of masturbation. It was an idyllic period that rapidly drew to a close.

Shortly before the end of Jack's stay in Boston he received a letter from Hannibal where along with the usual letter of credit was an invitation to the marriage of the newly graduated Lieutenant William Arbuthnot Watson and Bethany Abigail Winston on behalf of the Very Reverend Doctor R. B. A. Winston (he had almost forgotten his Christian names). This was to be celebrated just a fortnight after Merry was due to report to West Point.

On their final day together, Jack accompanied Meriam to the very gates of West Point: a huge collection of buildings staring down at the Hudson River and situated in 24.7 square miles of woodland territory. They sat gloomily in their carriage, the window curtains closed, kissing their goodbyes. They didn't make hand love as it would have been an inappropriate moment for Merry to have wet patches on his trousers, but Jack opened his shirt, then Merry's and pulled his ancient coin over his head and placed it round the neck of Merry.

"For love and for luck," he whispered.

There was a last kiss, the carriage door was opened and Merry stepped down and without looking back he marched through the gates. Jack watched sadly as he disappeared into his military career. He did not return to Boston but hurried directly south to New York where he caught a train towards the Mississippi. A few days' travel later he was in Hannibal and once more standing before the door of the Reverend Doctor's house.

The door opened and there was Bill, tall and handsome in his brand-new uniform.

***

"Well, well," said Bill, "the cat's bin at it again." And they gave each other a hug a little less ardent than the last time. Beth came forward for a kiss, nursing a tiny child and following behind was Judge Thatcher, leading two others by the hand.

"Despite your military duties, you've been busy, I see," said Jack with a broad smile. The Reverend Doctor roared with laughter.

"A fine boy! A fine boy!" he declared. "Time you should be getting busy too," he added.

"Too busy travelling," replied Jack, robbing the eldest child of the judge's hand with two of his own. He was kissed on the forehead.

"Come, tell us of your new adventures." He could not think of any that were repeatable other than his hand in the fate of John Brown, which was adventure enough.

At dinner that night he regaled the company that included Joe Harper and his wife with the history of Harper's Ferry, the death of Dan and the hanging of Brown. Bill was once more disconcerted by his absence from all these adventures.

"That negro Dan was always a strong-headed boy," commented the Reverend Doctor, "and rather intelligent, it seems, if all you say is true. Fancy him meeting all those philosophical folk, writers and poets and such." He shook his head in wonder.

"Yeah," added Bill. "He always was kinda extraordinary for a nigger. I never knew what to think of him. One minute all obedient and that and then there would be a sudden flash in his eyes that denied it — a true uppity nigger look."

"Well, you did rather force him with all your adventure games: particularly the escaping Greeks one. He should've strangled you."

"Hey, watch it, Jack Penn or I might think up something for you. Like a kick in the butt." There was a hint of anger in his voice despite his smile.

"Now, now boys," admonished Beth. "You aren't still at school."

"Yeah, a genuine Lieutenant should treat all that with disdain," said Joe and he laughed.

"He's right, Bill," added the Reverend Doctor. "Dignity! Dignity!" Bill blushed slightly and Beth took his hand. "More wine?" he added and Jack nodded. "But that Brown fellow, he seems to have been off his head. Never heard such a mess of contradictions: bandit, revolutionary, Holy Joe, murderer, Abolitionist, rustler — no end to it."

"I don't think he was entirely sane," said Jack, "There was a lot of psychological problems in that family. But there's one thing where he'll have you beat, Bill. He fathered twenty children." Everybody laughed, and even Beth giggled.

"Just you wait and see!" exclaimed Bill, joining in the laughter.

"A fine boy! a fine boy!" chortled the Reverend Doctor's voice above the general hilarity.

"And up North, they think he's a damned hero."

"Oh shush, Bill. Watch your language, there are ladies present," admonished Beth.

"They're even singing about him, I hear," added Joe.

"And down South he's a hero too, certainly among ill-treated slaves," said Jack.

"You become a 'bolitionist, Jack?" said Joe.

"Don't know exactly what I am."

"Slavery ain't all bad," said the Reverend Doctor. "It gives a lot of people bread to eat and a bed to sleep in. And if they're all freed, what will become of them?"

"Well, I think Dan could've replied to that," Jack said coolly. "He thought that some of them, particularly those from the crueller plantations might be lost, but not more so than many white trash." There was a silence as they finished their dessert.

"Ah! If the ladies will retire, I think a drop of whisky and cigars are called for. It often calms spirits more than it excites them." And the Reverend Doctor hurried over to the drinks cabinet where he collected four glasses and a bottle. Beth picked up the dessert plates and left the room with Amy Harper. A few seconds later a knock on the door and a black servant came in and quickly cleared the table of its remaining debris.

Jack looked around him, fondling his whisky. "Sorry about that," he said. "But I've seen a lot of things that the quiet citizens of Hannibal couldn't imagine. If this town was the image of slavery, it wouldn't be too bad a thing, I imagine, except perhaps in principle, that is, no one here has yet accepted that blacks are human, with human needs, hopes and rights."

"Yes, no less human than the half-breed son of white trash," murmured Bill into his glass.

"Bill!" exclaimed the judge.

Jack raised his hand in appeasement. "My Pap suffered from syphilitic dementia and so you can't really compare him with anybody. I've met people who knew him way back in the thirties, before he was infected. He was a very respected trader. And my mother, she was an Indian princess."

"Let's not talk about war and slavery," said Joe. "It makes me uncomfortable."

Jack stiffened. "It'll soon make everyone uncomfortable. There's a lot of over-excited people talking of civil war."

"Surely not, Jack," interrupted the Reverend Doctor. "That's sheer lunacy."

"Lunacy or not," added Jack, "ever since the Nebraska Act and the breaking of the Missouri Compromise and thus the line keeping slavery from the North, the South has been trying to push slavery further up — as in Kansas, and threatening secession when thwarted, which is seen in the North as high treason. And the death of John Brown has created an Abolitionist Free-Soil martyr that many are not being slow to exploit."

"Yeah," said Bill, "from what I've seen and heard in the North, I reckon it'll be war within the next six months. I'll fight for our right to hold slaves if we want or not to if we don't. Trying to impose one or the other on everybody is stupid."

"I doubt if that'll be the choice," said Jack. "Compromise seems to be drifting further and further away. In the end I think we'll have to decide which side we're on. I'm going to find that very difficult. I don't like slavery, but then I don't want to end up shooting old friends and neighbours.

"Yes, that is going to be a very difficult choice," added the Reverend Doctor.

"Not that difficult," said Bill. "When it comes to it, you fight for the Government and the Constitution and do your duty as a soldier. They are elected to make the decisions we must follow. If it means shooting a few people, well, that's always been the case as we need law and order. I reckon Jack here has become a bit soft headed, been hanging around niggers and intellectuals too much."

"Not soft headed. I've just seen a lot of war and you haven't. It's not something to enter lightly. It's horrible! It's terrible — you're still playing at soldiers, like you played with Dan and you could do with a bit of intellect," said Jack sharply.

Bill jumped up and his chair fell with a crash. He seized the half empty water jug from the table and threw its contents in Jack's face. The Reverend Doctor sat aghast. Joe stood up; but was uncertain as to why he had. Jack just shrugged; stood also, pushed back his chair and calmly left the room. Bill swallowed his whisky and went to follow him; but the Reverend Doctor took him by one arm and Beth by the other and were not to be shaken off.

Next day Jack left Hannibal with the Reverend Doctor's blessings, apologies and a promise to pass over his affairs to Jack's attorneys at law in New York.

"I don't know what got into the boy. Too much whisky, I guess. But a fine boy! A fine boy!" he added a little uncertainly.

Jack didn't see Bill again and ignored his note proposing a duel.

"Still a fucking kid," thought Jack. "Cowardly half-breed," thought Bill. "Oh dear, oh dear," thought the Reverend Doctor, not at all sure that a military career had helped Bill to his own liberal and open view of life.

Beth did not wish to form an opinion and was glad Jack had refused to fight as her children needed a father and thus her to be married, which she was a few days later.

\*\*\*

On arriving in St Louis, Jack went straight to the docks where were situated the steamboat offices. He soon found the company that, for the moment, employed Sam Clemens and asked of his whereabouts. The clerk before him looked bored and was reluctant to give the information.

"But I'm his brother Henry," protested Jack.

"Not possible," replied the clerk.

"Why so?" demanded Jack.

"'cos he's dead in a boiler explosion, back in fifty-eight. Nah bugger off." There was a momentary silence as Jack gathered his thoughts.

"Not that Henry," protested Jack.

"Oh yeah! Which of 'em then?" asked the clerk with an incredulous smirk.

"I'm another Henry, Sam's half-brother. His mother died when he was three and our father remarried. Sam, Henry and the other kids had been farmed out to various uncles and aunts, so when my mother insisted that her first son should bear her father's name, nobody really objected. When the family regrouped a couple of years later, I simply became Henry Two."

The clerk stopped smirking. This Henry seemed to be too well informed to not be able to cause him trouble.

"Wahl, in thet case I s'pose I could tell yah. He's doin' the Missouri run on the *A.B. Chambers*, wi' the Captain Bowman."

"Whereabouts?"

"Hmm! I reckon if you catch the *Mary Jane*, what's leavin' north this evenin', you should find him coming back down from Omaha at Kansas City. If'n they're not late thet is. Then jest wait 'cos it's no use going up to Omaha as you'll jest cross him on the way up and him goin' down."

"Thanks a lot, mister," and Jack tipped him five dollars, which even the clerk felt was rather excessive.

That afternoon Jack went aboard the *Mary Jane*. She was a

fairly small boat, no more than 300 tons and rather old. Some said too old for the Missouri run, which meant fighting against fast currents. She left St Louis as the late winter sun was setting, shining flame red across the smooth waters of the Mississippi and where a current ruffled the surface, revealing a reef or a snag; each wavelet was tipped in gold. In the distance, on the far Missouri bank, the trees were lost as mauve and violet shadows reflected in the waters where their coldness was occasionally flecked with bright wavelets. The sky was as vivid as the river with a few dark clouds floating along the western horizon. But very soon the water became turbulent as the fast, muddy current of the Missouri entered the broad Mississippi. The sun-stained water became a changing pattern of moving colour. The boat then turned into the current straight at the setting sun. She hugged the Iowa bank where the waters were calmer and less rapid. The sun gone, the river lost its brilliant reflections, and the water assumed its habitual dull, muddy yellowness. Jack turned away from the rail against which he had been leaning and mounted the stairs leading to the dining room on the upstairs deck. Above him the boat's twin chimneys spewed out massive clouds of black smoke as the ship's boilers were force fed to create the energy needed to fight the Missouri.

Despite the smallness of the boat, at first view, the dining room seemed luxurious, being elaborately decorated with many swathes of purple velvet and elaborate gold mouldings covered the ceiling. The furniture, however, was rather worn and tired. The lacklustre upholstery of the chairs was thin in places and even the occasional small hole was to be found. Evidently, thought Jack, this boat was soon to be laid up and forgotten. On closer inspection even the flamboyant decoration could have done with some retouching and darning. Nevertheless, the food was good: roast game, fresh river fish and a fruit pudding running with a pale treacle. He accompanied this with the black stout much favoured by the Irish population. After dining Jack retired to his cabin rather than join passengers gambling or gambolling to the music of a three-piece band in the saloon. He was very tired after a strenuous day of travel and enquiries. He lay down on his bed with a bottle of whisky to hand, but almost immediately fell into a deep sleep. He awoke in the night, still dressed and feeling cold. Rapidly he got into pyjamas and crept beneath his blankets; however, getting back to sleep was not easy — the noisy vibrations of the boat's struggling engines, not ten yards from his cabin, assaulted his ears and shook his bed. As the first light of dawn made his window curtains glow, he gave up on the idea of more sleep, heaved himself from his bed and got dressed again. He went up to the saloon which was still warm and well lit, and where the more enthusiastic of the gamblers were still playing. He sat down and watched a desultory game of blackjack. It was still an hour before he could expect breakfast to be served. Sitting across the room with his back half turned towards Jack was someone he had at first thought to be an old man because of his silver hair that hung below his shoulders; but on closer examination, as he looked towards him, he became a young man, in fact an attractive young man, also a rather familiar young man. Jack was still staring in disbelief when Black Crow Killer stood up and came towards him.

"So you're still with us. Thought you were dead."

Jack opened his mouth to speak in Mandan: "Black Cro…"

"Call me Steve and speak English," he interrupted in a low voice.

"Okay, Steve, so what happened? Why did you disappear?" Jack asked, rather coldly.

After a short handshake Steve began his explanation. "Well, shortly after we left the village we were attacked by Crows. Everywhere was crawling with 'em. We fled south hoping to circle round towards the north and so come back to the village by the opposite bank of the Niobrara. But it weren't no good, everywhere just seethed with 'em. So we waited and while we waited the village was destroyed and almost everybody killed — except, of course, the cunning Jack." He smiled and added, "We live by thieving and hunting now. Which is okay — because everything we do is either blamed on the Missouri Roughs or the Free Soil folk. That depends on who gets hurt or robbed." Jack nodded and smiled back not wishing, at this moment, to show disapproval.

"Looks like you're takin' a leaf from that John Brown's book."

"No, nothing to do with abolition and that — just surviving me and the other two over there, Pete and Buck," he said, indicating two other long-haired young men seated next to the stove. He then beckoned them over.

"We haven't done too badly, can even afford to disguise ourselves as whites and go for boat rides. Can we all have breakfast together?" he added.

"Be my guests," said Jack.

As the day progressed, Jack began to re-find the warmth he had for Black Crow Killer, now Steve. The other two spoke little English and both Steve and Jack felt it unwise to converse in Mandan. Jack's Mandan was also becoming a bit rusty. He was intrigued as to why these three Indians were hanging around St Louis, where they had obviously caught the boat and Kansas City, their declared destination. For the moment he refrained from enquiring and simply exchanged reminiscences of Mandan life until Steve finally volunteered a few more details of the history of his life after the attack on the village, but the reasons for his presence on the *Mary Jane* stayed unstated. Was it just a boat ride or were they reconnoitring for a robbery?

Several times Steve guided the conversation back to the assault of the Mandan village by the Crows and how Jack had escaped, but Jack had nothing new to add. He didn't mention recuperating his coin as he thought Steve might not appreciate that as he'd taken it from the Holy Lodge. He then learnt that the survivors of the Crow assault, largely old men, women and children, had been absorbed by the Mandan Crow people and they themselves had become more and more indistinguishable from the Crows; and that, in the end, Steve and his two companions had made peace with the Crow Mandan and the Crows, there being little other choice as the Sioux had long stopped recognising the Mandan as friends and had become somewhat hostile towards taking in refugees who had once abused their hospitality by declaring themselves independent. So now, Steve, Pete and Buck were Crows.

After dinner that evening, Pete and Buck retired to their cabin as they wished to avoid having to make conversation with the other passengers. Jack and Steve continued chatting and finally went back to Jack's cabin for a goodnight drink. Jack poured two whiskies, while Steve watched him. He handed one to Steve and then sat down on the bed leaving the chair to Steve. Steve eyed him quizzically, got to his feet and placing his glass on the bedside table joined Jack on the bed and placed a hand on his knee.

"Do we continue reliving the past?" he asked. Jack nodded and kissed him on the cheek laying his own hand over Steve's. They stayed like that for a minute or two. Jack felt his desire mounting. He then kissed Steve on the neck, wondered again why he found necks so attractive and moved his hand slowly up Steve's thigh until it covered his genitals. He was already hard, as was Jack. Jack lay back on the bed as Steve unbuttoned his waistcoat and shirt. He kissed his nipples which caused Jack to give a little shudder and his penis to swell a little more. "Well, Jack, you're still a very pretty lad even if you've sprung up a bit. How old are you now? You must be eighteen or more." He stroked Jack's belly appreciatively.

"Gosh, I'm almost there," Jack whispered as the boat's steam valves let off a high shriek and the engines started racing jerkily. The bed shuddered as Steve undid Jack's belt and trousers. Jack ejaculated as Steve took hold of his penis still hidden in his woollen long johns.

"Well, now that the impatient boy has lost his first lust, we can get to work properly," and he began to resuscitate the deflating member which readily became firm again.

"Oh! The wonders of youth, ever ready, ever full of sap." Jack was disturbed by the note of sarcasm underlying these comments.

Steve then turned Jack over, undid the back flap of his long underwear, dropped his own trousers and spat on his penis. He entered Jack rapidly and began a steady thrusting. This was a lot rougher than Jack was used to: for him the act of sex was something gentle and cajoling — except with Pap, of course. Steve was being aggressive. The entry had even hurt more than a bit.

"Careful'" he said. "That hurt me."

Even so his body responded, even responded energetically, matching Steve's thrusts with receptive pushes of its own. His anus was tightening towards orgasm as Steve ejaculated. Steve continued his thrusting and the massaging of Jack's penis through the wool, until a minute later Jack again squirted his pleasure. Steve continued thrusting. Jack was beginning to get a little sore and his prostate protested exhaustion.

"Hold on a bit," cried Jack. "It hurts." Steve ignored him and even increased his rhythm, his hips banging violently against Jack's buttocks and sending an unpleasant shock through his belly. The thrusting went on for some minutes, until Steve began groaning and pulling hard on Jack's penis. Jack was now definitely in pain. He tried to pull away from under Steve, but Steve had him pinned down.

"Jesus, Steve, stop that, will you," he cried. But Steve continued a while longer until having finally ejected and lost his erection he rolled off, leaving Jack sobbing alone on the bed.

"Have a drink," said Steve, already standing, still in shirt and waistcoat with his trousers and drawers around his ankles. Bottle in hand he gave Jack a nearly a full tumbler of whisky. "It'll give you strength for the next round," he added as he started re-buttoning the lower part of his shirt with his free hand. Jack waved negatively, and turned his back on Steve, who placed Jack's whisky and the bottle on the bedside table. Jack pulled the covers over himself. After a few minutes and as the pain lessened, he pushed aside sheet and blankets and sat up slowly. He then saw that Steve was now accompanied by the other two Indians who were rummaging through his luggage. Jack was suddenly very angry.

"Hey, Crow Killer, what the hell are you at?"

"Looking for something," he replied without the least appearance of embarrassment. He was speaking Mandan now.

"You robbing me?"

"No, just taking back what's ours. But it ain't here."

"What ain't there?"

"The great Mystery Medicine of the Mandan."

"The revolver? I lost that at Harper's Ferry."

"Don't act naïve, Jack. You know what I mean: the coin."

"Don't have that anymore, gave it a friend who's a collector."

"Sold it?" demanded Dancing Black Crow (his name had been modified out of respect for his Crow hosts).

"So what if I have?" said Jack angrily.

"As Four Bear's warriors once said: just like a white man: the only thing in your Medicine Bag is money. He was too soft on pretty boys, that Four Bears. As if Trader Penn's child could be anything but a sacrilegious thief."

"Superstitious thief yourself," he shouted back, this time in English. He didn't have a Mandan word for "superstitious"; however, he had begun to feel guilt. He should have realised how very important such medicine was to these people.

"Tell us who's got it now and I might not kill you."

"I'm not about to tell you," Jack answered furiously, his guilt increasing his anger. "You come here, chat, make love simply to rob me. You're just a bloody, immoral savage." These were not the words he really wanted, but they would have to do.

"I don't recall anything about making love. I hard fucked you, that's all. The fucks you've just enjoyed were despising fucks, fucks of scorn, a sort of rape by consent. Now we can try some real, angry rape," and he moved towards Jack.

"Tell me who has the coin, or you'll be dead before tomorrow. You've stolen the soul of the Mandan and you will suffer for it. The old men in the Holy Lodge saw you come in and snatch it just after the Crow attacked. You don't seem to have learnt anything of our beliefs. You committed sacrilege and think nothing of it. I was your teacher, I was to blame, cosseting you rather than beating the truth and faith of the Great Spirit into your icy little soul. All you wanted to learn was how to be fucked and then re-fucked. The ritual of initiation that you escaped is nothing to what you are about to receive. Fucked and fucked again you will be, by me, by Howling Wolf and by Run with the Buffalos; and after we've finished with you, it will be the turn of the broomstick in the corner," he said pointing, "and the fire axe handle at the door and that's just for a start. Your innards will just be a mess of shit, blood and torn flesh."

Jack raised his hands, placating palms towards Black Crow Killer. Then after a moment's silence he said, "Okay, okay, I'm very, very sorry. I won't tell you who has it, but I'll try and get it back for you, which may take time. It was important to me too, which is why I took it, but obviously not as important as its Medicine is for you. You could have explained more before you attacked me."

"Not good enough. I think I know where it's gone, but I'd like to be certain. There's a pansy rich boy you were humping in Jamestown and I reckon it's him. I reckon we could find him easily enough, but I want to be certain. I want to know who and where. AND NOW. And I want to avenge the GREAT HURT YOU'VE DONE TO MY PEOPLE." As he shouted these last words he moved forward and raised his hand to strike. The other two were beginning to unbutton their trousers.

At that moment there was another long shriek of escaping steam, followed by a series of small explosions, like gunshots, as bolts flew from bursting metal. The other two Indians, hastily re-buttoned their trousers, picked up their guns, rushed to the door and once outside stared about them seeking the source of these disquieting noises. There were further small explosions. Was it the militia, come for them? Suddenly there was an enormous roar and a whirling cloud of boiling steam and fire enveloped the two men who fell to the deck screaming. Only a little steam entered through the doorway as the racing flames and steam had sucked it shut. Dancing Black Crow turned towards the door as he struggled to pull up his underdrawers and trousers. Jack seized his opportunity, slid from the bed, took up the whisky bottle and brought it down violently on his head. Dancing Black Crow shuffled forward, stunned but not unconscious. He tried to turn but Jack took him by his collar and the half-raised drawers across his thighs and rushed him stumbling to the door which he pulled open easily lowering the handle with his elbow. Once the Indian was thrust outside, where entangled in his trousers he tripped and fell, Jack shut, locked and bolted the door. He heard Dancing Black Crow shower kicks on the door. Then there was a momentary silence followed by a wood-splintering crash. He had taken the fire-axe fixed to the wall next to Jack's cabin. Jack searched the room for a weapon and saw, unopened, the bag in which he kept his revolver. Taking it to the bed he fumbled in panic at its fastenings.

"Calm down, calm fucking down," he shouted to himself.

There was another crash and the axe head appeared near the lock of the door. Jack fumbled on as Dancing Black Crow tried to extract the axe.

Then there was another series of explosions and another great roar as the second boiler burst, drowning out the screams of the burnt and broken. Jack saw an even larger sheet of flame and steam rush past his window. The axe head vibrated, surrounded by spurting fire, and then fell still. As the reverberations of the final blast died away, the screaming slowly started up again. Those in agony had momentarily been surprised into forgetting their pain or had simply ceased to exist.

Despite his sore and aching anus, from which ran a trickle of blood, Jack hurriedly finished dressing. Flames began to lick up the wall behind the bed. Quickly grabbing what he could of the more precious of his possessions he opened the door and ran to the far end of the boat. The engine room, the main saloon and the pilot house were all in flames. The boat was slowly turning on itself in the dark as it floated with the current unguided.

It began to rain, at first a few drops, followed by a regular downpour. Jack looked up at the blackened heavens and whispered his thanks. The fire ceased spreading but was still too hot around its source to be to be more than dampened. The boat then caught on a snag, the head of a twenty-yard sunken trunk, and was pulled round to finally be grounded hard on a reef below a high muddy bank against which it began to lean. The twin chimneys collapsed.

The boat's crew began to get organised, started fighting the fire and with a few planks, organised a rickety bridge, from the roof deck of the dining saloon, thus connecting the boat to the shore above the mud bank. Jack helped remove the injured from the boat. The dead remained uncounted as the rain had stopped and the fire once more took control and the remaining crew and passengers fled to the refuge of the shore. He hadn't seen any sign of the three Indians. They were probably among the unrecognisably burnt, of which there were many. By mid-afternoon, rescue parties had reached them, both from the river and across land. The explosions had been heard as far as Kansas City.

Among the craft that had come to their aid was the *A.B. Chambers* with its pilot, Sam Clemens.

# CHAPTER EIGHTEEN

Some days later Jack and Sam were dining together at their hotel in St Louis. Both had told their tales of love and adventure. They were discussing Jack's future on the steamboats of the Mississippi complex.

"You could be a mud clerk and after a bit when you're seen as acceptable become a cub pilot with me."

"What does a mud clerk do?"

"A bit of everything nobody else wants to do. That's why they're called mud clerks, because every time we're accosting a stop where there's no jetty to offload cargo to a plantation or something, it's the mud clerks that get down with ropes to fix the boat and are usually up to their knees in mud. You don't get paid but you have board and lodgings on the boat. It's more or less how everybody gets to start on steamboats. It's what Henry was doing when he got killed. He was going to be a cub pilot."

"Yes, I heard about that. I'm very sorry for you and your family."

"It's the major hazard of the trade, as you have just experienced. At least I haven't lost you."

"I imagine there are no alternatives?"

"Well, you could just be my cabin boy," and he suddenly smiled. Jack frowned. "Your duties would be very light. Just unmake my bed each night and lend a hand when necessary." They both laughed.

By this time Jack's "injuries" from the "consented rape" were more or less healed. He could now walk normally, and defecating was no longer painful or bloody. Steve had been a nightmare, but he still had some fond memories of Black Crow Killer, now Dancing Black Crow, his Mandan mentor. He was glad they had different names. He wondered if he was ever to be an ephebe again now that he was eighteen and maybe older. His chin still only sported a few downy hairs that he took off once every week or ten days. Sam had done nothing more than give him a chaste kiss since they had re-found each other. Which was understandable, a delicacy that allowed him to heal without embarrassment. But he still had to tame his adolescent penis each night and as Tinker had said, it was more fun with two. He wondered if Sam now thought of him as too big and too old for the fun they used to have. Or was he just waiting for encouragement? The cabin boy joke was perhaps the signal he awaited. They had separate rooms as Sam had to entertain a lady from time to time. She was young and rich and married to a steamboat owner more than twice her age. Sam thought he was probably the father of her second child. Jack didn't know jealousy as he had always shared his friends and lovers: Bill and Joe Harper; Tinker and Rosie; Eliza and her betrothed; Sam and the widow; it was only Dan that was his alone except perhaps for the servant girl in Topeka, but that had been due not only to his absence, but to the fact that Dan's girls were in a different, less intense world to that of him and Jack and it didn't matter anyway.

Today, however, there was no lady in sight. Should he make a move, he wondered; but he couldn't risk a rebuff, as that would hurt too much. He decided to wait. He preferred having Sam as just a friend rather than lose him by suggesting something he didn't want. Once offered and rejected it would lie uncomfortably between them.

"Sounds as if I could like being a cabin boy," answered Jack giving Sam a grin and the possibility of an encouraging response.

299

Sam just looked at him and smiled as he reached out and touched Jack's hand across the table.

"How's the backside these days?" Sam then asked. "Still suffering from the Indian raid?"

"No, it's more or less back to normal, I reckon. However, it would need testing to be certain about that," and Jack grinned warily. Sam winked back. It began to seem to Jack that he had worried about nothing.

After dinner they sat in the bar for a while. Sam had wanted a nightcap. Jack was clasping his hands round his knees to stop them jumping and tried not to show his impatience. They finished their drinks and mounted the stairs together. Sam's was the first of their adjoining rooms, where they stopped. Sam gave Jack a quick kiss, unlocked his door, hurried in and closed it behind him.

Jack was frozen with disappointment. For moment he couldn't move. Then with a stifled sob went to his door and with a fumbling hand put his key in the lock. He struggled with it a minute. It always seemed to get stuck. Finally, it turned, the door flew open and he stumbled in. He went to the bed and lay down staring at the ceiling, slow tears filling his eyes.

Then there was a tap on the door, and it opened and there was Sam with a bottle and two glasses.

"Sorry about that," he said. "I was desperate for a pee and I thought we might need this." He waved the bottle.

Jack jumped from his bed, ran over and with a real sob of joy hugged Sam to him and buried his head in his shoulder.

"You bin crying again," said an astonished Sam. Jack gave a shamefaced little nod.

"If ever you want to grow up, not that I'm sure that you do, that's a habit you'll have to give up." He then pulled the neatly folded handkerchief from his top pocket, lifted Jack's head up and tenderly wiped his eyes and then enfolded his nose.

"Blow," he said, and Jack blew. Then giving Sam a huge smile began kissing him all over the face and neck.

"That's what I call a welcome. And if I'm not mistaken, that downstairs beast has been bidding me welcome too." He stuttered through the kisses and then began to return them. They stood pressed together clasped mouth to mouth for a long while. They parted.

"You have been growing up," remarked Sam. "Three years ago, you'd 've come by now." They both laughed. It had very nearly happened, thought Jack.

They undressed, erections a-waggle, and got into bed. It didn't last long. They barely had hold of one another and it was all over for both of them.

"That's a good start, it shows enthusiasm," said Sam. "Let's have a drink to celebrate. Then we can begin a long, slow quaking and tremble into an enormous eruption." He swung his legs out of bed and fetched the bottle and glasses.

"Would your volcano like to be inside me for that?"

"We'll see how it goes," murmured Sam as he poured their drinks.

"It should be really explosive. The magma has been building up for a long time."

"That I know, my cool and spicy Jackson. I missed you a lot."

They sipped their drinks in silence and then exchanging a look they clambered back into bed and lay down, each in the arms of the other. Then, after a while, Jack turned over and pressed his eager behind into Sam's belly.

"Be gentle," he whispered.

"Very, very gentle," was the reply as he entered slowly and

there began the eager climb to an eruption, a deep explosion of pleasure-filled affection refound.

***

Two days later, Sam learnt that his next boat was to be the *City of Memphis*. This was a magnificent ship of 865 tons, probably the largest on the Mississippi at that time. He had found a place for Jack as a mud clerk. Jack wondered whether he would like living rough again; but then Sam had his own cabin and he wasn't obliged to sleep with the other mud clerks. Sam said that this wouldn't bother anybody as "cabin boys" were fairly usual on these boats where women were in very short supply and puritans didn't go to sea.

The *City of Memphis* was splendidly luxurious, gold leaf; silk and velvet was to be found everywhere. Even the dormitory of the mud clerks had real beds with sheets and blankets; whereas the pilot's house, normally a spare little cabin boxed in by windows, was a broad spacious glass covered affair with even an oil painting, along with the potted palms and other pretentious decorative objects (miniaturised copies of the *Venus de Milo* and such), armchairs and even a sofa for the boat's other pilots and those that had come to "look at the river". These latter were pilots hoping for an appointment and always ready should an employed pilot fall ill or other, to fill his shoes. In the meantime, they "looked at the river" learning of its latest follies, as this at least gave them free board and lodgings and this boat provided the best food and lodgings on the river.

Life as a mud clerk had its advantages, as they weren't paid and were thus simply expected to be as limitlessly helpful as possible in order to forward their careers, life was only as hard as their ambitions pushed them. Once a mud clerk Jack had to decide where his ambitions lay. He could become a cub pilot, which seemed to be the best option or a cub engineer or "striker", but that was hard, dirty, hot and dangerous, if very well paid; or there were the lesser paths: a night watchman, which needed no great talent other than to stay awake and remember the calls to be made; a servant, cleaner of saloons, maker of beds, sweeper of alleyways; or maybe a real or professional cabin boy, which, if one was pretty and complaisant enough, with one's skin-tight pants and jacket, showing off your little round butt and holding and moulding your genitals attractively, could lead to generous recompense among high ladies and gentlemen, sometimes even a permanent post in a rich household. One waiter, now fallen from such heights, told Jack of six months he had spent in a great house in Memphis where he paraded naked all day long being caressed and fondled by the house guests and was even, on special occasions shaved (not his head of bright yellow curls) and painted gold to serve the aperitifs — but afterwards carefully cleaned with turpentine and soap, then hosed down before he could die of asphyxiated pores, as had the child slaves of Nero when plated with gold leaf. Jack decided, after not too much reflection, that it was indeed cub pilot that he wished to become. After a few months as a mud clerk, having a friend in high places, he became a cub with Sam on the *Alonzo Child* and with much pleasure found himself being sir'd by the lesser echelons. And when Sam was occupied by his rich lady, he could find solace and salacious moments with the cabin boys of his acquaintance and even, every now and again, as he was among the highly regarded, with a pretty servant girl.

\*\*\*

With the attack on Fort Sumner the Civil War had started. Neither Jack nor Sam felt a need to fight for one side or the other. They had both been born into the more northerly slave culture where, on the whole, slaves were reasonably treated. The Widow Wilson's sudden flush of avarice in wishing to sell Dan off south was an exception and indeed frowned upon by many, which had encouraged her change of heart. Whereas, in principle, neither of them approved of slavery, they didn't wish to find themselves shooting the neighbours they had known and loved as children; nor indeed fighting for the economic benefit of the plantation owners and the advancement of slavery towards the North and the new territories. But fate was to force their hands; however, for the moment they continued to sail the river. The war was being mainly fought on the other side of the Appalachians. Nevertheless, for the pilot new skills were to be acquired, notably avoiding the time-wasting blockades set up by one army or the other.

From the 14th December 1860 to the 8th January 1861, they were aboard the steamboat *Sunshine*, a small ship of some 354 tons, where Jack continued his apprenticeship under Sam and was beginning to know the great river, its ever-changing course and its fickle moods. After this voyage Sam had no more work until mid-May. This was the normal course of events for a pilot, who found himself with frequent holidays, which didn't create problems, for when they were working, they were very handsomely paid, often even more than the Captain. Jack and Sam thus enjoyed the last of winter and spring together and without interruption as the lady friend had gone south for the cold months and then to New York for the spring.

The South became increasingly intransigent and accelerated the war; thus, the river became less and less safe. They left New Orleans on the 14th May and struggled north against the fast currents of a river in flood. They managed to avoid a blockade at Memphis and thought they were clear, until, when they were not far below St Louis and passing Jefferson Barracks, there was the explosive sound of cannon and water spouted up ahead of them. Sam and his co-pilot Zeb Leavenworth decided to ignore this intrusion on their peace. Jack, who had been dozing off his generous lunch, woke up. Almost immediately a second shot followed, hitting the boat on the foredeck causing the pilot house windows to cave in and shower its occupants with wood and glass.

"Good Lord Almighty," cried Zeb. "What do they mean by that?"

"I guess they want us to wait a minute," replied Sam.

"Shouldn't we stop?" asked Jack.

"Guess so," said Sam as he began to turn the boat in towards the shore.

The inspection of the boat by Federal forces took the rest of the day, after which they were free to finish steaming up to St Louis.

Once in St Louis it became evident that steam boating, as they had known it, was finished. Sam thought that perhaps he could join the Confederate army as just a peaceful pilot guiding troop and supply boats along the difficult length of the Mississippi and Missouri, but soon regretted his naivety as the military had other ideas. They never really thought about using the talents at their disposal and were in need of fighting men to people their murderous battles. Jack watched this process anxiously and was relieved when Sam decided to desert and go with him to New York; where Sam hoped to find work with a newspaper or by simply writing and selling humorous articles. Jack wanted to find out what was happening to railways as his source of income seemed to be drying up somewhat. But his main reason for wanting to go north was the news that Francis Meriam had been badly wounded and risked losing a leg.

# CHAPTER NINETEEN

To avoid having Sam arrested and shot as a deserter, they took a ferry across the Mississippi and thereafter progressed slowly north-east on horseback, staying well to the north of the Ohio River. The weather was fine and sunny, and they had plenty of cash in their pockets. It was not so much a flight as a sort of Waldensian stroll. They felt free to linger where they would, appreciate the plains, rolling hills, woods and simple farmlands and admire the fauna and flora. Very often they didn't even bother to mount their tent at night and lay under a shared blanket, only sleeping once they'd finished making love and admiring the flights of bats and owls in the starlit sky. From time to time they met with wolves, but the horses would warn them of their presence and if their fire was not enough, a few shots would send them scurrying off without their having to kill any of the svelte creatures.

Another thing that would slow their progress a little was Sam's habit of addressing a few words to any personable female they might encounter. Mostly, these encounters went no further than an exchange of greetings at a farm gate, but on several occasions, Jack found himself alone under his blanket while Sam was somewhere being cosseted by a friendly girl. This did not trouble Jack too much. There was a fire to keep him safe and warm or sometimes even a place elsewhere in the farmhouse; besides which, from time to time he also profited from Sam's systematic soliciting of female passers-by: twice, a pretty girl decided that Jack deserved to sample her charms rather than Sam —- he being young and elf enough; and once, Sam's canvassing found them two sisters who travelled along with them for several days and Jack had ended up with the youngest and prettiest. He was quite sad when finally, they had to part.

They had started out in mid-June and were still quite far from New York by the end of September; however, they were well within Federal territory and had no fears that Sam might be hunted down and arrested. They finally arrived on the shores of Lake Eyrie and at Cleveland they sold their horses and caught a train.

On arriving in New York, they had to seek lodgings and after three days they found an apartment on 8th Avenue overlooking Central Park and the Cricket Field. It was large and not too expensive if rather broken down. Sam set about visiting newspaper offices and Jack about finding Merry in his military hospital.

The conditions in the hospital left much to be desired at the level of hygiene and nourishment even if Meriam had been a Captain, officer of a black regiment. Jack suggested he could come and live in the apartment with him and Sam. But the regimental doctors thought that Captain Meriam should stay with them at least until the leg was no longer suppurating and he could begin to walk. Jack insisted that he was quite capable of ensuring the leg was regularly cleansed and could provide a wheelchair. The doctors would see. So Jack came every day with supplementary food, books and conversation. He would also close the side curtains of Merry's bed to gain a little privacy. Only the patient opposite could see them, and he was often asleep. When this was so, Jack would slip his hand between the sheets and caress Merry's sex and bring him as much pleasure as inventiveness could achieve. Merry would sigh and shiver and finally ejaculate into the handkerchief Jack had provided to avoid alerting the nursing staff to their illicit activity. Quite often he could manage the same for himself and give Merry surreptitious kisses while his hand worked rhythmically in his pocket and under the sheets. This led to wet underdrawers, but he could usually avoid too obvious stains on his trousers, which anyway could be hidden by the newspaper he always carried. This situation continued for several weeks until, at last, the medical authorities, needing beds for the rising number of casualties, relented and allowed Jack to take Merry to 8th Avenue. After a few weeks Merry was still limping a little from sinews that were healed but weak. Other than that, there was a long scar that ran the length of his right thigh, well closed and noticeable but not disfiguring. For Jack he was quite as beautiful as ever.

Their "ménage à trois" was a success. Jack had feared that Merry would be jealous of Sam. But no, and after a while Sam and Merry would get together and then the three of them would sometimes crowd the same bed. However, for the most part it was just Jack and Merry as the rich young lady was still in town and Sam paid her court.

Merry had connections among the Abolitionist intellectuals frequented by his father. Thus, they often found themselves at political or literary "soirées" where Emerson might divulge his latest notions or Whitman give a reading. These latter performances were much appreciated by Merry; whereas, Jack and Sam favoured those of Emerson. At the end of each of the readings of Whitman, Merry would join the group of young men surrounding him. The ladies found Whitman a trifle vulgar, or so they said, but Jack thought their scorn arose from the lack of compliments and interest he bestowed on them.

Some months further on, at a similar event, Jack noticed, across the room, leaning against a pillar and looking rather bored, an elaborately dressed young man whose visage, although changed with the years, was very familiar and incited the resurgence of an almost forgotten instant yearning. Jack walked towards him hesitantly unsure that he could believe his eyes. As he approached the young man smiled encouragingly and extended his hand.

"Tinker," said Jack uncertainly taking the friendly hand.

"Ephraim Tinkerton, at your service," was the reply. "But Tinker if you wish; however, nowadays my friends call me Effy."

"You seem to have done all right for yourself."

"And you too, my pretty Jack."

Jack turned and beckoned to Sam and Merry, who came over and shook hands with Tinker.

"You probably remember Sam. And this is Francis Meriam or rather Merry."

"Glad to re-find you, Sam, and to make your acquaintance, Mister Meriam."

"Call me Merry, as I imagine we're going to be friends."

"Certainly, and you may address me as Effy or Tinker, whichever takes you best." Then turning to Sam, he said appreciatively, "Lucky man to find yourself burdened with two such attractive youngsters."

"No burden, I assure you. And you, sir, what have you been contriving these last years? If I remember correctly, you were ever one clever enough a cat to fall on his feet."

"Well, I went into business with Rosie and she proved to be a very enterprising partner. She's now retired, and we've been married some little while."

"Married!" exclaimed Jack. "I rather thought you to be a permanently independent jouster."

"Not so. I domesticate very easily. But onto other things: I must be off soon, business, you know! Are you all free to come and dine with me and Rosie tomorrow?"

Jack, Sam and Merry looked at one another nodding agreement.

"That seems settled then. Here, take my card. Let us say five o'clock, which gives us time for a bit of chinwag before eating — and a look round the house too, which I think you'll find interesting."

"Oh! Really!" said Jack raising his eyebrows inquisitively. Tinker just smiled widely and muttered his goodbyes as he took their hands again and then hurried off.

Merry looked at his retreating back. "Who's this Tinker then?"

"An old associate," answered Jack with a smile.

"And a disappointment as lover," added Sam with a grin.

"Really! I must say that he has a rather well-mounted behind."

The following evening, they arrived at Tinker's Fifth Avenue address. It was a tall four-storey, not very imposing building. It was narrow: just broad steps up to a double door and a window with a fancy wrought iron balustrade on each side. This, as they were to find on entering, denied the actual grandeur of the house as it spread behind the buildings on either side, which were shops, a tailor's and a "parfumerie". Standing at the top of the steps was a tall barrel-chested black in a long, green tailcoat with gold piping on the lapels and cuffs and with trousers and top hat to match along with very shiny black shoes.

"Good evenin', gen'lmen," he called as they mounted the stairway, while opening the doors.

"Washy," cried Jack.

"Mistah Washin'ton, now sah, if yo' please."

"Well, well! So you're still with Tinker and my, how you've grown."

"Wid Mistah Tinkerton, indeed, sah. He awaits yo' widin." Saying which, he gave a large gesture which ushered them through the doorway. As he passed Jack gave him a big smile and pressed a five-dollar piece into his hand.

"Oh! Yo' realy shouldna, sah," said Washy as he slipped it into his pocket and gave a similar smile.

Once inside they began to realise the true splendour of the Tinkerton property. The vestibule was as wide as the house front and nearly twice as deep. Gilt-framed paintings and yellow silk hangings decorated the violet floral-patterned walls. There was a cloakroom and a bar. A pretty young servant opened the doors to the "salon" which stretched almost the whole width of the house front and two shops, in the middle of which stood Tinker in impeccable evening clothes. He took off one white glove as he shook hands with each of them.

They looked around them, dumbfounded. On the many gilt sofas and chairs sat and lounged thirty or forty girls. All of them were very pretty and two or three quite beautiful. They were mostly in a state of undress and a few were nude. The decoration here was in pink silk on pale green walls. The paintings that had been mainly landscapes in the vestibule were here almost all of Boucheresque naked women, some of whom were being caressed by startlingly well-endowed young men.

"Come along," he said and led them into a second equally elaborately decorated if slightly smaller room. There they found twenty odd men and boys ranging from muscular mountains, though elegant adolescents to frail cupids. All the younger ones were completely naked and the others in leotards designed to show off well-moulded genitalia as if hairless. Here the décor was of blue silk drapes between which could be glimpsed silver grey walls. Lining one of the walls and placed between the sofas were statues, copies of Greek kouroi and on the walls themselves paintings, copies after the Michelangelo *Ignudi* from the Sistine Chapel.

"As you might imagine," said Tinker, "this is the most expensive and most fashionable 'bordel' in town. What do you think?"

"I think the French have a word for it," said Sam. "Epoustouflant."

Jack said nothing but gazed lingeringly at a slim, blond youth of about fourteen of fifteen that had ignited a strong torch of "instant yearning".

"Well, then let's go up and meet Rosie," and Tinker led his rather reluctant guests who followed him with many a last look at the sensual feast they had left behind, where many welcoming smiles glowed at them. Jack caught the eye of the blond youth who pursed his lips and gave a little wave. They mounted to the top floor. The other two floors were devoted to "cabins particuliers" as Tinker like to call the trysting rooms.

On reaching the top floor, they found Tinker's sumptuous apartment where they were greeted by Rosie and three boisterous little boys. To Jack's eye she had grown from a very pretty girl into a beautiful woman. Sam also looked impressed. Meriam was still gazing back down the stairs as if they were transparent and he could still see the living *kouroi* and Zeusian mountains that were there below.

Rosie gave Jack a very warm kiss on the lips as she hugged him to her. The erection that had begun in the salons below stiffened to full size. Rosie grinned and hugged him a little harder.

"Put that boy down, Rosie Tinkerton," said Tinker. "You don't want to spoil the look of his pants." Sam and Merry laughed.

"Yes, he's a very susceptible lad," added Sam.

"You could say that," contributed Merry.

"So we all know the randy Elf," grinned Tinker and gave Jack a kiss himself, but this was on the cheek.

The dinner was as luxuriant as all else in this house, with some very fine wines and off-season fruit raised in his own heated greenhouses. When at last they came to the end of its eight courses and were just nibbling at the savouries, Tinker started explaining his rapid rise to riches. It was mainly Rosie's work. At first, she had worked and knew how to select clients that were clean and prosperous and was also good at recruiting girls, choosing only those of some education and beauty from among the numberless workless immigrants roaming the city.

This was a boundless resource as by 1860 more than half New York's population consisted of those born in other countries. It was also a time of rapid economic growth that created tens of rich men practically each week, who came to seek pleasure. The country's population had been doubling or more every twenty years and Tinker had known how to profit from a busy demographic and economic expansion.

Tinker's house had rapidly become known for the quality of its girls and their cleanliness. All were inspected once a week by a doctor. The girls also were content as they were well paid and if they did fall ill or pregnant were nursed back to health rather than thrown out into the street. Tinker had also discreetly expanded to meet the pederast and frustrated wife market, which was very profitable. The two shops and several others connected to them were owned by Tinker and were mostly a front whereby clients could enter the brothel without being seen to. Thus, Tinker became a respected citizen, received by the rich men that he helped to fulfil fantasies without risking their reputations. He was known simply as a successful businessman of the retail trade. Only the highest, thus in need of most protection, ever learnt of his main source of income; for, although he had an apartment above his brothel, his official residence was a large house that he had built in the fashionable suburb of Coney Island. For these special customers he organised a delivery service and very often prolonged "rentings" that gave the impression of a love affair.

Dinner over and Rosie departed to look after and bed the boys. The four men took up cigars and passed the port between them. They chatted of the increasing lawlessness of New York where the Bowery Boys (mainly German immigrants) and the Dead Rabbits (mainly Irish immigrants), the two most powerful of the New York gangs, fought for control of the city, little hampered by the small and largely corrupt police force; and where Tammany Hall was becoming an increasingly powerful political organisation. This was the base of the Democrats and had become Irish immigrant dominated. It owed its popularity to the help it gave the poor and its willingness to ignore rules and red tape when it came to business. Tinker was much impressed by it as without it, what he considered to be its benign corruption, New York could not have had the rapid growth it had known since the 1850s. It had also been the not-so-secret force that had created his wealth. Sam and Jack, both being of a practical nature, were inclined to agree with Tinker. Merry, however, with a stronger religious and puritan background, was not so sure. He felt that somehow Tinker ought to have had to struggle a bit more.

The evening wore on and as all were by then more than a trifle inebriated, Tinker suggested they stay the night. There were plenty of bedrooms, he said, and each would have his own. This individualism didn't seem such a good idea to Jack, but he complied with the general wish for a quiet night. He entered his room unsteadily, one of the "cabins particuliers", briefly rinsed his hands and face and began slowly to undress. He was down to vest and trousers when there was a knock at the door. Jack opened it, expecting to find Sam or Merry there, but to his astonishment he found the slender blond from down below.

"Can I come in?" asked the boy. Jack stepped aside with a slight stagger and waved him in.

"To what do I owe this visit?"

"Mr Tinkerton sent me as a present." Jack found his slight German accent very fascinating.

"That was very kind of him, but I'm not sure that I'm in a condition to truly profit from it and besides, what do you think? Did you have choice?"

"It was by my choice. When Mister Tinkerton came down and asked us if anybody would like to entertain one of his guests, I immediately volunteered to accompany you. I think Mister Sam got a lady and Mister Merry a lot of muscle. It is rare to have an attractive partner and even one that might love you. I saw you looking at me a lot." Jack sighed.

"I would love to share my bed with you, but don't hope for too much activity. We've had rather a lot to drink."

"Don't worry, and we have all night and as much of tomorrow as you might wish." With these words he began to help Jack finish undressing. He was already nude himself other than for a light blue silk dressing gown. Once naked, Jack clambered into the wide, satin sheeted bed, immediately followed by the boy.

"What's your name?" murmured Jack.

"Well, my 'nom de guerre', as Mister Tinkerton likes to call it, is Carpos (a pretty Greek boy that got drowned in the Meander for some reason), but I began life as Hans."

"Then Hans it is," and saying this Jack put his arms around the boy and even as he felt desire mounting fell asleep.

When he awoke sun was shining through his window. Hans was still sleeping next to him, half uncovered, as Jack sat up. Jack was mildly surprised to find he only had a very slight headache. The high quality of the alcohol, he thought. He looked down at Hans. He wasn't sure if he had ever seen anyone quite so beautiful before: the pink/white skin of his slender body and his golden curls were gleaming in the sunlight that filled the window. Jack bent down and gently kissed his cheek. He then got out of bed, found the chamber pot, which he placed on the bedside table so as to make less noise, and had a long piss. As he shook himself dry, thus beginning to create an erection he turned and saw Hans watching him.

"Nice, comfortable-sized dick," said the boy reaching out and touching it. Jack just gazed at the little god and ran his hands through the gleaming curls.

Hans wiped a drip from Jack's penis with the sheet and then squeezed it tentatively. Jack took his hand gently, pulled it aside, and climbed back into bed. He lay on his back, looking up at Hans, who was leaning over him and smiling. He touched the boy's hair again and lightly ruffled it, at which the boy bent lower and kissed him on the mouth, staying there a while. Jack moved his hands to rest them on Hans' shoulders, at which the boy lowered his kisses to the neck and then to the crook of the clavicle and on to the nipples, nibbling at each one. Jack felt great lassitude along with his rising desire, dropped his hands to let the boy linger, while making wider and wider little circles across his belly, until his lips settled on the penis, now full and hard with a little bead of pre-seminal fluid at the eye. Hans licked this off and slowly enveloped the gland with his mouth. He stayed still a full minute before beginning to play with his tongue.

Jack's penis, fully engorged with blood, became a little more swollen as the eye opened anticipatively. Hans gripped it with his lips and then pushed slowly down. Jack's hard, tense desire exploded and spurted desperately five times before trembling to a stop. Hans looked up; smiling as he swallowed.

Jack, his eyes once more open, smiled back. "Did you like that?" he stuttered, as he recovered his breath.

"Yes," said Hans. "It's like eating oysters. It lacks the dash of lemon juice, perhaps."

Jack laughed. "Come here," he said, pulling the boy up and sliding down under him.

"Lift your pretty backside and come up here. I'd love you to fuck my mouth, just like you fucked my dick. Which was wonderful and for which I thank you. Thanks, thanks."

"Bitte, bitte," murmured Hans.

As the boy moved above him, Jack grasped his buttocks and guided the boy's penis into his mouth.

"Do you want me to come?" the boy whispered.

Jack nodded, holding the boys member firmly with his lips.

"That usually costs fifty dollars more," Hans giggled.

Jack gripped him harder, parting the buttocks and caressing the anus.

"I'd pay double," muttered Jack with difficulty

Hans gave three delicate little thrusts and then, as the orgasmic paroxysm seized him, arched his back and became rigid as he convulsively flooded into Jack's mouth. They rolled sideways, clinging to each other by head and buttocks. They lay like that for several minutes until slowly sliding apart, and then together until face to face.

"I see what you mean," Jack said. "Definitely a lack of acidity — but delicious none the less.

Neither of them did, but momentarily, lose their full erection. Then the boy began caressing Jack again carefully, kissing his neck and ears. Then he once more stroked his belly, touching just now and again at the newly swollen gland. Jack returned his caresses, squeezing the firm little behind and placing his sex between the boys thighs, whereupon Hans pulled Jack forward by his sex to join him. They moved together, penis against penis, until just as Jack was approaching a critical point of pleasure, the boy pulled away, turned around, and thrust his behind into Jack's stomach. Jack lost control and his sperm spurted in hurried jerks against the firm warmth of the boy.

"Did you want to come in?" Hans whispered apologetically.

"Oh! You little God. How could I? I'd love to, but you've just emptied me."

"I think I can do something about that. Just lie still." And he restarted his caresses with a slow gentleness and assiduity that astonished Jack, used to a more peremptory and energetic loving. He had never felt so loved. He was again the baby in his mother's hands, and it was not long before an urgent desire surged into him demanding its accomplishment. Hans saw this and turned, so that with his aid, Jack entered him.

"Oh my god, how I love you, my Hans. I want to melt into you. I want to be you." And he pulled the boy furiously against him, kissing at his neck and shoulders. Then, as the orgasm came, it was unlike any he had ever had before — even with Tinker. Exquisite pain and fierce pleasure mingled as his tortured prostate fought to fulfil desire, convulsively seeking an ejaculation from almost nothing. As this struggle stopped, with a series of hard spasms that left him limp and feeble, Jack began to weep. This time, he did not want to stop.

"Are you alright?" Asked Hans

Jack nodded, and between sobs he said, "Oh! You beautiful little whore. You could seduce the Saints. You could make Paul renounce of his sainthood and remount, once more a great lecher, on his heathen horse. I love you so much, I weep with happiness. I'm surprised I'm still alive after what you've done to me." His sobs went even deeper. "I love you, Hans, I truly do." He finally managed to stutter.

"And I love you," replied Hans, turning and pulling Jack against him. And they wept together a long moment.

"I'm no longer a virgin, as this is the first time I've fucked for love. All the tricks the girls taught me have suddenly begun to mean something, become a language of love, and not just incitements to spunk."

"Come and live with me, darling Hans."

Hans shook his head.

"Why not?" pleaded Jack.

"Because I don't want to find myself on the street again being beaten and fucked by any randy bastard who comes along — otherwise, I starved. My parents died on the boat. I don't want to be like I was before Mr. Tinkerton found me and taught me to be his top whore. I've perhaps another six or seven years being a beautiful boy and by then I want to have enough money to start my own business. Whoring is the only trade I know, and my looks will change. Will you still want me as a hairy man, with a gut that grows?"

"Of course, my darling child — I'll never abandon you."

"You believe that now. I don't doubt. I think we should wait a bit and just enjoy what we have. And later we'll see. My love will always be now, forever now. I'm sure Mr. Tinkerton won't mind you being around. He likes me to be happy . . . And then there are your friends. I'm sure that you and Mr. Meriam are having rumpty-tum, and what about Mr. Clemens? Him too, I bet. I could see all three of you were linked, more than just friends. Friends don't touch each other like you do. What are they going to think. Am I to share you with two others?"

"Am I to share you with your clients?" The boy blinked and stayed silent as tears once more started from his eyes.

Jack felt a little deflated by the boy's practicality and came down out of his dream. He had just relived his one night with Tinker, only multiplied by ten. He had fulfilled a dream and could continue it. Why not do as Hans said? Why demand the jealous exclusiveness of total possession? He had demanded nothing of Tinker — just lived with a melancholy hope — and now he had upset his heavenly little beloved.

"You're right," Jack muttered, and pulled the boy against him to kiss away his tears.

As they made love a final time, Jack murmured continuously, "my angel, my angel, my angel," while Hans relaxed into total surrender, caressed into sleep by two gentle hands and this low chant of love.

\*\*\*

Time passed and 1863 was upon them. Merry was spending more and more time with the acolytes of Walt Whitman, a group of young philosophers and poets. He would usually be home late and/or sexually exhausted and would sometimes be absent for two or three days at a time. Sam was often with his lovely, rich lady whose husband was rapidly declining. And so, Jack found himself quite at a loose end, or rather, simply free. On these occasions he would walk across the park and call in on Hans. Tinker did not object, in fact, he rather encouraged the relationship as it made Hans happy who, when happy, was twice as beautiful. A sulking boy, however well made, is never very attractive. Beauty was valuable. Jack got on well with the girls too and if Hans was engaged, they would see to his needs in his stead. He learnt much of the workings of Tinker's brothel.

For example, it was forbidden to try and penetrate the little cupids or the nymphets. This was not allowed until they became pubescent. They were for caressing and fondling only. If any client tried to break this rule, the children were instructed to scream loudly. The client was then ejected by Washy, whatever his riches or status and forbidden further entry for six months. There were two reasons for this: the first was to protect the children from injury; and the second, almost as important, to protect their virginity, because as they matured this could be sold for a small fortune — not only the female hymen, but also the tight little anus of an unpenetrated thirteen- or fourteen-year-old boy, the former having a slightly greater value, of course. Nevertheless, sometimes Tinker's plan was foiled by the children as they sought affection amongst themselves. The house was a little maze of rooms and corridors where it was not difficult for a little couple to find solitude. Tinker understood.

There were the mirrors in the two salons, which were in fact one-way windows through which discreet gentlemen and now and again, ladies could choose their partners without having to appear in the public rooms. Some very timid clients even preferred to stay and simply masturbate while watching the sexual riches below. For this there was a special cabinet with washing facilities and various lubricating unguents. There was also the vestibule which served as a bar and booking office as well, in which rich young libertines could show off to one another and where regular clients could reserve the whore they desired. Jack often strayed there, because it was also somewhere to chat up a potential lover who would come to him for free, or so he imagined.

With Merry and Sam distracted by other matters Tinker's little palace became his home. Here he was comforted and cherished as he had been by Dan. He had become almost the house mascot and would help clients make their choices informing them of the house rules: above all no violence. He would often chat with Rosie telling her of his life with Sam and Merry, who seemed to be drifting away. He told her of his father and of Dan and the ice flower in his heart that kept him from any total attachment to another. He thought he could love, but not love completely. He wanted to but had a great fear of abandonment that always kept his heart's centre aloof and distrusting, secret and for him alone. When he made love, however full and deep the pleasure, it was almost always masturbation. Rosie listened and caressed him, made him coffee and poured him whisky. They never made love again. She asked Tinker what to do. But he replied that there was nothing to do; only Jack could find himself by giving a little more of himself each time he loved another.

***

Then things changed again: one morning Merry came home and

after marching about hesitantly for a while, Jack and Sam watching and wondering what was coming, stopped directly in front of them and started talking about Walt Whitman, for whom he had a great respect and who was his inspiration.

"He has asked me to become his amanuensis," he added taking on a touch of self-importance. "Unfortunately, this would mean leaving here and living at his place, which is in Washington. He just visits New York. I'm dreadfully sorry, Jack, but there you are. I feel in need of an objective in my life, a worthwhile activity. I'm even starting to write things. There're lots of new ideas floating about and I need to be among them. But I'm not abandoning you. I'll come and see you."

"Thank you," said Jack rather coolly.

"There's this new member of the group," Merry continued in a rush, "who's just come from London where all the radicals are talking about a certain Karl Marx and his critique of Hegel. He says that Hegel's notion of alienation is stood on its head and that his idea of de-alienation is in fact the real alienation; whereby man, the subject, has become dominated by his own objects. That is to say, man has become the object of his own objects become subjects. This explains everything about how money or capital has become the directive subject/object that runs our world, in which we are just slaves to one of our own not very brilliant economic notions — competition! I suggest you try and get hold of some his economic and philosophic manuscripts from 1844. Especially the Critique of Hegel." With which words and a rather patronising smile, he left the room to go and pack his things.

"What's an amanuensis?" asked Jack.

"A sort of classy unpaid secretary, I think. I should also think there would be some venereal duties for any young man contracted chez Walt." He smiled, and Jack also, but rather sadly.

Jack was rather hurt and distressed by Merry's sudden departure, but solace was just around the corner. The ailing husband of Sam's lovely lady had died and so she thought it appropriate that Sam should stay away for a week or so or maybe longer, while she became the bereaved widow, not adding that it would also leave her free to seek out a replacement among the rich old men of her acquaintance. Sam complied without too much reluctance as he was beginning to get a trifle bored with her incessant demands upon his presence and sexual prowess.

Jack helped Sam with his writing, making suggestions and also copies to be sent about. They started a joint article on negro emancipation and a peaceful means of achieving it through civil disobedience. As such thinking often brought about attacks, even physical, they decided to use pseudonyms. Jack reminded Sam of an old pilot, now dead since a while, they had known on the Mississippi who wrote rather untalented stories under the pseudonym of Mark Twain, an expression used by sounders indicating about two fathoms of water. This, he suggested, was more serious than names Sam had used for comic articles in the past, such as Thomas Jefferson Snodgrass or W. Apimondas Blab. Sam agreed. Jack, who was beginning to learn some colloquial French from Sam and Tinker, the latter of whom obviously thought French names and titles added class to his establishment, had decided to be Fay Sheaigh, an insupportably opinionated Irish woman who promoted anything that might render their more conservative readers furious. Sam doubted if one in a million Americans would see the joke but concurred anyway to please his companion. However, he was very pleased with his own new pseudonym and congratulated Jack for having unearthed it for him. The article, however, though much commented on in news editor circles didn't seem to get published.

So Sam and Jack had become a couple again, almost like brothers but for the occasional love making as and when their other commitments permitted. Jack had his Hans and Sam quickly found an obligingly lonely girl who would sometimes oblige Jack as well. This situation suited them both and filled the fine days of late spring and early summer. But troubles were grumbling under the never tranquil surface of New York. Not only was there much discussion of Darwin's *On the Origins of the Species*, but there were also certain signs of reluctance towards the exigencies of the Civil War.

# CHAPTER TWENTY

July 1863 came, and the temperatures rose unbearably high, causing the stink of the city and its thousands of cesspits and other less sophisticated dumping places of human defecation, to create a nauseating effluvium, mostly arising from the poorer areas of the city, namely from lower Manhattan. Elsewhere, especially if you were stinking rich, you didn't make much stink. Jack and Sam were lucky to be overlooking the Park. But it was not just the weather that made New York so very uncomfortable.

Since Lincoln's Emancipation Proclamation in January 1863 there had been racist protests and attacks in the docks, where white, in the majority Irish immigrants, feared for their livelihoods and a depression of wages if masses of freed slaves came north looking for work. Many longshoremen refused to work with black labourers. Then in March 1863 came the Enrolment Act, for the war had become increasingly costly in men's lives and the flow of volunteers from among the poor immigrants had dried up. More often than seeking glory, they had preferred the risks of war with three meals a day and warm clothing against the winter cold to the abject poverty and near starvation in the city's slums. But now, with an enforced drafting, those that had work protested and those that had managed to install themselves as artisans and shopkeepers protested even more loudly as their businesses would be threatened by an absence with the army. But that which provoked the population even more was their resentment of the fact that wealthy men could escape drafting by paying $300 for a replacement — a sum well outside their own economic possibilities. There was also much sympathy for the Secessionists as much of New York's economy was tied to the South's cotton production and it was even suggested that New York secede from the Union along with the South.

The first drawing of draft numbers on the 11th July passed peaceably enough, but with the second drawing on the 13th riots started: firstly, with some attacks on the houses of the rich, largely a matter of screamed abuse and stone throwing, followed by a similar assault on the black population and along with them supporters of emancipation.

However, what had begun as a simple protest over the new draft laws became a generalised resentment that rapidly increased in fury as the days passed: rich quarters were looted and burnt; churches were set on fire; an orphanage for black children sacked and destroyed; and many blacks were lynched and often given hideous wounds — fingers and toes cut off; bodies slashed; and emasculations. The city became totally out of control as the small police force of about 2,500 ill-armed men for a population approaching 850,000 could, or for many, wanted to do little. The city was empty of soldiers as Lincoln had sent every available man and the city's militia to Gettysburg, which battle had been fought at the beginning of July.

\*\*\*

Jack and Sam were largely unaware of these events and despite the heat and because of the smell worked together behind closed windows. It was only late on the first day of the riots that lasted from the 13th to the 16th July that they recognised something was amiss. At about four o'clock they noticed a straggling, noisy crowd approaching across the Cricket Field towards the more opulent houses to their left, many of its members obviously drunk. Their house boy Herbert, a young black, was with them at the window.

A small group came out of the Park just below them and turned down the road to join the others. Herbert opened the window to see what was happening along the avenue. A member of the group below then pointed upwards.

"A fucking nigger," he screamed. The entire group turned, rushed to the front door and started hammering on it and were almost immediately joined by others distracted from their destructive activities, where they had set fire to a neighbouring house. Very quickly paving stones were dislodged and broken and hurled at the ground floor windows and several men attempted to clamber through into the downstairs rooms. Jack, Sam and Herbert grabbed their coats, wallets and Jack also his gun. They fled to the back of the house and the servants' staircase and from there descended to the tradesmen's entrance at the rear of the building. By traversing the small garden, they entered an alley running parallel to $8^{th}$ Avenue. Once in this narrow alley that only gave onto storage sheds and stables, they ran until they came to an adjoining alley through which they could reach the avenue.

Sam peered cautiously round the corner of the further end of this alley. The rioting crowd, now some two hundred yards away, was busy ransacking their house. The three of them ran unnoticed across the avenue and into a group of trees. Young Herbert was terrified and had to be dragged along. Now that they were hidden and gathering breath, they peered around them. There were still other small groups scattered through the park. They decided to try and make Tinker's brothel which was just on the other side of the park as they could think of no other nearby place where they could find shelter. But to get to 5<sup>th</sup> Avenue they had first to traverse the park which was mainly open ground. After a brief discussion it was decided that the best course was to be bold. They started walking with Herbert between them so as to hide as much as possible his dark face. They had already made half the distance when they came across a group of youths whose presence had been hidden by a cluster of bushes. They were sharing looted bottles as they lounged under a tree. There were six of them. They all stood up and took on threatening postures.

"Okay, assholes, hand over the nigger," the largest member of the group said. Jack drew out his gun.

"One step nearer, shithead, and I fire," he said. And it was obvious he meant it. Five of the youths retreated, looking around them for support, but the nearest of the other drunken groups was a good hundred yards away. The big youth, unable to accept the shame of defeat from this pretty boy made to throw the large stone he was carrying. Jack fired and the youth fell dead. The others just scattered; the noise of the shot disappeared among the dozens of others coming from the streets. The three of them then turned and jogged across to the southern boundary of the park without further incident. On reaching 5<sup>th</sup> Avenue they started towards Tinker's house, but soon met with another little mob. These had captured a black and were attempting to string him up on a tree without a great deal of success as the accessible branch was too flexible to sustain the poor man's weight. His knees were still touching the ground and with each pull on the rope the branch bent a little further. The victim was no doubt being strangled, but this did not satisfy the mob and certain of them started kicking him. There was a roar of laughter as he lost control of his bladder. Jack shot in the leg one of the two men pulling on the rope, who stumbled against his partner and the black fell to the ground. The little mob pulled back. One of them tried to draw a gun and Jack shot again and he fell dead. Sam came forward and loosened the rope around the black's neck. Herbert, again petrified, wet himself. This time there was no laughter as Jack waved the smoking gun from side to side.

"Clear off," he shouted. "There're four rounds left, and it'll soon be four dead men." A man with an iron bar made a threatening move and Jack shot again. The man's face imploded spraying blood on those near him. The iron bar fell and nobody picked it up. Jack was obviously an expert with his revolver. Those at the back of the mob started to drift away. Jack spoke again:

"I'm gonna count to ten, after which I will kill anyone within range." He began to count, and the rest of the mob fled. Once they were 50 yards off, Jack reloaded his revolver to replace the two missing rounds.

"Let's be off," he said. The hung black was giving signs of life and so Sam and Herbert carried him between them, while Jack turning around slowly as he walked kept the gun ready for use and the rioters at bay. They came across another crowd looting one of Tinker's shops, but the sight of Jack's gun was sufficient to dissuade them from attacking other than by hurling racist insults. Sam was silent, disconcerted by Jack's cold efficiency with the gun and apparent lack of reticence before the idea of killing his like. It was a side of Jack, seemingly sensitive and without aggression, of which he had had a few intimations in the past: for example, his distancing, encapsulating away from himself, the terrible deaths of his Indian wife and child; his indifference towards the acts and end of his father; but this overt evidence of a cold distancing of the lives of others, of those he condemned without appeal, was a revelation. What, he demanded, was in this normally gentle not yet quite a man? But Jack wasn't questioning his actions. He was thinking like a warrior, simply cold, alert and lethal. He had been well trained.

Just beyond Tinker's house a large crowd was gathering. They saw Herbert and the black being carried by him and Sam, set up a howl and started towards them. Tinker, who had been watching from a first-floor window, called down to Washy to let them in. At the sight of Washy in the doorway the rioters became even more agitated. But they were still thirty yards away when the double doors were slammed to. They began hammering at them. Tinker came down from his observation post to greet Jack and his companions, squeezing past a Gatling gun mounted at the end of the corridor between the cloakrooms and facing the front doors. Behind it was the door to the vestibule. The two cloakroom windows, Jack noted, were already boarded up. Sam and Jack stared at the Gatling gun. Tinker patted it.

"Bought this a few weeks ago as things seemed to be getting untidy," he said. "It belonged to an old man who was once a reporter on the *New York Times*. He told me it had been used to protect them in the Shakespeare riots in '46."

"Where's Rosie?" Jack asked.

"Rosie and the boys are at Coney Island — so safe and sound. And take that boy into the salon so that the girls can take care of him." Herbert complied.

The hammering on the doors suddenly intensified and became a series of heavy crashes as the assailants had evidently found something to use as a battering ram.

Tinker signalled to Washy and Hans who were stationed on each side of the doors. They threw them open and Tinker started turning the crank of the gun. The first bullets hit two men holding the head of a heavy bench. They fell and the bench with them.

One rolled down the steps and the other fell between the doors. The bench slid down to the roadway taking its other bearers with it. A second burst was aimed over the heads of the mob which ran off to reform at a little distance.

Washy and Hans started pulling the fallen man out of the way of the doors when there was clear, sharp sound of a rifle shot from among the crowd. Hans dropped dead, a neat round hole in the middle of his forehead.

There was a moment's stillness among the defenders, then Jack and Tinker trundled the Gatling gun to the doorway and its tac, tac, tac, started again with Tinker turning the crank and Jack feeding in sticks of bullets. The crowd fled, stumbling and falling against one another in the rush. The avenue in front of Tinker's establishment emptied, except for a dozen dead and twice as many wounded. Their screams, some so high as to be silent, filled the evening air confusing the bats.

***

Once the doors were again shut Jack flung himself at Hans's body, hugging it to him and showering his still warm cheeks with kisses and tears. He spent the next hour like that, until, finally, as the body grew cold, he allowed himself to be pulled away. They sat him in the vestibule with the girls (those that weren't upstairs as fire fighters). They gave him a large glass of whisky, but he was inconsolable, and the whisky was ignored. He was bent double weeping silently. Sam sat next to him with his hand on his shoulder. There were obviously things Jack couldn't encapsulate. Inside Jack something had broken, the warrior crumpled and the ice flower wilted, melted a little, confronted by the unexpected warmth of his total sorrow.

***

There were no more attacks on the front of the house that day and in the rear of the property, with its yard surrounded by high walls topped with broken glass, the occasional attempts to gain entry were easily repulsed by Washy and some of the male whores firing a motley collection of pistols and hunting guns from the first and second floor windows. The ground floor windows, like those of the façade on 5th Avenue, presented no danger as they were boarded up and further protected by their iron bars. The only danger was from the mob hurling burning torches at the higher windows; however, the many girls and their buckets, bowls and chamber pots full of water very quickly stifled any torch lucky enough to find access. Tinker and Sam could relax and while watching over Jack could enjoy a fine malt whisky, a twelve-year-old Cardhu imported from Scotland.

After a while they began talking of Jack as if he wasn't there. Which in reality he wasn't; at first at least, as he was oblivious to all but his mourning of Hans.

"He's a strange boy," said Sam gently squeezing Jack's shoulder. "I find it difficult to understand him. He seems to be more than one person. There's the Jack I love dearly who is gentle, almost afraid of life, who needs much affection; then this almost monster I saw this afternoon, a sort of avenger, killing in cold blood without any sign of reflection, much less remorse."

"I don't think he knows what he is, or who. In his moments of ruthlessness, he's like me. It comes from a hard life: slave or orphan. At least I had a pretty clear idea of who my father was and there was even some reluctant affection, even love perhaps, when the old sod called me Tinker when he wanted to bugger me.

But that syphilitic nut that fathered Jack and murdered his mother was no longer even human. He's had to pick up how to love on his own. So the sweet gentle Jack is his own fabrication, probably — with a lot of help from being beautiful and I reckon, from that nigger Dan — who was a big person in every sense. In a way the Jack we love is just a surface, a two-dimensional soul, the depths of which are hidden even from himself, or were perhaps never created."

"Yes, I think our Jack is a construction of wishing to please, of dependence. Fortunately, he's a sexy little bugger. If it wasn't for his hungry sex pushing him on, he'd have become a little nut, a nut without a kernel."

"You're right, saved by his nuts," said Tinker with a smile. Sam gave Jack's shoulder another squeeze, and laughed.

"We got our souls naturally, as children, and we've grown from the inside out. He's got to create his soul from the outside in."

"I'd like that whisky now," said Jack suddenly straightening up. "So what do I have to do to get a soul?"

"Just go on fucking," said Tinker with a grin.

"You might be right. That's how Merry got his." And Jack gave a little smile too as he reached for his whisky. His dream had ended. After all, he knew that it could only have been a dream. Hans was an angel, a sort of fallen one perhaps, thus destined to go early to nature's heaven, and not that loveless Christian place. He had been sent to show Jack love and where it began in unselfish adoration — just as they had adored one another. He looked at Sam with renewed affection. Sam had always adored him and he knew he now shared it, but at a different level to that which had existed with Hans. Hans had very definitely been a dream.

***

The next day, the third day of rioting, there was once more a crowd in front of Tinker's property. This time many of them were armed and there was a small cannon that had been captured that morning in the fighting with a party of marines from the naval base. There was much discussion what to do with it as they weren't quite sure how it worked and didn't wish to risk an explosion. Finally, someone who had once been a soldier was found and he charged the cannon which was now facing Tinker's house. It fired, bent a bit of wrought iron near the window and chipped a little stone from the solid wall.

"Aim at the fucking doors, you idiots, this ain't a siege gun," shouted the ex-soldier.

In the meantime, the defenders having seen the arrival of the gun and its slow mounting and charging, carried the Gatling up to the first floor and set it up behind a curtained window, the barrels angled down in the direction of the mob. The cannon fired again and a panel of the door buckled. There was a cheer from the crowd and Tinker began cranking. The cheers turned into shouts and screams. For a while the cannon stood alone, until under the cover of shots from multiple guns, the ex-soldier and two or three others returned to load it. Tinker and Jack had ducked down below the window and now they pushed the angle of the Gatling a little to the right towards where they knew the cannon to be. They didn't have to expose themselves to reach up, load and fire. The cannon and the Gatling fired simultaneously. The buckled panel became a hole and the soldier and one of his companions lay dead. Furious bursts of gunfire riddled the curtain at the window, but nobody came forward to re-man the cannon that had been scarred by Gatling bullets in several places.

There was a stalemate, with desultory firing at the windows and the occasional bursts from the Gatling. Jack, Tinker and Sam sat under the window sipping whisky until, after an hour or so, there was suddenly a series of explosions out in the avenue and the gunmen in the mob stopped firing. There was then a silence only interrupted by a few screams. There followed another series of explosions echoed by the cries of the mob as it fled down the avenue. Sam lifted a corner of the tattered curtain. In the distance, stationed to the right was a battery of light cannon, now being re-harnessed to advance on the rioters. In front of the cannons were rows of infantry, bayonets fitted, preparing to charge the fleeing mob. Soldiers and militia had finally arrived from Gettysburg and elsewhere.

On the fifteenth and sixteenth of July the army, with much violence, put down the rioting. In lower Manhattan where the rioters were well installed and barricaded, the navy used its great cannons to blast them into submission. By the seventeenth the troubles were over, and the postponed draft began. The numbers called were lighter than expected and Tammany Hall helped some of the most threatened businessmen and skilled artisans to find the $300 they needed. Thus, the people were placated, and feelings calmed. The black population was more than halved, because, other than those killed, many left Manhattan for safer areas of the city such as Brooklyn and others left for Canada. The official figure of those killed in the fighting was put at 119 or 120. However, more realistic observers thought that even 2,000 would be a rather conservative estimate, certainly if the total number of murdered blacks were to be included.

\*\*\*

On the 18<sup>th</sup> Jack and Sam went to inspect their home. It was gutted. Nothing but the walls remained. They returned to Tinker and despite his protests, after a few days, installed themselves in a cheap hotel. There were decisions to be made: were they to re-establish themselves in New York or try somewhere else? New York had suddenly become empty; Hans was dead; Merry had disappeared into a world of poesy and intellectual pretention; Sam's woman was courting rich old men; and whereas they loved Tinker dearly, the world of dissolute riches and bawdy houses had lost its appeal. In the end they opted for going elsewhere. For these reasons and also because they were threatened with conscription — and to avoid that they would have to leave soon; because once drafted, leaving would no longer be possible without risking arrest as deserters. They both came from the moderate South and could not muster the violent abolitionist fervour that could make them kill their neighbours on behalf of the industrial North; nor could they embrace the cause of slavery. They were in a world of conflict where they couldn't take sides; in a world that demanded they did take sides. The obvious solution was to leave that world.

Jack remembered his plan to go to the goldfields with Dan before they had been captured by the Missouri Ruffians. As Dan had put it, they were going to "light out West". The idea of escaping East Coast sophistication and hypocrisy appealed to both him and Sam. Sam's brother Orion had already gone to Denver and the silver mines as the Territorial Governor's Secretary. He had asked Sam to accompany him as Sam had just lost his employment as a Mississippi pilot; but at that time Sam had not long re-found his Jack, was classed a deserter by the Southern states and also his rich mistress had gone to New York and so declined the invitation, as his situation encouraged him to think North and East rather than South or West. Now it seemed a good idea to take up the invitation which still existed. The idea appealed to them, to once again set out on a Waldensian stroll: to live at nature's hour; to escape tiresome fears and worries; to live as free animals far from the soft comforts, insidious corruption and the continuous violence of New York. It also meant that having lost their worldly possessions they now had no need to find new ones. They set out as before on horseback, with knapsacks, a hunting rifle and inevitably Jack's gun. For all the good intentions borrowed from Thoreau, total pacifism seemed a trifle impractical in the Wild West. Living in sympathy with nature and its denizens would have to be enough. As they set out Sam quoted Thoreau:

*"We need the tonic of wildness ... At the same time that we are earnest to explore and learn all things, we require that all things be mysterious and unexplorable, that land and sea be indefinitely wild, unsurveyed and unfathomed by us because unfathomable. We can never have enough of nature."*

They were going "Roughing It".

# EPILOGUE

FRANCIS MERIAM aka MERRY

Merry died unannounced in 1865. No reason could be found for his sudden decease. He was found collapsed across his desk, where he had been organising a new collection of Walt's poems. His chair was turned over and his collar and top fastenings of his shirt torn open as if he had been struggling against asphyxiation. The doctors who examined the body suggested, maybe a heart attack, maybe a stroke. He had always been of a frail disposition and perhaps some genetically inherited and undiscovered weakness had finally claimed him victim.

Walt being of greater imagination had other ideas: the eyes were staring almost thrust out of their orbits; the mouth open, as if in a scream; his hands clenched; but what made Walt reach his conclusion was the heavy sag in the seat of his trousers. He had obviously died of fright, but frightened by what or whom? Walt had no idea.

DANCING BLACK CROW aka STEVE aka BLACK CROW KILLER:

Two or three months later in the same year of 1865 the Crow were holding a great welcoming dance. Their chief Medicine Man, Leaping Over Lions, was orchestrating the ceremony dressed in his finest plumes and decorated deerskins. He held aloft his well-feathered Medicine Pipe to demand total silence. Silence fell and then there was movement among the group of Mandan Crow People, who were the objects of this ceremony. A terrible creature came out from among them with only half a head of red tinted silver hair and naked but for a few chaste feathers. His right-hand side was a mass of weeping scar tissue from his scalp to his foot. He had practically no nose, just an open sore on one side, only one ear and his torn right cheek revealed some broken yellowed teeth. In his good hand was a small silken bag. As he approached the Chief Medicine Man, with the two remaining fingers of his right hand, he pulled from this bag the Great Mystery Medicine of the Mandan, which he ceremoniously handed to Leaping Over Lions who then tied it about his neck. At this point the terrible creature started dancing, screaming his thanks to the Great Spirit for having kept him alive long enough to deliver this medicine to their hosts. He then pleaded that he might be relieved of his suffering, be avenged and die. His last wish was to be granted as he danced round the great fire and with him the entire tribe were now dancing. The Chief Medicine Man again lifted his Medicine Pipe and the dancing slowed towards a stop. The Mandan had at last become entirely Crow. But Dancing Black Crow was dancing on, dancing his last, and in his head, he was once again Black Crow Killer. He had circled the great fire twice and now approached the Chief Medicine Man, a rather frail creature, whom he grasped by the arm and with a final piercing scream of triumph, "for you, Four Bears", he danced into the furnace with him. The old man's scream was not one of triumph.

## CAPTAIN WILLIAM ARBUTHNOT WATSON aka BILL

Bill Watson fathered only five children; thus, his ambitions were unfulfilled in this capacity when he met his death on the 25th June 1876. His ambitions also went unfulfilled in another capacity, that of soldier: he never made it to general.

His unjustly unsung, heroic end was the very stuff of his imaginary boyhood adventures; but, unfortunately, on this occasion he did not control the game. It was that damn fool Custer that spoilt it for him. Bill was a Company Commander under Lt Colonel Custer recently re-appointed to lead a regiment of cavalry against a Sioux uprising, after a brief disgrace caused by a romantically inspired desertion. He had let his ravenous desire for the embraces of Elizabeth Bacon, his wife, take precedence over military duty — being rather bored by Indian wars and loss of status.

Captain Watson had a plan for demoralising the Indian horde that confronted them through the capture of their supreme Chief, Sitting Bull and his aid, Crazy Horse, by seizing them from amidst their warriors in a surprise raid by his company of 50 men with Gatling guns mounted on carts with wheels bearing sickles and each pulled by ten racehorses or as near as was available. Custer considered his plan crazy and suicidal and forbad it and so Captain Watson was forced to follow his leader into an equally stupid plan of conquering the Sioux nation with 210 soldiers with single shot breach loading rifles against thousands of Indians, many with Sharpe's and Winchester repeaters.

Poor Bill remained unsung, while Elizabeth Bacon Custer worked hard to ensure the glory of her husband aided and abetted by Buffalo Bill.

Beth, of course, was no hand at telling lies or encouraging exaggerations or putting on circus performances.

And, if truth be known, Custer's Last Stand was fleeting, a one-nighter in St Louis three weeks before the Battle of Little Bighorn or of Greasy Grass as the Indians would have it.

MISTER WASHINGTON aka WASHY

Washy remained the devoted servant of Ephraim Tinkerton and assured his rise in society, politics and business by ejecting, maiming and very occasionally killing, on his behalf, those that sought to interrupt this ascension or mar the calm of his six houses. He married three times, fathered twenty-two children (he wasn't sure how many survived their infancy) and lived to be ninety.

## EPHRAIM TINKERTON aka TINKER

Tinker remained in New York for the rest of his life, rising swiftly to the top of the heap. Questions raised as to the rather radical defence of his property at the time of the Draft Riots were rapidly quashed and the use of a Gatling gun declared to be legitimate self-defence (after all, there were children in the house) by his friend the Chief Justice with a taste for caressing and being caressed by small girls. And in fact, the Gatling gun found its place as an historical attraction and conversation piece mounted in the centre of the vestibule of the first of his houses. Tinker was once elected Mayor of New York, that is, when professional advantage demanded it. He remained faithful, if not always showing great fidelity, to his Rosie who gave him 12 children, all but one of whom survived infancy. If, from time to time, he did stray from the nuptial couch, he had Rosie's unspoken consent (men, she thought, needed a little variety as chicken at every meal was a dull diet) and he never took advantage of his whores — this, he decided, would have been bad for discipline — and so generally satisfied his needs among the young and beautiful wives of the rich, old and sexually boring. He expanded and eventually had six brothels situated at key points around the city. His first and main brothel on 5th Avenue became three (all within walking distance and surrounded by numberless luxury emporiums for discretion). The first house was exclusively female, which resolved the problem of jealousy and difficult alliances with the male whores. The second house was exclusively male, with two salons: one for the pederast trade and the other for ladies. The third was peopled entirely by the young who, on coming to full maturity at about the age of fourteen, were transferred to one of the other houses and a working life.

Certain righteous souls complained that the exploitation of children was an evil trade. Tinker called them hypocrites and explained that his child brothel was in fact an enlightened bawdy orphanage where the children were well fed, cared for and even loved by the gentle ladies he employed for this purpose; that the house rules protected them from injury (anyone attempting violence or prepubescent penetration was banned, while in serious cases and if they threatened or protested too much, they were dealt with by Washy — a few greatly admired and respected citizens disappeared permanently).

He demanded of the righteous if he should put these children back on the streets where he had found them to sell their small bodies on windswept corners like thousands of other little, starving and beaten New Yorkers. Quite a number of his clients, he insisted, were elderly men who missed not having grandchildren and would come simply to dangle a pretty child on their knee, ruffle its hair and give one or two loving kisses on its rosy cheeks. And if they asked for other caresses, it was no more than the things children often did amongst themselves.

Finally, when any of his subjects wished to leave to do other things, they received a lump sum that represented 10% of their earnings over the years (over and above the very reasonable salaries they had already received), which could come to several thousands of dollars — enough to set up a business of their own. He suggested to the righteous that they adopt a few street urchins to demonstrate their good faith and forget the religious nonsense that sex and sin were synonymous. His advice was very, very rarely followed and probably not at all.

## DAN BROWNE

Dan had a not very long moment of posthumous fame and even glory when an article appeared in the *New York Tribune*, later reproduced in a host of other Abolitionist periodicals under the name of a certain Sergeant Fathom. The Article's title was "Dan Browne's Body Lies a-Smouldering in his Grave" in which Dan's life, learning and his lengthy, ever fiery, speeches on emancipation of the American negro were much lauded. This gave rise to a popular song among the negro regiments of the Federal Army and even among the Abolitionist generality. The chorus and title of this song was the title of Sergeant Fathom's article, followed by a series of Glory, Glory Alleluias. However, this did not please many of the rather conservative Abolitionists, who felt, with the help of phrenology and some over-interpretation of Darwinian Theory, that certain persons were more equal and thus allowed to be more emancipated than others. They also felt that the hero of Emancipation should necessarily be a white man rather than one that was black. And so, by the surreptitious introduction of numerous, seditious editions of song sheets, where slight modifications were made to the original title and chorus, they gradually caused the fame and glory of Dan to go elsewhere: "Dan Browne" became "John Brown" and the "s" disappeared from "smouldering". This latter change rendered the chant less warlike or revolutionary and would not raise the fire of black revolt from its glowing ashes. Who ever heard of mould as combustible? Thus, poor Dan was finally forgotten. Printers who insisted on being faithful to the original, even in rejecting generous bribes, found themselves either beaten up and/or bankrupt.

## PROFESSOR JACKSON PENN aka JACK

Jack and Sam spent two or three years roughing it among the Denver silver miners, found nothing of value, as was the case of the vast majority, and thereafter went to the Pacific islands, sampling the beauty of the islanders long before the syphilitic Paul Gaugin came to infect them. Sam had also been having some success with humorous and travel articles for magazines and newspapers, which along with Jack's railway investments, now much enhanced, gave them much liberty.

From the Pacific they went to Palestine and then Europe. It was at this latter point their lives separated. They remained great friends, often exchanged letters and Sam would visit Jack whenever he was in Europe; but the adolescent ephebe desires of Jack and the tutorial ones of Sam had faded and they no longer shared sex, or at least, very infrequently and when in inebriated nostalgia.

In passing through England Jack had found a girl he very much liked and desired and his thirst for knowledge originally awakened by Dan came to be dominant in his ambitions. Thus, with the aid of one or two well-placed endowments on a Cambridge College he became a student that went rapidly through the academic rituals of diploma gathering, ending with a doctorate and a much admired but unpublishable thesis entitled "Slavery and Infantile Sexuality in the Ante Bellum Society". Finally, after publishing a more conservative work on the American railway system and its contribution in the slaying of buffalos, he received the chair in American History at one of the more recently founded non-denominational universities. He re-adopted the name "Jackson" which added a quaint but appreciated American authenticity to his academic pretentions which simple "Jack" lacked.

Occasionally, a student would ignite an "instant yearning" and now and again this would develop into a series of torrid tutorials lasting well into the night. The most successful series lasted the whole five years of the youth's university career. And Jack continued to watch over the boy's further career for several years afterwards. Nevertheless, Jack's main erotic activity was with his lovely wife with whom he created ten children, eight of whom survived infancy (if not up to the Tinkerton survival rate it wasn't bad for those times and in this everybody shared the same lethal hand of fate). These survivors then created the infants that warmed Jack's old age. He lived to see the First World War, just.

Upon reflection the ageing Jack realised that as from about 1865 it seemed that fate had begun to smile upon him and thereafter, none of those he loved or adored came to violent ends. Even if adventures continued to find him, he prospered and was much admired.

## SAMUEL LANGHORNE CLEMENS aka MARK TWAIN aka SARGEANT FATHOM etc. etc.

Well, everybody knows what happened to Sam! Or at least they should do: the randy old bugger went on to write lots and lots of very American literature; became rich, then bankrupt and finally assuredly comfortable. He really did prefer girls even if boys would occasionally offer a brief interlude of delight; especially those he classed "as pretty as a girl", as were many of the pages in *A Connecticut Yankee in King Arthur's Court*.